Love that is Blind

AYRIAN STONE

Love

that is

Blind

VMI Publishers • Sisters, Oregon

Published by
VMI Fiction
a division of VMI Publishers
Sisters, Oregon
www.vmipublishers.com

ISBN: 1-933204-69-9
ISBN 13: 978-1-933204-69-7
Library of Congress Control Number: 2008933073

Cover design by Juanita Dix

Dedication

TO THE HOLY SPIRIT:
This is Your book. Thank You for Your passion for me.

AND TO THIS GENERATION:
The Lord is fully able to meet and satisfy
your desire for true freedom.

Prologue

The shrill beeping of the fire alarm jerked fifteen-year-old Cora Abrams out of a deep sleep. Acrid smoke hit her nostrils.

Fire! She coughed hard as she stumbled out of bed, the smoke activating her chest cold. She hurried to the door of her upstairs bedroom in central Los Angeles, then froze when a man shouted outside.

"Burn the Jews' homes!"

She gasped in horror. Glass shattered downstairs, and trembling assaulted her. *Oh, God, what am I supposed to do?* Everyone else from the neighborhood had driven to the synagogue to celebrate Hanukkah.

Staggering downstairs, she coughed harder from the thickening smoke. Then she entered the kitchen.

Fire licked up the wall near the phone. A cold December wind blew in through the broken window, intensifying the flames.

She swayed as dizziness swept over her, but she had to get to the phone. It was her only hope.

Flames darted close. She grabbed the receiver and frantically dialed 911.

Someone shouted near the window. She clutched at the gold cross on her necklace. *Dear Jesus!* What if the men came inside? What if they found her?

A calm, professional voice spoke over the line. "911. May I help you?"

"My house is on fire, and a gang is vandalizing—" The heavy curtain rod above her suddenly crashed down, striking the back of her head. She screamed as she plummeted into darkness.

"Cops!" Rye Tyler grabbed the scrawny arm of his teenage cohort as sirens screamed close. "We gotta run!"

"Yeah!" Dish threw his can of gasoline to the ground and tore across the residents' lawns with the five other gang members.

Rye raced after them, but whirled around when a girl's scream pierced the air. "What was that?"

Dish swore, racing faster. "Forget her!"

Rye stood, petrified. Flames billowed out the windows of the first house they had gassed. Dish had said all the Jews were gone. What if a girl burned to death because of what they had done? His mother had died in a fire, and her terrified screams still haunted him.

Anguish ripped through him as he sprinted to the girl's house. Locating a broken window, he shattered it with his elbow. Heat poured over him as he vaulted inside. Smoke stung his eyes, but he located the girl on the far side of the kitchen. She lay collapsed, fire licking at her nightgown.

He ran across the room. Flames singed him as he scooped her up. He staggered toward the door, and the metal knob scalded his palm when he opened it. He plunged through the doorframe, but the top beam broke loose, knocking him to the ground.

He fell on the girl, white-hot heat arcing into his chest from her cross necklace. Gasping, he stumbled to his feet, the unconscious girl flopping in his arms. His legs burned as he bolted away from the collapsing house.

Flashing red-and-blue lights lit up the neighborhood, but escape didn't matter anymore. He dropped to his knees on the dry lawn, cradling the girl against his chest.

A cold voice said, "You'd better let me have her."

He looked up at the uniformed paramedic, who took the girl from him. Her arms dangled limply, and blood matted her long, dark hair. Had he been too late to save her?

His self-control fragmented. Covering his shaved head with sooty hands, he broke down and wept.

Chapter One

"Where's the boy, Grandpa?" Cora pleaded, pitch blackness surrounding her.

"He ran away."

"We have to find him."

Hezekiah's voice hardened. "No."

"But he saved my life, and I didn't even get to thank him."

Cora woke to familiar darkness, tears streaming down her face. Poignancy filled her heart as the dream receded. She longed to meet the boy who'd rescued her from the fire seven years ago, but he had fled the hospital. Perhaps he had feared having charges pressed against him, though the police had been unable to prove his participation in the arson beyond circumstantial evidence.

Despite the boy's rescue, her grandfather's anger had not abated. Holding her hand as she lay in the hospital bed, he had told her coldly, "He was one of them, Cora. A skinhead and a Jew-hater. Put him out of your mind and focus on what must be done now."

Cora winced at the memory and pushed her covers back. Birds chirped outside her window. She knew it must be morning, though no light filtered into her sight. She swung her feet to the floor, and cool floorboards met her bare toes. Five years ago, her grandfather had sold their home in Los Angeles and moved to a small town three hours north. Telling her he was sick of the continual violence plaguing the city, he had plunged all his savings into starting his own shoe store.

His son, Caleb, had helped with the initial expenses. Only five years her senior, Caleb was more like a brother to her than an uncle, and he'd wanted to get her out of the big city as much as Hezekiah had. Since his one-man detective agency had been doing amazingly well, he'd pushed his dad to accept a loan from him.

Grandpa paid back the loan within two years, and three months later Caleb hired a partner. Cora couldn't remember his name since Caleb always called him "the kid." He spoke of him like a younger brother, though he had yet to bring him to meet her and Grandpa. He said it was difficult for them to visit together since The Private Spy Agency maintained a steady flow of clients, but Cora wondered if there was more to it than that.

The need to use the restroom pressed, and Cora padded toward the bathroom, touching the doorframe instinctively. Ever since the fire, blackness had enshrouded her, forcing her to recognize her surroundings through touch and hearing.

She had come to accept her blindness, but she often wondered if the neo-Nazi boy would have rescued her if he'd known she would end up an invalid. Hadn't Hitler wanted to annihilate those who were handicapped in any way? And her blindness made her dependent on others for so many things.

She sighed as the toilet flushed with an odd little clang that neither Grandpa nor Caleb could hear. While both of them had reacted with righteous anger to the tragedy that had struck her life, she clung to her faith in the sovereign goodness of her Savior.

She touched the deep, cross-shaped scar over her heart. Although it was too low for any of her modest clothing to reveal, the severe burn had given her what a simple gold cross on a chain could not: a permanent reminder of her deceased mother, who had worn the necklace first.

Tracing the outline of the burn from so long ago, Cora whispered the prayer that often accompanied the gesture. "Please, Jesus, watch over the boy who saved me, wherever he is. I pray he did not go back to that hate group. Please allow him to find You. I love You. Amen."

"Wow. Are you sure we're at the right place?"

Caleb smiled at Rye Tyler's surprise as he drove their Ford truck up to the security gate of a secured estate in the upper-class area of Los Angeles.

Three years ago, he had met Rye while the blond-haired, blue-eyed kid was working as a gigolo in a business operated by one of LA's cold-blooded drug lords. Caleb had offered to get him out of the underground world and train him in private-eye detection if Rye obtained inside information for him. Rye had provided enough specifics to put several drug lords in prison, then joined The Private Eye Agency as an assistant. Since then he had helped with scores of investigations, and Caleb appreciated his quick wit and enthusiasm.

"It's the right place," Caleb assured him. "Patrick Sunnel owns a billion-dollar computer enterprise." He pressed the button on the intercom set up three yards from the large electronic gate. "Caleb Abrams and Rye Tyler here to see Patrick Sunnel."

"Come in," a guard spoke from the other side of the high brick fence. The gate swung open.

Caleb drove up the long, paved driveway. Palm trees and manicured lawns spread to the sides. A three-story stone mansion towered in front of them.

Rye gave a low whistle. "We haven't had a customer with this much dough in a long time. Do you know what he wants us to investigate?"

"He wants us to find his missing granddaughter." Caleb opened his door, then stepped out of the truck. Rye joined him as he walked up the stone steps to the porch.

The oak door opened, and a gray-haired man in a crisp suit nodded. "Mr. Abrams. Mr. Tyler. I'm Yancey, Patrick Sunnel's butler. Thank you for coming so quickly. Mr. Sunnel is in the parlor with Mrs. Brinnon. This way, please."

Caleb followed him down the carpeted hallway, not sure who Mrs. Brinnon was. Patrick had mentioned only his missing granddaughter during his phone call an hour ago.

The butler paused at the parlor door and gestured them in. A tall, thin man with white hair, who looked to be about seventy years old, paused from speaking with a blonde-haired woman in her mid-thirties, her eyes red and teary.

The white-haired man strode forward, and Caleb accepted his hand. "Patrick Sunnel, I assume."

"Yes. A pleasure, Caleb. Rye. A colleague of mine recommended your agency to me. He knows how much I value high ethical standards in business. In the area of private investigation, honesty is even more critical. Please, have a seat."

"Thank you."

Patrick gestured toward the blonde-haired woman. "Allow me to introduce Dana Brinnon. I made her acquaintance yesterday, and her story is the reason I called you. Dana, I'd like you to tell these men the reason you came to me."

She knotted a handkerchief in her slender fingers. "Three days ago, my husband was murdered. A man came into our home around ten o'clock at night. I had gone upstairs to get ready for bed, and Alan was finishing up some paperwork. He was a lawyer."

She stopped, fighting tears. "When I went downstairs to check on Alan, I saw a man in the study. He was breaking into my husband's safe. Alan lay crumpled on the floor."

She pressed her handkerchief to her mouth. "I didn't realize he was dead. I thought he'd just been knocked out. I ran upstairs and called the police. By the time they arrived, the intruder had left."

"Do you know what he was after?" Caleb asked.

She nodded, her face pale. "A letter Alan was supposed to hand deliver. It was the only item missing when I went through the safe. I was planning to go with Alan the next morning to Summerland Resort to give it to Patrick's granddaughter."

Rye frowned. "I thought she was missing."

Patrick leaned forward. "She's missing in the sense that I don't know who she is, and neither does Dana. Dana told me that my son, Douglas, hired Alan several months ago to draft his will and deliver a letter to his daughter after his death. Everything was to be kept strictly confidential since Douglas didn't want his daughter contacted while he was alive. He died a week ago in the state prison, stabbed by another inmate. The prison warden called me since I was the closest known relative."

Patrick paused and bitterness swept his face. "I gave legal authority to my nephew, Jackson, to handle all the details. He's the vice president of Sunnel Enterprises and my heir. I wanted nothing to do with Douglas in life, and I didn't care about his death. He was serving a life sentence for two murders and a rape. He had never been married. I didn't know he had a child until Dana came. But now I'm worried. There seems to be only one reason for someone to steal the letter and kill Alan. That person doesn't want either me or my granddaughter to find out about our relationship. However, I'm determined to find her."

Caleb pulled out a notepad and pen. "Do you have any idea who would fear the discovery of a Sunnel heir?"

Pain crept into Patrick's pale blue eyes. "Unfortunately, Jackson is my sole heir, and the only one who had access to Douglas's will. I'm assuming Douglas left everything to his daughter and that when Jackson read the will, he became afraid that I would greatly decrease his inheritance in favor of Douglas's daughter. Jackson and I have had a number of arguments because of his tendency to deal underhandedly in the business. I've warned him to stop acting outside the law. Five months ago, I threatened that if he did so again, I would disinherit him. However, it never crossed my mind that I shouldn't trust him to take care of the details involved with Douglas's death. Douglas had no earthly possessions, and he never cared about any of the people in his life."

Rye shifted in his chair. "Do you know what Jackson did with your son's will?"

"The will that Jackson showed me is in my safe. It didn't mention a daughter. I believe Jackson forged a new one in order to fool me, then hired someone to silence Alan and steal the letter mentioned in the will. He didn't realize Dana knew about the girl as well."

Caleb scribbled a note. "We'll need to get DNA samples from the prison, then test the women at Summerland Resort to see if any of them could be Douglas's daughter."

Patrick shook his head. "I already thought of that. I contacted the prison, but they say there's no DNA on record. The prosecution didn't use it to convict Douglas, and the mortuary cremated Douglas four days ago. I'm sorry."

Caleb tapped his pen. So much for the easy route. "We need to narrow the field somehow. Do you know what race she is? What age? Any distinguishing features?"

Dana bit her lip. "I remember Alan saying once that Douglas injured himself. He had to have stitches, and Alan said he made the comment that now he matched his daughter because she also had stitches in the shape of an x."

"Do you know the location of the scar?" Caleb asked.

She shook her head.

"What about her age?"

She shrugged. "I don't know."

Patrick leaned forward. "Douglas started sleeping around at seventeen, but he had a hunting accident at twenty-nine that left him unable to have children. So she would have to be between eighteen and thirty."

Caleb jotted down the information in his notepad. At least they had something to work with. "Any idea what race she might be?"

Patrick grimaced. "Douglas hated blacks. But the girl he raped was Hispanic."

"Did she have a child?"

"No."

Rye shifted in his seat to face Dana. "Were you able to identify your husband's murderer?"

"I caught a glimpse of his profile. He looked to be in his thirties, with black hair and dark eyes, although I suppose he could change his looks. I didn't recognize him in the wanted pictures the police showed me."

"Did they draw a sketch from your description?"

"Yes, but I don't have a copy."

Caleb scribbled a quick note. "I should be able to get a copy from them." He looked up to study Dana's face. "I'd like you to come to the resort with us."

She startled. "Why? I don't know who the girl is."

"I know. But there's a chance that your husband's murderer may have been hired to kill her too."

Patrick struck his hand on his armchair, pain and anger washing over his face. "Then it's probably too late. Alan was murdered three days ago."

Caleb remained calm. "Most likely the assassin is lying low right now. I've seen the case on the news, and since he thinks you don't know about the granddaughter, he can take his time getting to her. My guess is that Jackson wants her permanently removed from the situation. But he'll be willing to let the assassin choose his timing. Neither of them will want to draw attention."

Patrick slowly exhaled. "I hope you're right. Dana, please go with them. I'll pay for all your expenses."

Fear filled Dana's eyes. "If the assassin's there, he's sure to recognize me."

Caleb nodded. "Perhaps. But your husband already reserved a room there, didn't he? You're going there to think of him and grieve, away from pressing memories. And the assassin has no reason to think you know the real reason Alan picked Summerland Resort for your vacation."

She shook her head. "You don't know what it was like—going over to Alan's body and staring at his blank eyes. I don't know if I can do this. I'll be alone. I can't be with you, or he'll guess something's up."

Rye glanced to Patrick. "Does Summerland have an escort service?"

"Yes, it does. Why?"

"Dana's a widow. It might raise the assassin's suspicions if she comes with a man. But he's not going to suspect her motives if she requests companionship from the resort. I could spend time with her and sleep at her cabin without raising any suspicions if I work as part of their hospitality department."

Caleb blew out a hard breath, not liking the idea at all. However, he couldn't argue with Rye's logic. "In that case, Dana will need to rent a beach house rather than a hotel room so you can sleep in separate beds."

Dana clasped her hands. "Actually, Alan rented a beach house."

"All right."

"I should warn you," Patrick inserted, "that Jackson and his wife, Aurora, spend every summer at the resort. They went there three days ago with their daughter, Arianna. They have a large house they always rent near the beach."

Caleb pondered the information. "If they vacation there every year, their presence now is coincidence. I don't think it will make a difference in how we handle the case."

"What happens when we find the granddaughter?" Rye asked.

"I'll come get her," Patrick promised. "I want her safe."

Caleb looked at Dana. "Come to Summerland in a couple of days. Ask for Rye Nelson."

She swallowed. "What if the assassin gets to the granddaughter before you figure out who she is?"

Caleb nodded. "Let's pray he isn't ready to risk another murder just yet."

That night, in his upstairs bedroom in the home Caleb owned in south LA, Rye stared at the ceiling with a frown. Ever since he could remember, murder and hatred had been part of his life. Anger, greed, jealousy, racism…all were motives for acts of violence. Caleb said that evil came from the hearts of men who had turned their backs on God.

Rye gave a humorless laugh. How ironic that his worst crime had been committed in racism against Jews, yet it was a Jew who had rescued him from his life of degradation and given him hope and purpose. Sometimes he feared what Caleb would do if he knew Rye had almost caused a teenage girl's death because of his participation in a hate group. Despite their camaraderie, Rye had no doubt Caleb would kick him out the door if he ever learned about his history before he became a gigolo.

Rye sighed. As it was, Caleb knew enough of his background to keep him from bringing Rye with him whenever he visited his family up north.

Rye absorbed every word that Caleb let slip about his father and niece, but he understood the unspoken boundary his past had erected between him and those whose lives were untainted by the depths of sin.

He didn't blame Caleb for maintaining that boundary. The older man had demanded he stay clean of drugs, alcohol, sex, and crime. Though Rye had found the strict rules tough to follow at first, Caleb's kindness had been reason enough to rein in his free-and-easy lifestyle. He had been a drifter, tasting everything life offered yet satisfied with nothing, having no idea why he existed. Then the quiet, devout Jew had entered his life and given him purpose.

Rye felt a strong debt of gratitude. Honoring the boundary between himself and Caleb's family was a small price to pay to have a secure friendship.

Caleb kept conversation about his father and niece to a minimum. But from the few words he had let slip, Rye had discerned that Caleb's teenage sister had died giving birth to a baby girl when Caleb was five, and that Caleb had grown up as more of a brother to the baby than an uncle. Caleb's mother passed away shortly before his sixteenth birthday, and the two men continued raising the girl as best they could.

Whenever Caleb talked of his father and niece, it was with such incredible love and respect that Rye yearned to be part of the family. But Caleb closely guarded them from wrong relationships. Rye couldn't shake off the heartache he felt because Caleb believed he had to guard his family, and especially his niece, from *him*.

Caleb's niece was only a year younger than himself, and over the last three years, her name had become etched into his soul. *Cora.* Whenever Caleb mentioned her in even the briefest of phrases, he spoke of her as everything a woman should be—pure, sweet, and full of selfless love. Caleb planned to marry a girl of the same caliber, but apparently finding such a young woman was an extreme rarity since Caleb had not so much as dated in his twenty-seven years.

Cora was the opposite of any woman Rye had ever spent time with. Anguish ate at his soul whenever he thought of the chastity he had sacrificed for momentary pleasure and survival. Girls like Cora were sacred, chaste, set apart. They were protected by fathers and brothers for the right men to win their love. Men who weren't like Rye—tainted, guilty, and condemned.

Rye held his head in his hands. As Caleb had taught him about God's standards, the weight of condemnation had crashed down on him. His sins reached up to heaven, and chains of guilt wrapped around him every time he looked in the mirror. The cross-shaped scar burned into his chest kept him from ever forgetting the girl he had almost killed. Because of the blackness of his soul, he had forfeited every right to meet, let alone love, a girl like Cora Abrams.

Chapter Two

Well, here we are." Rye stepped down from the Ford pickup and glanced around at the sprawling wood buildings of Summerland Resort. On his right, a stone-tiered restaurant with beautiful landscaping sat near several tennis courts. To his left, a casino attached itself to the five-star hotel. On the other side of the hotel, palm trees shaded an open pool area with lush lawns.

Caleb headed toward the front door of the building marked Administration. "Ready to apply for a job?"

"Sure. Are you trying for the stables?"

"Yes." He frowned as something past Rye caught his gaze.

Rye turned in the direction of the pool and noticed a teenage girl whose eyes seemed riveted on Caleb. She stood near several sunbathers, wearing a revealing bikini over her voluptuous form.

Knowing Caleb's aversion to women who flaunted their bodies, Rye couldn't resist teasing him. "I guess you caught her attention."

Caleb jerked his gaze forward, lengthening his stride. "I just hope she's not a candidate for Patrick's granddaughter."

Rye laughed, following him into the office building.

Caleb embodied everything he admired and respected. But in the world of money, sex, and power, Rye had the advantage. He had committed himself to upholding Caleb's moral standards, but he knew the importance of integrating himself into each case's situation. Since there was nothing he could do to change his past, he might as well use his knowledge wherever it gave him an advantage.

Arianna Sunnel stared at the brown-haired man as he jerked his gaze away from hers then strode into the administration building. His towering height had snagged her attention when he stepped out of a beat-up truck. Few men were taller than her six-foot frame, but the stranger appeared to be several inches over six feet. He was also handsome and powerfully built. When his eyes met hers, the intensity of his dark stare had electrified her like lightning. Men rarely met her gaze so fully. They were usually too busy staring at her body.

"Nan, are you listening to me?" Next to her feet, her best friend, Rebecca, pushed herself up from her sunbathing position. "I don't think you've heard a word I've said."

"Sorry." Arianna sat back on her towel but felt too distracted to ask what Rebecca had been telling her. "I wonder if he's going to work here."

"Who are you talking about?"

"The guy I just saw. He went into the administration building. I doubt he's a guest. Rich people never drive trucks that old."

Rebecca eyed the weathered Ford. "He definitely isn't going for class. Why are you interested in him? I thought you hooked up with that English lord's son yesterday."

"I did, but rich boys are all the same. They just want to get laid. Then they move on to the next girl."

Rebecca laughed as she settled back onto her towel. "That's life, Nan. You should know that by now. Besides, relationships never last. It's better just to have fun and get all the pleasure you can."

Arianna nodded but continued to mull over the depth in the stranger's gaze. Even though he had looked at her for only a moment, he had made her feel like a real person. What would it be like to gain his interest? Have his passion?

She had lived for pleasure since her first date at fourteen. The boy had been several years older and had promised to make her feel more wonderful than she'd ever felt before. And he had been right. The experience hooked her. After all, nothing mattered in life except feeling good. Contrary to what the religious generation before hers said, absolute right and wrong didn't exist. Each person was free to discover his or her own truths, realities, and purpose. But so far, Arianna hadn't discovered any purpose to her life. Sometimes the randomness of her existence frightened her, but pleasure always drowned out the fear.

The boys she had slept with over the years hadn't filled the hunger for acceptance that drove her. Today, the stranger's gaze had reawakened the longing to be wanted not just for her body but for who she was.

"I'm going to have him."

"What?" Rebecca angled her head to look at her.

Arianna tipped her chin. "I'm tired of rich boys. If he starts working here, I'm going to find a way to get him."

Rebecca rolled her eyes. "Go ahead. Try someone different. But you'll see. Men are all the same, no matter how old they are or how much money they have."

Arianna shrugged. "Maybe."

But hope tightened her heart.

Rye knocked lightly on the door to Room 214. His application for a position in "hospitality" had been accepted three hours ago, and at eight o'clock a request for companionship had come in. His new boss, Nat Gilligan, had passed him the information with a stern warning. "You're on trial for the next month. Please our clients and you'll please me."

Rye smiled as the door swung open. Let the drama begin. He had learned that women didn't automatically want sex. Many who requested companionship were lonely. They wanted to talk and feel loved. They had been neglected by husbands or cheated on by boyfriends. They wanted to feel valuable again. Of course, there were also the ones addicted to sexual pleasure. Thankfully, he had sleeping powder in his pocket should he need it.

The redhead who opened the door gestured him inside a luxuriously furnished room. She appeared to be in her late twenties with an athletic build and toned muscles. She cocked an eyebrow. "Care for a drink?"

"Water's good for me. Are you vacationing alone?"

She gestured toward the sofa as she walked to a small credenza. "Yes. My husband's in Scotland with his mistress. Have a seat."

Rye's gut tightened. Married women had been half of his patrons before Caleb pulled him out of his immoral lifestyle. He accepted the water glass when she brought it and forced his gaze to stay on her face as she sat next to him.

"So, what's your name?"

"Rye. And yours?"

"June. How long have you been working at the resort?"

"Actually, I just started." He smiled. "But don't worry. I haven't disappointed a woman yet."

Her green eyes glowed. "Well, that makes things easier."

She slipped off her blouse, and Rye startled. An x-shaped scar gleamed on her left shoulder. He gestured toward it. "How'd you get the scar?"

She eyed him. "An operation."

Rye forced a roguish smile. "Scars fascinate me. I have a similar one." He unbuttoned his shirt so she could see the white cross etched into his chest.

She relaxed. "Looks like we're a matched pair."

"Mind if I ask how long you've had yours?"

"Five years. You like to talk, don't you?"

Rye grinned. "Most women don't get enough conversation from their men. Being interested in each other is the first step to intimacy, isn't it?"

She reached for her glass then swirled the amber liquid. "I think a drink together is usually the best start."

Rye smiled. "It's definitely the quick way. Maybe I will have a glass."

She set her glass to the side and stood. "Good."

She walked to the credenza. As she poured his brandy, he slipped the sleeping powder into the last of her drink. Since she didn't seem to want to talk, he would find her driver's license to identify her name and age once she slipped into unconsciousness. Hopefully that would confirm whether she was in the running to be Sunnel's missing granddaughter.

"Hey there, Pompay. How you doing, girl? You had quite a long ride, didn't you?" Caleb soothed the heavily breathing mare that had just been returned to the stables. He took fifteen minutes to walk out her excited heartbeat, then led her into the Summerland Resort stable. He brushed her coarse hair until no dirt or sweat remained. Then he repositioned her wooden gate.

"Excuse me. Could I get some help with my horse?"

At the feminine voice, he glanced to his left then slowly turned.

The girl from the pool held the reins of a black filly. Red lipstick glazed her sumptuous lips, and glossy black hair bounced over her bare shoulders. She wore a too-small halter top and too-short shorts. Her blue-green eyes flirted with him.

He pressed his lips together. He had been raised to revere modesty and a chaste attitude. Both characteristics were becoming rare in the modern world, but he refused to compromise his belief in God's standards. "What kind of help do you need?"

Her smile teased him. "I want an escort."

"Sorry. I'm not in that line of service."

"Mayflower's jittery today. I want someone to ride with me in case I fall and break a leg."

Caleb doubted the high-strung filly was worse today than any other day. However, he couldn't ignore the fact that the girl looked the right age to be Sunnel's granddaughter. "What's your name?"

Her eyes glowed beneath heavy eye shadow. "Arianna. What's yours?"

"Caleb Lindon," he said, using the last name he had created for undercover jobs. "Who are your parents?"

She cocked her head in surprise. "Jackson and Aurora Sunnel. But don't worry. They don't care who I date."

So Douglas wasn't her father. Relief touched him. "Sorry, but I can't go with you. I need to clean the stalls."

She pouted. "Maybe I should tell your boss you aren't giving complete customer satisfaction."

He put his hands on his hips. "Do you always manipulate people to get your way?"

She smiled coyly. "Usually I don't have to."

"You manipulate just by the way you dress."

She stared at him as though shocked by his blunt assessment.

A deep chuckle sounded behind him. Arianna narrowed her eyes. Caleb turned, taking in the eavesdropper.

A man in his early twenties with long blond hair stood a foot away. He looked to be about five foot ten, with a barrel chest and long arms. He wore dusty jeans, and Summerland's logo graced his faded shirt. He grinned at Caleb. "I'm Darrell. I work here in the stables. Been here three years."

Caleb nodded. "Caleb. Nice to meet you."

Darrell glanced slyly at Arianna. "Nice to see you again. If you're tired of rich guys, I'm available any time you want."

Arianna tipped her chin up. "If I'd wanted you, I'd have come and asked."

Darrell's lip curled. "You've always been Miss High and Mighty, haven't you?"

Arianna's gaze shot bullets. "You'd better watch your mouth. I can have you fired before today's over."

Darrell's hazel eyes gleamed. "All that fire's gotta be good for something. I'll be waiting when you change your mind about church boy here."

He swaggered past them while Arianna looked at Caleb, her gaze questioning. "Do you go to church?"

"No. But when I can, I attend a synagogue."

Arianna scrunched her nose. "What's that?"

"It's the worship center for believers in Judaism. I'm a Jew."

She cocked her head as if studying him anew. "So you are religious."

"Yes. Excuse me. I need to get back to work."

Caleb brushed past her, striding to a stall several yards away. He picked up a pitchfork then forked fresh hay out of the overhead bin.

Arianna remained there for several minutes, watching him, but he ignored her. The last thing he wanted to do was pay attention to a teenage girl trying to seduce him. As soon as he was off work, he would use his laptop to search the resort's database for real candidates for Sunnel's granddaughter.

Rye knocked on Caleb's door at a quarter past five.

"Come in."

He stepped into a small employee cabin similar to his own, with kitchenette, table, couch, and television. The bedroom door hung ajar, the bed neatly made. He smiled wryly. He had headed for bed at six that morning and hadn't bothered straightening the covers after getting up to meet Caleb. "How was your day?"

"It was fine." Caleb didn't look up from his laptop where he sat at the round table.

The screen rolled through a long list of names and dates. Rye studied them. "Is that the guest register?"

"Yes. I'm compiling a list of female guests and employees based on age. In a couple minutes, the program will give us their social security numbers, which I'll use to track down their medical records by hacking into hospital databases."

Rye pulled out a chair. "I ran into a woman last night with an x-shaped scar. Her name's June Moore. Her driver's license said she's thirty."

Caleb finally met his gaze. "How'd the night go?"

Rye shrugged. "I drugged three women and had 'deep, meaningful' conversations with two others. I'm glad Dana's coming soon, or I'd lose my job. Sleeping pills don't exactly make the women want to recommend me."

Caleb glanced back at the computer screen. "The list's ready. I'll plug in June's social first."

The computer screen blipped as the hack program surfed through medical databases, looking for June's social security number. Minutes passed, then the database for Wheaton Hospital blinked onto the screen. Caleb followed several links to read her medical history. "No operations listed. When did she get the scar?"

"She said five years ago."

Caleb shook his head. "It's not listed. I'll run the program again. Maybe she's been to other hospitals."

Rye sat silently as the computer worked again. But after ten minutes, the program reported no other finds.

Caleb tapped the table. "Her medical record is very short. Wheaton didn't fill in many of the usual details. I wonder..." He minimized the hospital database, then instructed the program to do a broad search of all databases for June's social security number. "This could take a while."

Rye leaned back in his chair. "She said her husband's in Scotland. Maybe she had her operation abroad."

"Could be. But usually hospitals like to keep each patient's full history."

The New York Police Department database popped onto the screen. June's social security number stood in bold at the top.

Rye leaned closer. "June Moore, age twenty-two, reported missing seven years ago. Disappeared during a hiking excursion in Scotland with friends." He whistled.

Caleb drew in a deep breath. "The file doesn't say she was ever found. I'm going to search for a marriage certificate."

He ran the search, and a few minutes later, the screen reported that there was no record of June's social security number being listed on a marriage document. Caleb leaned back in his chair. "She could have married abroad and only recently returned to the States. But I think we need to verify that the woman you met last night is the real June Moore. If she's not, we'll have to find her true parentage and age."

"You think she might have stolen June's identity?"

"It happens. Did you search her room?"

"Yeah. She didn't have much. No pictures of hubby or reference to any other family. Maybe I should go back to see if she's hidden documents inside her luggage."

Caleb nodded. "Take our fingerprint kit when you go. Just don't get caught."

Rye grinned. "You know me. I have the best excuse in the world for being in a woman's room."

Caleb turned back to the computer screen. "Let's load in the other socials and see who else is a candidate."

Two hours slowly ticked by. Rye read off social security numbers, then crossed off the names of women who didn't have x-shaped scars. He read the next name on the list. "Arianna Sunnel. Well, she's not a candidate. We know her father."

Caleb sighed. "Yes, but I don't want to leave any loose ends. What's her social?"

Rye repeated it. Moments later, her medical record displayed on the screen.

Caleb pressed his lips together. "Looks like we need to investigate further."

Rye scanned the information about an x-shaped scar low on her left hip. He double-checked her birth date. She had turned eighteen six months ago, putting her within the age range for Patrick's granddaughter. He glanced at Caleb. "I guess we need to find out if Aurora slept with Douglas."

Caleb rubbed the back of his neck. "I can't believe she's a candidate."

"Why?"

"She's the girl from the pool."

Rye grinned. "Did she hit on you?"

"Yes. She's an audacious flirt."

"What are you going to do if she asks you out?"

Caleb sent him an annoyed glance. "My job. Let's get back to work. What's the next social security number?"

Rye read it. An hour later, they had eliminated all the other female guests and employees as possible candidates for Patrick's granddaughter.

Chapter Three

S o, will you go riding with me today?"

At the teasing voice, Caleb turned from raking hay around one of the stalls. Arianna leaned on the gate, her blue-green eyes twinkling under heavy makeup.

He set the rake to the side. Although he doubted she was the missing granddaughter, he couldn't risk ignoring her. "Sure. I'll go with you. But first, change into something that doesn't expose any skin from neck to knees. And wipe off all that makeup."

"What?" She stared at him, stunned.

Caleb braced his hands on his hips, daring her to argue.

She hesitated a moment before taking a step backward. Then she turned and sprinted from the stables.

Caleb watched her go and wondered if she would return. Perhaps he had pushed too hard. But he didn't like the idea of spending time with a girl who dressed and acted like a prostitute. Although he could do nothing about the latter, hopefully she would acquiesce to his demand about the former and make his job a little easier.

In her family's luxurious beach house, Arianna soaked a washcloth in warm water, then rubbed vigorously at her carefully applied makeup. When she finished, she stared at her reflection in the bathroom mirror.

Considering how bland and unattractive she looked, she half regretted giving in to Caleb's stipulation. How could she lure him looking like this? But she was willing to try anything to gain his interest.

She headed to her bedroom, where she tore through her wardrobe, trying to find clothing that matched his strange requirement. After several minutes, she scowled in frustration. None of her clothes qualified. And she couldn't borrow any of her mother's clothing since Aurora Sunnel was nearly a head shorter than she was. The resort's small store only carried skimpy beachwear, and a drive into town would take too long.

"Arianna, is that you making all that racket?" Her mother's plaintive voice drifted from the master bedroom. "I've got a terrible headache, and I'm going sailing with your father and Uncle Benjamin in an hour, so I really need to rest."

Uncle Ben! Of course. Arianna ran to the far guestroom. Her mother's older brother had a slim physique and shared her height. His clothes would surely cover her curves and meet Caleb's demand.

Grinning, Arianna made her raid.

Caleb caught sight of Arianna as he helped an older woman mount her horse. For a moment he forgot what he was doing and stared at the cheeky girl.

With the heavy makeup gone, the fine planes of her face appeared softer and her natural beauty shone through. She had donned a man's denim shorts and oversized T-shirt and had pulled her jet black hair into a crazily leaning ponytail. The effect made her look like a farm girl out for an adventure.

"Could you hand me the reins, please?" The elderly lady's voice jerked him back to his task.

"Of course, Mrs. Normandy." He handed her the reins, then stepped back so she could take off on her ride.

"So, what do you think?" Arianna bounded to his side with contagiously youthful enthusiasm, her eyes aglow. "Will I do?"

Irritated by the sudden attraction he felt, he scowled. "Who'd you rob for the clothes?"

"My uncle. I didn't have anything that met your approval, so I thought of Uncle Ben. Aren't you glad?"

Caleb ignored her question as he strode to the Sunnel stall. "Your uncle's here too?"

"He says it's not really a vacation, 'cause he and Dad are working on business. Uncle Ben's a lawyer for my grandfather's business."

"What's his full name?"

"Benjamin Dean. He's my mom's older brother. He's a lot more fun than my parents, though. I'm glad he's going to be here this summer."

Caleb threw Mayflower's saddle on the filly. "He doesn't usually come?"

"No."

Caleb tightened Mayflower's girth. If Dean worked with Jackson, could he be involved in Brinnon's murder? What if Jackson had asked him to draft the forged will? Dean might even be the assassin. His presence at the resort where he didn't normally vacation raised suspicion. Dana would need to get a visual of Dean as soon as she arrived.

Finished with Mayflower, Caleb headed down the stable corridor to choose a mount for himself. After settling on Painter, a six-year-old gelding, he joined Arianna in the stable yard.

Reining in Mayflower's impatient prancing, she looked at his horse with obvious disappointment. "Why'd you choose a slowpoke? I wanted to go for a good gallop. Or don't you ride well?"

"I ride fine. But if you're afraid of taking a spill, I don't think I should be on as temperamental an animal as your filly."

Arianna laughed, reaching forward to pat her mount's sleek neck. "Mayflower's not temperamental. Are you, baby? Come on. Let's go."

Caleb stayed close to her until they reached the riding path of the resort's forest. Then he allowed Painter to drop back several yards. Arianna didn't seem to notice. For the next fifteen minutes, she gazed at the passing scenery and caressed her mount.

Caleb found himself watching her and told himself it was because she was a candidate for the case. Had Aurora ever implied to her daughter that Jackson might not be her real father? Did Arianna know that her mother had slept around? Considering her lack of morals, she had probably modeled herself after her mother's behavior.

It seemed odd she could flaunt herself one minute and act as if she were a kid the next. Caleb grimaced and looked away from her. He hadn't been interested in a woman in a long time, and he resented the attraction he felt for this promiscuous girl.

"I think we should take a break here."

Alerted by her voice, Caleb glanced around. It was an ideal picnic spot, full in the sun yet sheltered from north winds and filled with the fragrance of sweet clover and daisies. He would have enjoyed lingering except for the warning he felt because this part of the trail wasn't well traveled.

Arianna slid off her mount then let the reins trail. The sweet clover caught Mayflower's attention, but Caleb kept Painter's reins in a loose grasp after he dismounted.

"Isn't it lovely?" Arianna turned toward him, intimate warmth in her eyes.

Caleb's throat tightened, and he looked away.

She came and stood before him. "It is lovely, isn't it?"

"I don't know." He glanced at the surrounding trees as though they held far more interest for him than she did. "I'm sure this meadow has hidden dangers in it. A flash flood, a fire, maybe a wolf."

Her laughter interrupted him. She stepped up to his chest and draped her arms around his neck. "I think I'm in love with you, Caleb Lindon."

A muscle jerked in his jaw at her nearness. Avoiding her gaze, he reached up and unclasped her hands. "I'm not in the habit of robbing cradles, Arianna."

He pushed her back a foot, expecting her to react to the rebuff with hauteur. Instead, she asked softly, "Will you ride with me again tomorrow?"

The tender longing in her voice stunned him. The softness came across as less manufactured than the brazenness.

Frowning, he let go of her wrists and stepped away from her.

"I'll behave myself. I promise."

His throat tightened. He wanted nothing more to do with her, but what choice did he have? Until she was disqualified as a candidate for inheriting Sunnel's wealth, he couldn't risk alienating her. He might have to guard her if she was the assassin's target. Although questions about her background might seem odd, he needed to start gathering information about her parentage. "How does your father treat you?"

She raised her eyebrows. "My father?"

"Yes."

She shrugged. "He acts like I don't exist. Why'd you ask?"

"Understanding people is a hobby of mine. Has he always treated you that way?"

"Pretty much. He didn't want to have kids. I don't think my mom did either."

"So you've heard them talking?"

She gazed at the trees. "They fight sometimes about whose fault it was that I was born. Dad says Mom should have had an abortion. But since she didn't, he says he doesn't care what I do as long as I stay out of his way. All he cares about is business deals and making money. Mom just cares about having money to spend on casinos and drinks."

She glanced at him coyly. "But she likes it when I bring home a cute boyfriend. She says I should have fun while I can."

Caleb held her gaze gravely. "Life's about a lot more than having fun. It's about pleasing God."

"So you don't want to have fun?"

"It depends on what you call fun. I enjoy God's creation, and I like helping people."

Her eyes twinkled. "Well, you're helping me. I get bored hanging out with the same kind of people all the time. But I'd like it if you'd go out with me tonight."

He shook his head. "Sorry. I have work to do."

"You have two jobs?"

He refused to lie in his personal life, but considered his investigative work another matter. "I'm doing research on the Internet for a breeding company."

"Horses?"

"Yes."

Her eyes brightened. "I'd love to breed horses! Someday I hope I'll have enough money to buy a ranch of my own."

As Caleb swung onto his horse, he wondered if perhaps she would get to have the ranch of her dreams. The Sunnel inheritance would enable her to buy anything she wanted.

Chapter Four

"Cora, dear, you're looking a little wan."

Cora felt embarrassed that her fiancé's stepmother had noticed her tiredness. Esther had brought her to the Summerland Resort restaurant after their morning on the golf course with David and his father, Paul.

She and David had been friends since preschool, and according to Jewish custom, Paul had suggested the betrothal when she turned thirteen. Grandpa Kai had agreed. David remained committed to her during the years she struggled to adjust to her handicap, and this summer he'd encouraged her to join the family during their vacation.

Not wanting to wile away the next three months, she had also volunteered at a nearby YMCA campground. She enjoyed her days at the Y more than her time at the resort since David tended to fill his schedule with meetings and sports activities. Although her blindness prevented her from participating in most of the activities that David and his parents enjoyed, she'd also agreed to spend the afternoon at the tennis courts. After the long morning, however, she felt emotionally and physically drained.

"Would you like to lie down?"

Cora accepted Esther's suggestion gratefully. "Yes. Thank you for lunch."

"My pleasure, dear."

Esther's chair scraped across the floor, and Cora stood as well. She took Esther's arm for guidance across the restaurant, then Esther headed them into the sultry outdoors.

A few minutes later, they stepped into the cool air of the resort's hotel lobby.

"Oh, dear," Esther lamented. "I'm already late for my appointment at the tennis courts."

Self-conscious about her dependence on others, Cora offered, "Why don't you go ahead? I'm sure I can find the room myself."

"Really?" Esther sounded pleasantly surprised. "Thank you, dear. Why don't you ask the clerk for an extra key so you can go to the room anytime you want?"

"Thank you, I'll do that. Enjoy your match."

"I will. Take care, dear."

Esther's heels clicked on the wood floor, and Cora drew in a deep breath. She prayed she hadn't acted too hastily in offering to find the Hauzens' room without assistance. She'd been in and out of the hotel a number of times, so she knew the general layout of the building. She also knew that every floor and room number had Braille underneath it. She didn't think there'd be a problem.

Cora trailed her fingers along the wall to the registration counter. Sensing that her cane was repellant to Esther, she'd left it at the Y.

Grandpa often said she had a natural gift for reading people, something her blindness had enhanced. Caleb called it a sixth sense that he wished he had for his sleuthing, but Cora knew the gift had more to do with her relationship with Jesus than some mystical ability. The Lord had apparently decided that with her sight gone, she needed another way to read the world around her.

She waited patiently until a clerk asked her in a harried voice, "May I help you, Miss?"

"Yes. I'm Cora Abrams. Esther Hauzen said I could get a spare key to her room."

"Of course. One moment."

Cora sensed him hurry away. A few seconds later, he came back. He handed her a cool metal key. "Here you go, Miss Abrams. Room 214. Enjoy your stay at Summerland."

Cora hesitated. 214? That didn't sound right. But surely the desk clerk knew better than she did. "Thank you."

She trailed her fingers on the counter until she came to the wall. From there, she walked on the smooth floor until her toes hit the base of the stairs. She reached the second floor after twenty steps. Keeping her hand lightly on the wall, she brushed the room numbers as she walked past each door.

210. 212. 214. The walk didn't seem long enough, but she had always been with someone else before. She must not have paid close enough attention.

She found the doorknob, then inserted the key. The door clicked open, and she breathed a sigh of relief. She stepped into the air-conditioned room, then shut the door behind her.

Rye startled when he heard the key turn in the door lock. June Moore had left for town a half hour before, and he had taken the opportunity to slip into her room. He was searching her suitcase lining for any hidden documents when the lock clicked, warning him he was about to be discovered.

He zipped the suitcase shut, then straightened. Thankfully, he had already cleaned the area where he had dusted for June's fingerprints.

A girl in a modest sundress stepped into the room. She didn't seem to notice him as she slipped off stylish sunglasses then leaned the back of her head against the door. She closed her eyes and lifted her face toward heaven as if in prayer.

Rye doubted he could hide anywhere in the room and remain undetected until she left. So he slid into character with the ease of old habit, deciding to initiate instead of giving the girl time to question his presence. He moved silently across the plush carpet, then planted his hands against the door on either side of her shoulders.

Her eyes flew open. "Who—?"

Figuring that actions would answer her question better than words, he dipped his head and kissed her.

She responded hesitantly, and warmth spiraled through him. Unlike June's demanding lips, this girl's mouth was kind and gentle.

When he ended the kiss, she drew in a ragged breath. "David, I thought—"

"I'm not David."

Her dusky complexion paled, and horror filled her dark brown eyes.

She stared through him as if he were a ghost, and regret filled him. To keep his cover, he murmured, "But I can be your Prince Charming."

"Oh, Jesus!" She pressed her hands against his chest. "Please let me go."

He wound a strand of her long, dark hair around one finger. "Don't you want to stay, baby?"

"No!" Tears spilled onto her cheeks. "I must have the wrong room."

Reluctantly, he eased back. If her paleness was any indication, it would be cruel to keep her in torment any longer.

"Okay, Hershey," he said. The nickname suited her chocolate-brown eyes. "Just remember, I work here, and you can ask for me anytime."

Red burned across her high cheekbones as she groped for the doorknob with a slender hand. As soon as she found it, he stepped away.

The strand of dark hair fell from his fingers. A moment later, she was gone.

Outside Room 214, Cora held on to her composure by a thin thread. Her lack of sight had caused a few embarrassing moments in the past, but her mistake this time outdid every one. The last thing she wanted to do was go back to the desk clerk and ask for the correct room number and key, but she had to. The Hauzens wouldn't be back for hours, and she desperately needed the sanctuary of Esther's room.

"Can I help you, honey? You look like you're lost." An older woman's kind voice broke into her thoughts, and Cora caught the scent of rose perfume as she pushed her sunglasses on.

"I'm blind, and I was given the wrong room key."

"Oh, you poor dear." The woman clucked her tongue in grandmotherly fashion and put a wrinkled hand on Cora's arm. "Now, you come with me, and I'll get you to the right room in a jiffy."

Ten minutes later, Cora followed her into room 218 and immediately smelled the sweet fragrance of Esther's French perfume.

The kind woman rustled around the room, apparently checking something. "The luggage tags say Paul and Esther Hauzen. Are they your folks?"

Cora nodded. "Thank you."

"No problem at all. Now, why don't you lie down and rest? You look awfully pale."

"Thank you."

"Bye, dearie."

The door clicked shut, and Cora sank onto the plush couch near the door. There was no way she could take the woman's advice and rest. Her mind swirled with a cacophony of thoughts, none of them peaceful.

She had just received her first kiss... and not from David! Memory came rushing to the forefront of her thoughts, triggering a disturbing range of emotions.

She would never have guessed that a respectable, high-class resort would offer escort services, but apparently she had much to learn about the world of high society. If only she hadn't found out firsthand!

She trembled as her emotions demanded release from her tight control. She pressed a hand against her mouth to try to keep the sobs inside.

She chided herself for not knowing the man in the room wasn't David even before he kissed her. David's musky cologne was nothing like the clean, fresh pine scent of the stranger. But she hadn't been able to think outside her little world, where only the man who had the right would dare to kiss her.

Cora bowed her head in her hands as tears slipped down her cheeks. David had wanted to save their first kiss for their wedding day, and she had agreed to hold back in physical interaction. But over the years, she had often imagined how she would feel when he finally took her in his arms and kissed her. Tender, warm, precious. How horrible that she had felt exactly that way when kissed by a complete stranger!

There should have been some warning that the man was kissing her out of lust. But there hadn't been. And she had made the mistake worse by returning the stranger's kiss.

"Oh, Jesus, forgive me!"

She wept brokenly into the silence. Then a gentle presence drew near, and she breathed in deeply. The sweetness of the Lord's closeness eased the condemnation she felt and reminded her that He had been in that room, watching and protecting her.

Her tears slowed. As calm returned, she realized that He also saw the need of the young man's soul.

Child, I love him too.

She trembled at the revelation. Whereas she had only been able to see the stranger in light of his reason for being in the room, the Lord looked past the sin to the need of his soul.

She felt a burden for the young man's salvation press upon her, and she bowed her head.

"Jesus, I hate the fact I let him kiss me, but if there's a reason You allowed it, please move in his heart. He needs You to satisfy whatever drives him. Please bring him to a saving knowledge of You, and please remove him from the life he is living."

The silence lingered as she waited quietly for the Lord's reply. She felt the Spirit remind her that even after she knew the man wasn't David, she had felt no fear.

She didn't understand the revelation, but somehow it released her to set aside her turbulent emotions. She moved to the bed and lay down. Moments later, she fell into an exhausted sleep.

Chapter Five

Caleb met with Rye over dinner that night at a roadside café several miles from the resort. Cutting into his steak, Caleb asked, "Have you made it to June's room yet?"

Rye stabbed a slice of roast beef. "Yeah. I have the fingerprints, but she didn't have anything hidden in her luggage."

"Okay. I'll mail the fingerprints to Glendon in LA. He'll be able to tell me if they're on record."

Rye chewed another bite. Will Glendon worked with the police department in downtown Los Angeles. He valued the tips that Caleb had given him over the years and didn't mind helping Caleb out in return.

After a few minutes of eating, Caleb said, "Arianna told me her uncle is here. He's a lawyer for Sunnel Enterprises, but it's unusual for him to join the family on their vacation. I looked him up on the Web. He works hand-in-glove with Jackson. I want Dana to get a visual of him as soon as she arrives. We need to know if he's the assassin."

Rye took a sip of his Sprite. "What's his name?"

"Benjamin Dean. He's staying at the Sunnel beach house. I thought you could search it during the day when the family is elsewhere."

Rye nodded. "Good idea. Do you know Arianna's schedule?"

"She wants to go riding with me again tomorrow. We'll head out at two o'clock since the Sunnels have a habit of all going out in the afternoon. While you're at the Sunnel beach house, search through Aurora's belongings for a diary or something that might tell us if she had a relationship with Douglas. I called Patrick and asked him to search their home in LA."

Rye cocked an eyebrow. "How did he respond to the idea that Arianna might be his granddaughter?"

Caleb grunted. "He said we shouldn't waste our time with her. I wish we didn't have to. But we have to eliminate every possibility."

Rye knocked on the door of Beach House 14, the stars twinkling in the night sky. It was nine o'clock, and his boss had said that the resident in Beach House 14 had requested him by name. Patrick had phoned earlier to tell him that Dana would be arriving that night, and Rye hoped she was the woman who had called his boss.

"Who is it?"

A woman's fearful voice called through the door, and Rye drew in a deep breath. "It's Rye Nelson."

"Oh, thank God!"

Dana swung the door open, and Rye stepped into the beach house.

Dana's relief mirrored his own. He was fast tiring of accepting the advances of women he had no intention of sleeping with. He had half feared that after too many encounters, he would lose the willpower to resist their seductions. But thankfully Caleb's morals had embedded themselves strongly within him, reminding him of the consequences of immorality. And ever since his encounter with Hershey, he hadn't felt any attraction to other women. The memory of her sweetness made the women's coy seductions all the more crass and repugnant.

Dana locked the door then stepped farther into the living area. She gestured toward the couch, where a pillow and blankets sat folded on the end. "It's not a hide-a-bed. I'm sorry. But I found extra blankets."

Rye smiled. "Thanks. When do you usually get up?"

"Nine or so. I suppose you want to spend most of tomorrow exploring the resort."

"First Caleb wants us to watch the Sunnel beach house. He needs to know if you recognize either Jackson or his brother-in-law, Benjamin Dean, as the intruder in your home."

Dana looked fearful. "He won't notice us, will he?"

"We'll watch the house with binoculars. If you see the killer, warn me. If neither of the men is the assassin, we'll trail the two women candidates."

She swallowed. "There's coffee in the pot if you want it. And snacks in the cupboard. I'm going to bed."

"All right."

She headed into the hall then disappeared into the bedroom.

Rye walked to the couch. He set the heavy blanket aside and unfolded the sheet. In the bathroom, he changed into the sleeping shorts and T-shirt he had brought. Going around the house, he checked the locks on the doors and noted the security system in place. He studied it thoughtfully. Most likely, the Sunnel beach house also had a security system.

He pulled out his cell phone and called Caleb. "I need the code to the security system for the Sunnels' beach house."

"I'll access it tonight and give it to you at lunch tomorrow. Has Dana arrived?"

"I'm at her place."

"Good. Let me know how it goes."

"I will."

"It's not him."

Rye sighed as Dana lowered his binoculars from peering out her car window at the Sunnel beach house. She had parked the sedan across the street near several other vehicles. "You're sure?"

"Yes. The intruder was heavier than both of those men."

Dana passed the binoculars to him, and Rye focused through the windshield on the slim frame of Benjamin Dean. He appeared to be in his early forties with modernly styled brown hair and tanned skin. He wore designer golf clothes, though he held his laptop as he unlocked his flashy silver Mustang. Earlier, Jackson had left the house with his laptop in hand, dressed in suit and tie, apparently for a business meeting.

Rye lowered the binoculars as Dean drove away. Too bad neither of the men were Alan's murderer. It would have made his job simpler. Now he would need to trail June while Caleb kept tabs on Arianna until they knew who the assassin was after.

He glanced at his watch. One o'clock. "Caleb wants me to search the beach house as soon as everyone is gone. Arianna's supposed to meet him at two. Aurora usually leaves before then."

Dana shifted uneasily. "Do you need me to do anything?"

"If someone drives up while I'm inside, call my cell phone. That should give me time to slip out the back door."

Dana leaned her head against the back of her leather-upholstered seat and soon fell asleep. A half hour dragged by. Then a wispy-looking woman in her late fifties stepped out of the house on three-inch heels. She threw a silk cloth around her neck as though chilled despite the ninety-degree weather. Arianna's mother had probably been a beauty in her youth, but the roots of her red hair showed gray and her heavy makeup failed to cover the lines around her blue eyes.

Rye tapped his fingers on his shorts as she headed down the gravel road toward the main buildings. At one-fifty, Arianna appeared on the porch, locking the door behind her. She wore a man's shorts and T-shirt. Neither failed to conceal the fullness of her figure or the sway of her walk.

Rye waited until she disappeared into the stables, then woke Dana. "I'm heading in."

Dana nodded, and Rye stepped out of her sedan. He headed toward the Sunnels' beach house, then angled around it. He walked up the back steps of the wraparound porch, perusing the neighborhood. No one lingered in their yards, so at the back door, he punched in the code for the Sunnels' alarm system. The red light blinked off, and he slipped in the master key he had smuggled out of hospitality. The lock clicked, and he entered the dim interior. Thankfully, the blinds were drawn. He went upstairs first.

Jackson and Aurora had separate bedrooms, both lavishly furnished. He searched Aurora's drawers first, discovering high-dosage medications and a spiral-bound journal. He glanced through the dates, but the entries had been written over the last several months. Hopefully Patrick would discover older journals in her home in LA. Several depleted alcohol bottles stood on the vanity along with a number of used glasses.

He discovered little in Jackson's room except half a dozen books on running a corporation and managing stocks. It appeared Jackson kept all documentation of his business dealings on his laptop.

Rye glanced in Benjamin Dean's room. Designer clothes and three-piece suits filled the closet. An address book on the dresser contained mostly women's names. Rye searched the dresser drawers quickly, discovering an addiction to pornography but no information pertinent to the case. He headed to Arianna's bedroom.

High-school memorabilia filled her dressers and horse posters covered her walls. Letters from friends were jammed into a keepsake box, and makeup accessories cluttered her dresser. He searched her drawers, but didn't find a journal.

As he headed downstairs, his cell phone vibrated. He checked the caller ID. It was Dana, obviously warning him that someone was coming.

He jogged to the back door and slipped out. He didn't take the time to reset the alarm system. Hopefully the new arrival would assume someone in the family had forgotten to set it.

Minutes later he joined Dana in her car, where she gripped the binoculars nervously. "Thank God you made it out of there. I wanted to faint when I saw Jackson pull up."

"Thanks for the warning. I didn't get to search the main rooms, but it didn't look like there was an office downstairs. Everything must be on their computers."

Dana nodded. "Did you find anything suspicious?"

"No. But this is their summer home. Patrick will probably have better luck than I did."

"I behaved today, didn't I?"

Caleb sighed as Arianna slid gracefully off Mayflower in the stable yard after their second ride together. "Yes, you behaved."

"So you'll race me tomorrow, right? And you won't ride that slow old Painter?"

"Arianna…" Caleb wrestled with his obligation to his job. He didn't want to ride alone with her again. His thoughts had already been on her too much. But for now she was under his protection.

Apparently Arianna misinterpreted his reluctance. "Oh, Caleb, I'm not going to fall off Mayflower if we race. Why don't you ride Starr tomorrow? He's a fast runner."

He squelched his personal preference. "Fine."

He led his plodding mount into the stable, and Arianna turned her attention to unsaddling her filly. As he finished taking care of his horse, he noticed a slight abrasion on the gelding in the next stall. He entered the stall, then lifted the gelding's left foreleg to examine the wound. Thunder was the property of the resort, which meant one of Caleb's coworkers had put the horse away without taking care of the scrape.

"Is he okay?"

Caleb looked up and saw Arianna leaning against the gate. He frowned. "What are you doing over here?"

"Watching you." She smiled sweetly at him.

Irritated by the warmth in her eyes, he lowered the gelding's leg and approached the gate. Arianna moved slightly so he could open it. "Don't you have something better to do?"

"There's nothing else I want to do."

He walked to the medicine cabinet and grabbed a large jar of animal ointment, then carried it to Thunder's stall.

As he applied the ointment, she asked, "Are you free tonight? There's a dinner-and-dance we could go to."

He frowned. Although she was making it so easy to guard her, perhaps the best way to find out if she was really Douglas's daughter would be to catch the assassin in a murder attempt. But the assassin wouldn't go after her while she was with someone.

"I'm not going out with you."

"Why not? Do you already have a girlfriend?"

"No."

"Did you just break up with someone?"

"I've never dated."

Her eyes widened. "Never? But you've slept with a girl before, right?"

He grimaced as he snapped the lid back on the ointment. "No, I haven't. I believe in abstinence until marriage." He strode to the gate, but she didn't move away from the latch.

She stared at him. "I didn't think anyone believed that way anymore."

"Well, they do if they want to honor God. Excuse me. I need to keep working."

She moved just enough for him to exit the stall.

He headed over to several saddles that needed oiled and rubbed ointment into them. She lingered, asking him questions about the horses and his breeding research. Customers rescued him occasionally. Her presence bothered him more than that of other women he had worked with. Why did her youthful curiosity and coy attention get under his skin? Was it because beneath her selfish exterior he sensed that she had a deep-seated need for someone to really care about her?

He didn't want to get entangled emotionally, and as soon as he was off work, he made a beeline for Rye's employee cabin. "Did you find anything at the Sunnels' beach house?"

"Aurora had a journal, but it was recent stuff. Nothing about the past."

Caleb grabbed his cell phone. "Maybe Patrick found something." He punched in the long-distance number.

"Hello, Caleb," Patrick answered. "Glad you called."

"Did you find something?"

"Nothing that should have surprised me. Douglas cared nothing about decency."

Caleb's gut tightened. "He slept with Aurora, didn't he?"

"Yes."

"When were they together?"

Bitterness touched Patrick's voice. "Nineteen years ago. But I don't believe Arianna is Douglas's daughter. He never showed any interest in her. Forget about her and focus on that other woman—the one who disappeared seven years ago but is now at the resort."

Caleb struggled with his desire to cross Arianna off the list. He understood Patrick's aversion to the girl's selfishness and promiscuity. And what he said made sense. If Arianna were Douglas's daughter, wouldn't he have interacted with her at least a little? Unless Aurora had kept the secret until recently. He sighed. There was no point arguing over suppositions. "We'll focus on June for now. Thanks for your help."

"Not a problem. Call me when you have something more."

"I will. Bye."

Caleb pressed End, then rubbed the back of his neck as Rye watched him. "Aurora slept with Douglas. But only she can tell us if Arianna's his child or Jackson's."

Rye nodded. "She likes to drink. I'll see if I can get her drunk enough to talk about the past. But I'll need to wait until tomorrow night when I have time off. It could take a while to loosen her up."

"That's fine. Arianna invited me to a dinner-and-dance tonight. I declined, but I'm going to keep a close watch since I think it'd be a good opportunity for the assassin to make a move. Patrick doesn't think she's the granddaughter, but I don't want her dead if he's wrong. Can you and Dana keep tabs on June?"

"Not a problem."

Rye headed out, and Caleb showered before getting ready for the evening festivities. As he swung his tie over his white-buttoned shirt, a knock sounded at the living room door. Finishing the loop, he crossed the living room and opened the door.

A FedEx delivery man glanced up from his handheld computer. "Caleb Abrams?"

"That's me."

"Envelope for you."

"Thank you." Caleb glanced at the return address of the police department where Dana had given her testimony.

He shut the door then tore open the envelope. He slid out a photocopied sketch of a lean-faced man with sharp brown eyes who looked to be in his early forties. His black hair waved slightly over his forehead. His features held a slight European cast.

Caleb punched the Memory button on his cell phone. It rang several times before Rye answered.

"Can you drop by again? I have a sketch to show you."

"I'll be right there."

Caleb snapped the phone shut as he studied the sketch. If Dana's memory was correct, he and Rye now had an edge in identifying the assassin. However, they couldn't get too cocky. If the man dyed his hair, slipped in contacts, and grew a beard, his looks would change drastically.

He laid the paper down just as Rye rapped on the door and entered.

Caleb waved at the sketch. "This is our man."

Rye picked up the paper and studied the picture. "Should we tell Dana she can go back home?"

"No. If the guy has changed his appearance, Dana might still recognize his expression or walk."

"Nan, you're intoxicating."

Arianna smiled as her date held her close on the lantern-lit outdoor dance floor.

"Do you know how badly I want you to come to my room?"

Timothy Holdan had enchanted her at the beginning of the week with his chiseled features, golden hair, and aristocratic bearing. The son of an English baron, he had accompanied his family on their vacation to the California resort and had introduced himself at the pool.

However, since joining him on the dance floor in her shimmering, low-cut, slit-to-the-hip evening gown, Arianna had had difficulty keeping her focus on his ardent compliments. Her thoughts kept slipping to her conversations with Caleb at the stables. She couldn't stop wondering what it would take to get him to say the words Timothy had just spoken.

It baffled her that Caleb could exude such raw magnetism while holding to some ridiculous moral standard. The two images simply didn't mix. Abstinence belonged to people too ugly or weak to captivate anyone's desire.

She had gone home that afternoon, hoping to pester Uncle Ben for an idea on how to persuade Caleb to give up his strict moral code. But she had found out that her uncle had left the area for several days. Disappointed, she'd readied herself for her date that night, hoping an idea would come to mind amid the romantic atmosphere.

In response to Timothy's ardent question, she asked flirtatiously, "If I did go to your room, what would we do?"

Sparks leapt into Timothy's cauliflower blue eyes. "Come with me and I'll show you."

A wave of desire passed through her, activated by his sensuous touches. Perhaps she should go with him. After all, she had no idea how long it would take Caleb to come around, and Uncle Ben said she should always live for the moment.

"When do you want to go?"

He smiled. "Now." He led her off the dance floor and into the shadows. But when they passed a number of tables set up for drinks and refreshments, she froze. Caleb sat at one of the tables, and the scorn in his gaze cut into hers.

"Nan, aren't you coming?" Timothy stepped in front of her and kissed her neck, seeking to reclaim her attention.

Behind him, Caleb's gaze blackened. He stood and walked away.

"Forget it." Arianna pushed away, ignoring the confusion in Timothy's eyes. Heedless of her high heels, she sprinted in the direction that Caleb had gone.

Just as she caught up to him, he swung toward her. His eyes narrowed.

She spoke before he could. "Caleb, Timothy was my date for tonight, but I don't want him. I want you."

Anger darkened his eyes. "You're shameless, you know that? You let that guy put his hands all over you, and you have the gall to say that you want *me*?"

Fear that she had ruined any chance of having him caused tears to spring to her eyes. "None of the guys I've liked before would've gotten angry."

His face hardened. "Give up your infatuation with me, Arianna. You're the last girl on earth I would give myself to." He strode away.

Arianna stood frozen as he disappeared into the darkness.

She started to go find Timothy so he could ease her hurt pride, but a sudden realization struck. Caleb had said, *"You let that guy put his hands all over you."* A tingle ran up her spine. He had been watching her on the dance floor.

During their rides together he had acted indifferent to her presence. But if he was as disinterested as he indicated, why would he have watched her from the shadows?

Her heart raced in sudden, intense hope. She resolved to keep every other guy at a distance so Caleb's anger would cool down. It might take a few days because of the depth of his passion, but hopefully during that time, she would get a chance to talk to Uncle Ben about the best way to integrate herself with someone whose religious convictions made him fight his own desires.

Caleb watched Arianna enter her house, shutting the door behind her. He had walked away from her in anger, but he had not been able to desert the situation as he wanted. The shadows of the dance floor provided too prime an opportunity for her to be assaulted. However, she had unexpectedly headed home after his tongue-lashing.

He circled the beach house, noting her bedroom light as it flickered on. He grimaced as her shadow passed by the window. Too bad detective work made him a Peeping Tom. Perhaps Patrick was right and he was wasting his time with her. If she was an heir to the Sunnel billions, wouldn't Jackson simply manipulate her instead of kill her?

He circled the beach house again. Jackson pulled up in his luxury car and headed into the beach house, laptop in hand. Caleb watched, troubled. Arianna had spent many hours alone with that man. Jackson could easily find a way to kill her and make it look like an accident. He wouldn't need to hire an assassin. Teenagers overdosed on drugs all the time.

Caleb shook his head. Even if Arianna were Douglas's child, she wasn't the daughter Douglas had willed his few possessions to. He wouldn't worry about her anymore.

Chapter Six

Rye whistled as he strolled along the outer path of the resort's beautiful rose garden. Caleb had offered to take over the responsibility of trailing June with Dana since he had the day off. Rye was grateful for the break.

Last night, he had spent four hours with Aurora, drinking vodka and managing to get her to open up to him. She admitted to sleeping with Douglas Sunnel, but brushed aside the notion that Jackson wasn't Arianna's real father. "She looked just like him as a baby."

Rye didn't consider her reasoning to be conclusive evidence since the two men were related, but he doubted Douglas would think Arianna was his child unless Aurora told him so.

On the other front, Caleb's friend at the LA police department had phoned Caleb that morning. The fingerprints Rye had obtained from June's room did not match any on record in the United States. Since the FBI would have filed June Moore's fingerprints at the time of her disappearance, Caleb decided their June was an imposter. He had e-mailed an old friend who worked in Europe as a reporter, asking for his help in discovering "June's" real identity.

Rye wandered toward the long patio of umbrella-shaded tables adjoining the garden's refreshment bar. A number were occupied, with feminine voices drifting past the roses and orchids. Whistling again at the pretty picture, Rye stuck his hands in his pockets as he continued to walk with no particular purpose.

Then he saw her.

He paused, his heart jumping in his chest.

The chocolate-eyed maiden who had entered June's room by mistake sat alone at the end table, her hands reposing in her lap. She seemed to drink in the sun, her head tipped back and adorable round sunglasses shielding her eyes from its brightness.

Her presence pulled him like a magnet, and his heart beat faster as he headed toward her.

Cora had asked to be seated at a table near the fragrant rose garden when David told her he had a meeting with a potential employer. He had apologized for the poor timing, but she said she understood. He had hurried off to the appointment as soon as he settled her at the table.

Cora's thoughts drifted to her work at the Y. After losing her sight, she had learned how to play violin pieces by ear and even earned a scholarship to a local college. During the summers, she worked as a volunteer with the children's programs at a nearby YMCA campground. She loved sharing about Jesus with spiritually hungry children while teaching them singing and violin. She'd eagerly accepted the Hauzens' invitation to join them at the resort, seeing it as an opportunity to volunteer at the Summerland YMCA.

Music had become her primary outlet for the love she felt for her Savior, though Grandpa and Caleb didn't understand why she wanted to worship a God who required her to forgive those who hurt her. They didn't realize that holding on to despair after her accident would have destroyed her soul.

Letting the sun's warm rays soak into her skin, she prayed for the Lord to reveal Himself to her family. Hezekiah had been raised in staunch Judaism and had passed down to Caleb his strong belief that the Messiah would come as a powerful King, not a sacrificial Lamb. The dearest desire of her heart was to see both her grandfather and her uncle embrace the healing grace of the risen Messiah, Jesus of Nazareth.

A shadow fell across her face, and she drew in a sharp breath when she caught the scent of fresh pine much too close. A moment later, her lips were grazed with a warm kiss.

"Hello, Hershey."

Amusement colored his tone, and she didn't need sight to identify him as the man from the hotel room. She felt speechless.

"Well," he teased, "aren't you going to say something?"

She searched for adequate words. "Why did you do that?"

"What? Kiss you?"

"Yes."

He settled with a lazy sigh into the patio chair beside her. "Because every princess should get a kiss. And I told you—I'm Prince Charming. But you can call me Rye."

Cora's cheeks heated at the open flirtation, but for the life of her she couldn't put him in the class of repulsive predator or would-be seducer. Something in his manner offered no threat. However, neither could she sit peacefully beside him. She didn't want David to return and find them together.

She stood, hoping she could make it safely to the rose garden. It was surrounded by a short brick wall that began only a few feet from the table. She moved quickly for the wall. In her haste, her foot caught on something that felt like outstretched legs.

She cried out as she fell, but relief poured into her as Rye caught her. He pulled her safely onto his lap. "You know, Hershey, if you wanted me to hold you, all you had to do was ask."

She blushed, then realized he didn't know. She took off the sunglasses that hid her unfocused eyes from the world. "I'm blind."

He sucked in his breath. A gentle ripple of air stirred in front of her face as if he were testing her sight for himself.

His knuckles brushed lightly against her cheek. "I'm sorry."

She didn't know if he was apologizing for tripping her or if he felt bad for her handicap, but embarrassment flooded her as she realized she was allowing a stranger to hold her. She found the arm of the chair and shifted to her feet.

Rye wrapped warm fingers around her right hand and stood with her. "Why don't you have a dog or a cane or something?"

"I left my walking stick behind. I'm usually with someone here, and

Esther feels uncomfortable when I bring it."

"Who's Esther?"

"My fiancé's stepmother."

Rye rubbed his thumb over the pulse in her wrist. "You mean David?"

"Yes." A tingle ran up her arm. Unnerved by the feeling, she pulled her hand out of his hold.

"So, where were you going so quickly?"

She hesitated. "The rose garden."

"I think it would be easier to tour with an escort."

Whether he meant the double meaning or not, Cora blushed.

He laughed. "Don't worry. I won't steal any more kisses—this time."

She almost refused his assistance, but a memory tugged at her soul. *My child, I love him too.*

She knew her Savior well enough to realize that two chance encounters were not mere circumstance. She also knew she had nothing to fear in this man's company. On the contrary, she felt the burden of the Holy Spirit for his soul rest upon her.

She nodded consent to his help, and Rye tucked her arm under his. "On to the roses. And after that, an acre of heavenly fragrance."

Rye gazed at the ceiling over his bed in the small employee cabin. He had left Hershey fifteen minutes ago, slipping away per her request before David made an appearance.

He smiled wryly. Although she had agreed to walk with him in the rose gardens, she had not wanted to introduce him to her fiancé. But then, he hadn't wanted to meet the other man in her life either, preferring to hold on to her sweetness without pulling himself out of his dream world.

She hadn't told him her name during their walk together, and he hadn't asked. He feared the spell connecting him with her might break if he obtained too many concrete facts.

When he shared her appreciation of the velvet-soft roses, she had quoted a poetic verse. *"Every good and perfect gift is from above."* He'd asked what it meant, and she had said that everything good was a gift from God.

He couldn't remember any goodness in his life until he met Caleb, who also believed in God. Rye wondered if his own fledgling belief was the reason God had allowed him to taste Hershey's serenity of soul.

Chapter Seven

H ey, Caleb. Chris here."

Caleb straightened in his seat as the Instant Message popped open on his laptop screen from his friend who worked as a reporter in Europe. He quickly typed an answer. "Hey, Chris. Good to hear from you. Where are you?"

"London. What's this dame look like that you want me to find?"

"I'll e-mail you a couple pictures." Caleb grabbed the digital camera he had used during his surveillance of June that morning. Although he had been careful not to get close, the zoom had provided several clear shots of June's face and profile. He inserted the digital card into the laptop and downloaded the images.

Another message popped up from Chris. "I'm stuck here for a few days, but I can start browsing databases. Where should I look first?"

"Scotland. She mentioned that her husband's there. It's also where her family said she disappeared seven years ago."

"Interesting. Any recent airline tickets?"

"Didn't find any."

"Know when she arrived in the States?"

"She checked into the resort here a week ago. That's all I've got."

"Okay. Hey, good-lookin' chick. What do you want her for?"

Caleb smiled as he tapped the keyboard. "That's confidential. But it looks like she's stolen another American's identity. Don't want to involve the Feds yet, though. They don't cooperate with PIs very easily."

"Know the feeling. Any chance she's not American?"

Caleb frowned. "Good question. She doesn't have an accent."

"Scottish look, though. I'll see what I can do."

"Thanks. Let me know when you need a favor from our end."

"Will do."

"Lindon!"

Caleb looked up from pouring feed into a mare's trough, then stepped out of the stall as his boss strode toward him. "Yes, sir?"

Flannigan looked to be in his sixties, his face weathered under his cowboy hat. A scowl filled his gray eyes. "The Sunnel filly just came back with a foreleg badly cut and no rider. I need you to find the girl."

Caleb's heart rate escalated. For two days, he had ignored Arianna as she came and went at the stables. Although uncomfortably aware of her presence, he had reminded himself that she probably wasn't Patrick's granddaughter. However, Flannigan's announcement shocked him.

Mayflower may have thrown Arianna, but she was an excellent rider. She had ridden out alone on the south trail an hour ago. What if she was the granddaughter after all? His negligence might have left her wide open for the assassin to attack. Fear flooded his soul. He quickly saddled Star and an extra mount, then galloped to the trail Arianna had taken.

A trio of riders emerged from the woods. The couple looked to be in their fifties and the young man in his twenties. Caleb reined Star to a halt and hailed them. "Have you passed a girl in her late teens with black hair?"

The older man shook his head. "Sorry."

"Have you heard anything that sounded like a gunshot?"

The woman startled. "There's not supposed to be any shooting around here."

The younger man frowned. "I haven't heard anything like that."

Caleb nodded. "Thank you." He urged Star into a gallop, passing the family.

As he continued down the trail, he battled his fear with logic. Surely the assassin wouldn't risk attacking a guest on resort property where someone might see. But what if he had lured Arianna into the trees? Would she have been stupid enough to cavort with a stranger?

Caleb's chest tightened in a mixture of fear and anger. If she had gone into the forest with the assassin, it might take days to find her body.

At that moment, distant crying reached him. It came from off the trail to the left. Relief touched him, but he frowned as he dismounted. The pine trees were too dense to take a horse into. Why had Arianna gone into the trees? Was she with someone?

He slipped off Star and moved as quietly as he could through the thick undergrowth. He pushed branches out of his way and stared at Arianna where she sat alone in a small grassy area. Her shoulders shook as she cried, but she didn't appear hurt except for a long scrape on her right calf.

Fear receded, and logic told him she had left Mayflower on the trial to meet with someone. Only it hadn't been the assassin. Apparently she had found another man to seduce, but her romantic interlude had gone awry. Anger stirred, and he strode forward, heedless of the twigs and leaves that snapped underfoot.

Arianna jerked her head up. Her eyes dilated.

He stopped a few feet from her and asked coldly, "Did you know Mayflower got away while you were meeting with your latest lover?"

Her face flushed, and she winced as she pushed herself to her feet. "I wasn't meeting with anyone. Mayflower threw me."

Anger flared full force, and he grabbed her arm, wanting to shake her. "Don't lie to me! There's no way you rode Mayflower in here."

Arianna glared. "She didn't throw me *here*." Tears filled her blue-green eyes. "I've been trying to get back to the resort."

"You've been walking off trail? You'd better come up with a better story than that."

"I was *riding* off trail farther up the hill. If you won't believe me, just leave me alone!" She yanked out of his hold but lost her balance. She fell with a strangled cry and grabbed her left ankle.

The desire to help her washed over him, but he covered it with irritation. "If your ankle's hurt, why have you been walking on it?"

"Just go away!"

He smiled grimly. Apparently he had wounded her pride too many times. "I've got orders to take you back, so come on. Get up."

She refused to look at him. "It hurts too much. I can't walk on it."

"Then I'll help you." He reached down, but she jerked away.

"I don't want your help!"

He gritted his teeth. "Fine. Have it your way. There's a horse on the trail for you."

He strode away. Once the pain subsided, she'd be able to make it to the extra mount. She wouldn't be far behind him.

What if she was Cora?

The quiet thought filtered into his turbulent emotions. A muscle jerked in his jaw. He would never leave Cora to her own devices, but that was different. Cora was sweet, submissive, and willing to accept help from others. The opposite of Arianna.

However, he couldn't ignore the prick of his conscience. He slowed his stride and glanced back. Tears trickled down Arianna's cheeks as she nursed her ankle. She looked lost, rejected, helpless. Pressing his lips together, he turned back.

Her eyes widened as he neared. He grabbed her waist and hauled her up, hoisting her over his shoulder as though she were a child. She gasped and struggled.

"Don't you dare, Arianna Sunnel!"

She stilled immediately, and as soon as they reached the trail, he threw her onto the extra horse. He strode toward Star while Arianna hissed at her mount, then galloped past him toward the stable.

Caleb didn't spur Star to catch her.

"Is she going to be okay?" Arianna asked the stable manager as he examined Mayflower.

Flannigan nodded. "She'll be fine, miss. Just need to keep that bandage fresh. She took a nasty gouge in the foreleg."

Arianna buried her face in the horse's silky mane. This was all her fault. If she hadn't taken that last jump, Mayflower wouldn't have injured herself. She hadn't seen the dead wood until it snapped under the filly's weight, causing her to rear up. If only her frustration over Caleb's prevailing reticence hadn't made her reckless.

Flannigan stood. "Don't worry, miss. I'll see to it that the stable hands change her bandage every day and watch for signs of infection. You can ride one of the other mounts until she's better. It might be a couple weeks."

Fresh tears sprang into Arianna's eyes. She stroked the filly's neck as Flannigan headed back to the front of the stable. "I'm sorry, Mayflower. I'm not gonna let your cut get worse. And I won't go riding until you're better."

Feeling somewhat better for her promise, she wiped away her tears, then located a grooming brush. Mayflower loved its gentle, soothing strokes, and she let the rhythmic motion draw out her ragged emotions.

Caleb had come for her. He had made it clear that he had done so against his will, but her pulse had jumped anyway. His disbelief in her cut her pride, and it angered her that he would resent touching her. However, her defensiveness had crumbled when he hauled her over his shoulder. The memory of his primordial behavior made her stomach flip.

He had accused her of meeting with a new lover. His reaction tasted of pure jealousy. If only Uncle Ben had been around the last few days to advise her.

Somehow she needed to convince Caleb that giving in to his attraction to her would be well worth any cost to his religious convictions.

She finished with Mayflower's right side, then limped to the filly's left side to continue brushing.

A horse trotted into the stable, and she glanced toward the wide doorway. Caleb dismounted, then talked in a low voice to Flannigan, who glanced her way and nodded. She fixed her gaze on the sweaty hair of her horse.

Brush, Arianna. Just brush. He doesn't like you throwing yourself at him, so you're just going to have to find a different way.

Determined not to risk another humiliating mistake, she pretended to ignore Caleb as he walked Star past her. But she felt his presence with every fiber of her being.

He finished with Star before she was willing to leave Mayflower, and by the time she patted her horse good night, her left ankle hurt so badly it was the only thing she could focus on. Caleb hadn't spared any compassion for her injury, and she refused to give herself any pity either, not when Mayflower had sustained a far worse wound.

She wanted to cry, however, at how much it hurt just to cross the stable yard. Near the hotel, she sank onto a bench, her ankle throbbing. Putting her head in her hands, she gave in to tears.

"Ready for help this time?"

Her sobs caught, and she jerked her head up. Caleb gazed at her with an expression she couldn't read. She smeared her tears away.

He gestured an impatient hand at her silence. "Come on, Arianna. It's not that hard to say yes. Besides, if you want to help take care of Mayflower tomorrow, you need to get that ankle on ice."

She swallowed. He cared about horses as much as she did. Perhaps the filly could provide the connection she needed with him.

She pushed herself painfully to a standing position. As she shifted her weight, a stab of pain shot up her leg.

Caleb stepped close. "If it's this bad tomorrow, I'm going to have to get you a crutch."

"A crutch!" Arianna pretended offense, but her heart hammered as he slipped his arm around her waist, bracing her injured side.

She tried not to betray the wave of desire that ran through her as she hobbled alongside him. But halfway along the path to the beach houses, she risked a glance up to his face. He seemed oblivious to her, his gaze centered straight ahead.

She glanced again, and this time a muscle bunched in his strong jawline. An electric current sizzled into her, and her pulse skittered wildly. She had been right! He felt the same pull she did. She broke pace, seized by an incredible yearning for him to swing her around and press her against him as his mouth found hers.

His gaze cut down to hers and darkened. "So, what did you do to Mayflower to make her cut herself?"

Arianna sucked in her breath. Horrid man! He must know how much she loved her horse and that she was ashamed of having hurt Mayflower. She averted her gaze. "I took a jump before I knew what was on the other side."

Caleb said nothing more until he delivered her to the front steps of her parents' beach house. He released her to the support of the pine railing, then stepped back. "We feed the horses at eight. I'll mix up an oatmeal mush with some antibiotics in it for you to give Mayflower."

"Thank you."

With seeming reluctance, he met her gaze again. "I'm sorry I didn't believe you."

The unexpected apology made Arianna tremble.

His gaze flickered over her, then he turned and strode away. She sank down onto the bottom step of the porch, overwhelmed that she had finally received his amity. Clenching her fist, she resolved to do nothing to cause it to falter.

Rye walked into Summerland's red-carpeted casino, his thoughts grim. Caleb wanted him to get the pseudo June Moore to talk. Time was of the essence, and it could take a while for their reporter friend in London to unearth more leads.

A few days ago, Rye wouldn't have minded the assignment. He knew women. Knew how to get them to talk. A few drinks and a few nudges in the right direction had been all it took to get Aurora to divulge her past dalliances with Douglas. But June could handle her alcohol better than Aurora, and she wasn't interested in chitchat. Which made playing her a dangerous game.

Resort guests stood at the slot machines lined up on both sides of the casino. In the center, several poker games ensued while to the far back half a dozen guests leaned over a long table where the larger bets were wagered. June hung on the arm of a lanky black man dressed in designer slacks and jacket.

Rye found a place in the shadows and leaned casually against the wall, watching the game of chance. If June had a boyfriend, his chances of gaining her attention were slim. He hadn't exactly given her a heart-throbbing night to remember the last time they were together.

He grimaced. Try as he might, he didn't have an ounce of desire to draw her interest. All he could think about was a pair of chocolate eyes behind adorable sunglasses. During his short hour with Hershey, the subtle strength of her character had reminded him of the one type of woman he had no experience with. A woman of virtue.

In the back, June laughed. Luck had played into her hands. She leaned forward to gather her winnings, her low-cut dress exposing far too much. Rye looked away. But he also remembered the scar on her shoulder and the mission before him.

He squared his shoulders. If he had the chance, he'd play June with all charm and skill he had.

Chapter Eight

How's my baby girl doing?"

"No sign of infection yet." Caleb held the oatmeal bucket for Mayflower as Arianna hugged her filly. He was glad to see she was limping only slightly this morning, but he felt bothered by the tight tank top and shorts that revealed way too much of her long legs. "Why aren't you wearing one of your uncle's outfits?"

She glanced down at herself, then looked back to his face with apparent contrition. "I'm sorry. I didn't think about it."

Caleb decided not to chastise her for the lapse. But by the time he finished instructing her on how to change Mayflower's bandage and clean the wound, he knew he had to find another solution to what she wore. He had always believed that the sanctity of marriage was preserved not only through purity of deed but also through purity of thought. But every time he looked at her, his thoughts slipped in the wrong direction.

Determined to stop the lure of temptation, he asked, "Do you have time to go shopping this evening? After I get off work, I'd like to take you somewhere to pick out some modest clothes."

Something sparked in her eyes. "Okay."

"I can pick you up at the beach house a little after five."

She kept her gaze fixed on his face. "My parents bought me a ticket to go with them on the yacht cruise tonight, but I'd rather go with you."

He nodded and focused on Mayflower's eating.

Arianna's infatuation appeared to be back in full force, but he had decided last night that even though the chances of her being Patrick's granddaughter were slim, he couldn't handle ignoring her the way he had. The jolt of fear when Flannigan reported her missing had convinced him to give her what she wanted: his presence if not romance. If she thought he was interested in her, at least he wouldn't have to worry about her going out with strange men. She also needed positive affirmation in her life for something other than flirtation and manipulative ploys. Something few men would supply. He might as well be a positive influence while he kept her out of harm's way.

He patted Mayflower's side. "You did a good job helping me today. Thanks."

She blinked rapidly as if fighting tears.

"Does your ankle hurt?"

She shook her head. "No. It's a lot better."

"Okay. I'll see you at five then."

He left the stall and turned his thoughts toward the e-mail Chris had sent that morning.

"No records of marriage for June Moore in Great Britain. Fingerprints have no match here either. Will travel to Scotland in four days and inquire at Scotland Yard about disappearance. More info would help, especially town where husband is."

Caleb hefted a feedbag off a shelf on the far wall, then walked to the line of stalls to ration the oats. Dana had stayed home last night so Rye could engage with June. Caleb grimaced over the compromising position he had asked the kid to assume. But with a girl's life on the line, what else could he do? Hopefully last night had given Rye enough information for Chris to find the answers they needed.

When his break came at ten o'clock, Caleb headed to Rye's cabin. He rapped on the door, then knocked harder when there wasn't an immediate answer.

"Coming," Rye grumbled through the door, then threw it open and blinked against the bright sunlight. His feet and chest were bare, the brand of a cross outlined on his chest from his ghetto days.

Caleb entered the cabin, noting the wrinkled clothes on the chair and floor. "Sorry for waking you."

Rye slid onto a nearby chair and put a hand to his head. "It's all right. I talked with June last night. Got myself a hangover doing it."

Caleb grimaced. "What'd you find out?"

"Said she married her husband during a spontaneous, romantic fling. But hubby isn't a nice guy. Started slapping her within a week. She filed for divorce, but he beat her up over it. She decided to flee to the States. Hates his guts."

"Find out a name?"

Rye squeezed his nose. "No. That's what makes me suspicious. Even drunk, she was careful what she said. No names, not of family or of towns."

"How long has she been married?"

"Couldn't get a definite on that either. Sounds recent, though. Maybe a month."

Caleb nodded, his mind churning. "An abused woman might steal someone else's identity. But she must have connections somewhere to get hold of the real June's passport and identity. I'll tell Chris what you found out. Hopefully it will help us find out her true identity so we can figure out if she's the heiress. Thanks for doing what you could."

"Yeah." Rye winced. "I'm starting to think I'm not cut out for this detective game. Last night stunk."

Caleb's throat tightened. "How far did you have to go?"

"Further than I will again."

Caleb raked a hand through his hair, upset with himself. "It's my fault. I shouldn't have asked you. Nothing merits breaking God's laws. Just forget the job next time, okay? God can watch out for the granddaughter."

Rye rubbed his eyes. "Don't worry. It wasn't anything close to what I've done in the past. I just…" He drew in a deep breath and looked away. "We're doing our job. That's what matters."

Caleb wasn't sure anymore. He justified breaking the rules for the sake of others' safety, but he knew his strength. Rye, on the other hand, wasn't that far removed from his old lifestyle. And he already had too many marks against him come Judgment Day.

Rye shifted in his seat. "I have to take Dana on a cruise tonight. June's attending some posh event the resort schedules every summer. I doubt the assassin will strike on board where he can't get away, but I know you want all bases covered."

"Speaking of all bases…" Caleb sighed. "I'm taking Arianna into town tonight. I don't like the way she throws herself at guys without a thought to her safety. If she's hung up on me, at least she probably won't try something stupid with someone else."

Rye rubbed his forehead, his gaze pensive. "So you still think she's in the running?"

Caleb shrugged. "I don't know. But it's my responsibility to keep her safe. At least until we know."

Rye started to nod but winced at the motion. "At least you don't have to pretend to be a playboy."

Caleb cleared his throat in discomfort, but didn't apologize again. "Call me tonight if anything happens on the cruise. Otherwise, I'll see you tomorrow."

"Esther," Cora said when she heard the woman's cell phone click shut after her conversation with Paul, "if David's sick, maybe I shouldn't go to the cruise tonight."

"Nonsense, dear. Just because he's down with the stomach flu doesn't mean you can't attend. No girl in her right mind would give up a chance to dress up and flirt with the who's whos of society."

Esther had taken Cora by surprise two days earlier when she told her that her husband, Paul, had bought all four of them tickets to attend the resort's yacht dinner and dance. Cora had mentioned that she didn't have anything suitable to wear, so Esther had offered to take her to pick out a dinner dress. However, upon their arrival at the Summerland mall, Paul had called to tell them that David wouldn't be able to make it.

A rustling sound told Cora that Esther was sorting through taffeta dresses. Suddenly she wished she hadn't given in to her childish wish to look like a princess with Prince Charming at her side.

Prince Charming. The phrase made Cora think of the man in the rose garden. *Lord, I still don't know why You had me walk with him. I thought I was supposed to witness to him, but I didn't get the chance. Or maybe I'm just not for-*

ward enough. I should have started preaching, I guess, because there's no other reason for me to have spent time with him.

She sighed. She didn't want her thoughts on any man but David. *Lord, why did You have to let him get sick?*

"What about this one, dear?" Esther's voice interrupted her prayer. "It's a gorgeous blue and has a v neckline." She gave a rueful laugh. "Never mind. I know you want something that doesn't show cleavage."

Cora listened to her replace the dress, then they moved to another rack. Esther described the dresses she thought would look good on Cora, but put each one back because they were all too revealing in some way.

At last, she exclaimed, "This one's perfect for you. It's pure white with a round neckline and frothy skirt. Wait here while I check to see if they have it in your size."

Esther hurried off, and Cora fingered the silk of a nearby gown. Esther didn't understand how overwhelmed she felt about the evening ahead of her, meeting dozens of strangers who would only feel pity for her.

She sighed and let the sleek material slip from her fingers. If only she could tell Esther that she didn't want to attend. But that would probably offend the older woman, who had gone out of her way numerous times to help her. David had also mentioned that the tickets were incredibly expensive and that it was very generous of his dad to include them in the evening's grandeur. There was no way she could pull back from what the Hauzens considered a generous bequest.

Esther came back, accompanied by a professional saleswoman who whisked Cora in and out of the soft, filmy dress in no time.

"We'll take it."

Cora silently accompanied Esther to the cash register. Once the purchase was made, Esther draped the long dress bag over Cora's left arm before taking her right arm. Cora submitted to her guidance through the mall to the parking lot. Outside, the sun blazed down upon them.

"Oh, no."

Cora moved her head at Esther's worried tone. "What's the matter?"

"My keys aren't in my purse." Her tone switched to one of annoyance.

"They must have fallen out in the dressing room. Can you wait here while I run back in?"

Cora didn't like the idea of being left alone in the parking lot, though she often walked alone at her university campus. She swallowed her discomfort. "Sure. I'll be fine."

"Thanks, dear. I'll be back in a jiffy."

Esther hurried away, and Cora struggled against a sense of exposure. Drawing a deep breath, she reminded herself that such a feeling was foolish. The Lord was always with her, no matter where she was. She might as well use the time to pray instead of letting fear prey upon her soul.

Rye shrugged back into his loose-fitting T-shirt, then went to the cashier to purchase the black three-piece suit he'd found. He hated trying on clothes, but he didn't own anything that would stand up to the scrutiny of the wealthy guests at tonight's cruise.

With his suit zipped into a dress bag, Rye headed back to the truck. His stomach hinted that it didn't like the tequila he'd had last night any more than his head did. He winced at the brilliant sunlight as he strode across the parking lot.

His mood wasn't improved by the fact that he'd crossed a line with June, even if he hadn't slept with her. Never mind that the woman had only started talking after he'd crawled in bed with her. And never mind that the heiress might be the next target for Alan Brinnon's killer. Rye knew God's rules, but once again he had broken them.

Reaching the truck discouraged and frustrated, he threw the suit across the passenger seat. As he started to climb in, he noticed a slender girl standing alone by a silver Crown Victoria. She held a long bag similar to his. Her pink sundress fluttered in the warm breeze, and her dark hair hung in a long braid down her back. Round sunglasses sat on her delicate nose, the gold in their frames blending against her dusky skin. She used her fingers to feel her way around the car, then settled the dress bag on the top of the trunk.

His pulse quickened. This had to be the blind girl he'd run into at the resort. But what was she doing out here alone?

He put his foot back on the ground and closed the cab door. Sticking his hands in his pockets, he made his way across the parking lot. His guilt and his hangover faded to a dull sensation in the back of his head.

He noticed various shoppers coming in and out of the mall. Hershey appeared to be waiting for someone. He slowed as he neared her, not wanting to startle her, then paused a couple of feet in front of her. "Hi, Hershey."

She startled and turned her head toward him. "Rye?"

"Yeah."

Relief flickered over her features. "What are you doing here?"

He smiled and stepped closer. "I have a crystal ball that told me I might find someone with chocolate eyes if I waited here long enough."

Her breath caught for a moment. "Is that why you call me Hershey?"

Rye stepped close enough to touch her hair with his fingertips. "That and your ravishing dark hair."

She blushed and acted as if she wanted to step back to break the contact, but the Crown Victoria held her in place.

He dropped his hand. "Who are you waiting for?"

"Esther."

Her fiancé's stepmother. He was glad she left the reminder unsaid. He glanced at the dress bag on the trunk. "Going to a party?"

"Yes."

He wanted to ask what party she would be attending, but caught sight of an elegantly dressed woman of about forty making a beeline for them from the mall doors. Regret touched his heart. Hershey would feel awkward about introducing him. "Guess I'd better go. Esther's coming."

"Thank you."

He hesitated a moment longer. "For what?"

"For staying with me until she came back."

He smiled, the guilt in his heart slightly assuaged. "No problem."

He headed away from Esther as she approached. He returned to the truck and started the motor, his headache reemerging with pounding force.

Chapter Nine

Arianna poked her head into her uncle's room, glad to see him back from his trip. "Can I borrow a T-shirt and shorts again, Uncle Ben?" He looked at her in the mirror as he swung his silk tie into a loop. "Shouldn't you be getting dressed for the cruise party tonight?"

She hung on the doorframe, watching him slip the tie into place over his silk shirt with expert ease. "I'm not going. Are you?"

He picked up the gold Rolex on the vanity and slipped it over his wrist. "I wasn't planning on it, but an old friend invited me at the last minute. She has an extra ticket since her stepson became ill."

For a moment Arianna felt disappointed that she wouldn't be joining the festivities. But even Uncle Ben's company couldn't match Caleb's. "So, can I borrow your clothes?"

Uncle Ben looked amused. "If you're joining the new trend of cross-dressing, I've got spiffier clothes than old jeans and T-shirts."

Arianna laughed. "I'm not cross-dressing. There's this guy I like, and he's taking me out tonight, but my clothes aren't modest enough for him."

Uncle Ben turned to face her. "You're dating a prude?"

Arianna smiled slyly. "He's gorgeous."

Uncle Ben gestured toward his dresser. "Go ahead, take whatever you want."

"Thanks." Arianna made her raid, then returned to her room to change.

Caleb's kindness made her long for his affirmation. Although he was taking her tonight to purchase clothes he liked, she figured that changing her attire now would show him how much she wanted to please him.

Caleb saw Arianna sitting on the steps of her parents' beach house when he pulled up in the Ford.

She jumped to her feet, her eyes bright with anticipation. To his relief, she was again wearing her uncle's shirt and shorts.

She smiled as she opened the passenger door and slipped in. "Hi."

He nodded toward her clothes as he put the truck in reverse. "Thanks for changing. Did your uncle mind?"

She looked pleased that he had noticed. "No. But he was surprised that I was going to hang out with someone who has standards about modesty."

No resentment showed in her expression over the fact, and she reminded Caleb of Rye when they first met. Rye had been eager to do all he could to please his new friend. Arianna's infatuation might very well be a chance to show her God's perspective on relationships.

During the half-hour drive to the mall, she chatted about horses and various equestrian events across the country. Caleb relaxed. He enjoyed the subject as much as she did, and she had apparently decided to let go of her manipulative ways.

They arrived at the mall and walked across the parking lot. She kept pace with his long strides, but glanced at him in astonishment when he held open the mall's glass door for her. He met her gaze for a moment, understanding a little more about her. She wasn't used to even the simplest of gentlemanly courtesies.

He directed her to a department store that held a wide selection of family clothing. She meekly accepted his suggestions for half a dozen shirt-and-shorts outfits.

The outing hadn't taken very long, and Caleb hesitated. Should he take her back to the resort? She had been so compliant, he guided her to the Chinese restaurant in the mall.

Like Rye used to, she acted the way she did because there was no inner compass to align her with God's righteousness. Although he would have preferred not to be the object of her infatuation, he could take the risk of being with her…at least until the heiress was found.

"Ben!"

Cora paused on Paul Hauzen's arm as Esther greeted her long-time friend on the deck of the yacht.

"I'm so glad you could join us for dinner tonight."

"The pleasure is mine," he said smoothly. "Paul, it's good to meet you. I'm glad Esther found another good man."

"Cora," Esther said, "this is my long-time friend, Benjamin Dean. Ben, Cora is engaged to Paul's son. She's graduating from college next spring with a music major. She plays the violin by ear." She lowered her voice to a whisper. "She lost her sight in a fire when she was fifteen."

"A pleasure, Cora."

"Nice to meet you, Mr. Dean."

"Call me Ben. All my friends do. What activities have you found the most enjoyable here at the resort?"

Esther laughed. "Oh, Cora doesn't participate in any of the activities. But she loves the rose garden. Don't you, dear? And the beach. Whenever we go there, she tells us how soft the sand is and how briny the air. I think she enjoys everything in nature."

Cora felt embarrassed at Esther's description. She wasn't used to having her deepest pleasures laid out in front of a stranger. Perhaps Esther didn't realize how much God's creation had come to mean to her after losing her sight. The busyness of the world required sight to function well and therefore produced a certain level of tension within her. But the sounds and smells and textures of nature reminded her of the beauty of her Savior and rejuvenated her soul.

She walked with her hand on Paul's arm as the group headed inside to the dining area.

The murmur of hundreds of voices reached her as well as the tinkle of glass, but she had to imagine the ornate setup of tables and decorations. It had to be exquisite since the cruise catered to the finest of society. She wished someone would describe the details for her. Caleb and Grandpa always did, but neither of the Hauzens or David usually thought to do so.

Paul directed her into a cushioned straight-back chair at one of the tables.

"Thank you." She sat down, settling the filmy material of her dress beneath her.

Other chairs scooted over what sounded like a polished wood floor, and she rested her hands in her lap as Esther and Dean conversed. Paul seemed caught up in conversation with a man farther down the table.

The first course was served as soft orchestra music wafted from one side of the room. Cora forgot to eat as she listened to the sentimental tune.

"I see you enjoy Mozart, Cora."

Dean addressed her from her left, and Cora smiled. "Yes."

"Have you played many of his pieces?"

"A few." Cora remembered the salad on her plate and reached for her fork. She touched warm flesh and startled, surprised Dean's hand was in such close proximity to her plate.

"What do you think you'll do with your music after you graduate?"

She tentatively located her fork. "I want to teach grade-school music."

"Cora's volunteering at the local YMCA campground," Esther inserted. "She volunteers at the Y near her home every summer. We're very proud of her for reaching out and influencing the next generation."

Cora smiled politely but wished that Esther hadn't mentioned where she worked. For some reason, Dean's attention made her nervous.

He asked her several more questions about her work and her relationship with David. "Where do you and David make your home?"

She frowned slightly, uncertain of the question. "I live with my grandfather. David has an apartment near the college."

"So you don't live together?"

Cora put her fork down. Where had that question come from? "No."

Esther laughed, a little nervously. "The Abrams hold to the Mosaic moral code. I know it's a rarity in these times, but Cora and David both desire to wait for marriage."

"I apologize if I offended you."

Cora nodded and stabbed a forkful of lettuce. When the next course arrived, she had little appetite. She could sense Dean's appraisal of her throughout the meal, increasing her nervousness. Why was he interested in her? Was it because she was blind? Or did her stand on morality make her an oddity?

"What about you, Ben?" Esther asked during the third course of lamb and potatoes. "Do you have an ongoing relationship with anyone?"

He laughed lightly. "I'm too carefree to be tied down. I enjoy the freedom of coming and going as I please. Women expect some sort of accountability as soon as a man hints at a long-term relationship."

"I suppose so. Still, there are advantages to having a steady partner."

His voice held an amused smile. "I'm glad you think so. Paul seems to be a good man."

When the four-course meal finished, Esther asked, "Ben, would you mind being Cora's partner for the evening? Paul and I are going to head to the dance floor."

"It would be my pleasure." He stood and pulled Cora's chair out for her. Her stomach knotted, but a refusal would be rude. He touched her arm as he asked, "Would you join me for a stroll around the deck?"

Though Esther had entrusted her into his care, something about him warned her not to be alone with him. "I'd like to go to the dance room."

"Will you honor me with a dance, then?"

"I don't really dance."

"I assure you a two-step would be easy to manage."

She flushed at the idea of him holding her close. "I'd rather not."

"Well, perhaps after a while." He guided her across the room. But instead of the music growing louder, it faded.

A warm breeze touched her face, and she stopped. "We're outside."

"It's so stuffy in there, I thought we'd get a breath of fresh air."

"Mr. Dean, I asked to go to the dance room."

He ran his hand over hers, as though to reassure her. "Don't worry. Esther knows you're with me."

The scent of his cologne increased, and his warm breath touched her neck. Alarm spiraled through her. She stepped backward. "I really don't want to be out here."

"Why? The breeze feels amazing, doesn't it? It's like a caress on the skin." He ran his hand down her neck.

In a panic, she jerked away. "I—I want to use the ladies' lounge. Now."

He laughed softly. "Okay, Cora. You don't need to be so worried."

He rested his hand on her waist as he led her back inside. Her stomach churned until he directed her hand to the doorframe of the lounge. "I'll be watching for you. Then we can go dancing."

She had no intention of going anywhere with him. The music faded as she slipped into the lounge, where quiet greeted her. She leaned against the wall. Her whole body trembled. Dean wasn't to be trusted. He had ignored her wishes and would probably do so again.

Oh, God, what am I to do? I don't want to go back out there, but I can't stay in here forever.

Surely if she said she was sick, he would return her to Esther. And the declaration wouldn't be a complete lie. Her stomach was twisted into a thousand knots.

Chapter Ten

Rye arrived on the cruise ship with Dana ten minutes before the yacht pulled out of the harbor. His black suit coordinated well with her deep red dress, and he noted with a touch of amusement that the long, tight skirt had a slit up one side so she could walk in it.

He shed his suit coat as soon as they sat at their table, then rolled up the sleeves of his gray silk shirt. Despite the air conditioning, he felt overly warm and attributed it to the discomfort of the new suit.

Dana glanced around the dining area nervously, and Rye looked with her. More than two hundred men and women were present, dressed in elegant evening apparel and adorned with glittering diamonds and other gems. The whole room sparkled of glass, silver, and polished wood.

He located June seated several tables to the right. She wore a low-cut, silver dress that sparkled with every movement. A gray-haired man sat on her left, and a young blond man leaned toward her on the right. She tittered, and Rye grimaced. She flirted with every man who gave her attention, and if her actions with him were any indication, she had probably slept with most of them.

He continued to scan the room. Toward the back, Jackson sat at a table with Aurora. He engaged in close conversation with two men wearing expensive suits, their expressions intent. Aurora displayed disinterest to their conversation as she took a long drink from her wine glass. Though the evening had just begun, her scrawny arm looked shaky as she lifted the flute to her red-splashed lips.

Rye studied the men at their table. Either of the two could possibly be the assassin, but it didn't seem likely that Jackson would socialize with the killer so publicly. He glanced to Dana. "Do you see him?"

She shook her head.

"Dana, is that you?" A petite brunette of about thirty sitting several seats down their table squealed in delight.

Beside her, an angular-faced man with premature balding nodded. "Good to see you, Dana."

She looked surprised. "Ellen, Stan. I didn't know you were here."

"We arrived this morning," Ellen answered. "But we thought sure you would have cancelled after what happened. You poor thing. I'm so sorry."

Dana twisted her napkin. "It's been hard. But Alan wanted so much to come here."

Ellen nodded sympathetically. "I'm sorry we didn't make it to the funeral. Our tickets back from Paris were already set."

Dana smoothed the napkin. "It's all right."

"Have the police caught the murderer?"

"No. It's—it's very difficult for me to talk about."

Ellen made a comforting sound. "I understand. We enjoyed our time in France. So much to see. And of course, all those stores to visit!"

"Thankfully," Stan said dryly, "Ellen let me stay at the hotel and enjoy the fine wine while she shopped."

Dana smiled weakly.

Ellen continued to chat about the newest fashion styles in France as the first course arrived.

Rye gratefully bit into the warm bread. His stomach hadn't allowed him to eat much during the day. The salad drenched in ranch dressing also tasted good, and he finished before the arrival of the second course. Dana paid him no attention as she engaged with her friends. He had the feeling that she didn't want them to know he was her partner for the evening. Leaning back in his chair, he let his gaze drift toward the rest of the tables.

Warmth flooded him when he saw Hershey sitting at a table a hundred feet to his right. She looked utterly enchanting in her flounced white dress. A simple pearl necklace lay across her collarbone, and her dark hair fell like a waterfall to her waist. She wasn't wearing her sunglasses, and her chocolate eyes sat like transparent pools in her oval face. Amid all the flaunting and flirting in the room, she seemed to stand out like an oasis of purity and sweetness.

The dark-haired man on her left leaned toward her, touching her hand. Rye frowned. Was that Benjamin Dean, Arianna's uncle? The stylish clothes and debonair manner looked all too familiar, and Rye remembered the magazines in Dean's drawer. He gripped his Coke glass harder. The guy was gazing at Hershey like he couldn't get enough of looking at her, but she didn't seem to be welcoming his attention. In fact, she didn't smile once during the next three courses.

Rye remembered to check on June as the meal ended. She took the arm of her date, and they sashayed to the bar at the far right of the room. The barkeeper poured both of them martinis, and Rye glanced back to Hershey's table. To his surprise, Esther was heading toward the dancing room with a silver-haired man, leaving Hershey with Dean. Rye frowned as the two exited the room onto the decorated yacht deck.

Dana continued to converse with her friends, her back turned to him, and Rye struggled between an intense desire to go after Hershey and his obligation to monitor June.

He straightened when Hershey returned. Dean's hand rested on her waist, and her face had turned pale. Rye stood, his heart beating fast. What had happened out there?

Hershey slipped into the women's lounge, and Dean angled over to talk to Jackson at the nearby table.

Rye cast a swift look at the bar. June giggled as she accepted another tall martini from the bartender. Rye pressed his lips together. If he guessed right, June would be at the bar for a while. And if the assassin was on board, he wouldn't assault her while she was with her date.

Rye turned back to the women's lounge and followed his heart.

Dean glanced in his direction as he neared the lounge, but Rye pretended to head into the men's room. Dean returned to his conversation with Jackson, and Rye slipped into the corridor between the two doors.

He waited, glad that Dean had shifted to face Jackson rather than keep an intent eye on the door. Several minutes passed before Hershey emerged, her fingers trailing the wall.

Rye lightly caught her hand. "Hey, Hershey."

She startled. "Rye?"

"Yeah. Come with me a minute, will you?"

She let him draw her into the hallway, then asked, "Is something wrong?"

Rye guided her around a corner, then positioned her against a wall. He leaned over her, hiding most of her from view. "Nothing's wrong on my end. But you looked like you didn't want to be with that guy."

Her breath caught. "How did you know?"

He combed light fingers into her hair. "You were only gone five minutes, and your face was pale when you came back. What happened?"

She shivered and rubbed her hands over her bare arms. "He took me outside when I asked him to take me to the dance room."

"That's all?"

Strain washed over her face. "I thought he was going to try to kiss me. Or... or worse. I didn't want him touching me."

Rye dropped his hand and studied her. "Dean's a womanizer. How'd you end up with him as your partner?"

"David caught the flu, so Esther invited Benjamin instead. He's an old friend of hers." She shivered again. "I was praying about how to avoid being with him. I'm glad you came."

Warmth ran through him. "I'm glad too." He touched her cheek. "You're trembling."

"Only because of him."

"Forget him, then." Rye didn't care whether his actions would be considered right or wrong. He lowered his head and kissed her.

She inhaled sharply, then broke away as though in consternation. Her voice was a breathless whisper. "You shouldn't do that."

Her shivering had stopped. Apparently he had the opposite effect on her that Dean did. He smiled. "I do a lot of things I shouldn't."

She went so still that he realized what his careless words had made her think. Pain touched his heart.

Taking both of her hands in his, he said softly, "Hershey, I can't explain all the details, but please believe me that I'm not a gigolo."

"Really?" Relief flooded her face. "I'm glad."

His heart tightened again. At least the words were true for the present. He wrapped a silken lock of her hair around his hand. Being with her was the only time he experienced peace, and he knew it was because it hung like an aura around her. Whenever he kissed her, that peace seemed almost tangible.

"Are you okay?"

Apparently he had been silent longer than he realized. "I'm fine."

He longed to spend the remainder of the evening with her, but June remained a priority. Perhaps he could take a little time with Hershey, though. June's drinking episodes usually lasted an hour or so. Besides, Dana was still keeping watch. He took the risk. "I was just wondering if you'd be missed if we went for a walk."

"Oh."

She stayed silent a moment, and he could almost read her struggle. Did she continue to hang out with a man who kept kissing her, or did she return to Dean? Apparently he was the lesser evil, for she said, "I don't think anyone would miss me."

Well, Dean would. But extricating her from his presence was the whole point.

Rye smiled. "How 'bout we visit the other side of the ship? We should be able to hear the waves lapping over there."

An odd look crossed her face. "All right."

He tucked her right arm under his to guide her down the hall. They walked onto the bow of the ship, where a half dozen other couples lingered. Some leaned against the railing as they looked down at the shimmering water, while others stood within each other's arms, unaware of the world around them.

His heart rate quickened, and he glanced at Hershey's soft face. He tore his gaze away. He had not brought her out here to make love to her.

He found a place at the high railing, then broke contact with her. He let his gaze center on the dark night sky, sparkling with hundreds of stars. Remembering that his companion could see none of their surroundings, he observed softly, "It's beautiful out here, Hershey. The sky's like black velvet with hundreds of glittering diamonds. The water reflects the moon with shimmering waves. It's amazing that something so dangerous can be so beautiful."

"The heavens declare the glory of God, and the firmament shows His handiwork."

He glanced at her. "You mentioned God last time we were together."

She nodded. "God made everything that is good. He made us, too, and wants a relationship with each of us." She paused as a breeze lifted tendrils of hair off her neck. "Do you believe God exists?"

"I didn't used to. But if there isn't Someone in charge of things, there's no reason to uphold right over wrong, is there?" He parroted Caleb's words, but meant them as his own. What else explained the depth of guilt his sin had entwined around his soul?

She nodded. "'The law of the Lord is perfect, converting the soul. The testimony of the Lord is sure, making wise the simple.' God gave us His written Word, the Bible, so that we can know His character as well as His desire to cleanse our hearts from our wrong thoughts and actions."

Rye stared at her. Although she spoke simply, the words sounded like a foreign language. His only positive instruction in religion had come from Caleb, who had emphasized God's supreme holiness. That formed the strong moral code of Caleb's life, and Rye copied the code as best he could. But he carried little hope that God would overlook his former transgressions.

Hershey's words held no congruency with the little he believed about God. Feeling like a first grader, he asked, "What do you mean—His desire to cleanse our hearts?"

Though she couldn't see him, she turned from the railing toward him. Earnestness filled her face. "God desires for us to freely give Him our love. But we all make wrong choices. So He had to provide a way to purify our hearts."

"There you are! Dear, we've been looking all over for you."

Rye turned at the interruption. Esther and the silver-haired man hurried across the deck, worry pinching their faces. Hershey turned with seeming reluctance.

The silver-haired man gave Rye a once-over, then took Hershey's arm. "Why didn't you tell us where you were going? Ben said he couldn't find you after you went to the ladies' lounge."

"I didn't think you'd miss me." She hesitated. "Rye works at the resort, and I wanted to talk to him."

Esther cast him an appraising glance, and Rye wondered if she recognized him from the shopping center parking lot.

He smiled, but before either of them could speak, Esther's husband propelled Hershey past him. "You shouldn't have left the banquet hall without telling us. We were very worried about you."

"I'm sorry."

He hurried Hershey away, Esther following.

Although he hadn't been given a chance to say good-bye, Rye felt thankful that at least Hershey was with her guardians now and not Dean.

He needed to return to Dana, but he took a moment to glance out once again at the night sky.

The heavens declare the glory of God.

A whimsical longing touched him as he headed back inside. It seemed he had fallen in love with one of God's angels.

Chapter Eleven

So, how did last night go?"

Rye shook his head in response to Caleb's question as he opened the roadhouse menu. "Nothing happened to help the case. June drank the night away, and Dana didn't see the assassin. What about Chris? Has he e-mailed?"

"Just a quick note to say he's at Gretta Green. That's the only place in Great Britain where an expedited marriage can be performed. However, he didn't find June Moore's name listed. I told him to compile a list of women in the same age range so we can examine their medical records. Hopefully, if he finds a woman with an x-shaped scar, we'll have June's real name."

"Are any of the new guests candidates?"

"No, but we'll keep checking."

"How'd it go with Arianna?"

Caleb shrugged. "I found her better clothes to wear, which will make things easier. We went bowling, and she didn't push for something more romantic afterward, so that's good. But I'd still like to wrap this case up."

Rye stared at his menu. If the case ended, they'd leave, and he doubted he'd ever see Hershey again. If only he could justify pursuing her. But she was engaged, and Caleb didn't want him fantasizing about women.

"Can we do something after you're off work today?"

Caleb glanced up from mucking out Mayflower's stall to where Arianna held a bucket of oatmeal mash while her filly gulped down the medicated breakfast.

She had been disappointed that he hadn't spent time with her the evening before, but at least she hadn't made a big deal out of it. He deliberated about what type of outing would be best. "Would you like to hike one of the trails?"

"Sure! I have some good hiking boots. Can we eat supper together before we go?"

Caleb shook the old hay into the large disposal bucket. "I suppose. Let's meet at The Summer House."

The resort's restaurant had higher prices than he would normally pay, but he supposed he could include the dinner under job expenses. After all, any time spent with Arianna doubled as acting bodyguard, even if Patrick didn't consider her an option.

After work, Caleb showered, then arrived at The Summer House ten minutes early for his meeting with Arianna. He stayed outside, waiting for her, until he saw her heading from the direction of the beach. At the same time, he caught sight of Paul and Esther Hauzen coming from the tennis courts. Behind them, David walked with Cora on his arm.

He startled. When had Cora arrived? He had seen the Hauzens' names listed on the hotel's register and had prayed they wouldn't come in contact with him. He had no wish for them to blow his cover. But Cora wasn't registered at the resort. He would have to call his father to find out where she was staying.

"Who are you looking at?" Arianna approached, following his gaze as she neared. "Do you know those people?"

"Yes." Caleb hesitated, not sure how much he should tell her. Whenever he was undercover, he tried to separate himself from anyone who could identify him.

It irked him, though, when Arianna guessed, "Is that an old girlfriend of yours?"

"I don't have any ex-loves." He headed toward the restaurant's double doors, hoping she'd drop the subject.

Arianna hurried to catch up with him. "Then who is she?"

When he held the restaurant door open for her, she paused in front of him. Her blue-green eyes searched his face, and he sighed. "She's my niece."

"Your niece? But she's not much younger than you."

"No, she isn't." Caleb put his hand on her arm to direct her inside so she'd stop blocking the doorway.

The host ushered them to a table for two, leaving menus. But Caleb could see that Arianna wasn't interested in hers. She looked at him with something akin to poignancy in her eyes. "Do you have a brother or a sister?"

Caleb realized there was no getting around it, not if he wanted her to believe him about the relationship. He opened his menu but didn't see any of the words on it. "I had an older sister. She died when Cora was born." He paused, then added quietly, "Hannah was fifteen."

"Oh." Emotion flickered across Arianna's face as if she was thinking of what it would have meant if she had suffered the same fate. Unusual gentleness filled her eyes as she caught his gaze. "I'm sorry."

Caleb's heart constricted. "It's okay." He looked back to the menu. "Shall we order?"

But he still couldn't focus on the words listing the restaurant's entrees. He was too distracted by the worry that he might not be doing the right thing in spending so much one-on-one time with a girl who kept impacting his heart.

"Cora, there's a guy here to visit you. Says his name is Caleb."

Cora lifted her head from where she sat in the dormitory-style bedroom in the Y cabin she shared with several other female volunteers. She stopped tracing the Braille in her Bible at her roommate's words. "Caleb?"

"Yeah. Who is he?"

Cora reached for the walking stick propped next to her chair and stood, amazement filling her. She could scarcely believe it. Caleb was here! She answered Sandy's question joyfully. "He's my uncle. I had no idea he was here."

"He's waiting on the porch."

Cora smiled with delight. "Thanks." With her walking stick, she traversed the wooden floor of the cabin's narrow living room. Perhaps Caleb's arrival was the Lord's answer to her prayers of late.

For the last few days, her emotions had been in turmoil. No matter how she sought the Lord's presence, the fragile peace she attained there was often fragmented by unruly trains of thought. Although she dearly loved working with the fourth to eighth graders who engaged in the Y's music and drama program, she felt as though her personal life was in shambles.

After finding her with Rye on the deck of the cruise ship, Paul had made certain his son knew about the other man. David had been undisturbed, stating with his usual calm that he trusted her implicitly. His words should have relieved her, but instead Cora fought the feeling of not mattering enough to be jealous over. However, she had always accepted David's laid-back personality before, and she pushed away the disloyal thoughts.

She also resented the fact that Paul hadn't had any problem handing her over to Dean, yet he had a major problem finding her in Rye's company. Once again, she hadn't been able to hold on to her resentment. In Paul's mind, Dean was too old to be considered a threat to her engagement. Only Rye had recognized the motive behind the other man's behavior.

For the hundredth time since that night, Cora pushed back the longing that threatened to pull her under whenever Rye came to mind.

She had been determined to forget him after their first meeting, but after the second, she had known she was supposed to witness to him. The Lord had given her an opportunity to do so on the deck of the cruise ship, but the Hauzens had found her before she was able to share the whole redemption story. If she could think of Rye only in light of his soul, she wouldn't struggle with the other doubts and feelings that kept resurfacing since that night.

Every day she pushed herself to remain content with her life, especially with her engagement to David. She had never compared him with anyone else before, and she didn't want to start now. Especially not with the much-too-charming man who didn't even know her name. She felt certain her present agitation would leave if she staunchly refused to feed it with memories of Rye's stolen kisses.

She swallowed as she swung open the door to the front porch. Perhaps Caleb's presence would help her get her emotions back under control. At least his visit would pull her attention away from the tempting thoughts that lurked in the back of her mind.

Caleb stared at Chris's e-mail. Chris had compiled a list of three women who had married at Gretta Green and matched June's age and description. However, his current e-mail said that none of the women's medical files listed an x-shaped scar.

"Dead end. Sorry. However, I have a contact in the underground who might be able to find out who bought June Moore's identity on the black market. He costs a pretty penny, though."

Caleb punched in Patrick's phone number. The billionaire answered within two rings. "Caleb. How are things going?"

"Not so great. But I have a contact in Europe who can get us information about who bought June's identity. He'll cost some money, though. I wanted to double-check with you before I hire him."

"Expense doesn't matter. Just tell me where to wire the money. I want my granddaughter found."

"Yes, sir. I'll get you the details. Thank you."

"So, what's the word from Chris?"

Rye pulled back a chair as he joined Caleb at the table in his cabin. Caleb had just called and asked him to come over. It had been two days since the underground contact had been paid to search for information.

Caleb read off his laptop screen. "June Moore's passport and social security number were sold to a Heather Winston twenty-five days ago. Heather's marriage certificate lists her maiden name as Down. Her medical records validate surgery. Birth certificate lists her mother as English; father unknown. Will visit Marie Down to discover the father's identity. Hope to be reimbursed."

Caleb hit reply. "Reimbursement no problem. Call me as soon as you know identity of Heather's father. Thanks for all your help."

He leaned back in his chair, and Rye tried not to show his disappointment. "I guess the case is almost wrapped up."

"Yes. I'm calling Patrick."

Caleb placed the long-distance call, and while he relayed the news to Patrick, Rye struggled. He had spent hours with Dana trailing June around the resort and the town of Summerland. But never had his attention been further from a case.

He found himself watching the milling guests more than June, hoping to catch a glimpse of a brown-haired girl with dusky skin and round sunglasses. But over a week had passed since he had talked with Hershey on the cruise. Although he saw Esther and her husband from time to time, Hershey was never with them. If he wanted to see her again before he returned to LA, he would have to ignore Caleb's rules about pursuing a girl and initiate his own search. But even if he found out her name, there was a chance she had finished her vacation and left. The thought depressed him.

Caleb snapped his cell phone shut. "You look a thousand miles away."

Rye averted his gaze. "Just wondering how much longer we have here."

Caleb typed an e-mail to Chris. "Depends on whether Heather's mother identifies Douglas as the father."

Rye frowned. "What if he isn't?"

"We'll cross that bridge if we come to it."

"Hey, Caleb, where's your shadow?"

Caleb glanced up from pouring feed into Mayflower's trough. One of the other stable hands, Darrell, stood there, watching him with a smirk on his square face. Caleb hadn't associated with the man much, mostly because of Darrell's foul mouth. But Caleb knew what he referred to.

Arianna had spent hours at the stable since Mayflower's accident, not just with the filly but talking to Caleb as he worked. The other hands had noticed, though no one made any remarks when she was around. Flannigan would fire them on the spot if they insulted a guest. But today Arianna was late in making an appearance, and Flannigan was nowhere around.

Caleb continued raking out the stall.

"Arianna's quite the tasty morsel. Young and easy. That's the way I like them."

Caleb's temper erupted. "Shut your mouth, or I'll shut it for you!"

Darrell, who was big if not tall, narrowed his eyes. He might have pushed the confrontation except Arianna walked into the stable at that moment. Her gaze cut into him, showing she had heard every word.

Caleb almost wished Darrell would give him reason to throw a fist in his face. Instead, fear of losing his job shot across the other man's eyes. "Sorry," he muttered, then strode away.

Caleb lifted the gate to Mayflower's stall. He hated Darrell's reminder of Arianna's previous promiscuity, but his upbringing demanded that he give his own apology for letting a woman be insulted. "Sorry, Arianna. I should have stopped him sooner."

She slipped her arms around his waist and gazed up at him with adoration. "Thank you, Caleb."

He winced. He wanted to shield her from gossip, but here she was adding fuel to the fire. He unwound her arms from around him. "This isn't the best way to show your gratitude."

Her eyes said she didn't care, and he sighed. Since she had dropped her coy behavior, he had come to enjoy her company. Though his time with her was coming to an end, he was proud of her for letting go of her worldly attitude. Even when he ran across her with her parents or her uncle, she always had on the clothes he had bought for her. She ignored the whistles that came her way and seemed content to be in his company without manipulative ploys. Nor could he find any irritation over her grateful hug. She was simply being Arianna, impetuous and demonstrative.

She gazed at him with a mixture of adoration and longing, and his throat tightened. He let go of her wrists. "Maybe you are hanging around here too much."

Distress overtook her finely cut features. "Don't make me leave. I promise I'll be good."

She had been good, and it wasn't her fault that Darrell had a filthy mind.

Caleb sighed. He couldn't bring himself to tell her to stop coming to the stables. After all, in a few days, it wouldn't matter, because he'd be gone.

Rye stared at the four names on the screen of Caleb's laptop. After struggling with his conscience, he had decided that Caleb couldn't be angry at him for seeking the friendship of a girl who loved God.

However, he didn't want to explain himself before he found Hershey, so he had slipped into the cabin while Caleb was at work and logged into the resort's guest list. He instructed the computer program to search for guests logged in as needing additional service because of a handicap. It came up with only two women. Neither was Hershey's age.

He frowned. If she hadn't listed her handicap, he needed another way to narrow the field. There were hundreds of young women at the resort in her age range. Perhaps her room was registered under her in-laws' names.

Although he didn't know Esther's last name, he typed in her first name. Hope returned as three names came up. One of the Esthers was too old to be Hershey's stepmother-in-law-to-be, and one wasn't married. But the third fit all the information he knew about her. She was married to a man named Paul Hauzen, and his son was staying at the resort as well. His name was David.

Rye drew in a deep breath. He had found Hershey's family. But why wasn't a girl mentioned as part of their group? He did a backward search, but no other name showed up from earlier dates.

He tried to remember all the investigative tricks Caleb had taught him. He logged out of the resort's database and signed into an Internet search. Wealthy families often had Web sites or articles written about them. Perhaps he would learn something about their personal lives.

The Hauzen name popped up, and he clicked on the first link. A swift perusal of the business article told him that Paul Hauzen had made his money by investing in pharmaceutical equipment. The article ran on about his plans for future improvements.

The second link looked more promising. It was an article about Paul's recent marriage to Esther, the widow of anchorman Hugh Reane. Though the author referred to David's studies at Biola University in Southern California, a fiancée was not mentioned.

Frustrated, Rye stared at the Web page. Was he never to see Hershey again? She hadn't wanted to introduce him to any of her family, but would she be angry if he ignored her wishes and asked Esther for her name? Would Esther give it to him? Or would she want to protect Hershey from him just like Paul had the night of the cruise? Paul had whisked Hershey away from him as though afraid she would be contaminated by some plague. He hadn't even had the chance to say good-bye.

Rye's chest tightened. Paul's protection was valid. Hadn't he felt the same way when Dean had sought Hershey's attention? But he wasn't like Dean. He didn't sleep around anymore or allow lustful desires to preside in his thought life.

Esther seemed more liberal minded than her husband. Perhaps she would share Hershey's whereabouts if he asked her without Paul or David present. If she did, he would find Hershey. And if Hershey seemed glad to see him, as she had all the other times, he would tell her how deeply he had fallen for her. Then it would be up to her if he had any kind of chance of staying in her life.

Caleb drew in a deep breath as he stared at Chris's final e-mail. So that was that. There was no use arguing with the evidence. All these weeks, he and Rye had been watching the wrong woman. He didn't look forward to his phone call to Patrick. He needed to be as prepared as possible.

He hit Memory on his cell phone, and a moment later Rye answered. The kid's voice sounded tired even though the evening had just begun.

Caleb didn't waste time on pleasantries. "Chris e-mailed. He talked with Marie Down. Douglas isn't Heather's father."

"So June isn't a candidate after all?"

"That's right. Heather was born out of an affair Marie had with an English lord. There's no chance that Douglas is the father. Marie has never traveled outside Great Britain, and Douglas never left the States."

"So that must mean Arianna's the granddaughter."

Caleb winced. "Patrick isn't going to like that conclusion. I'm running another check of current guests. I need you to start taking Dana around the resort. Different places at different times. If the assassin's lurking here, hopefully she'll catch a glimpse of him."

"It stinks that we've been trailing the wrong woman this whole time. At least none of the guests has been murdered while we've been sidetracked."

"We weren't sidetracked. June was our best bet. I'll call you again after I talk to Patrick."

"Okay."

Rye disconnected, and Caleb frowned as he waited for the computer to finish its search of the newest resort guests and employees. He was going on a hike with Arianna in a half hour. She didn't pay other men attention, so even if she was Patrick's granddaughter, she wouldn't be easily lured by the assassin. Although he had thought for sure June/Heather would end up being the missing heiress, it seemed he had been right to follow his instinct to hang out with Arianna. He needed to make sure she was safe.

The computer beeped, and he focused on the screen. Several new female guests fit the age range, so he jotted down socials. Then he hacked into medical databases again. Two of the women had had surgeries, but the operations had resulted in straight slices. Their fathers' names were also listed. He pressed his lips together and punched in Patrick's number.

"Caleb! I was hoping to hear from you today. When do I go pick up my granddaughter? Heather's her name, right?"

Caleb rubbed the back of his neck. "Uh, Patrick, we've run into a difficulty."

A frown touched the billionaire's voice. "What do you mean? Do you need more money? I'll send it. No problem."

"No, it's not that. Chris talked to Heather's mother and confirmed her story. Marie never slept with Douglas. They weren't even in the same country."

After a long exhale, Patrick said, "You're sure?"

"I am."

"Now what?"

"I've searched the medical records of the other women in the age range. Arianna's the only one here who has an x-shaped scar."

"I'm telling you, it's not her! Jackson wouldn't be afraid of my giving any money to that girl. Arianna's a selfish, immoral brat. I didn't put her in my will before, and I won't now." His tone hardened. "You and Rye stay there. When my granddaughter comes, you find her."

Caleb breathed in slowly. "All right. Rye and Dana are still watching for the assassin. I'll let you know the moment we have another lead."

"You're a good man, Caleb. You're honest. I appreciate that. I just don't want you wasting your time on the wrong girl."

"Yes, sir." Caleb hit End, then stared out the cabin window. In spite of Patrick's assurances, he couldn't shake the feeling that Arianna was Douglas's heir. She had been at the resort from the beginning, when Alan Brinnon was supposed to have arrived. It didn't make sense that Alan would come when the granddaughter wasn't present.

Unless the granddaughter had been delayed for some reason. But if that was the case, she might not come at all. The assassin may have located her at her home and finished the job there. If so, he needed to track down women who had cancelled and see if any of them fit Dana's description.

He focused on the laptop and typed in a new search, looking for cancellations. A list of twenty guests appeared. He immediately deleted all the men. He plugged the women's socials into his software program and narrowed the search to two women in the correct age range.

He hacked into their medical databases. The first woman had stitches from a childhood diving accident. The wound had been a deep but straight cut. The second woman had a surgery five years before on her stomach. A tumor of some sort had been removed, but the scar was listed as crescent shaped.

He pressed his lips together in frustration, not at the lack of candidates, but at Patrick's stubbornness. What would it take to prove that Arianna was Douglas's heir? A murder attempt? At least Jackson didn't seem willing to kill her himself, which meant Brinnon's assassin would sooner or later appear on the scene.

Chapter Twelve

W here are you headed, Nan?"

Arianna paused as Uncle Ben met her on the beach house steps. Even dressed in shorts and a T-shirt from his day at the beach, he looked debonair and sophisticated.

She smiled. "I'm going riding with Caleb. We're celebrating because he said Mayflower's healed."

"Celebrating, huh?" He held the railing with a tanned hand as he regarded her in amusement. "And how does your straight-laced boyfriend celebrate?"

She laughed. "I told you, we're riding horses. He even promised to race me on Star. Caleb said he's the fastest horse in the stable, but I bet Mayflower can beat him."

"And is racing the most passionate thing he'll do with you?"

Arianna's smile faltered. His cynical words cast a shadow over her emotions.

It had been two weeks since Caleb had begun spending time with her, and she had been so happy with his kind affection she hadn't thought about what was missing. Until now.

Before she could come up with an answer to her uncle's question, he surprised her by asking, "Do you think Caleb will mind if I join you for the ride?"

Arianna's spirits brightened. "Can you come right now?"

"I'll meet you there. Just give me ten minutes."

"Okay." Arianna hurried down the stairs and jogged all the way to the stables.

Caleb had insisted they ride after he was done working so he wasn't short-changing his job. Though she had been surprised that he would consider the issue a moral one, she had happily accepted the evening date.

She saw him leaning backward with his elbows on the corral fence and noticed he had changed into fresh jeans and a T-shirt. She thought he looked gorgeous no matter what he wore, and when he smiled at her, her breath caught in her chest.

"Hi." She slipped close to his arm, which was draped over the top fence bar, and gazed adoringly at his handsomely chiseled features.

He raised his eyebrows, not moving away from her. "You look happy."

She sighed with contentment. "Uncle Ben asked if he could come riding with us. I said you wouldn't mind."

He hesitated. "No, I guess not."

She felt her pulse quicken. "He doesn't have to. Not if you just want me with you."

His gaze swept down to her. Emotion darkened his eyes as though he knew what she was thinking. He straightened, breaking their light contact. "I said he could come."

He looked toward the road to the beach house, but Arianna didn't take her gaze off his face. Her uncle's words had stirred up her old desires. Caleb treated her with more respect than any other man, but she hadn't given up her former friends just to have a platonic relationship.

A muscle bunched in Caleb's jaw as though he was aware of the steadiness of her gaze. Satisfaction touched her. She hadn't seen the passionate side of him in what felt like ages. Uncle Ben was right. A horse ride was only the beginning of what she wanted from Caleb.

"Your uncle's here." Without waiting for a reply, Caleb crossed the stable yard to greet the other man with a handshake.

Arianna followed a few feet behind him, watching Uncle Ben's face as he appraised Caleb. When she stopped at Caleb's side, Uncle Ben winked at her. "So, shall we ride?"

Arianna enjoyed the next hour of sunshine and hot breezes on her face as she galloped Mayflower over clover-scented hills. She teased Caleb into keeping his promise to race, and Uncle Ben joined in on his older gelding.

She laughed when Star flew past her close to the finishing spot. She had a feeling Caleb had held his horse back just to keep the race close.

Caleb let Star prance in small circles to slow the horse's heartbeat. Arianna did the same. She laughed as their legs touched when the horses passed each other.

Uncle Ben rode up, and she beamed at his amused face. "Well, Star won. And I think Caleb held him back."

Caleb didn't correct the statement.

Uncle Ben smiled with apparent ruefulness. "And I wasn't even close."

Arianna slid off Mayflower. "Maybe we should rest the horses for a bit."

Both men accommodated, and the horses grazed on sweet-smelling clover, their reins trailing behind them. Uncle Ben reposed against the trunk of a tree, and Arianna sank down close to where Caleb sat cross-legged on the soft grass. He kept the conversation centered on her uncle.

After three hours of intermittent galloping, walking, and resting, they returned to the stables. Uncle Ben handed his horse to a stable hand, then waved good-bye. Arianna took the next half hour to brush Mayflower. Caleb did a quicker job with Star, and she smiled when he paused by Mayflower's stall. He watched her with an enigmatic expression.

"Did you want to go out to dinner?"

He shook his head. "Not tonight."

"Are you going to see your niece again?" He had told her he visited Cora on the evenings they didn't spend together.

He rubbed a hand over his neck in a gesture she found fascinating. "Probably."

She continued brushing Mayflower as he strode away.

Ten minutes later she left Mayflower eating from her trough and headed to the beach house. She found Uncle Ben reclining in the living area, the television on. At her entrance, he muted the sitcom. "You were right about him being attractive."

She settled onto the couch beside him.

"But after two weeks of being with this guy, don't you think you're wasting your time?"

His words pulled her emotions off their high. "Why do you say that?"

"He treats you like a little sister." He pushed the mute button again, and the TV spat out a toothpaste commercial.

Arianna wished his words hadn't taken away all the happiness she had been feeling.

The next morning, she arrived early at the stables. She had barely slept the night before, thinking about what it would be like for Caleb to take her in his arms. His friendship meant a lot to her, but she had no desire to live without pleasure.

He smiled at her as he approached Mayflower's stall, and desire washed over her. Blatant come-ons hadn't worked with him before, but there had to be a way to turn his thoughts toward romance.

"Morning." He entered the stall.

She smiled. "How was your night?"

"Fine. How's Mayflower?" He picked up the filly's injured leg and examined it.

Arianna stroked the horse's neck. "She's doing great. Do you want to go out this evening? We could go swimming."

He shot her a glance. "Not riding?"

She shrugged and pretended nonchalance. "I don't want Mayflower to overdo it. She's not used to running every day."

He dropped the leg. "Then we'll go hiking. Or bowling."

"Swimming is exercise too." She knew the reason for his reluctance. He didn't want to be allured by seeing her in a skimpy bikini. "Didn't you tell me God made us?"

He swung her a confused gaze. "I did."

"Then He made me the way I am, didn't He? I mean—my body."

He looked away. "What's your point?"

She gave him her most innocent look. "I don't see why the clothes thing is such a big deal. If God made me look the way He did, why should it bother you to see me?"

He pressed his lips together. "Modesty matters. Not just in clothes, but in actions." He held her gaze for a long moment. "Look, if you want to go swimming, you need to get a decent swimsuit, and there won't be any flirting. Understand?"

"I promise." Excitement scampered across her veins. Bringing God into the conversation had worked. Even without flirting, she was certain she could get Caleb's thoughts to go in the direction she wanted them to go.

Caleb met Arianna at five-thirty on the beach near her house. She waved as soon as she saw him striding down the path. "Caleb!"

As he walked closer he noticed her new swimwear. She wore a shimmery blue one-piece with a short, scalloped skirt, completely modest. She was right—it wasn't her fault men turned to take a longer look at her. However, noticing her long limbs and full carriage didn't mean his thoughts had to stay there.

He turned his attention to the white sand that spilled out of caressing slopes then darkened, pressed by the flowing tides. Sparkling blue water stretched out as far as the eye could see, with dozens of motor boats pulling skiers. Two sailboats rocked gracefully on distant waves.

Arianna ran up to him almost as if she were going to hug him. She stopped inches away, her blue-green eyes sparkling. "Do you like the swimsuit?"

"It's fine. How far out do you want to swim?"

She laughed. "I can do two miles easy. What about you?"

He stripped off his shirt and strode toward the water. The surf sloshed around their legs, and he was thankful when he could throw his whole body into the rolling waves. Arianna stroked easily beside him, her brilliant smile flashing to him every few minutes.

He lengthened his strokes, and Arianna kept up, reaching the two-mile mark with him. He glanced to her as they treaded water. "Ready to race?"

She grinned. "Last one back to shore has to buy water."

"On three. One, two, three."

She shot off, and he let her have the lead for the first mile. Then he gradually overtook her. She didn't seem to notice when he passed, her black hair glistening against the evening sun.

He stayed slightly ahead of her, glancing back several times in the last quarter mile. Undertows could be dangerous. Nor could he forget about the assassin.

His feet touched bottom, and he took several strides on solid ground, then waited. She laughed as she pushed her way past the oncoming tide. Water ran down her legs and off her arms. Her face glowed with beauty.

"Good job. You stayed close."

"And you held back again. But I don't mind. You never make me feel like you want to be better than me."

"Winning's not important. Kindness is."

"I'll get the water."

He sat on the towel she had left on the beach. Five minutes later, she returned with two ice-cold bottles.

"Thanks."

"You're welcome." She sat beside him. "It's pretty here, isn't it?"

He took a long swallow. "God's creation always amazes me."

She glanced sideways at him. "*All* of God's creation?"

His throat tightened. "Why are you fishing for a compliment? You know you're beautiful. But character is more important than outward appearance."

"What do you mean?"

"Character is who you are inside. Your beliefs and standards. The way you live your life."

She ran sand through her fingers. "You don't think I live my life the right way, do you?"

"I know you weren't raised to honor God. Our culture has told you that you can do whatever you want. That morality and eternal values don't matter. But our souls are eternal. If we live to please God, He'll bless us. And after we die, we'll live with Him. But if we live selfishly, not only will we hurt other people with our choices, we'll hurt ourselves, because God created us for His purposes, not our own."

She frowned. "I don't think I've hurt anyone."

He studied her. "Have you been hurt?"

"Well, sure. That's part of life. Everyone gets hurt."

"Some pain we don't have control over. But most the hurts in life are because of a choice someone made. A choice to not care about another person's feelings or do what is best even if it's hard."

She shook her head. "You talk about things most people don't even think about. Everyone else I know just talks about money or relationships. Don't you get lonely sometimes?"

He looked away. "I have people in my life."

"But don't you want someone special?"

"I want what God wants." He stood. "Come on. We're here to swim."

They raced several more times, using different stroke styles. Caleb made sure to stay close. He couldn't shake the need to protect her, not just physically but in other ways as well. She seemed young and naïve about the way men would treat her if she returned to her promiscuous lifestyle.

He was grateful God was giving him a little more time with her, though the assassin was sure to surface soon.

Caleb's feet touched sand, and he glanced around the beach, analyzing the inhabitants. Children frolicked between mothers on quilts, and men and women stretched out to tan in the hot sun. Two men lounging in beach chairs watched Arianna as she sloshed through the tide toward him. The lust in their gazes angered him, and a deep desire kindled to do everything in his power to keep her out of the arms of men who would only use her.

"Gotcha!" Arianna laughed as she snagged Caleb's arm. "Who were you frowning at?"

"No one."

She glanced toward the two men who had been gazing at her. The tanned, blond one grinned, a come-on in his blue eyes.

She couldn't help smiling back just a little.

"We're leaving." Anger touched Caleb's tone. He clasped her arm, heading away from the men.

A mixture of security and delight washed over her. He was jealous! She glanced toward him with more coyness than she had allowed herself in weeks. "Don't worry. I'm not interested in them."

He glanced at her, and she let her smile say the rest. *Just you.*

He didn't respond.

When they reached their spot on the beach, he let go of her arm and picked up the towels. She walked with him up the path, wondering how much she could push. Did he still feel the need to keep his attraction for her at bay? Or with a little help, would he follow the desire she saw at times in his eyes?

At the beach house steps, he handed her towel to her. "See you tomorrow." He turned to leave.

"Caleb, wait."

He stopped. "What?"

She stepped closer and touched her fingers to his bare chest. "Will you come inside? We could make popcorn and watch a movie."

Struggle reflected in his eyes, and she realized she needed to make this easier for him. She took her hand off and looked away. "I don't like being alone, especially if one of Dad's business friends drops by."

"Do your dad's friends bother you?"

She shrugged. "Dad tells me to be nice to them. I think he hopes I'll sleep with them so they'll owe him. But they're too old."

"I thought you said your dad didn't notice you."

"He doesn't. But he knows his friends notice. I guess he figures that since he has a daughter, I might as well be of some use to him."

Anger filled Caleb's eyes. "Arianna, don't ever give in to them. Do you understand? They'll use you and leave you."

She gazed at him, loving his passion. "I know. They're not like you. Oh, Caleb…" She swayed toward him, and he dragged in a shallow breath. For the barest instant, she thought he might reach out to her.

He stepped back. "I'll go change clothes. Then I'll come back, and we can watch a movie."

She pulled in a steadying breath. "I'm going to take a shower, so if I don't answer, just come in."

He nodded, then strode down the road to his cabin.

Anticipation filled her. He wanted her. She could read it in the tension of his body and the darkness of his eyes. But she had to be careful. She had to keep his attention on how he felt around her and off the restrictions of his religion.

Caleb changed swiftly into a dry T-shirt and denim shorts, then grabbed his USB jump drive. If Arianna was in the shower, he might get the chance to access the Sunnel laptops.

Five minutes later, he rapped lightly on the door to the Sunnel beach house. When no one answered, he let himself in.

He glanced around the dim interior, noting the kitchen to the left, stairs in front, and a carpeted living room to the right. He entered the living room, taking in the leather couches and the large flat-screen TV. A laptop sat on the desk near the window. He walked over to it and powered it on. The request for a password flickered onto the screen. He inserted his jump drive, then accessed the decoding program saved on it.

Two minutes later, the simple password popped into place. He opened My Documents to search the files. He found several legal documents with Dean's name on them, plus a list of expenses, apparently for taxes. He scrolled past a dozen files that didn't look informative, then opened one named with the date of Douglas's death.

Finally! His assumption had been right. The document was the falsified will Jackson had shown Patrick. Although Dean may not have participated in the murder, he had agreed to fake a legal document.

Caleb hit Save As and copied the file to his jump drive. When the file finished saving, he scanned the rest of the documents, but none were relevant to the case. He slipped his jump drive into his pocket and powered down the laptop.

Light footsteps sounded on the stairs, and he turned his attention to the selection of DVDs that filled the TV cabinet.

Arianna slipped her arms around him from behind. "Find anything you want to watch?"

He forced himself to focus. Most of the movies were horror flicks or sexual dramas. "Do you have a suspense or action section?"

"Bottom right." She loosened her hold, and he squatted to look at the two dozen films she had indicated.

"I haven't seen this one in a while." He straightened and handed her the DVD.

She slipped it into the player, then settled onto the couch beside him, shifting close as she tucked her legs under her. Jasmine wafted to him from her hair, and her bare arm rested against him.

The plot gave him a safe place to center his attention. At the end of the movie, Arianna faced him. "Did you enjoy it?"

"Yes." He drew in a shallow breath. She was so close. Desire surfaced, stronger than it had been yet. Was it wrong to be attracted to her?

"Caleb..." She leaned into him, her lips parting.

God, is this right?

She brushed his lips with hers, and her hand slipped to his inner thigh.

A sick feeling hit his stomach. The intimate touch brought back the reality of his situation. She was ready to go way too far, and he didn't want to be seduced into making a choice he might regret. He pushed her hand off and stood, not looking at her.

"I'm going to head home. Good night, Arianna. Lock the doors after me."

He headed out before desire returned. But instead of going to his cabin, he drove toward the Y. He needed to clear out the emotions churning inside him.

Arianna sat on the couch in shock. Caleb's command to lock the door after him barely registered.

She had waited until the desire in his eyes was as strong as any of her ex-boyfriends', then thrown herself in his arms. But he hadn't even kissed her.

She didn't understand how he could walk away from her. How could she have failed?

A sick feeling washed over her. She had always been a failure. To her father. To her mother. Nothing she did ever pleased them or earned their love. After her first date, she had learned that drowning herself in pleasure covered the fears inside her. Her boyfriends approved of her body and offered her enough affection to momentarily satisfy her need to be loved.

But she was never satisfied. Not really. The depths in Caleb's eyes when he looked at her had offered her a refuge, a place to nestle where she wasn't wanted just for her body. But he had rejected her.

Pain twisted her stomach. Why had she let herself get so besotted over one man? She should have known better. Rejection hurt too much.

There was no way she could let the pain stay. She had to get rid of it. But she knew only one way to do so.

She strode to the phone and called her closest friend. "Hi, Becky."

"Nan! I haven't heard from you in an age."

"Is there a party going on tonight?"

"Richard's throwing a doozy. You want to come?"

"Yeah."

"Great! I'll be at your place in twenty minutes."

Arianna dropped the cordless back in its stand and stared at it. She didn't want anyone except Caleb. But if he didn't want her, she had no other recourse. She couldn't bear to live in the pain of being unwanted.

"Have you solved your case yet?"

Caleb shook his head as he sat on the porch of Cora's cabin at the Y, a glass of lemonade in his hand. "Once the case is wrapped up, you can ask me all the details you want, but you'll have to wait till then."

She nodded, her face reflecting her understanding.

He gazed at her, feeling the tension of the evening drain away. Her inner serenity calmed his ragged emotions. She often affected him in such a way. She said he was sensing the peace of Jesus, but he knew it was the sweetness of her own heart.

Crickets sounded somewhere alongside the porch, and he smiled at a long-ago memory. "Remember our first campout? We were with the Hauzens. When it got dark, you wouldn't go into your tent. You insisted on sleeping with David and me in ours."

She smiled. When the smile faded, she asked quietly, "Caleb, why didn't Dad arrange a marriage for you like he did for me?"

Caleb sighed. "Mom didn't approve of prearranged marriages. By the time she died, I think Dad figured I was too old to convince. But you always interacted well with David. When Paul suggested the idea, Dad assumed God had put you together from the start."

He hesitated, troubled by the expression on her face. "Are you and David having difficulties?"

Clasping her hands in her lap, she shook her head, her long hair falling over her shoulders. "No." She turned her face away and whispered, "We're fine."

He had the impression she was saying the words more to convince herself than him. He wondered what had happened to make her doubt the wisdom of his father's choice.

She shifted the conversation to her work at the Y, talking warmly about the children. But an uneasy feeling grew inside him. He wondered if Arianna had stayed in her house as he'd instructed her to.

He tightened his hold on his glass. What if she resented his abrupt departure?

As soon as Cora finished her description of the day's recital, he stood. "I need to get back. But thanks for talking with me."

She stood, her walking stick in hand. "Are you doing okay?"

He forced a smile. "I'm fine." He crossed the porch to kiss her cheek. "Take care of yourself."

"I will. I love you."

"I love you too."

He headed down the steps then slipped into the Ford. At his cabin he stepped out of the truck and stared up the road toward the Sunnel beach house. He didn't want to talk again tonight, but the heaviness sitting inside him pushed him to check on Arianna's safety.

He walked up the road, wondering how he could salvage the situation. Should he apologize for leading her on or just remind her of the importance of friendship?

His steps slowed as the beach house came into sight. She was leaning on the back railing of the wraparound porch, talking with a redheaded girl. Both of them held cigarettes and were dressed to flaunt every inch of the bodies God had given them.

Anger flared. He had walked away from her, and now she was walking right back into her worldly lifestyle. But he couldn't believe one-night stands were what she really wanted. She had given up her manufactured worldliness and had become a simple, sweet girl who loved horses and craved positive affirmation. She had accepted his friendship, not pressing for more until today. What had changed? Why had she tried to seduce him again?

Realization hit. Yesterday evening, Benjamin Dean had ridden with them. Caleb had ignored many of his suggestive comments about their relationship, but he wouldn't be surprised if Dean had said or done something to make Arianna believe their friendship wasn't worthwhile unless Caleb succumbed to her.

Focusing his anger on her Uncle Ben, Caleb strode up the porch's back steps. She gasped when he plucked the cigarette out of her fingers and trampled it on the deck. Her friend took a frightened step back from his angry presence.

Caleb glared into Arianna's stunned eyes. "What do you think you're doing?"

The shock receded from her face, and anger sparked. "Enjoying my life again."

"Who thinks that ruining yourself brings enjoyment? Your uncle?"

"I'm not ruining myself. I'm just not letting life pass me by, like you are."

He grabbed her bare shoulders. "If you follow your uncle's example, life will take everything that's precious from you and throw you on the street when you have nothing left."

She glared at him. "Uncle Ben gets everything he wants and so does everyone else I know. I'm the only one who's been stupid enough to wait for something I'll never get." Tears surged into her eyes, hurt and disillusionment gleaming through the anger.

Bright headlights flashed onto them. Caleb glanced over as a silver Corvette squealed up to the porch. Two college-age boys in the front seat.

Arianna's red-haired girlfriend ran down the porch steps. She hopped into the backseat while the boy Arianna had danced with weeks ago called in an inebriated tone, "Hey, Nan, what's going on? Aren't you coming with us?"

"Yeah."

She tried to pull away from Caleb, but he tightened his grip on her shoulders. "You're not going."

Hot anger flushed her face. "Why? So you can be proud of yourself for making me like you?" Tears slipped down her cheeks as raw longing overtook her. "You want to change me, but you're never going to want me."

Pain clenched his heart. He did want her. But the woman he wanted was the sweet Arianna who had enjoyed his company and hadn't been intent on getting him to make love to her.

More than anything, he wanted to protect her. But he wasn't going to be able to save her from the influence of seductive forces like Benjamin Dean and her worldly friends unless he yielded at least a little to the desire inside him.

For a moment he wavered... a split second when he wasn't sure. What kind of dangerous temptations would he set himself up for? But he was strong. He had always been strong. And she mattered too much now. He couldn't let her go back to the world that would consume the vitality of her soul and leave her an empty shell.

He drew in a shallow breath and softened his hold on her shoulders. "Stay with me." He pulled her to him, and her eyes widened. Desire kindled, but he wouldn't let it get the upper hand. He lowered his head and kissed her.

Behind him, a man swore. The Corvette squealed away.

Arianna melted into his arms, her kiss offering so much more than he was going to take. Slowly, he broke away. Amazement filled her eyes.

He brushed her cheek with his fingers. "I care about you very much. Promise me you won't choose them again. Let me help you be the beautiful woman I know you are."

Tears slipped down her cheeks. "I promise, Caleb. I just want you."

He cradled her close to him, and she sighed with contentment. Caleb stood with her a long moment, praying he could make the difference she needed.

After several minutes, he murmured, "It's late. I'd better go."

"Okay." She looked up at him with obvious longing but loosened her arms.

He kissed the top of her head, thankful that although she had thrown herself at him for all she was worth, her young heart had been won back with a simple kiss. "See you in the morning."

"Good night."

He walked off the porch, feeling her gaze follow him.

At his cabin, he powered on his computer, then pulled the jump drive from his pocket. He loaded the file he had found on Dean's hard drive and reread it. Finally, he punched in Patrick's home number, despite the late hour.

"What do you have, Caleb?"

"I copied a document from Benjamin Dean's laptop. It looks like it's the forged will that Jackson gave you. I'm e-mailing a copy for you to verify."

"Great."

A few minutes later, Patrick told him, "It's the same one. I wish my guess hadn't been right. Should I press charges?"

"Not yet. We don't want them to realize we're searching for the grand-daughter."

"I'm guessing you don't have any new candidates."

"No, sir. Are you sure you won't consider Arianna? She'd be safer if you'd bring her to your compound and change your will. Then we could start to prosecute."

"Arianna's perfectly safe. If Jackson wanted her dead, he'd have found a way to kill her weeks ago. My granddaughter is still coming. Just keep looking."

Caleb sighed. "Yes, sir."

Chapter Thirteen

Rye pulled the Ford to the front of Caleb's cabin and glanced at the digital clock on the dashboard. 5:25. He felt bad about breaking the speed limit on his drive from town, but at least he'd made it back to the resort by the time Caleb had requested.

Depressed by his fruitless trip to town, Rye killed the truck motor, then stepped out, slamming the door. Ever since he decided to approach Esther to find out Hershey's name, he hadn't seen the older woman without Paul or David. When Caleb gave him the day off, he had trailed Esther into town, hoping for a chance to corner her. However, she had met Paul at the Chinese restaurant within five minutes of her arrival.

Rye had wandered the nearby stores, waiting for Paul to leave, but the couple exited the mall together. Frustrated, he slipped into a showing of the most recent action flick. But even the intense plot hadn't been able to dissipate his growing depression, and he had driven back to the resort wondering if God even heard his prayers.

Caleb had said once that God wouldn't listen to the prayers of the wicked, of those whose hands were stained with blood or whose souls were soiled with impurity. Rye knew he was disqualified from being heard by the Maker of heaven and earth in both regards. Yet he couldn't keep from begging for another chance to see Hershey. But the days slipped by, leaving his prayers unanswered.

"Hey, Rye, thanks for watching the clock." Caleb came out of the cabin and clasped his shoulder.

"Sure. Have a good night."

He moved to step away, but Caleb tightened his grip, holding him in place. "Are you okay? You haven't seemed like yourself in a while."

Rye gave the first excuse he could think of for his moodiness. "Guess I'm just bored. This case has been standing still for way too long."

"Eager to leave and get on with other things?"

Rye shrugged and looked away, not wanting Caleb to know the real reason for his depression. He caught sight of Arianna coming toward them and frowned. Caleb said he spent so much time with her because of the case, but that didn't explain the warmth that filled Caleb's gaze as he watched her approach.

Caleb smiled when she hugged him. "Hi, Arianna. Ready to head out?"

"Definitely. I can't wait to meet your niece."

What? Rye jerked his gaze to Caleb, stunned. Cora was here? And Caleb hadn't said a thing to him?

Caleb shot him a hard glance as if daring him to question his decision.

Rye swallowed his hurt, but had to plead, "Can I come too?"

Caleb's gaze darkened. "Not tonight."

Rye's heart tightened in pain. The answer was as good as saying, "Never." Caleb hadn't told him Cora was close by because he didn't want him near her. Rye wasn't worthy to meet her, not tonight or the next or the next.

Caleb helped Arianna into the truck and drove off.

Rye inhaled deeply, then headed toward the beach, his chest hurting with every breath. He told himself over and over that Caleb's reticence shouldn't matter, but his heart refused to accept his argument. Combined with the depression of knowing Hershey was no longer near, Caleb's distrust wound like a thick cord around him, choking him until he thought he couldn't bear it a moment longer.

He walked until the beach narrowed away from the more popular coastline and into the quieter sand dunes. Dim voices filtered through the sound of lapping waves.

"They're late," a man said. "I'm going to go get my cell phone."

A girl's voice drifted on the breeze. "I'll come with you."

"It won't take more than a minute. Just wait here."

"But…"

Rye looked toward the voices and saw Hershey and David sitting in a secluded sandy spot. His heart lurched at the sight of them. David stood, then jogged up the sand dune toward the parking lot.

Rye caught his breath at the look of abandonment that crossed Hershey's face. She drew her legs up under her sundress and hugged her arms around them. He looked back up the sand dune that hid her fiancé from view. If the guy didn't care enough to keep her with him, he didn't deserve her.

She must have heard Rye's footsteps in the soft sand, for as soon as he neared she drew in a startled breath.

His heart beating heavily in his chest, he bent close to her. "It's Rye, baby."

Awareness flooded her face, and he slipped his hands under her elbows then drew her up.

"Rye. . ." She said his name in a breathless whisper, and her voice held the same longing that gripped his heart.

He slid his fingers into her hair, giving release to some of the poignancy that filled him. "I've missed you so much."

She trembled as the longing intensified on her face, and he followed his deepest yearning. He pulled her into his arms, close to his heart, and kissed her.

Cora melted into him, all resistance swept away.

For days, she had battled to remain content and satisfied. She had pushed herself to resist the longing that filled her whenever Rye came to mind. But the shock of his presence had stolen all reason. She found herself drowning in the heady scent of his skin and the honey taste of his mouth.

His left arm pressed her to him, and his right hand cradled her head as his kiss deepened. He seemed to be looking for something in her...something she desperately wanted to give him.

Her hands slid up his back, feeling its muscled smoothness through the fabric of his shirt as she responded with her own desire.

But in that moment, reality came crashing down on her. With a strangled cry at the depth of her folly, Cora broke loose. She pressed her palms into her forehead and wept. What had she done? How could she have kissed him so completely?

"Hershey?" Rye's voice sounded broken. "I'm sorry. I'm sorry, baby."

She shook her head in anguish. "I shouldn't have done that. I shouldn't have let you…" Tears choked her words. She deserved to have David come and say that he had seen it all. That she wasn't pure anymore or worthy to be married to him.

Child…

A gentle voice whispered into her mind, but a tumult of guilt and condemnation threatened to drown it out.

Child, the voice spoke again. *I forgive you. Do you forgive him?*

Cora sought to gain control of her weeping. She knew the voice was the same one that had calmed the raging sea so long ago. Slowly, she lowered her hands and lifted her head.

She turned back to where Rye had been standing, not knowing the reason but knowing what she needed to say. "Rye?"

She waited, listening. Her heart tightened as she realized what the stillness around her meant.

He was gone.

"Oh, there you are."

Caleb nodded as David waved at him and Arianna from beside his teal rental car in the coastal parking area where they had arranged to meet. "Sorry we're late. Had a flat tire. Where's Cora?"

David gestured toward the beach. "With the picnic stuff. Go on over. I'll join you in a minute. I need to make a call to a business contact."

"Okay."

Arianna trudged up the sand dune beside him. As they neared the top, she grimaced. "I'm getting sand in my shoes." She bent down to untie her tennis shoes, and Caleb took two more strides to reach the top of the sand dune. The magnificent blue of the ocean spread before him, its waves lapping at the coast.

Movement caught his gaze, and he looked down the sand dune just as Cora broke away from Rye's embrace.

Fury sent the blood rushing to his head. He couldn't believe it. How had the kid found her? And had he actually dared to kiss her?

"Okay, I'm ready…" Arianna trailed off as she caught a glimpse of his face. "Caleb?" She turned to look at what had captured his attention. "Is that Rye?"

Caleb curled his hand into a fist. The kid was striding away from Cora, his head down. More than anything, Caleb wanted to lay into him. But Arianna didn't know what had happened, and he had no desire to cause Cora further humiliation.

He worked to keep his fury under control. "We need to go back." He strode down the dune toward the parking lot.

Arianna hurried to catch up. "That was Rye, wasn't it? Why don't you want him meeting Cora?"

Caleb had no desire to explain the situation. Over the years it had become obvious that Rye had a crush on Cora, but Caleb would never have expected the kid to act on his infatuation the moment he met her.

David paused in his phone conversation when he saw them. "Where are you guys going?"

Caleb waved a hand. "I forgot an appointment I had. Tell Cora I'll see her later." He opened the Ford's passenger door, and Arianna slipped in. She seemed to realize he wasn't going to talk about what was upsetting him and remained silent on the short trip back to the resort. Caleb dropped her off at her house, then parked at his cabin. He strode toward Rye's place.

The kid wasn't back yet, but Caleb picked the lock and entered. He wasn't about to let Rye escape his wrath.

There was only one moment in his life when Rye had hated himself more than the moment when Hershey had pulled away from him, sobbing because she had succumbed to his kiss.

She had taken the blame on herself, but he knew it was completely and utterly his fault. Caleb was right. His past had tainted him and made him someone no one should trust, not even himself.

He should have known that her commitment to David would stand regardless of the emotions he stirred within her. But instead of honoring her strength of will, he had given in to his own desperate need and used all he knew about temptation to try to seduce her as soon as he saw her again.

He pressed his fists into his forehead as he hiked back the way he had come.

Her embrace had eased his depression, but now he knew seeking peace from her was futile. Anything he took from her only cost her, and he couldn't bear the thought of hurting her again.

He arrived back at the cabin. Not knowing how he would be able to live with himself any longer, he unlocked the door and stepped inside.

"You!" Caleb strode across the living room, his face livid. He spat out a filthy name.

"What's the matter?" Rye stopped as sudden realization dawned. Caleb's fury could only be from one thing. He must have seen him with Hershey. "I'm sorry." He swallowed hard. "I know I promised no girls—"

"Sorry!" The word seemed to release something in Caleb that Rye had never seen. "You try to seduce Cora, and all you can say is that you're *sorry*?"

Horror swept Rye. Spots danced in front of his eyes. *Cora?* He had battled to honor her at all times, even in his thoughts. He never wanted to demean her, though his heart ached to have the love of a girl like her.

When he had encountered Hershey, she seemed like a dream come true, one he could surrender to without fear. But never would he have let himself behave toward Cora as he had his chocolate-eyed angel.

He fought Caleb's declaration with all he had. "I didn't go see Cora. I don't even know where she is."

Caleb swore. "Don't lie to me! I saw you plain as day. She was saving her first kiss for her wedding day, did you know that? And you just took it without a pang of conscience! You lecherous..."

He cursed Rye's lineage, but Rye barely heard him. There was no way

Hershey was Cora. Hershey was a Christian. Cora was a Jew. And Hershey was blind. Caleb had never mentioned Cora having such a life-altering handicap. "Caleb." He looked at his partner in desperation. "I was with a woman today. But it wasn't Cora. This girl is blind."

The muscle in Caleb's jaw spasmed. "Cora lost her sight in a fire seven years ago," he said in a brutal tone. "If you so much as think of touching her again, I won't leave you a life worth living." He stalked to the door and threw it open. It slammed shut as he exited.

Rye stared at the door. He collapsed onto the edge of the couch as anguish rushed through him. The angel he had sought had finally materialized before him, only to be snatched away. Cora was the one girl in the world he could never pursue and in no way deserved to have.

Caleb strode up the road to the Sunnel beach house. Benjamin Dean's Mustang sat in the driveway, and the TV shone through the living room window. The back of Arianna's head was visible through the front window, where she sat watching the television.

He stopped in the middle of the road, tense and frustrated. Although Arianna might expect him to return, he didn't want to answer any questions she might have. Nor was he in the mood to be pleasant company.

He strode back to his cabin, not feeling the need to stand guard over her. Her Uncle Ben was home, and Caleb doubted Arianna would leave the house. She had promised to stay away from her old friends, and she liked to be at the stables early with him, which meant she went to bed at a decent hour.

He shoved open the door to the cabin and paced in agitation as his mind returned to the scene between Cora and Rye. Renewed anger bubbled inside him. Even if Rye hadn't known who Cora was, he had devalued her character with his cavalier treatment. He had taken advantage of her trusting nature and encroached upon her innocence, something Caleb couldn't forgive.

He had been right to keep Rye away from his family all these years. He had to do whatever it took to protect Cora from the kid's fickle morality, no matter how much his young partner might beg to see her.

Chapter Fourteen

Arianna stared at the TV as she waited for Caleb to return after his talk with Rye. At eight o'clock, she realized he wasn't going to come back. She snapped off the television.

Uncle Ben glanced up from working on his laptop. "If you're bored, why don't you call one of your friends?"

She shrugged, not wanting to admit she was waiting for Caleb.

"Can't spend your whole life waiting on that guy. Take my car and get out." He tossed her a silver-ringed set of keys, and Arianna stared at them. She had never confined herself to the house before, and being around her family was depressing. She clenched the keys in her fist. As much as she hated going out by herself, it was better than sitting around doing nothing. She stood. "Thanks."

She slipped into Uncle Ben's Mustang, then took the highway toward the town of Summerland. The movie she had wanted to watch with Caleb was showing again in twenty minutes. She might as well go see it.

The movie didn't hold her interest the way she had hoped, and annoyance settled over her. Why couldn't Caleb have come to find her after he finished talking with Rye? She didn't like being ignored. Caleb had said he cared about her, but so far he had only kissed her once. How much longer did she have to wait for him to give her the love and intimacy she craved?

The movie ended, and she trudged out of the theatre, her head down.

"Hey, Nan! Where's your boyfriend?"

Arianna lifted her head. Her best friend, Rebecca, hung on the arm of the guy she had been dating since the night of the dance. Arianna walked up to the couple. "He had something else to do. Where are you guys headed?"

Rebecca giggled and looked up at her boyfriend. "We're heading to Vance's place. His parents let him rent a cabin of his own. Do you want to come hang out?"

Tempted, Arianna forced herself to shake her head. She had promised Caleb she wouldn't hang out with her old friends.

She walked off while Vance pulled Rebecca into a juicy embrace. Arianna's stomach twisted with jealousy. She had wanted a guy who valued her for more than just her body, but it wasn't fair that Caleb's religion kept him from sleeping with her at all.

She slipped her key into Uncle Ben's Mustang, but glanced up at a deep voice. "What's a sweet thing like you doing here alone?"

A stranger leaned against the red Mercedes parked on the other side of the Mustang. A sensual smile curved his mouth, and he gazed at her with dark, bold eyes set in European features.

Her pulse jumped at the desire in his gaze. "Do you always pick up girls outside movie theatres?"

His black eyes glinted. "No. But then I don't normally see one as gorgeous as you."

The compliment salved her wounded pride, and she let a smile flicker.

The stranger straightened, his mouth curving further. "You won't forget me, I promise. And I know I'll never forget you."

Desire washed over her. She ached for the pleasure he was offering, but she wanted it to come from Caleb. She just had to wait a little longer. "Maybe another time."

"In that case, let me give you my number." He took a piece of paper out of his pocket and walked close enough to offer it.

Her throat tightened in sudden conflict. She shouldn't take it, but Uncle Ben always said she should leave her options open.

"Thanks." She tucked the paper into her jeans pocket and opened the Mustang door.

The stranger stepped back. "See you. Soon."

Arianna slipped into the Mustang and drove away.

"I saw him!"

Rye halted inside Dana's door. She wrung her hands, her face filled with fear. His heartbeat quickened. "Where?"

"At the theatre. I went out with some friends. I figured it was safe. I mean, you said he would be lying low since Patrick's granddaughter isn't here. But he was there!"

"Give me the details. Try to stay in order."

She swallowed. "I had just walked out of the theatre with my friends, and I happened to glance across the parking lot. I saw him leaning against a red sports car. A Mercedes, I think, with 'Big Jim's Rentals' on the license plate."

"Did he do anything?"

"He was talking with that teenage girl your partner's dating."

"Arianna?" Rye stared in shock. So Caleb had been right. His stomach tightened. "Were they still together when you left?"

"No. She took off while I was talking with my friends. He drove away shortly after."

Rye exhaled in relief. "I'm gonna call Caleb, and I want you to tell all this to him. More if you can remember anything else. Even something insignificant might be important."

She nodded, eyes wide with fear.

He flipped open his cell phone and punched Caleb's speed-dial button. He clenched his hand into a fist as Caleb's wrath-filled words of three hours ago replayed in his mind. But he couldn't keep Dana's news to himself. Identifying the assassin was crucial to solving the case, and Caleb needed to know that Arianna was definitely the target.

Caleb answered on the third ring with a hard tone.

Rye swallowed. "Dana saw the killer. He was talking to Arianna at the theatre."

"Is he with her now?"

"No."

"Where is she?"

"I don't know."

Caleb swore and ended the call.

Dana paced the room, wringing her hands. Not wanting to escalate Caleb's anger by making him try to get facts out of a tormented mind, Rye asked, "Want a cup of coffee?"

She stared at him as though incapable of thinking about such mundane matters, and he moved to her kitchenette. He had made coffee for her the night she'd been overwrought about his delay in coming to her, so he put out the sugar and cream he knew she liked. He figured this was the best way to achieve a calm, relaxed atmosphere, not just for her but for himself too.

He didn't want to think of life without Caleb's camaraderie or wonder if he could resist temptation without Caleb's constant reminders. After his folly that afternoon, he was all too aware of the weakness of his will.

A hard rap sounded on the door, and Dana jumped.

Rye opened the door and Caleb strode past him. "She's home."

"Did you ask her about that guy?"

Caleb sent him a cutting look. "I wanted to get the details from Dana first."

Dana related everything she had told Rye.

Caleb frowned. "Did you hear anything the man said to Arianna?"

"He asked her what she was doing by herself and told her that she wouldn't forget him."

"What did she do?"

Dana looked uncomfortable. "She told him maybe another time, then drove off."

"Did he follow her?"

"No. He went in a different direction."

"Did he look the same as the last time you saw him?"

"Yes." Dana gave a sudden shudder.

"I'm calling Patrick." Caleb snapped open his cell phone. "He'd better not argue about coming to get Arianna now."

Dana frowned. "Why does Patrick need to get her?"

"Now that the assassin has approached her, she's in grave danger."

Dana looked confused. "But she's not the granddaughter."

Caleb's face darkened. "How do you know?"

"Arianna is already related to Patrick."

"But she has a scar shaped like an x from an incision," Rye said. "And her father could have been Douglas Sunnel."

Dana looked apologetically at Caleb. "I'm sorry. The granddaughter is an outsider. I didn't realize Arianna was one of your choices." She swallowed. "There's something else. I guess I should have told you this right away, but I'm not entirely sure the x-shaped mark on Patrick's granddaughter came from an operation."

Caleb didn't bother covering his anger. "Dana! That means it could be a brand or tattoo. Something that wouldn't necessarily be on a medical record."

She winced. "Look, I've done my part. I identified the killer. Can I go home now?"

Caleb ran his hand through his hair. "Sure. Rye can take you to the bus station in the morning."

"Thanks." She hurried to her bedroom, closing the door behind her.

Caleb clenched his cell phone. "We're back to square one. We'll have to recheck the guest registry and make a new list of all female guests and workers in the right age range who were scheduled to be here from the first day we came and are still here now."

Rye hesitated. "You're sure the granddaughter's here?"

"The assassin is, so it's a good guess she is too."

"How are we gonna narrow down the candidates?"

"Douglas knew about his daughter's mark. If it's not listed on a medical record, it must be in plain sight. After we compile a list, we'll track down each of the women. Not many young people stay at a resort for more than a week or two, and it's been three."

"Are we going to try to find the assassin too?"

Caleb headed to the door. "You can focus on him until I get a complete list of the women. Go to Big Jim's rental agency. Rent a car. That way we'll each have a vehicle. Try to find out the name the assassin's using. I'll log into the databases of all the hotels in the area. Meanwhile, you can go to all the bed-and-breakfasts to see if anyone recognizes his photo. Unless he has a friend in the area letting him stay at his home, we'll find him."

Chapter Fifteen

Although tormenting thoughts about his impropriety toward Cora kept Rye awake most of the night, at nine o'clock the next morning he drove Dana to the bus station in her rental car so she could return home.

She accepted her two suitcases from him with a sad smile. "Thanks, Rye. If you hadn't helped me, I couldn't have stayed here."

He nodded. "No problem. Take care."

She headed into the bus station, and he slipped back into the sedan. He returned it to the rental agency, then walked ten blocks to Big Jim's Rentals, where the assassin had rented his car. Determined to shove his depression to the side and focus on the case, he strode into the small office building.

A bald, overweight man with "Big Jim" on his shirt sat behind a wide desk, talking with a man in a business suit. At the service counter, a blond kid who looked to be eighteen straightened. The name Heath was embroidered on his company shirt. "Can I help you?"

Rye walked to the counter. "Yeah. I'd like to rent a car for the next week."

"What kind are you interested in?"

Heath recited the qualities of the higher-priced rentals, but Rye shook his head. "The Pinto out front works for me. How much is that?"

Health quoted a price and walked outside to inspect the Pinto with Rye. After he had noted the few dings, they returned inside, and Heath rang up the transaction.

"Thanks." Rye accepted the keys, then pulled out the sketch the police had done of Abel Brinnon's killer. "There's something else you can help me with. I'm looking for an escaped convict. He was seen driving a red Mercedes with your rental company's name on the license plate. Have you seen him?" He slid the paper across the high counter.

Heath stared at the picture. "He was here two days ago. I didn't know he was a convict. His ID cleared."

"He stole someone else's name. He's certain to rob another bank if I don't find him. What name did he give you?"

"I can look it up." Heath's fingers shook as he accessed the computer database. "He said his name was Kenneth Sweeney. He had a Texas driver's license."

"When is he supposed to return the rental?"

"He paid for a month." Heath lowered his voice to a tremulous whisper. "Do you think he'll steal the car? My boss will have my hide."

"Won't be your fault. Thanks for your help."

Heath nodded, looking sick, and Rye strode out of the building. He slipped into the Pinto and drove a couple of blocks before calling Caleb.

"Lindon here."

"Our guy's going by the name of Kenneth Sweeney. He rented the Mercedes for a month. Seems odd, doesn't it? Wouldn't he want to get the job done and get out of here?"

"He might not be sure about when he can get to the granddaughter. Maybe she's here with friends or family who are always with her. Or maybe he wants to give himself plenty of time to leave the country before the rental agency starts looking for their car."

"I'm heading to the two bed-and-breakfasts listed in the Yellow Pages."

"My break's in an hour. I'll start the computer search of the local hotels. Of course the assassin might have used a different name and ID. Hopefully he's not that cautious."

Rye grimaced. "I'll call you when I have something." He ended the call.

Fifteen minutes later, he pulled to the curb of the Victorian three-story home that had been converted into Lindsey's Bed-and-Breakfast. Tulips bloomed in the flower beds under the bay windows.

He strode up the wooden porch steps and thumped the brass knocker. A few seconds passed before the door swung open. A silver-haired woman in her sixties smiled. "Hello. Richard, right?"

Rye gave her his most charming smile, assuming she was expecting a boarder of his age. "Actually, my name's Matt, and I'm supposed to meet my uncle here. He made a bet with me that I couldn't find him in the first twenty-four hours of my arrival without using his name."

The woman's eyebrows flickered in confusion. "You can't use his name?"

Rye chuckled. "I'm enrolled in the police academy, and he's trying to prove that I'm not getting my education's worth. I also can't use a photograph, so I sketched a simple picture. Could you tell me if he's here?" Rye withdrew the police sketch.

The woman eyed it uncertainly. "You draw well. But that doesn't look like any of my boarders. I'm sorry. Maybe he's at the bed-and-breakfast across town. Or one of the hotels."

Rye shrugged. "Okay. Thanks for your time."

He skipped down the steps and started the Ford. The Yellow Pages had given him the address of the second bed-and-breakfast, but he took several wrong turns before finding the obscure side street where the long Georgian manor sat behind a high stone wall.

Eyeing the metal gate, he pressed the entrance button. The gate swung open, apparently in place to keep animals out more than people. He drove up the circular driveway and parked in front of the four-stall garage. A young woman in a straw hat looked up from hoeing in a blooming flower garden. Rye smiled as he walked closer. "Hello. Do you work here?"

She straightened, assessing him with pale blue eyes. "Yes. Are you looking for Ann-Marie? She runs the bed-and-breakfast."

"Yes."

"Okay. Follow me." She rested the hoe against the fence and headed up the sidewalk.

Rye followed her inside, noting the expensive furnishings. It didn't seem the type of setup that an assassin would want, since wealthy homes usually ran background checks. Perhaps Sweeney felt confident in his false identity.

The young woman rapped on an oak door, then pushed it open. "Mom, someone to see you about a room."

Rye nodded his appreciation as the girl gestured him into the room.

The older woman had apparently dyed her abundant hair an impressive blonde. He smiled and held out his hand. "Kyle Johnson. Ann-Marie, I assume?"

"That's right." She studied him critically, her eyes scanning the holes in his jeans and T-shirt. "Are you interested in a room?"

Rye smiled as he shook his head. "Actually, I'm looking for my uncle. He rented a room in the last day or so. Do you mind if I show you a sketch I drew of him?" He drew out the sketch and casually turned it toward her.

Her eyes narrowed as she glanced at it. "I'm sorry. I can't help you."

Her answer wasn't the concrete no or yes he'd hoped for. He tipped the corner of his mouth ruefully. "Okay. Guess fifty bucks isn't that much to lose. Thanks."

Ann-Marie didn't nod or say good-bye as she watched him go. In the living area, Rye eyed the back hallway. It appeared to lead to several bedrooms. A glance toward Ann-Marie's office showed that she hadn't followed him, so he scurried down the hallway.

Each of the doors was closed, but the hallway ended in a stone patio. He stepped outside. A thin man in his fifties sat at one of the tables, reading a newspaper. He glanced up when Rye approached.

Rye smiled with casual friendliness. "Hi. Have you seen Ken around?"

"Is he the gardener?"

"No. He's renting a room here."

The man frowned. "I didn't know there was another male boarder. Who are you?"

Rye shrugged, keeping his attitude light. "Reporter for the *Summerland Daily*. I was told Kenneth Sweeney had a room here. He tries to keep a low profile, so maybe he hasn't introduced himself. Have you seen a man who looks like this?" He showed the sketch again.

The man shook his head. "He doesn't look familiar."

"Well, thanks anyway."

Rye headed down the patio steps and found his way back to the circular driveway in front of the house. He drove off the property, hoping Caleb would have better luck than he had in tracking down the assassin.

Caleb studied the list of seven young women that his software program had compiled from the resort's database. Two of the women worked at the resort—one as a lifeguard, the other as a clerk. He had plugged all seven women's social security numbers into his program to pull up their medical records, but none of them had an x-shaped mark listed. No wonder their names hadn't come up during his previous searches.

One of the names looked familiar, though. Wasn't Mayla Rivers a rock singer? He typed her name into Google, and within seconds several Web sites popped up. He scanned the first two, but the third caught his attention.

"Mayla says her tattoo of the Roman numeral ten comes from her connection with a college fraternity. She's proud of the large insignia on her left shoulder…"

He continued to read, seeking a reference about a father. The sixth article he opened went into detail about her parentage. Apparently, her mother had worked as a backup singer in Reno, where she had slept with numerous men. She was quoted as saying, "I neither know nor care who Mayla's father is. She and I belong together. A man would only complicate our lives."

In bold marker, Caleb circled her name on his list. He accessed the resort's database and jotted down the suite where she was staying. A note stated that it was accessible only to invited guests and that Mayla had brought her own security guards.

He leaned back in his chair. If she was the granddaughter, she already had protective measures in place. On the other hand, a concert was scheduled that night in a city two hours away. The assassin might find a way to get close amid the craziness of a crowd. Although he didn't approve the topics that most rock stars sang about, Arianna would probably appreciate a night together with him. He could ask her to the concert and search for the assassin while they were there.

He called her beach house.

Her voice brightened as soon as she recognized his voice. "Do we get to go out tonight?"

"If you want. There's a concert at eight, but it's two hours away, so we'll have to leave soon to make it."

"I'll be over in ten minutes."

"Okay."

He pressed End, but the phone rang again. He glanced at the caller's name and pressed his lips together. Rye. He wished he didn't have to talk to the kid, but personal feelings had to be put aside while they searched for Patrick's granddaughter. He pressed Answer. "Yes?" He kept his tone cold.

"I've visited three small hotels. Nothing. Either Sweeney's checked in under a different name or he's staying with a friend."

"Forget him for now. I've found seven women who've been here for three weeks. One of them is a rock singer with a tattoo of the Roman numeral ten. I'm going to her concert tonight to see if Sweeney's hanging out near her. I need you to find out if the others have x-shaped marks of some kind. I'll leave the list on the table here with all the information. One of them's an office clerk who works at the resort and lives in town. Her shift ended at four. Check her out first."

"What's her name?"

"Karen Neilson." Caleb gave the address.

"I'll head over there now."

Caleb hit End, then strode into his bedroom. He tossed the cell phone on the dresser and then changed for the concert.

Anger stirred anew as he pulled a clean shirt from the closet. Rye's charming nature benefited the case since it enabled him to integrate himself easily with the women they were investigating. But Cora deserved better treatment from him. Rye should have been able to discern her virtue just by looking at her. She didn't dress, act, or talk like the worldly women the kid knew so well. Caleb should have known he couldn't trust the young man to give up his old ways. Why couldn't Rye have left Cora alone?

A light knock sounded at the front door. Caleb grabbed his money clip out of his jeans and stuffed it into his pocket as he strode from the room.

Arianna hugged him as soon as he opened the door. "So, what concert are we going to?"

"Have you heard of Mayla Rivers?"

"Sure, but I didn't know you liked her."

Caleb opened the Ford's passenger door. "She's not my style, but I thought a night out would be nice."

Arianna beamed. "I'd love a night out with you!"

"Sure is quiet around here."

"Everyone's gone for a campout." Cora listened to the gravel crunch as David drove onto the YMCA campground. She had spent the evening alone with him per her request. They'd eaten supper together, then walked along the beach. Their conversation had lagged within a short time, and Cora had sensed his impatience for the evening to end. That saddened her but also told her what she had been wanting to discover. David wasn't the man for her.

For years she had accepted her prearranged marriage and had trusted her grandfather's choice, especially since David had converted to Christianity in his teens. But since meeting Rye, she recognized the brutal truth that she had believed her blindness would make her undesirable to anyone else.

All through the painful years of high school, as she adjusted from a world of light and color to a world of darkness, the only boy who had paid her any attention was David. At her senior prom, he told her he was happy she was his girl.

She had accepted his desire to graduate college and get a secure job before they married. His studies occupied him so much that he sometimes forgot their dates, and his absentmindedness caused him to forget the help she needed because of her blindness. Unlike Caleb and Grandpa, who had swiftly adjusted their lives around her lack of sight, David had relegated her to a small section of his life.

Cora had sought to please David for so long she hadn't perceived the widening distance between them until the Lord brought her into contact with Rye. It seemed God wanted her to acknowledge that her reasons for holding to her prearranged betrothal were insufficient. Why else would He allow her to be found multiple times by a young man who not only needed a Savior but who had awakened in her the realization that love shouldn't be a lukewarm business arrangement?

The evening spent with David had solidified her conclusion that both of them would be better off with other people or even single. If one evening alone felt awkward and long, how would they survive a life together? They would end up living in separate worlds. She knew some marriages operated that way, but it was not what she wanted for hers, and she was certain David didn't want it either.

Her greatest struggle in breaking the engagement came from going against the expectations of the people she loved. Caleb and Grandpa would be stunned.

"We're here. Want me to walk you inside?"

Cora nodded, all too aware that he had had to ask, whereas Rye seemed to always know what she wanted, even when he had embraced her on the beach. Desire washed over her at the memory of the incredible way he had kissed her, but she yanked her thoughts back to the present. Breaking the engagement with David didn't give her license to think of any man in such a way, especially one who wasn't saved.

"Are all your roommates gone?" David accepted the key she gave him and the lock clicked.

Cora gave a small frown. "Sandy should be here. She wasn't scheduled to go on the camping trip."

The door squeaked open. "Doesn't look like anyone's here."

She waited a second before realizing David wasn't coming back to guide her in. She trailed her hand on the door frame. "Do you see my walking stick?"

"Yes, here it is."

"Thank you." She took it from him and moved toward the couch.

David's footsteps headed to the door. He paused. "When do you want me to pick you up next?"

She would be a coward if she didn't tell him now. "Actually, there's something I should tell you." Her mouth went dry. "David, I don't think I can do this anymore."

For a moment silence filled the room. Then he asked, "Do what?"

Tears stung her eyes. They had been friends for many years, and she had given him no reason to guess what she was about to say. Her voice cracked. "I don't think I can be engaged to you any longer."

His stunned silence pierced her, and she wanted to cry. But tears would only make the moment harder on both of them. Finally he asked in a strained voice, "Did I do something you don't like?"

Cora shook her head. "No, it's nothing you've done. I've just realized we don't have the same goals or enjoyments." Her voice dropped to a whisper. "And I don't want you to spend the rest of your life with a blind girl."

He walked over to her and touched her arm. "Cora, that's not a problem. You don't know that after all these years?"

She swallowed hard. "It's not a problem because our lives are so different and we're doing our own things most of the time. But I don't want to live separate lives." She paused, then said quietly, "I'm sure that eventually we would."

His hand fell away, and he stayed silent a long moment. At last he said, "You're right. It seemed to make sense that we get married since both of us believe in Jesus, but I think our faith is the only thing we have in common." His voice grew soft. "I'm sorry, Cora."

She smiled against her tears. "It's not your fault. It's not anyone's fault. I'm sure God has the right woman for you. Someone who will enjoy your giftings and support you in everything you do."

"You've always supported me. I'm afraid I'm the one who hasn't supported you."

She blinked at the tears. She couldn't deny it.

"Well…"

He seemed not to know what to say, so she filled the silence for him. "Don't worry about taking me to the resort anymore. After I finish the summer here, I'll return to college. I'm sure we'll see each other around. I know you'll do well wherever God leads you."

"Cora…"

He seemed to feel as if he shouldn't give her up too easily, but she shook her head. "Please don't try to change my mind. I'm going to be all right and so are you. Good night, David."

He didn't reply, but several moments later the door squeaked closed. Then his car motor started outside, and gravel crunched as he drove away.

A mixture of pain and anxiety swept her. She sank onto the couch, trembling. "Oh, Jesus, please take care of him. And please take care of me."

Fear leered at her. What if she had just given up her only chance of being married?

She buried her face in her hands and wept. The memories of Rye's embraces were just that—memories. Now that she wouldn't be returning to the resort, she doubted she would ever encounter him again...unless she sought him out.

She struggled to accept reality. Rye wasn't an option she could consider. The Word of God allowed no compromise. Marriage between a believer and an unbeliever was forbidden. Her heart broke.

"Oh, Jesus! Whatever the future holds, I'm going to serve You. I refuse to compromise my faith for fantasy. I won't cling to dreams that aren't Yours. Please help me rest in You and trust my future to Your hands."

She poured out her brokenness. At last exhaustion struck her. She wiped away her tears, grasped her walking stick, and stood. In her bedroom, she changed into the modest cotton nightgown she had bought for her co-ed living. Caleb had teased her about how she preferred dresses over pants and nightgowns over pajamas. "You're such a girlie-girl, Cora."

He was right. Something about the feel of free-flowing material made her feel graceful and feminine.

She undid her long braid and ran her hands through the thick tresses to loosen them for sleep. Memory swirled again. She had been standing beside Esther's car when she had asked Rye why he called her Hershey.

His fingers had brushed through her hair as huskiness coated his voice. *"Because of your ravishing, long dark hair."*

Cora jerked her hands out of her hair. Angry with the battle she couldn't seem to win, she turned back the covers of her bed.

A sudden rattle filled the air. Reptilian fangs buried deep in her left forearm, then disengaged.

Cora cried out in horror. "Oh, Jesus, help me!"

She staggered backward, weeping as her arm began to throb.

A wave of nausea swept her. She fumbled for the wall. Faintness threatened to pull her under, but she stumbled across the living area. It could be hours before Sandy found her.

Her fingers snagged the phone, and she pressed its buttons.

"911, may I—" The voice crackled, then the dial tone hummed.

Tears streaked down her cheeks. She tried again, but only static met her attempts to reach the police. *Jesus, no!*

The pain in her arm intensified. Nausea assailed her. Her focus blurred.

She punched in the cell number Caleb had made her memorize a long time ago. Agony gripped her as it rang and rang.

She began to shake. "Please, God, make him answer. Please…"

Chapter Sixteen

ountry music greeted Rye as he walked into Denny's Bar. He drifted to the side, scanning the numerous occupants. Karen Neilson, the woman Caleb had asked him to check on, had entered two minutes before him, accompanied by the fair-haired man who had picked her up from her apartment. Rye had trailed them to an expensive restaurant, but the maître d' had looked down her nose at his faded clothes as she said in a chilly tone, "Reservations only."

Rye had waited in the parking lot, hoping for a better look at Karen to see if she had an x-shaped mark. Her tight skirt and spaghetti-strap top would allow him a good view if he could get close enough. Of course, he didn't want the guy she was with to take offense, so he hoped to get close without drawing attention to himself.

The boisterous crowd in the bar provided the coverage he needed. He moved closer to the pool table, where Karen and her boyfriend were greeted by two other couples. Karen's boyfriend took a turn at the game and sent three balls into their holes. Their friends cheered, and Karen gave him a loud kiss.

A rosebud was tattooed on her left calf, and Rye changed angles several times before deciding she didn't have any other markings. Satisfied, he exited the bar and headed to the resort to pick up the list Caleb had left for him of the five other women.

Caleb had locked the cabin door, but Rye slipped the lock pick he always carried into the knob. The lock clicked open, and he walked to the table where Caleb's laptop sat.

He picked up the white sheet of paper that sat next to it and studied the names. One of them Caleb had highlighted was a lifeguard at the resort.

Rye planned a trip to the pool tomorrow to catch sight of her in her bathing suit.

Sadness touched him. Caleb had warned him many times not to ogle women, but now he was obligated to do so for his job. Being a private eye was becoming less appealing all the time, but he'd probably lose his relationship with Caleb if he quit. The older man certainly didn't see him as a worthy friend at the moment.

He noted the beach house number of Susan Jacobs, a twenty-eight-old who had registered with her husband and two children. He headed for the door, but startled when a phone rang.

He recognized the ring to Caleb's cell phone and scanned the room with a frown. He didn't see it anywhere. He walked to the bedroom, where he found it lying on Caleb's dresser.

He glanced at the Caller ID, but the number was unavailable. Assuming the caller would try again later, he turned to leave.

Answer it.

Rye whirled at the clear voice, even though no one else was in the room.

Answer it now.

The command was so sharp and urgent he grabbed the cell phone and hit Answer. "Hello?"

"Caleb, I need help. A rattler bit me."

At Cora's voice, fear jolted Rye's heart. "Where are you?"

"At the YMCA campground. In my cabin."

"Isn't anyone with you?"

"No. My roommates are all gone. Please come. I feel sick."

"What's your room number?"

"Ten. I don't think I can—" A dull thud, like a body falling, sounded on the end of the line.

Rye dashed out of the cabin and slid into the Pinto. Pealing onto the road, he dialed 911 on Caleb's cell.

"911 emergency."

"There's a girl with snakebite at the YMCA campground," Rye bit out.

"An ambulance will take forty minutes to get there. Could you get her to the Summerland clinic any quicker?

"I should be able to get her there in about thirty minutes."

"Do you know what bit her?"

"A rattler."

"Is she in shock?"

Rye gritted his teeth. "Yes."

"Immobilize the limb and make sure it stays lower than her heart. But don't cut off the circulation."

"Okay." Rye snapped the cell phone shut. He jerked the steering wheel to the right when he saw the sign for the campground. After passing several darkened buildings, he saw two rows of smaller cabins. He counted by twos and pulled up to the last cabin on the right. The Pinto's headlights illuminated a large 10 on a signpost next to the door. He jumped out of the truck.

He took the porch steps two at a time, then twisted the doorknob. It was locked. He slipped his pick into place and snapped the lock open within seconds. Stepping inside, he flicked on the light.

His heart jumped in his chest. Cora lay collapsed beside the end table, the phone dangling beside her. He sprinted to her and turned her onto her side. Blood trickled from a small cut on her forehead, and her right forearm was grotesquely swollen.

Riddled with anxiety, he laid her down, then ran to the kitchen. He pulled open drawers until he found a wooden spoon. Grabbing it and a dishtowel, he rushed back to Cora and carefully applied the splint.

She moaned, and he laid a hand on her shoulder. "Stay still, Cora. I'm gonna take you to the doc."

He hoisted her up, and she winced. He hurried outside and settled her into the passenger seat. Her face contorted. She grasped at her left arm, but startled when she felt the spoon.

Rye belted her in place. "911 said to splint your arm. Don't move it, okay?"

"Rye? Is that you?"

His heart twisted. "Yeah." He hurried to the driver's side and slid behind the wheel. The Pinto spit gravel as he backed out.

Cora leaned her head against the window. "Were you the one on the phone?"

"Yeah."

She seemed to struggle to concentrate. "What were you doing with Caleb's cell phone?"

He drew in a deep breath. She deserved the truth regardless of Caleb's preferences. "I'm Cal's partner. We're here on a case."

Her breath caught. "And here I thought I'd never see you again."

He stared at the road. After the way he had kissed her, he'd felt certain she would want nothing more to do with him. Was her pain the reason she hadn't remembered to hold his folly against him?

Another apology seemed trite, but he needed her to know that he really did regret the way he had taken advantage of her. He struggled for the right words. "Cora, I wish with all my heart that I hadn't..." He couldn't finish.

Her soft voice eased into the silence. "I forgive you."

He jerked his gaze to her face. No resentment or anger showed in her sightless gaze. Rather, a gentle smile curved her mouth. Her kindness poured relief into the depths of his being. He drew in a long, deep breath. "Thank you."

Strain washed over her face, but somehow she found another smile. "You're welcome."

A longing ache spiraled through him, but he didn't dare give in to it. Hadn't his desire wounded her enough already?

At least he had the chance to help her now. Focusing on the road, he accelerated as fast as he dared.

Ten minutes later, he saw the exit for Summerland. The clinic sat next to the mall. He pulled to the curb. Light shone through the window. He jogged to Cora's door. She inhaled when he slipped his arms around her, but he pushed his emotions down as he carried her inside.

A small man with wire-frame glasses glanced up from his desk. He narrowed sharp gray eyes on Cora. "Set her on the examination table."

Rye obeyed, and the doctor untied the spoon from her arm. "I'm Dr. Miller. What's your name, young lady?"

"Cora Abrams."

"Cora, I'm going to give you a shot of antivenom. It should work quickly and dissipate the pain, although perhaps not the nausea." He slid a syringe into her arm, and she winced.

"Now I'll bandage the puncture holes to prevent infection."

Miller cleaned the wound then wrapped a cloth bandage around her lower arm. He pressed his stethoscope to her heart and checked her pulse. The pain had lessened from her features. "You'll be fine, Cora. But don't go back to your cabin right away. Pest control will need to patch the hole where the rattler entered and make sure it didn't lay eggs."

"Thank you."

She slid off the examination table. Only then did Rye realize she was wearing her nightgown. Although it was more modest than any he had seen, he felt embarrassed for her sake.

He said good-bye to the doctor and guided her to the truck. Once again, he secured her seatbelt around her.

"I'm sorry," she said.

"For what?"

She touched the strap of the seatbelt. "I'm acting completely helpless."

She had no idea how much he desired to take care of her for all time. It was a moment before he could trust himself to speak. "Don't you dare apologize. You're the one with the snakebite."

She bit her lip, and he forced himself to close the door. He went around the truck, putting some distance between them. In the driver's seat, he started the motor and turned onto the street. The doctor's warning flashed across his mind. "I'm gonna take you to Caleb's."

"All right." She closed her eyes, resting her head against the passenger window.

He drove in silence, thinking about all the times he had spent with her. He doubted Caleb would let him anywhere near her in the days ahead. His throat tightened, and he wished he had been more careful when she had simply been Hershey. Her forgiveness only amplified his desire to be near her, but he couldn't think of any reason God would allow him a second chance.

Seeing the sign for Summerland Resort, he drove under the resort's large oak archway. Minutes later, he pulled the Pinto to a halt in front of Caleb's cabin. The Ford wasn't out front, so apparently Caleb hadn't returned from the concert.

He rounded the car to Cora's side and tapped on the window.

She startled, and he opened the door. "We're at Caleb's."

She held out her hand and he helped her out, much too aware of her for his own good. He should probably take her inside and then leave immediately.

But by the time they made it indoors, he knew he couldn't desert her. She looked ready to pass out just from walking with him to Caleb's bedroom. Tender concern overtook every other emotion, and he guided her to the edge of the double bed. "Go to sleep. I'll tell Cal when he gets here that he has to take the couch."

She lay down without resistance. Her eyes closed as soon as her head hit the pillow.

He drew the blanket over her shoulders, then exited the room, gently shutting the door. He went to the kitchenette to fix some coffee while he waited for Caleb's return. Hopefully his partner wouldn't yell at him for being with Cora after he learned about her desperate situation.

Arianna kept watch for the exit sign to a beach turnout she remembered from one of her past dates. As soon as she saw it, she pointed and asked, "Can we turn here? There's a lighthouse nearby with a beautiful view of the ocean."

"It's already late."

"Please?"

Caleb shook his head. "Some other time."

Disappointed, she watched the headlights of passing cars. The concert hadn't been as much fun as she'd hoped. Caleb hadn't appreciated the music and he'd seemed preoccupied with looking at the people around them. He had changed their location numerous times and frowned in disapproval at the lascivious displays of other couples.

Arianna wished he had taken the beach turnout. Her past boyfriends had never passed up an opportunity to make out with her. Caleb didn't act like a boyfriend at all. Did he give her any more affection than he gave his niece? The thought didn't sit well.

When they arrived at the resort, Caleb drove straight to her beach house. "Thanks for coming with me tonight."

She struggled to respond, wanting to communicate her feelings without chasing him off. Finally, she asked quietly, "Am I your girlfriend? Or am I more like a sister to you?"

He raised an eyebrow. "I kissed you, didn't I?"

"I know, but..." She trailed off, knowing she risked his anger if she complained further.

He stepped out of the cab and came around to her side. She accepted the hand he offered, relieved he wasn't angry. To her surprise, he wrapped his arms around her. She looked up into his eyes, wondering at his intention.

"I know I don't treat you the way you're used to. But a healthy relationship isn't focused on physical attraction. I'm proud of you for staying away from your old friends. They want to make you think fulfillment can be found in unlimited sexual experiences, but it can't. I spend time with you because I enjoy who you are inside. Your soul is more important to me than your body."

Arianna swallowed. His words made her feel significant, but... "I liked it when you kissed me."

He pulled her closer and rested his chin on her hair. "I know. But trust me. I'm only going to do what's best for you. I want to protect you and honor you."

Arianna struggled to see his point of view. She had never been forced to think past immediate gratification, but she reminded herself that Caleb valued her, whereas her other boyfriends hadn't bothered looking past her body. She drew in a deep breath, trying to fortify her resolve to be patient. He wasn't going to give her what she wanted if she pushed for it.

She withdrew from his arms and managed a wan smile. "I want to please you. It's just... Sometimes I get jealous of what everybody else has."

"Not everyone," Caleb corrected her gently. "People who think they can live without consequences to the rules God has set in place keep going from one person to the next, trying to find something God designed to be found in only one."

She stared at him. "Do you want to have just one girl all your life?"

"Yes."

The idea of Caleb taking care of her for all time filled her with a greater sense of security than she had ever experienced. She grabbed his hands in delight. "I love you, Caleb Lindon!"

Caleb's chest tightened at the joy in Arianna's eyes. He hadn't made a promise of commitment to her, but she had taken his answer as one. He pulled her back into his arms, mostly so she wouldn't see the anxiety that suddenly filled him. He wondered if her promiscuity had been a desperate search for the kind of love that would last.

He tightened his hold on her, wrestling with the need to protect himself. She didn't fit the ideal woman he wanted for a wife. At least not yet. He couldn't promise anything except to take their relationship one day at a time. He kissed the top of her head. "I'll see you tomorrow."

She stepped back, smiling warmly. "Good night." She backed up several steps, her gaze staying on his face, then headed into her parents' beach house.

Caleb slipped into the Ford and headed toward his cabin.

To his surprise, his living area light gleamed through the window and images danced on the TV screen. Frowning, he entered.

Rye lounged on the couch, his feet propped on a chair. At Caleb's entrance, Rye dropped his feet with a thud and turned off the TV.

"What are you doing here?"

Rye stood. "Cora was bitten by a rattler at her cabin. I had to take her to the clinic in town."

"What were you doing in her cabin?"

"Don't you want to know if she's recovered before you question my helping her?"

Caleb regarded him darkly. "How is she?"

"She'll be fine, but pest control is investigating her cabin, so I brought her here. She's in your room."

Caleb strode to the bedroom door. Cora was asleep, curled up under his blanket like a little girl, her dark hair spread out on the pillow. His stomach clenched. She looked like an angel, even if she wouldn't be considered a beauty by most people's standards.

He closed the door quietly, then walked back to his partner. "You'd better have a good excuse for why you were with her."

"I wasn't. Neither was anyone else. The campground was deserted when I got there after she called."

"She called you?"

Rye cracked a grin. "I wish."

Caleb growled.

The kid sighed. "She called your cell phone around nine. You left it in your bedroom. I heard it ring. I wasn't going to answer. But I think... I think God told me to."

Caleb stared. "God?"

Rye smiled. "I guess He wanted somebody to get over there before the poison killed her."

The seriousness of his words reminded Caleb he owed Cora's life to this young man. Suddenly weary, he lowered himself to the couch. "Why'd you drive her into town? You should've called 911."

"I did. But they said an ambulance would have taken too long."

Caleb stayed silent, unable to criticize the kid's response.

"I take it you didn't see the assassin at the concert."

Caleb sighed. "No. But I have tomorrow off, so I'm going to make some phone calls. See if I can get an interview with Mayla's mother. If she slept with Douglas, she should remember him. What about you? Did you get the chance to see Karen?"

"Up close. And in skimpy clothes. Near as I could tell, she's not a candidate. I figure I'll check out the lifeguard when she starts her shift tomorrow."

"Caleb?"

Rye jerked his head around at Cora's voice. Caleb sucked in his breath at the sight of her. She wore only her light summer nightgown. Angry that Rye had seen her dressed like that, Caleb sent a sizzling glare at him. Rye clapped a hand over his eyes.

Caleb scowled as he strode to Cora. "I'm sorry I wasn't here for you." In more ways than one.

She pushed her hair away from her forehead. "That's okay. Rye came."

Caleb studied her wan face. "How are you feeling?"

"My arm hurts a little." She paused. "I didn't know Rye was your partner."

"I didn't know you knew him."

A light pink crept up her cheeks. "We met at the resort." Her breath caught as if she had just thought of something.

Caleb frowned. "What?"

"Is he supposed to pretend to be a gigolo for this job?" she whispered.

Caleb rounded on Rye. "How does she know about that?"

The kid winced. "Cora came into June Moore's room by mistake while I was searching it. I thought she was one of June's friends."

That had been weeks ago. The rest of Rye's statement penetrated his understanding. "What did you do to her?"

"Caleb, it's okay." Cora spoke up before Rye could, but Caleb didn't like the light blush that once again stained her cheeks. "Rye couldn't have known, and it was nothing."

"Nothing?" He was certain now why Rye had accosted her on the beach. Apparently he had already taken one kiss from her. And if Cora's current defense was any indication, she hadn't given him the slap he richly deserved.

"He doesn't need to pretend to be a gigolo anymore." Caleb put his hand on her arm, eager to get her away from his partner. "Come on. Why don't you go back to bed?"

She surrendered to his guidance, but turned her head when she reached the bedroom door. "Good night, Rye. Thank you."

"Glad I was here."

Caleb helped Cora slip under the covers and kissed her head. "I'm glad you're safe."

"I love you, Caleb." She closed her eyes.

He stepped out of the room and shut the door. He glanced to where Rye sat on the couch and cast him a dour look. "Unless you have more earth-shaking news, I think you should go back to your place now."

Rye heaved an exaggerated sigh as he stood. "See you tomorrow." He walked by Caleb, then opened the door.

Caleb's conscience kicked in. "Rye."

He paused. "Yeah?"

Caleb sighed, letting go of his anger, if not his determination to guard Cora like a hawk. "Thanks."

A look of surprise crossed Rye's face. He gave a quick smile. "Anytime." He stepped outside, closing the door behind him.

Caleb dropped onto the couch for some much-needed sleep.

Chapter Seventeen

Rye whistled as he stepped out of his cabin the next morning. Despite his late night, he had woken at seven and felt exhilarated to start a new day. Thanks to Cora, the cloud of depression hanging over him had disappeared. Gratitude over her forgiveness buoyed his heart, and he rejoiced that Caleb seemed to have accepted the situation.

Although he had at first regretted that Hershey turned out to be Cora Abrams, he realized God had given him the opportunity he had longed for—to interact with Cora firsthand. He prayed the Lord would allow him to spend more time with her and vowed to honor her as she deserved.

Remembering that she didn't have any clothes with her besides her nightgown, he slipped into the Pinto and headed to the Y. Perhaps he could pack an overnight bag with a few things she might want.

A note fluttered on Cabin 10's door, warning about pest control's investigation. He kept watch for snakes while he went through her bedroom closet for dresses and shoes.

Only one bed had the covers pulled down. His stomach knotted at sight of the swirled sheets where the rattler had been.

He pulled open the drawers of the dresser next to her bed. Refusing to let his thoughts drift, he grabbed a few essentials, then hurried out of the cabin.

At the resort, he rapped on Caleb's door. When no one responded, he tried the knob and found it unlocked. Deciding to leave Cora's clothes where Caleb would find them, he entered the cabin and noticed the bedroom door hung open but the bathroom door was closed. He laid Cora's clothes on the coffee table next to where Caleb lay stretched out on the couch, breathing rhythmically.

The bathroom door clicked. He hastily turned his back. "Hey, Cora, I'm here. Are you decent?"

She gave a light laugh. "Yes. Do you know what time it is?"

"Twenty to ten." He picked up the bag with her clothes and turned to take them to her.

His pulse jumped when he saw her brushing tangles out of her hair. It hung like a damp wave down her back, and he groaned at the desire so easily awakened in him. He focused on the bandage covering the snakebite. "Does your arm hurt?"

"Enough to not want to use it. I'm just glad it's my left."

As she ran the brush through her hair again, he walked to her. Catching the intoxicating scent of lilac soap, he swallowed. "I got you some clothes and shoes." He pressed the bag into her hands, and she glided agile fingers over the various articles. "Thank you."

"No problem. I'll let you get dressed."

"Okay." She stepped back, then paused. "Is Caleb awake?"

He glanced to his partner. "Not yet. Do you need something?"

Hesitation colored her voice. "I'm supposed to help with worship at the church next to the Y, and the service starts at ten. The pastor's wife will be worried if I don't come."

He raised his eyebrows. "I could take you. I wanted to go back that direction anyway to look at your cabin, see if I can figure out how that snake got in."

A grateful smile bloomed on her face. "Thank you."

She closed the door, and Rye wandered over to the kitchen table. He took a seat, then realized he should leave a note for Caleb, explaining where he was taking Cora. Jotting down the information, he realized that Cora didn't have the reservations Caleb did about hanging out with him. Of course, since Caleb hadn't told him about her loss of sight, he probably hadn't told her about Rye's history either. Rye stifled a sigh. The past would only ruin the present, so he pushed the condemning memories away.

Cora opened the door, wearing a pink sundress. She walked forward, trailing her fingers across the wall. Rye hurried to her side and touched her arm. "This way. The room's kind of narrow."

She rested her right hand on his arm. At the door Rye turned to help her down the steps. She smiled, and he wondered if she knew how beautiful she was.

Somehow he got her in the Pinto without pulling her into his arms. As he started the motor, his chest finally loosened enough so he could breathe again.

Heading off the resort, he asked, "How are you helping out at the church?"

"I was supposed to play the violin in the worship service. I mentioned to the pastor's wife that I'm volunteering at the Y for their music program, and she asked if I would accompany her on piano."

"Will you be able to do that with your injured arm?"

She shook her head with a tinge of regret. "I think it would hurt too much."

"How long have you played?"

"Since I was five."

"You must really like it."

She smiled. "I've always loved music, but after I lost my sight, it became my one creative outlet. I'm able to play by ear, so I chose to major in music at college."

"What do you think you'll do after you graduate?"

"I hope to work in an elementary school as a music teacher, but it's not always easy to find an opening. If I need to, I'll teach private violin lessons until something else opens up."

"Are you a senior?"

"Yes. Just one more term before I graduate."

She fell silent, and he caught a shadow of sadness on her face. "You okay?"

"Why do you ask?"

"You seemed kind of sad for a minute."

She shook her head. "I'm fine." She bit her lip, then laughed softly. "You remind me of Caleb. I feel like an open book with him too."

Rye hesitated, wondering if he should apologize.

Before he could reply, she teased, "It's rather unfair, I think. After all, I don't get to see your thoughts written on your face. I have to wait for you to say them, and by then you've probably decided what you *should* say instead of blurting out what you really think."

As Hershey, she had never teased him. Stunned, he almost missed the sign for the little church. Jerking the wheel just in time, he turned into the little lane shaded by trees. He wondered if his platonic attitude was the reason for the change in her. She seemed more confident, more independent, more like someone he wanted to sit and talk with for hours on end.

He sought for a reply that wouldn't damage her new ease. "I think you read people quite well."

"You do?"

He only had one experience to back up his statement, but didn't feel like mentioning Benjamin Dean's name. "We're at the church." He jumped out of the car, wondering if she would wait for him to help her out.

She did. Apparently she was used to gentlemanly treatment from Caleb and David. At the thought of her fiancé, a flood of jealousy swept him.

She held out her hand as he opened her door, but hesitated after she stepped out. "Are you okay?"

"And you think you can't read people. I think you just have to be close enough…"

He trailed off as his gaze traveled over the softness of her face. The enticement of her lips beckoned, and only the arrival of another car saved him.

Directing her across the parking lot, he lectured himself about staying cool, calm, and collected. Behaving honorably was turning out to be harder than he had expected. Cora's sweetness and his own torrid past were a lethal combination that made self-control difficult.

He guided Cora up the church steps, then glanced around the old-style building as they entered. Several dozen pews faced a small podium near a battered piano. Homemade posters reflected the different phases of Christ's life, and the warm sun slanted through tall, narrow windows.

He directed Cora into one of the middle pews while several people glanced at them with interest.

"There you are, Cora!" A smiling man in his mid-fifties stood from the front pew. Presumably the pastor, he gestured toward a kind-faced woman talking with a parishioner on the side. "Zoe, Cora's here."

The auburn-haired woman excused herself from her conversation and hurried over. She took Cora's hands in both of hers. "Cora, dear, we were worried about you. Oh, what happened to your arm?"

"A rattlesnake bit me. I'm fine now, but I won't be able to play with you today. I'm sorry."

"Don't apologize, for heaven's sake! I'm just glad the Lord kept you safe. We'll try again next Sunday if you're feeling well enough by then." Zoe extended her hand to Rye with a kind smile. "I'm Zoe Robbins, Pastor Hal's wife."

Rye accepted the handshake. "Rye Nelson."

"It's nice to have you here. I assume you brought Cora?"

"Yeah. I must admit, I'm disappointed that I won't get to hear her play."

Zoe smiled warmly. "Then you'll have to come back next Sunday. Do you live in the area?"

"For now."

She studied him, and Rye wondered if she was trying to guess his eternal status. Not willing to open up to strangers, he sat next to Cora. It was all he could do not to take her hand and hold it as Pastor Hal announced the beginning of service.

Never having been in a church before, he watched everything with curiosity. He had no idea if Pastor Hal typified the normal preacher, but Rye felt his heart strings pulled when Zoe asked everyone to stand. She led the forty or so parishioners in songs praising Jesus. Joy shone on many faces as voices lifted in adoration. Rye's heart squeezed tightly. He knew God was righteous and demanded reverent fear, but he had never seen people worshipping Him as though He was the essence of love itself.

Beside him, Cora sang with a pure, sweet voice and raised her hands as though unaware of anyone except Jesus. Her worship of an unseen King made her seem even more beautiful, and Rye wrestled with a sudden longing to have the joy being experienced in this place.

However, he had no idea how to get to such an ethereal status, and Pastor Hal's sermon only confused him. It seemed directed toward those who had a special understanding of heavenly things. How could one walk by the Spirit and remain on planet earth? What did being crucified to sin and alive to Christ mean? It sounded like one of those fanatical cults where people pierced their hands and feet to be like Christ. Cora couldn't possibly be involved with a cockeyed group like that. Yet her face stayed intent throughout the sermon.

Rye felt glad when Pastor Hal led the congregation in a closing prayer. When the service dismissed, he put his hand under Cora's elbow and drew her into the aisle. They didn't make it very far. Pastor Hal and Zoe seemed determined to follow up on their morning visitor. Rye didn't feel like making up a bunch of answers to their probing questions, so he politely excused himself and Cora by saying they needed to get to an appointment. The Robbinses looked disappointed, but renewed their thanks that he had come with Cora.

In the Pinto, Cora asked, "So, who are we meeting?"

Rye started the motor. "I left Caleb a note saying we'd go to your cabin after church. He's probably already there."

"Oh. Did you understand Pastor Hal's sermon?"

He drove out of the parking lot. "Not really. What was it about?"

"Pastor Hal was encouraging us to listen to God more and live like Jesus every day, not just on Sunday. Do you know what salvation is?"

He frowned. "I suppose that's the term for what keeps us out of hell. Caleb's told me about how important it is to obey God's laws so that maybe God will have mercy on us at Judgment Day."

"No one can earn the Lord's favor," she said quietly. "But He freely gives His mercy to everyone who believes that Jesus is God."

He turned into the Y campground. "Wait a minute. How can Jesus be God? Caleb says there's only one God."

"There is." She smiled as though sympathetic to his bewilderment. "The Bible teaches a concept called the Trinity. Some people scoff at it because it's hard for our finite minds to comprehend. The Trinity means there is one God who is actually three Persons: God the Father, God the Son, and God the Holy Spirit. Jesus is God the Son, who took on human form and was born a baby on earth. He grew up like a normal child, but when He became a man, He performed many miracles and prophesied things that later came true. He proved that He was God, but many of the people who knew Him rejected Him and demanded that the government crucify Him."

Rye stopped the Pinto in front of Cabin 10 and saw Caleb leaning against the Ford, his expression filled with displeasure. "Caleb's here."

Rye stepped out of the car, but Caleb reached Cora's door first. "There you are."

She accepted his hand, surprise on her face. "We came as soon as service ended."

Hiding a smile at the way she came to his defense, Rye noted how Caleb kept his hand on Cora's arm.

Caleb pressed his lips together as he met Rye's gaze. "Your note said you wanted to meet here to figure out how the rattler entered Cora's cabin. Don't you think pest control will do that?"

Rye shrugged. Mostly he had wanted a reason to come back to Cora's place.

Caleb's eyes narrowed as though he had guessed that fact. "I don't think we need to perform our own inspection. Cora can stay at my place until the Y says the cabin's clear."

"Can I get some of my things?"

Caleb gazed at Cora as though realizing for the first time what her being dressed for church implied. "You're not going in there if there are snakes around."

"Okay. Would you mind getting me more clothes as well as my Bible and walking stick?"

"Sure. I'll just be a minute." Caleb sent Rye a warning look before striding up the porch steps.

Once he disappeared inside the cabin, Cora resumed their previous conversation. "Do you know why Jesus allowed Himself to be killed?"

"Allowed Himself?"

"Yes. Jesus could have stopped the process at any time, but He didn't. He chose to die for our sins. Do you know what that means?"

"It sounds like He got the death penalty instead of those who are guilty and should have." Like him.

"That's right. Jesus didn't deserve the death penalty, but He willingly took our place. Every person who has ever lived can be forgiven of their sins. All God asks is that we accept Jesus' death in our place and believe that He rose again."

The cabin door shut with a slam, and Caleb jogged down the steps, a stack of Cora's clothes in his arms as well as her Bible and walking stick.

Rye tried to process what she had said about forgiveness, but he couldn't concentrate with Caleb hovering over her like a burly guardian.

Caleb handed Cora her walking stick, and she smiled. "Thanks. Do you guys want to go to lunch? I skipped breakfast, and I'm starving."

Caleb grunted. "I can take you, but Rye has things he needs to do for the case."

Rye held up his hands. "Guess I'd better get busy. The day's already half gone. I'll see you later."

A frown crossed Cora's face, but she said good-bye, and Caleb helped her into his truck.

Rye climbed into the Pinto. Although he felt disappointed at missing lunch with Cora, he couldn't be too upset. It could take pest control a day to fumigate Cora's cabin and then maintenance would need to repair any openings. In the meantime he would see her whenever he visited Caleb.

However, first he needed to make a trip to the pool. After he ascertained whether Terri, the lifeguard, was a candidate, he would terminate his employment with the resort and move his belongings from the employee cabin to a hotel room in town. After that, he would track down the four other women on Caleb's list to determine if any of them might be Douglas's long-lost daughter.

Chapter Eighteen

Although thankful Rye hadn't pushed to join him and Cora for lunch, Caleb had a feeling the kid would find any excuse to drop by his cabin in the next few days. Fortunately, Cora's schedule matched his. He could drop her off at the Y for her volunteer work and pick her up as soon as he was done at the stables. If Rye did drop by, at least she wouldn't be alone with him.

He seated her at the table the waitress at the Summerhouse Restaurant had directed them to, then perused the menu for her favorites. "They have chicken Alfredo and roast beef sandwiches. Or would you like something else?"

"Alfredo sounds delicious." She unwrapped her silverware from the napkin, traced her fingers over the pieces, then picked up her fork, fingering it.

Caleb raised his eyebrows. Cora rarely fidgeted. "What are you thinking?"

She laid the fork down. "Why didn't you want Rye to join us?"

Caleb leaned back in his chair. "What makes you think that?"

A frown flickered over her face. "Don't play with me, Caleb. Rye has to eat lunch just like everybody else, even if he is working on the case."

Caleb's jaw bunched. "Time is of the essence, Cora. A girl's life is at stake."

She looked stunned. "Then I'm hindering your investigation. You don't need to babysit me. I can go back to the Y."

"Not until your fellow volunteers return from the campout. However, I do have some important phone calls to make today. As much as I want to spend time with you, it would be better if you spent the day with David. Do you know if he's available?"

She sat so quietly he began to wonder if she had heard him. "Cora?"

She twisted her fingers nervously. "I don't know if he's available. I broke off our engagement."

"What? Why? What happened?"

"I just realized we're not compatible. I told him I couldn't go through with it."

Caleb frowned. "Did he agree?"

"I don't think I left him a choice."

There was always a choice. David wouldn't let her get away that easily, not after ten years of betrothal. However, he would have to leave the reconciliation up to the two of them. "I guess that means you don't want to stay with the Hauzens today."

She shook her head.

"Don't worry about it. I can work while you're at the cabin if you don't mind."

"Of course not. Thank you."

Their food arrived, and she ate as hungrily as he did. After they finished, he stood. "I'm going to go pay for our food. I'll be right back."

On his return to the table, he caught sight of Arianna and Benjamin Dean entering the restaurant.

Arianna's face broke into a delighted smile. "Caleb!" She ignored the hostess coming to seat them and hurried over to him, giving him a full hug.

She glanced at Cora, who had turned her face toward the unfamiliar feminine voice. Caleb prepared himself to make introductions. Cora would be as stunned as Rye had been to learn he was dating someone, but at least she couldn't see Arianna and wouldn't have a clue how young or exotic she was.

He cleared his throat. "Arianna, this is Cora. Cora, this is Arianna. I've been... taking her out."

Surprise flooded Cora's face, and she held out her hand. "I'm delighted to meet you."

Arianna beamed as she shook Cora's hand. "I'm glad to meet you too. Caleb's told me a lot about you."

"Perhaps we can spend some time together, get to know each other."

"That'd be great!"

Benjamin joined them, and Caleb shook his hand, though he wished he could get Arianna to stop hanging out with her worldly uncle. Dean put his hand on Cora's shoulder and leaned toward her like an old friend. "Hello, Cora. I'm sorry I haven't had the opportunity to talk with you since the cruise."

A trace of strain crossed Cora's face, but she smiled politely. "I've been busy."

"Well, hopefully I'll see you around more, especially since your brother's dating my niece."

"Cora's my niece," Caleb corrected. "I take it you've met before."

Dean straightened without removing his hand from Cora's shoulder. "I'm a long-time friend of Esther's. She invited me to partner with Cora on the cruise two weeks ago when David came down ill." He looked at Cora again. Concern flickered in his eyes when he caught sight of the bandage on her arm. "What happened to your arm?"

"There was a rattlesnake in her cabin at the Y," Caleb explained. "Thankfully a friend helped her to the doctor."

Arianna's eyes widened. "Does it hurt?"

"A little."

Dean frowned. "If you're afraid to return to your cabin—"

"She's staying with me for now." Caleb thought he saw Cora wince, and he wondered about her odd behavior. She was keeping her attention straight ahead of her. Ever since she'd lost her sight, she had developed a habit of turning her head toward whoever was speaking in an effort to encourage communication. Apparently, she didn't want to talk to Dean.

Caleb decided to wrap up the conversation. "It was nice to see you again, Dean, but we need to take off. Arianna, I'll see you later."

"Can I come by the cabin after lunch?"

Caleb had a feeling that Dean would include himself in any invitation, but he didn't see how he could tell Arianna no when both he and Cora had said they wanted her company. "That's fine."

"Okay. See you later."

Cora smiled, and Dean pulled her chair back so she could stand. As he helped her to the aisle, the strain on her face increased.

Outside, Caleb tucked her arm under his. As he headed toward his cabin, he asked, "Did something happen on the cruise between you and Dean?"

She shivered. "No, thank God, but only because Rye rescued me."

The kid again. "Just how much have you hung around Rye?"

"Not much," she hedged. "He saw me on the cruise with Benjamin. Esther had asked Dean to stay with me while she and Paul went to another room to dance, but I didn't feel comfortable with him. Apparently Rye could tell." She shrugged. "So he came to my rescue."

Caleb studied her face as they walked down the gravel road. "Why did you feel uncomfortable around Dean?"

She swallowed. "He took me outside when I asked him not to. And I got the feeling he was going to try to kiss me."

Caleb frowned. Dean had acted too familiar at the table, but he doubted the guy would try to take advantage of Cora the first time he met her. She wasn't the type of girl to draw men's attention. He played down his concern, not wanting to feed her fears. "I wouldn't worry about him."

"I'm trying not to." She switched subjects. "How did you meet Arianna?"

"She keeps a horse at the stables where I work. The filly cut herself so I helped treat the wound."

"You like her a lot."

Caleb sighed. "We've only known each other a few weeks. She loves horses, which gives us something in common, but she's from a completely different background. I'm not sure I should even be dating her."

He hadn't meant to admit so much. Cora knew his high standards. He hadn't wanted any mistakes in his life. What was it about Arianna that made him willing to take a risk?

"She's different from the kind of girl you thought you'd fall in love with, isn't she?"

Had he fallen in love with her? He enjoyed her company and had a strong desire to protect her and take care of her. Was that enough to qualify as love? Even if it was, what about the standard he expected of the woman he married? Arianna longed for affection and lasting love, but her moral character had never been developed. What if pleasing him stopped being a priority in her choices? She could tear his heart to pieces with one wrong choice if he gave her the power. Yet at the same time, he didn't like the thought of not having her in his life.

"Arianna's incredibly passionate about life. But she often doesn't realize the long-range effects of her spontaneity. She seems to want to please me, though."

Cora was silent for a long moment, then said softly, "Well, I'm glad to know about her so I can be praying for your relationship."

"Thanks." Caleb unlocked the door to his cabin. He appreciated Cora's prayers, but a dead Carpenter wasn't going to be able to answer them.

A light rap sounded on Caleb's door, and Cora guessed that Arianna had come by as she had said she would. Removing her fingers from the Braille words in the first chapter of 2 Timothy, Cora listened to Caleb open the door. She looked forward to talking with the girl who had caught his attention, though he had surprised her when he shared his uncertainty about the relationship. Still, it was apparent he cared for this girl, and Cora hoped she could get to know her better.

After Caleb greeted Arianna, he said dryly, "Hello, Dean."

Cora tightened her hands on the Bible as a wave of fear washed over her.

Daughter, I have not given you a spirit of fear but of power and love and a sound mind.

She took a deep breath as the familiar Scripture flooded her mind. She realized the Lord wanted her attentive to the situation, not trying to get away from it. Willing herself to relax, she smiled as Caleb said, "Looks like a full house, Cora. Arianna and her uncle are here to visit."

Cora greeted Arianna warmly. "I'm glad you could spend some time with us."

"I haven't been in here before," Arianna said. "Caleb and I always hang out at the stables or in town."

Cora smiled. "What do you like doing together?"

"Oh, riding horses, hiking, and sometimes bowling."

"Arianna's idea of a good time has tamed down these days," Dean commented.

"Why don't you both have a seat?" Caleb sounded annoyed.

The conversation moved to issues involving horses, breeding, and ranching. Dean revealed a degree of knowledge about the subject, and Arianna's passion was obvious. Cora had a feeling Caleb hadn't told her about his true occupation, and she wondered what Arianna would think when she found out.

"What an interesting book you have there, Cora," Arianna said. "What are those little bumps?"

"That's Braille." Caleb's voice held amusement.

Cora smiled. "This is my Bible. It's my favorite book."

"Really?" Arianna sounded curious. "People have always told me it's boring."

"Do you enjoy the sections on philosophy," Dean asked, "or the stories about the Israelites?"

Keeping her thoughts focused on the promise of the Lord, Cora smiled with genuine warmth. "I enjoy reading about the life of Jesus the most, but the entire Bible holds truths that bring me hope and strength. Do you have a religious belief system, Mr. Dean?"

"I don't hold to any established religion, unless humanism qualifies. I believe man answers only to himself. But I admit the idea of someone rising from the dead is intriguing."

"Who rose from the dead?"

Cora's heart squeezed. Was Arianna's question the reason the Lord had made sure she didn't withdraw from this meeting? She had always hoped Caleb would be attracted to someone who was already a believer and could help him find his way to Christ, but Arianna needed to discover the truth as much as Caleb.

Not knowing how many opportunities she would have to share the gospel, Cora answered the question with soft intensity. "Jesus rose from the dead. He created everything, but He became a man and died in order to pay for our sins. Because He had never done anything wrong, He rose from the grave and conquered death."

"That's why the early Christians were willing to be fed to lions in Roman arenas instead of recanting their faith." Sarcasm tinged Dean's voice. "Christianity is the only religion I know that demands a person believe life on earth is worthless and only life in heaven has value."

"Not worthless," Cora corrected gently. "Every life has incredible value. But our time on earth is given for a specific purpose. Our true worth lies in our souls—here on earth and after we die."

Arianna drew in a startled breath. "That's what Caleb said!"

"God created our souls, minds, and bodies," Caleb explained. "He designed our souls to live eternally with Him, but sin blocks us from knowing Him until we walk in righteousness and earnestly seek Him."

"So you don't think my life's a random accident?"

Cora smiled. "Definitely not. God made you and longs to have a relationship with you."

"That's why it's important to hold to His standards," Caleb added. "He knows what's best for us and won't do anything that will hurt us."

"Like you." Awe touched Arianna's voice.

Dean changed the subject. "Will you be joining the Hauzens for their tennis match tomorrow, Cora?"

She shook her head, grateful that her decision to separate from David also spared her from Benjamin's company. Esther would always welcome him as a member of their party.

"Well, your volunteer work at the Y is commendable, but don't let it take up all your time."

"She won't." Cora heard Caleb stand. "Thank you both for coming over. But I'm afraid I have to ask you to leave now. Cora needs her rest. She's not totally up to par yet after her accident."

"Of course," Dean said smoothly. "We'll head out so she doesn't overdo it."

"I can wait for you, Caleb," Arianna offered.

Cora grasped her walking stick from where she had leaned it against her chair and stood. "It was nice to talk with you again, Arianna."

"You too."

"See you around, Cora," Dean said.

"Good-bye." She used her walking stick to find her way to the bedroom, then closed the door. For a long moment she leaned against it, eyes closed. Her heart felt heavy, and she lifted both Arianna and Benjamin Dean up in prayer.

"Lord, I feel so inadequate. I've lived with Caleb all my life, and if he won't accept my witness, why should they? But I believe you brought me into their lives for a purpose. Help me to be a faithful witness of Your character and the hope You can give them. Please soften their hearts to receive the truth and intervene in their lives so they can embrace You as Savior and Lord."

She lay down on Caleb's bed, but it was some time before her prayers gave way to sleep.

Chapter Nineteen

Caleb sat back down on the couch as soon as Dean left. He let Arianna snuggle up against him, her feet tucked under her. He rested his hand loosely against her hip and smiled when she said, "I like being with you. It's so much nicer here than at my parents'. My dad hardly notices me, and my mom is always complaining."

He pressed a kiss against her hairline, grateful for her positive response to all he and Cora had said about God, even with her uncle present. "I'm sorry your home life hasn't been a blessing to you. Parents are supposed to nurture their children and train them in godliness so they can love the Lord."

She tipped her head back and studied his face. "Is that what your parents did? I mean, before your mom died?"

"Yes. And my dad continued to raise Cora and me in godliness even after Mom passed away. He wanted to make sure we never strayed from God's will."

Sadness drifted over her face. "I wish I'd been raised like that. It seems like I learned all the wrong ways of doing things."

He brought her hand to his lips and kissed it. "It's okay. You're willing to change and do things God's way now. It's a lot harder than the world's way, but I promise God will bless you for it."

She stared at him, and he caught the sweet scent of the bath soap she used. He noticed again the clear beauty of her skin, enhanced with only the slightest touch of makeup. His gaze slipped to the exquisite shape of her lips, their color natural and alluring. They parted under his gaze, and his pulse quickened.

Despite all his logical analyses of the risks involved in loving her, his heart hadn't been paying attention.

"Oh, Caleb." When Arianna murmured his name, the sweetness in her breath overshadowed all the risks.

He lowered his head and tasted her lips.

She returned the kiss with deep longing. Her hands caressed his face then slid down his shoulders and arms. He lingered in the warmth of her embrace. But he knew not to go too far. He brought his hands to her cheeks and slowly ended the kiss.

She opened her eyes, tears mingling with joy in their blue-green depths. Gazing at him, she whispered, "I've waited all my life for a kiss like that. You make me feel beautiful, Caleb."

He trailed his fingers down her throat and shoulders, then took her hands in his. "You are beautiful. You're one of the most beautiful things God ever made."

He pulled her against him. She nestled close, and he leaned his head against the back of the couch, letting her joy over his embrace saturate him with warmth and gladness.

Rye stepped out of the Pinto after parking in front of Caleb's cabin. He wished he could have called it a day earlier, but he hadn't wanted to risk Caleb's anger by neglecting to investigate each of the four women on his list.

As evening had slipped into night, his hope of seeing Cora again that day filtered away, but he had driven to Caleb's cabin to give his report in person.

He rapped on the door, and it swung open within seconds. Caleb gestured him to a seat. "Want a Coke?"

"Caffeine sounds good." Rye sank down on one side of the couch and noticed the document open on Caleb's laptop. Only a few notes filled the screen. "Looks like you didn't get much time to make phone calls today."

"No." Caleb brought the soda can over, and Rye accepted it with a sigh. "All four women visited the beach today. Only the lifeguard, Terri, is a candidate. She has an x-shaped burn on her left thigh."

Caleb clicked open a new document. "I'll locate her mother's information so I can find out about her father. I called Mayla's mother. She lives six hours away, and she set up an appointment with me two days from now. It was the soonest she could manage, and she wasn't willing to give me information over the phone."

Rye popped the lid on the Coke. He let his gaze drift toward the closed bedroom door.

"She's asleep," Caleb said dryly.

Rye raked a hand through his hair, feeling guilty over how much she consumed his thoughts. "Sorry."

Caleb grunted. "I never thought of Cora as someone to catch men's attention, but between you and Dean, she's getting an entourage of admirers."

"Dean?" Rye spat out the name.

"Cora and I ran into him at the restaurant. He was with Arianna and followed her to our table. Arianna asked if she could visit me here, and Dean ended up tagging along."

Rye scowled. "You let him pester Cora?"

"I wouldn't say he pestered her. Except when she started preaching at him."

Rye couldn't imagine Cora being bold enough to tell Dean all the things she had shared with him. "What did he say?"

"He knew enough about Christianity to question her, but I'm sure his interest had little to do with religion."

Rye frowned. "That guy should stick to older women." He thought about what else Caleb had said. "So Cora met Arianna."

Caleb met his gaze.

"What did she think of her?"

"She liked her, just like everyone does."

"I didn't mean what Arianna thought."

Caleb sat in front of his neatly stacked piles of papers and picked one up, though he didn't seem to concentrate on it. "Cora shared her faith the way she always does. She thinks she's responsible for telling everyone that we're lost unless we believe in Jesus." He glanced up. "Has she preached at you yet?"

Rye nodded, taking a swig of Coke to avoid giving an answer.

Caleb leaned against the couch back. "How many times did you run into Cora before you knew who she was?"

Rye stared at the pop can and counted in his head. "Five times, maybe."

He could feel Caleb's astonishment. "Five *accidental* times?"

"Yes."

Apparently Caleb wanted to push some buttons. "Was your kiss on the beach accidental too?"

Rye put down his soda can and looked Caleb in the eyes. "I've already apologized for that, and Cora told me she's forgiven me, so just let it go."

Caleb's eyes darkened. "She forgives everyone," he muttered.

"Is that such a bad thing?"

"Obviously not for you." Caleb clenched his fist. "Other people have hurt Cora far worse than you did. And she just *forgave* them." He spat the word out the way Rye had Dean's name a few minutes earlier.

Though afraid to hear the answer, Rye asked, "What did they do to her?"

Caleb looked up with bitterness in his eyes. "They took her sight."

Caleb had said she had lost her sight in a fire. If it had been intentionally started, Rye understood why Caleb couldn't forgive the perpetrators. The weight of guilt he felt over another fire and another girl pulled on him. Not wanting to resurrect the pain, he stood. "I guess I'll go. Unless you need my help with anything."

"No. Just make Terri your top priority right now. I suspect Sweeney's going to go after either her or Mayla."

Caleb headed to the Sunnel beach house after dropping Cora off for worship practice at the church she attended. Rye was keeping watch on Terri, and Mayla had bodyguards who went with her wherever she went, relieving them of the need to follow her everywhere. Caleb had called Arianna to schedule a hike since he had the evening free, and she had readily agreed.

At his knock, she swung open the door. She gave him a long hug.

As tempting as it was to kiss her again, he didn't want to start focusing their times together on the physical. "Ready to head up the mountain?"

She nodded but didn't let go.

He brushed his knuckles over her cheek. "Think you can keep up?"

"Of course!" She drew back, ready to get going.

"All right, come on." He took her hand in his and set a strong pace toward the hiking trail.

Arianna chatted about candidates for the upcoming derby race. He smiled at her enthusiasm, but wondered if she ever thought much beyond the coming weekend. Heading onto the dirt path that led through the pine forest and up the mountain, he asked, "Are you going to college this fall?"

She shrugged, her gaze tracking a soaring hawk. "Yes. But I don't want to. It's just what everybody does after they graduate."

Hoping he could encourage her toward doing something of significance with her life, he said, "I'm sure you could find a field that would interest you. Veterinary medicine or zoology maybe. Even equestrian studies."

She laughed. "Here I am, excited to spend an evening with you, and you want to figure out what major I should take."

"Do you want to depend on your parents for the rest of your life?"

She sent him an amused glance. "I'll be depending on them in college."

"Yes, but after you graduate you can find a job and support yourself."

"Do you wish you'd gone to college?"

He had earned his bachelor's, but apparently she had made the wrong assumption because he was employed as a stable hand. Since she remained a candidate for the case, he didn't want to risk her knowledge of his involvement. Letting the question slide, he said, "College is always a good choice. It opens up a multitude of opportunities."

"I guess so." She glanced at him coyly. "Maybe I should transfer. What college is near here?"

He grinned, knowing her reason for suggesting the idea. "I won't be staying here. This is just a summer job." He wondered what he would do about their relationship once the case resolved and he needed to return to LA.

"Where will you go?"

"I live in Los Angeles. I'll probably be going back there soon."

"Oh." Disappointment filled her face. "Will I get to see you after you leave?"

He squeezed her hand. "You're from the LA area, too, aren't you?"

She nodded.

"I want you to come visit me, and I'll visit you too."

"Often?"

He studied her. Would she care that he had lied to her about his occupation after he told her the truth? He doubted it would matter as long as he kept giving her the attention she wanted. "If you want to."

"I do." She laughed as a light drizzle began to fall. She held out her hands in delight. "I love the rain. It always makes everything smell so clean and new."

Feeling his shirt getting damp, Caleb remarked, "It also makes everything wet. Come on, there's a small cave up here where we can wait it out. These clouds are moving pretty quickly."

She ran with him up the incline until he pointed to the left, where a recess had been carved into the side of the mountain. The hillside to it was steep, but remains of a path curved upward, and he helped her over the roughest spots.

She breathlessly climbed over the edge of the cave into its small interior. She leaned her hands on the jutting rock. "This is a great view."

Caleb joined her, gazing at the valley below. The expanse of hills was covered with pine trees and junipers, but areas of clover and bluebells peeked out at various intervals. "It's beautiful, isn't it?"

A passage from Isaiah came to mind, and Caleb quoted it. "'Thus says God the Lord who created the heavens and stretched them out, who spread forth the earth and that which comes from it, who gives breath to the people on it and spirit to those who walk on it: I the Lord have called you in righteousness and will hold your hand.'"

Arianna gazed at him.

"That's from the Torah. In another place it says, 'What is man that You are mindful of him and the son of man that You visit him?'"

He faced her fully. "God has no reason to watch over us. He has no need to preserve us day by day. But He does. And all He asks in return is our obedience. 'With my soul I have desired You in the night, yes by my spirit within me I will seek You early. For when Your judgments are in the earth, the inhabitants of the world will learn righteousness.'"

She drew in a ragged breath. "I want to believe like you do. I keep thinking about what you and Cora said yesterday. About how God created me for a purpose. I want to believe that I'm important and that there is Someone who wants to take care of me. But sometimes I think my life doesn't matter at all."

He took her hands. "It matters. You matter." With all his heart he wanted her to know how incredibly important she was, not only to him but to God. If she knew the value the Lord placed upon her soul, she would not be swayed to throw herself away on things that would only bring grief and emptiness.

She leaned toward him, a soul-deep hunger in her eyes.

Caleb let her slip into his embrace. A tremor ran through her body, and desire swept him at the memory of how sweet she tasted. Lowering his head, he took her mouth with his.

The passion of her response burned into the core of his being. Her kiss deepened, awakening a fire that he didn't want to extinguish. He forgot all the restrictions he had placed on himself. His every thought and action focused on the feeling she ignited within him.

Son...

She pressed against him, wanting more. She broke the kiss just long enough to whisper, "Oh, Caleb, I love you."

Son, I love you. Don't do this. Don't bring grief to Me. Don't bring this guilt on yourself or her.

Her hands slid under his shirt.

"Arianna, wait." He stepped back, trying to hear the voice that had called to him through the fog of his physical and emotional desire.

She pressed herself back into his arms, holding on to him with surprising strength. "You want me, Caleb. You know you do. Please make love to me. I've waited so long."

She pulled his head down, but Caleb avoided her kiss and drew in a deep breath, regaining control. She might not have been trained in what was right and wrong, but he had been. As clarity of thought returned, he knew he couldn't let a moment's pleasure ruin the very essence of who he was.

He disengaged her hands from around his neck and stepped back. His breath ragged, he held her away from him. "I can't make love to you. We're not married, and it would be wrong. I would be dishonoring you and defying God."

She drew in a soft, deep breath. "Then marry me."

Fear shot through him. His desire for her had pushed the risks of their relationship to the back of his mind, but her new faith hadn't been tried and strengthened by life's trails. What if he married her but her love for God didn't last? What if she began to chafe against the standards he would expect from her as his wife? What if he gave her what she wanted and then her old nature reasserted itself and she found something else, or someone else, more appealing?

He had waited his whole life to fall in love with a woman of excellence. A woman of character and chastity. Arianna had given up her chastity long ago, and even though she was now seeking God, she was still immature in many ways. He had no idea how long it would take for her to develop the strength of will he needed to trust her. Marriage was sacred, pure, meant to last a lifetime and not to be used just to validate a few weeks or months of passion.

God forgive him. In his delight that she was opening her heart to God, he had led her to expect more than he was ready to offer. But how could he explain his fear without angering her?

"Arianna, you're only eighteen."

She gazed at him, longing in her eyes. "Why does that matter? You kissed me. You were ready to make love to me. You weren't thinking of me as a child then, so why are you using my age against me now?"

What she spoke was truth, and the reality of what he had done tasted like bitter gall in his mouth. She had been content to be his girlfriend until he made the mistake of exploring dangerous waters. Fearful of her reaction, he sought for a compromise. "We've only known each other a short time. I want you more than I've wanted any other girl. But I also want a strong marriage. Will you be patient and wait for us to know each other better before we make a commitment that God intends to last a lifetime?"

She stared at him as though unable to believe what he was saying. "How long do you want me to wait?"

He looked away from her penetrating gaze.

"How long will it take for me to prove that I can be a good wife to you? A month? Two months?"

He stayed silent.

"You don't think I'll ever be good enough for marriage, do you?"

"No!" If she felt unworthy of marriage, she would return to her old lifestyle and give herself to every man who came her way. His voice hoarse, he said the only thing he thought would save her from such a fate. "I do want you, and I will marry you. But not right now. I want you to attend a year of college first. There are a lot of things we still need to learn about each other."

She brushed a tendril of hair back from her face. "Okay," she said in a subdued voice. "If that's what you want."

He turned from her, rubbing his neck. A year might seem like a long time to her, but he desperately needed to know that she wouldn't tear his heart to pieces after her infatuation had worn off.

Chapter Twenty

Rye knocked on Caleb's cabin at ten the next night, after Caleb returned from his appointment with Mayla Rivers's mother. After Caleb let him in, he sank onto the couch. "What did you find out?"

Caleb returned to the table, where a search program was running on his laptop. "Ms. Rivers recognized Douglas's picture, but she didn't remember his name. She said she slept with him a couple times when she was working at Reno, but she couldn't recall what year that was. Could have been the year she got pregnant. But she has no idea if he's Mayla's father. Since Mayla's definitely a candidate, I'm going to apply to be one of her bodyguards. That way I can keep a better watch out for the assassin. If she hires me, I'll quit my job here."

He gestured toward the computer. "I haven't been able to discover very much about Terri, the lifeguard. Her mother died two years ago, after being beaten by a boyfriend. But there's no mention of her father. You'll need to ask her about that."

Rye glanced at the closed door of the bedroom where he presumed Cora slept. Getting close to another woman was the last thing he wanted to do.

Caleb frowned. "Cora's not here. Her cabin was cleared for occupancy today."

Disappointment hit. "It's only been two days. Didn't they have to patch up some holes and spray or something?"

"Apparently they couldn't find any cracks. Nor did they locate a nest or droppings under the house. Pest control assumes the snake must have crawled in through the door when it was left open. Anyway, everyone's back from the campout, so Cora has others watching out for her again."

"And you thought my meetings with Cora were suspicious. A rattler slithering into an occupied cabin is highly unlikely."

Caleb raised his eyebrows. "You're only upset because Cora isn't here anymore."

Rye scowled and looked away, not wanting to admit Caleb had guessed right.

Caleb stood. "I'll call if I have anything else I need from you."

Rye strode from the cabin in irritation, letting the door slam behind him.

Rye dangled his sandals in one hand and carried two bottles of Coke in the other as he walked across the sand to where Terri sat alone. She had gone to the beach at the end of her morning shift at the pool, and he had purchased the colas in hopes of striking up a conversation.

She glanced toward him and shaded her eyes, watching him approach with a neutral expression.

He held up the sodas and smiled. "Would you like a drink?"

She studied him. "You work here at the resort, don't you? You're one of the gigolos."

Rye sat down a foot from her. "I was. I quit."

"Why?"

"I wanted to pick my own dates." He handed her a Coke, which she accepted.

She opened the bottle. "I've seen you a couple of times with a blind girl."

Rye's throat tightened at the reference to Cora, and he looked away from Terri's penetrating gaze to the blue of the ocean. "She wasn't a client. But the relationship didn't work out."

"Because of your job?"

"Maybe." He studied her. "What about you? Are you without a boyfriend right now?"

"I could have one if I wanted. I don't. No offense."

He drank some soda. "You must enjoy the water a lot. You work at the pool and spend your free time here."

"The ocean's unpredictable. I like the fact that I never know what mood it will be in. Sometimes peaceful and calm. Other times angry and dangerous. Life is the same way."

He studied her. "Sounds like you speak from experience."

"I do."

He waited as she drank more of the Coke, then asked, "Do you have family close by?"

She tilted her head as if assessing his reason for asking. "I never knew my father. And my mother died two years ago. One of the times when life got ugly. She died in the hospital from a cerebral contusion after a customer knocked her across her camper."

Since Terri seemed willing to talk about her personal life, he said, "I take it she was a prostitute."

"Yes." She gestured the bottle toward him. "You made the right choice, quitting your job."

He looked away. He had never suffered physically from his work under the drug lord, but Terri's frankness reopened emotional wounds. If not for his immoral past, Caleb wouldn't see the need to protect Cora from him. He forced himself to refocus on his reason for conversing with Terri. "Was your mother a prostitute while you were growing up?"

"Yes. It wasn't an easy life. I swore I'd never go down the same path."

"Did she ever talk to you about who your father might be?"

She looked him in the eye. "No. She had two abortions before me and three after. Don't know why she kept me. Maybe she wanted someone to love her. What about you? Any kids?"

Shame washed over him. Did he have kids? It was a possibility. On the other hand, the women who had visited him weren't the type to maintain unwanted pregnancies. If he had fathered any children, most likely they'd been aborted.

He shook his head. "I don't know."

She returned her gaze to the sea, and silence lingered between them.

He couldn't think of any more questions to ask. Terri had no idea who her father was, and Douglas was the type to frequent whores. He and Caleb would need to keep her under surveillance since she might be Patrick's granddaughter, but the pain in his heart kept him from making idle chitchat at the present.

She glanced at him. "Thanks for the Coke."

He took the statement as a graceful request for him to leave. He pushed to his feet. "You're welcome. I'll see you around."

She nodded, and he headed back up the beach to watch over her from a distance.

"You quit?" Arianna stared at Caleb in shock as he sat across from her at the Summerland Diner.

He stabbed a forkful of lettuce. "Today was my last day."

"Why so soon?"

"I took a different job. I'm going to be a bodyguard for Mayla Rivers. She's having me work from one in the afternoon till three in the morning, so I won't be able to see you as much. I'm sorry."

Arianna twirled her fork around her spaghetti, sorting out the implications. At least he wasn't leaving her right away. But she didn't like the fact that he wouldn't be easily accessible anymore. "Will we still go riding together sometimes?"

"Maybe. It might take me a while to get used to the new schedule. I'm not normally a late-night person." He reached for his Sprite. "I know you'd rather I stay at the stables, but Mayla pays better. I want to be able to save up over this next year, before we get married."

She studied him. "Is money the reason you want to wait? 'Cause if it is, I have an allowance—"

He frowned. "I'm not going to use your parents' money to start our life together. Besides, money isn't the reason I want to wait." He studied her. "It's Jewish tradition for engagements to last a year. The reason was not just to give the groom a chance to build his family a home, but to test the couple's commitment. Their faithfulness to each other prior to the wedding built a stronger endurance in them to handle the pressures of life afterward. Unlike today, divorce wasn't an acceptable way to deal with difficult times. I want the same degree of commitment in our marriage."

Arianna gazed at him. "I'll be a good wife, I promise. Can't we get married now?"

He looked away, struggle evident on his face. "Marriage is for a lifetime. I'm going to do everything to make sure ours will succeed. If you're really committed to me, you'll wait."

Arianna fell silent. There wasn't anything more she could say. She didn't like his prerequisite of waiting. But she was determined to have him, whatever it might take.

Arianna trudged the familiar path from the stables to the beach house, her head down. It had been a week since Caleb quit his job at the stables.

She missed the hours they had regularly spent together, and time hung heavy on her hands. He had moved out of his employee cabin into a tourist bungalow on the outskirts of town. Although he had promised to visit her often, he hadn't yet scheduled a date. She only saw him if she took a taxi into town during the morning, but he was usually tired from his late nights guarding Mayla. He didn't want to go out to do any of their usual activities, but neither did he want her hanging out at the small bungalow.

Staring despondently at the gravel under her feet as she walked, Arianna hunched her shoulders. If only he would let her move in with him.

She walked up the beach house steps and entered the silent house. She wandered to the fridge to pull out a Coke. After opening the can, she sat at the kitchen table, staring out the window.

Had Caleb even mentioned their engagement to his family? He hadn't taken her to see Cora lately, nor had he spoken to her about meeting his father.

But then, she hadn't told her family about their engagement either. She doubted her father would believe her, and her mother would probably beg her not to leave. Uncle Ben would laugh over the fact that she'd let the prudish Jew talk her into marriage. He preferred his single status, which allowed him to have as many women as he wanted.

She frowned. Caleb said Uncle Ben was searching for something he could never have. But once again, she seemed like the one on the losing end. If Caleb would marry her, all her fears and doubts would be chased away. But as it was, she struggled against the tugging pull of depression.

The front door opened, but she didn't turn around. Solid footsteps came close, and Uncle Ben glanced at her on his way to the fridge. "You look depressed, Nan. What's up?"

"Nothing."

He pulled out a beer and popped the top off, then leaned against the counter. After a few swigs, he said, "Boyfriend still hasn't laid you, huh?"

"We're engaged." She said it moodily, staring at the buttons on his polo shirt.

He raised his eyebrows. "When did that happen?"

"A week ago. He switched jobs, though, so I don't get to see him as much." She shifted in her seat, not sure why she was telling him except that she was tired of having no one to talk to.

"So when's the big date?"

"In a year. He says we need to get to know each other better."

He eyed her. "And now he's working longer hours, which allows no time for the getting-to-know-you-better part."

"He's not avoiding me," she said defensively.

"Of course not." His tone was smooth, which meant he thought his point was too obvious to have to defend.

She balled her hand into a fist on the table. "Unlike everyone else I know, Caleb keeps his word."

He pushed away from the counter, shaking his head. "I didn't realize you were so naïve, Nan. Even Jews lie. He's probably lying to himself more than to you, but whatever impulse drove him to propose isn't going to last a year. You're wasting your life waiting for something that's never going to happen. Trust me. Prudes don't marry girls like you."

He walked away, snapping the door shut behind him. Arianna sat totally still, his words washing over her again and again. *Prudes don't marry girls like you.* Uncle Ben knew the world. He knew people.

Her stomach twisted with sharp pain. How could she have been so foolish? Caleb was slipping away with every day that she sat around waiting for time to pass. He had agreed to her suggestion of marriage out of impulse, just as Uncle Ben had said. Fear that the rest of her uncle's words were true overwhelmed her. Caleb spoke about commitment, but with the passage of enough time apart, he would forget why he had agreed to marry her, and she would be left with only the memory of his passionate kisses.

Trembling, Arianna stood. She would force him to marry her before she let time steal him out of her hands. But what could persuade him to marry her if activating his desires hadn't been enough?

Heart hammering, Arianna gazed out the window. Slowly an idea began to take shape, coming out of the shadows of her mind. She still had the phone number of the stranger from the theatre. What if she called him? What if he came to get her in front of Caleb? What would Caleb do? Would he let her go with him? Or would the jealous protection she had seen in him come to her rescue?

She clenched her hand as opposing fears wrestled inside her. The plan could backfire if Caleb responded wrong. But the longer she mulled over what Uncle Ben had said, the more convinced she became that she had nothing to lose and everything to gain in forcing Caleb's hand.

Caleb stripped his shirt off over his head and tossed it toward the corner where a laundry basket sat in the small bedroom of his bungalow. It missed, but he was too tired to bother picking it up. After slipping out of his jeans, he sank onto the edge of the bed and held his head in his hands.

His plan wasn't working. He had felt certain that either he or Rye would catch sight of the assassin if they hung around Mayla and Terri during the women's waking hours. But so far Sweeney had stayed out of sight.

Tired from the long hours, he stretched out on his bed, falling asleep within seconds.

A loud pounding awakened him, and he sat up, disoriented. Yanking on his jeans, he strode through the bungalow's tiny livingroom. He jerked the door open.

Arianna stood there, dressed in clothes fit for a hooker. Bright red lipstick stained her mouth and dark mascara blackened her lashes.

Hot anger washed over him. He stepped into the cool night air and grabbed her arm. "What do you think you're doing?"

She shrank a little at his anger, then squared her jaw. "I'm leaving. I thought I should tell you good-bye."

"Leaving?" He couldn't believe it. "Where are you going?"

A tremor swept her body, but she threw her head back as though in defiance of her weakness. "That doesn't matter. I just wanted you to know that after tonight you don't need to worry about pretending to want to marry me."

"Pretending?" Caleb was so angry he couldn't think straight. "I told you I was going to marry you. Don't you believe me?"

She shook her head, tears splashing onto her cheeks. Was she acting or did she believe some lie that had been planted in her mind? Either way, she was after something if she had gone to such pains to provoke his wrath.

She raised her gaze to his. "I think you want me to believe you'll marry me eventually. But you don't really believe I'm good enough. So I might as well give up now. I tried things your way, but it wasn't enough for you. You want someone who's chaste and pure and—"

"Stop it!" He shook her before he could stop himself.

Her face whitened, but the rebellion didn't leave her eyes.

"I'm taking you back to your parents." Realizing he had no shoes or shirt on, he dragged her inside the bungalow, where he grabbed both. She watched him dress with surprising sobriety. Gripping her arm again, he strode out to the Ford, hardly able to believe she was forcing him to act like her babysitter.

She stood in silence as he unlocked the passenger door. When he opened it, she drew in a shuddering breath. "You can't force me to stay with my parents. The only way I won't run away is if you marry me."

He jabbed his finger at the open door. "Get in."

"I don't want to be with anyone but you. But if you don't think I'm worthy of marriage, I'll go to someone who doesn't care about that."

Raw fire snaked through him. She was pushing him too hard, even after he had been willing to compromise for her.

A red Mercedes drove into the gravel lot where the bungalow residents parked. Caleb drew in a stunned breath.

Sweeney stepped out of the car and strolled up to Arianna. "Is this the boyfriend you need my help with?"

Caleb gripped her arm hard, trying to think of a way to end this horrible nightmare.

Sweeney flicked open a cell phone. "Let her go or I'll call the police."

"No." No matter how deeply she had just cut into his heart, he couldn't let her go with a man he knew to be a murderer.

Sweeney punched a number into his cell phone.

"Get in the truck," Caleb seethed. "We'll get married in Vegas tonight."

She blinked. After she climbed in, he rounded the cab. He started the motor, thinking fast. Rye's hotel was across town. There wasn't enough time to have the kid come and help. He'd have to take care of this himself.

After heading out of the gravel lot, he switched off his headlights and pulled into the shadows of an old barn, where he watched for Sweeney.

Arianna stared at him. "Caleb?"

"Your would-be lover is a hired assassin," he gritted.

"How do you know?"

"I'm a private investigator. Patrick Sunnel hired me to track the guy down and stop him from killing his son's illegitimate daughter. Rye's my partner. He and I have been trying to locate Sweeney for a week. Now, thanks to you, he's finally where I can trail him."

She gasped. "You lied to me! Uncle Ben said you were a liar."

He threw her a hard glare. "Is he the one who put you up to this ploy?" He gestured toward her low-cut top and tight miniskirt.

"No. But he said you lied about being willing to marry me. Even if you don't let me go tonight, I'm still going to run away.". Choking on a sob, she pulled on the door handle.

Caleb caught her before she could escape. "I didn't lie about that. For some reason I love you, and I can't stand the thought of you throwing yourself away."

She turned toward him, amazement in her eyes.

His heart thudded in his ears. How could she look so vulnerable with her face smeared with makeup and her body displayed before him? He hated himself for his weakness but he couldn't deny the fact that he wanted her. Shameless and unabashed child that she was, so passionate to live every moment, she had given in to the fear that her life would be wasted waiting for a secure footing for their marriage.

And now she would get what she wanted. But he vowed it would be the last time she manipulated him. As his wife, she would do things his way.

A red car drove past. Caleb yanked his attention away from her. He waited several seconds, then edged out to follow the Mercedes. He stayed several car lengths behind as they drove down deserted side streets. At the main road, Sweeney turned left and entered the parking lot of a bar.

Caleb parked the truck a few spots away and flipped open his cell phone.

When the kid answered, his voice sounded sleep clogged.

"Rye, I've got our target. He's in Al's Friendly Bar on Main."

"Okay. Give me five minutes."

"Bring a spare shirt."

"Why?"

Caleb didn't bother explaining. He pressed End and looked at Arianna. "I'm sorry I lied to you about my occupation."

She gazed at him with affection and longing. "Are you really going to marry me tonight?"

"Isn't that why you pulled your little stunt? To get me to rush you to the altar?"

"I couldn't think of any other way to get you to do it."

"That's why I wanted to wait—so we could learn to trust each other. But now... I guess we'll learn the hard way."

A Pinto rental pulled in and parked. Rye climbed out and crossed the lot, carrying the requested shirt.

Caleb stepped out of the truck. He took the shirt, and tossed it into Arianna's lap. "Put this on."

Rye's eyes widened at sight of her. "Whose beat did you pull her off of?"

Caleb cut him an angry glance. "Watch your mouth."

Arianna slipped the loose-fitting shirt over her immodestly tight one.

Caleb focused on Rye. "Put the tracking device onto Sweeney's car. Then hang out in the bar and follow him when he leaves. I'll take over for you this afternoon."

Rye nodded, his eyes intent. "I'll call you if something happens before then."

"I have to go out of town for a while. I should be back by noon."

Rye looked surprised.

"I'll explain later."

He stepped into the truck, and Rye crossed the parking lot to plant the tracking device. Thankful that Rye knew how to blend into the bar scene, Caleb turned his attention to Arianna.

He pulled out the hankie in his back pocket and tossed it to her. "Wipe off the makeup. I don't want you looking like a hooker when I marry you. Is your birth certificate at your parents'?"

"No. I have it with me."

Grimly, he started the motor. She hadn't been bluffing about her plan to runaway if he didn't marry her immediately.

Although most girls would have wanted a gorgeous dress and an elaborate ceremony, apparently all Arianna wanted was his bed. It unnerved him and at the same time ashamed him. He wished he could believe differently, but it was what she had pursued from the start of their relationship. Considering her all-or-nothing scenario, it seemed he hadn't made much of a difference in her thinking. But now she was giving him a lifetime to correct her incredibly self-absorbed worldview.

Pulling away from the shadows around the bar, he drove back to his bungalow to pick up his birth certificate. Paper in hand, he returned to the Ford then accelerated to the interstate that led to Las Vegas and matrimony.

Chapter Twenty-one

When Al's Friendly Bar closed at three a.m., Rye tailed Sweeney to Porter Motel, where Sweeney headed up the stairs of a side entrance. He entered the door marked 206. Rye settled in his seat to wait.

After Caleb took over following Sweeney, Rye would break into the room and search it. Hopefully he would find something to identify which woman Sweeney was after. If not, he would take pictures of any weapons he found.

Although he assumed Sweeney wouldn't emerge again until late morning, he forced himself to ignore his own tiredness just in case Sweeney went somewhere. Several hours ticked by. At seven-thirty, Sweeney reappeared. He slipped into the Mercedes and exited the parking lot.

Rye followed him to Summerland's main street then onto the highway, going in the direction of the resort.

When the road curved, he lost his visual of the Mercedes. He glanced at the tracking monitor. Sweeney was slowing down. Rye geared down. A minute later, he caught sight of the Mercedes on the side of the road. A gray Volkswagen sat upside-down in the middle of the lane. No other cars were in view.

He jerked the Pinto to a stop several yards behind the Mercedes and jumped out, not caring if Sweeney saw him. Shattered glass lay everywhere, and a red-haired girl hung suspended by her seatbelt inside the crumpled VW. Rye ran toward her.

Sweeney hesitated several feet from the wreckage. "I'll call the police."

"Thanks." Rye jerked open the driver's door. The red-haired girl didn't smell like alcohol. What had caused her to take the turn so fast?

She moaned. "My foot. It hurts. I can't move it."

Rye examined it. Crushed metal pinned it to the bottom of the dashboard. "I think I can push the metal up enough to free it. Does your neck hurt?"

"It's fine. Just get me out of here."

Rye shoved on the twisted car frame. The girl grabbed her foot and pulled it free.

He reached around her to undo the seatbelt, then braced her as she dropped. Another girl hung in the passenger seat. Her long brown hair spilled down, covering her face. Rye glanced out her side window to see if Sweeney was coming to help, but he wasn't in view. "Great."

He helped the red-haired girl to the side of the road. The Mercedes was gone.

He couldn't just leave the other girl in the VW. He would have to use the tracking device to catch up to Sweeney later.

He jogged to the passenger door, but hesitated as he eyed the brown-haired girl. She hadn't moved. If her back or neck was injured, it could damage her more to take her out. On the other hand, her fingers looked unnaturally white from lack of blood circulation.

He flipped open his cell phone and hit 911. "Hello. I'm at the accident on I-5, five miles south of Summerland, that was reported a few minutes ago."

"We haven't received any call of an accident in that area."

Rye gritted his teeth. Sweeney hadn't reported it. He should have guessed Sweeney wouldn't want his voice on record with the police. "It's a single car. Two girls injured. I got one out, but the other's unconscious. Her fingers are white. Should I move her?"

"Go ahead. Ambulance will be there in fifteen minutes."

Rye clipped the phone to his belt and reached under the brown-haired girl to unsnap the buckle. He held her close as she slipped loose. His heart jumped at a familiar lilac scent. *Oh, God!*

He eased her out then carried her to where the red-haired girl sat, watching anxiously. He knelt on the ground and brushed long strands of dark hair away from the girl's face. His heart pounded as he exposed Cora's closed eyes.

Arianna felt as heady as if she had drunk too much wine. She was getting married to Caleb!

He had driven them to a marriage chapel in Las Vegas, then quietly requested the appropriate paperwork. The clerk pushed several legal documents across the counter with disinterest. Caleb filled in a long section, then handed the pen to her, his eyes dark with swirling emotion.

Her heart thudded as she filled in her name, birth date, and address. She signed next to Caleb's name with growing ecstasy.

Her idea had actually worked! For a few minutes she had feared it had backfired and that Caleb had lied to her to get her in the truck so he could follow Sweeney. But unlike everyone else she knew, Caleb kept his promises.

"Do you have rings?"

Caleb shook his head. "How much for gold bands?"

The clerk named the price, and Caleb paid the required amount. The clerk measured their fingers and found two bands in the correct sizes. He gestured them toward the chapel area, decorated with orchids and sparkling chandeliers. "Father Matthew will join you up front to perform the vows. Another attendant and I will sign as witnesses."

"Thank you."

Arianna slipped her hand into Caleb's as he led them down the aisle to the ornate podium at the front.

A minute later, a tall, gray-haired man in a white robe entered the chapel from a side room, carrying their paperwork. He smiled at them. "Welcome to White Dove Chapel. I'm Father Matthew. Would you like the traditional vows read or a modernized version?"

"Traditional," Caleb answered.

"All right." Father Matthew stepped behind the podium and opened a book that lay there. He cleared his throat. "Dearly beloved, we are gathered together today in the sight of God to witness the joining in holy matrimony of this man and this woman."

Arianna repeated the vows she had always laughed at before. Obey her husband? The modernized version wouldn't have had that part in it. Cling to and honor? The words sounded old-fashioned, yet in this time and place, strangely wonderful.

She gripped Caleb's hands and smiled at him in delight. Flickers of different emotions darkened his eyes, but he held her gaze unswervingly as he declared his own vows to love, honor, nurture, and provide for her all of his life.

"You may exchange the rings."

Her wedding band felt cool as he slipped it on her finger, and overwhelming emotion swept in. Never in her life had she thought she'd want so much to belong to one man. She placed his ring on his finger, and Father Matthew drew to a close, his voice strong. "What God has joined together, let no man separate. By the power invested in me by the State of Nevada and the blessing of the Holy Trinity, I now pronounce you man and wife. You may kiss your bride."

Arianna stepped into Caleb's arms and returned his kiss passionately. When she drew back, intense desire shone in his gaze, and her heart hammered wildly. Would he take her to a hotel here or drive the three hours back to his bungalow?

He guided her out of the chapel, a hand on her back. She slipped into the Ford and slid next to him as he started the motor.

He glanced to her, but didn't say anything. She didn't mind. She was his now, forever and always. She snuggled next to him as he drove past several hotels, finally taking the exit to the interstate.

The miles slipped by, and she closed her eyes as she envisioned the moments and nights ahead. There were no more reasons for him to withhold himself. He had given her the right to love him the way she had wanted to for so long.

His cell phone rang. She shifted slightly so he could answer.

Rye's voice jumped out of the receiver. "Cal! Cora's been hurt. She's at Bethel Hospital. How soon can you get here?"

"I'm three hours away." Anxiety filled Caleb's voice. "What happened?"

Arianna couldn't make out Rye's reply.

"Do you know where Sweeney is?"

Rye answered something, then Caleb snapped the cell phone shut, his face tense. "Cora's unconscious. She was returning to the Y from overnighting at a friend's house, and their vehicle flipped. Apparently the brakes failed. Rye's waiting with her until we get there."

Disappointed they couldn't go straight to his place, Arianna rested her head against his shoulder.

Her disappointment wouldn't last long, though. At least he would never send her to her parents' home again.

"Man, Cora, you scared me." Rye squeezed Cora's hand as he sat next to her in the hospital bed. After three hours of waiting for her to regain consciousness, he was too thankful she had stirred to care about Caleb's restrictions.

She wrapped her fingers around his. "Is Sandy okay?"

"Just a broken foot. You've been out of it for three hours, though. Does your head hurt?"

"A little. Is Caleb here?"

"He's been out of town, but he should be here soon."

Puzzlement crossed her face. "How did you find out I was here?"

Rye rubbed his thumb over her hand. "I guess God must think I do a good job rescuing you."

Her breath caught. "Thank you."

He brought her hand to his lips and pressed a kiss to the back of it. Surely even Caleb would do that. However, Caleb's heart wouldn't trip over itself at the way her lips parted in soft surprise.

Aching to hold her, he squeezed her hand as he laid it back on the bed. "I'm going to get a nurse to check you now that you're awake."

"Okay."

He headed to the nurses' station. An older nurse followed him back to the room. She smiled when she saw Cora sitting up. "Glad to see you awake, dearie. I'm going to call the doctor so he can check your contusion. You have a nasty lump on the head."

Rye used the restroom as the nurse recorded Cora's vitals. He double-checked the tracking monitor. Sweeney had returned to his motel room after a brief circuit around the resort. The Mercedes was still in the motel parking lot. Rye decided it was safe to presume Sweeney was sleeping. Thankful he could stay with Cora awhile longer, he reentered her room and lingered in the doorway.

The nurse had left, and a gray-haired doctor was asking Cora questions to check her memory. The doctor examined her eyes and nervous responses, then declared, "Your external injuries will heal quickly. However, the procedure for a cerebral contusion requires us to keep you here another twenty-four hours so we can make sure there are no complications, such as brain swelling."

"Okay."

"I'll see you in the morning." The doctor strode from the room.

"Rye?" Cora asked hesitantly.

"I'm here." He returned to her bedside.

"Why do you think God keeps having us run into each other?"

He caught his breath. But he doubted she was thinking what he was. He willed himself to think like Caleb. "I don't know. Maybe to keep you safe."

She smiled. "Maybe God also wants you to have the chance to learn more about Jesus."

He studied her. "Caleb says you think everyone who doesn't believe in Jesus goes to hell."

"God is just. He can't leave sin unpunished. But Jesus is God's free gift to everyone. A person doesn't have to be good enough or smart enough to get into heaven. They simply have to believe that Jesus took their punishment so that God's justice could be satisfied."

Rye sighed. "Caleb's taught me a lot about God's justice. He lives his life based on it."

"God is perfect, and He can't allow us to enter heaven tainted with sin. That's why Jesus died—to wash us clean so God can accept us into His courts."

The beauty of her words washed over him, and he held no resentment that she was once again 'preaching at him' as Caleb had put it. "It sounds wonderful to be accepted so easily by God, but I've done some horrible things."

He didn't want to tell her even the least of the sins that hung so heavily around his neck, so he put the focus back on her. "I am grateful, though, that He gave me the opportunity to meet you. Before I knew who you were, I thought you might be one of His angels."

She laughed softly. "I think Caleb can confirm otherwise."

He gazed at her wistfully. "I don't think I've ever seen you act selfishly or speak out of anger."

A troubled look crossed her face. "Rye, I'm human just like everyone else. I have thoughts I shouldn't have, say things I shouldn't say, do things I shouldn't do."

"Really?" He wondered if she was thinking of the way she had returned his kiss on the beach. But he was certain God laid all the fault of that episode at his door. She had been the innocent. He the exploiter.

He sighed, sure that whatever faults she had were so minor not even God would notice them. After all, she exuded a sweetness that could only come from a pure heart and mind. "I think you're everything God wants. Caleb told me you even preached at Dean."

She looked embarrassed. "I wonder why Caleb told you about that."

"Maybe he wanted me to get jealous."

She blushed. "I doubt that."

He smiled, enjoying the pink cast to her dusky skin and relieved the topic had moved away from the status of his soul. Even though Caleb said she always forgave, he had no doubt that her purity would recoil in horror at the depths of the depravity within him.

"Cora! Oh, thank God!"

Rye moved away from the bed as Caleb strode into the room, followed by Arianna. The teen barely glanced his way, keeping her gaze on Caleb as he leaned down and enveloped Cora in a tight hug. "I was afraid when Rye called that you wouldn't be awake."

She hugged him back. "God protected both Sandy and me. It could have been a lot worse. And Rye's the one who found us."

"He said your brakes failed. Didn't Sandy know they were bad?"

"I don't think so. She seemed stunned they weren't working."

"But you're okay?"

"Yes. The doctor wants to keep me here another day to make sure I don't have any brain swelling, though."

"God forbid."

Arianna sat in a chair against the wall. A ring glinted on her left hand. Rye shot a startled glance toward Caleb's left hand. A gold band rested there as well. He sucked in his breath.

Caleb looked at him then directed, "Arianna, come here."

She stood and crossed to where he sat on the edge of the bed.

"Cora, you and Rye are the first to know. Arianna and I were married this morning in Vegas."

"Caleb!" Cora held out her hands in delight. "I'm so happy for you! Can I have a hug, Arianna? You don't know how long I've prayed for Caleb to find a wife."

Cora embraced Arianna, happiness on her face.

Rye jerked his chin toward the door. "Cal, can I talk to you a minute in private?"

Caleb scowled but stood. "I'll be right back."

Rye exited the room. Caleb followed him into the hall. Rye turned, letting his disbelief spill out. "Cal, were you drunk? The last time I saw you with Arianna, she was dressed like a hooker. You can't tell me she won your heart that way."

Caleb pressed his lips together, his eyes dark. "She threatened to run away with Sweeney unless I married her."

"Then you're going to annul it, right?"

"No, I am not. I don't break my commitments. You should know that." He headed back into the room, and Rye forced himself to follow, questions swirling in his mind. Did Caleb actually want to be married to Arianna? Certainly he couldn't be pleased by her manipulation.

Cora and Arianna paused in their conversation as Caleb joined them. Rye hesitated. Caleb ought to go after Sweeney, but he doubted his partner wanted to leave Cora. And if Caleb actually wanted a honeymoon…

He grimaced at that train of thought. His partner deserved a far better woman than Arianna, and he wished Caleb had not been trapped by her manipiulations.

He pulled the tracking monitor out of his pocket. It indicated that Sweeney's car was still parked in the lot of Porter Motel.

Caleb glanced at him. "Is Sweeney on the move?"

"Not yet, but he'll probably leave his motel room soon."

Cora startled. "Who's Sweeney?"

"He's the man trying to kill the girl we were hired to protect," Caleb said.

Worry washed over her face. "Be careful, Rye."

He grinned, delighted at her concern. "Don't worry about me. You're the one who keeps needing to be rescued. I think you're beginning to owe me."

A tinge of color touched Cora's cheeks.

Caleb shot him a dark look, but Rye ignored it. "See you around, everyone." He waved and headed out the door.

Chapter Twenty-two

Arianna's pulse quickened when Caleb at last said good-bye to Cora. It was late afternoon, and she had forced herself to hide her impatience while Cora and Caleb talked. She had answered Cora's questions, but her attention hadn't stayed on the blind girl. She wanted so much to be in Caleb's arms.

She slipped her hand in his as they headed out of the room, and Caleb glanced at her. She smiled, and his gaze flickered. He guided them out of the hospital and across the parking lot.

On the drive to the bungalow, he stayed silent, but she didn't mind. She wasn't interested in talking anyway.

At the bungalow's cul de sac, he parked in front of his door. "Stay here." He stepped out of the truck and unlocked the bungalow.

Arianna waited until he came to her door. He opened it and looked at her. Intense emotion burned in his eyes once again, and her pulse jumped. She scooted toward him.

Her breath caught in her chest as he scooped her up in her arms and carried her across the threshold. She laughed softly. Trust Caleb to think of such a romantic tradition!

She held his face in her hands and covered him with kisses, barely aware of him setting her down or shutting the door. "Oh, Caleb, I love you so much. Thank you for marrying me. I promise I'll be a good wife."

He pulled out of her hold. His eyes were still dark, but the emotion in them wasn't desire.

She swallowed. "Caleb?"

He spoke in a low, tightly controlled voice. "You wanted me to marry you, and I have. But now we do things my way."

"Your way?" She didn't have a clue what that meant.

His gaze hardened. "I'm assuming the only reason you pushed for me to marry you now instead of waiting like I asked is because you want me to sleep with you. But that's not going to happen. Not right now."

A wave of dizziness hit her at the cold, unexpected words. She grabbed the back of a chair. "You married me, but you won't sleep with me?"

The muscle in his jaw jerked. "No."

She couldn't believe he meant it. She licked her lips. He must be angrier at her than she realized. He had been furious when he saw Sweeney, but had backed off once he agreed to marry her. She thought he had been fighting himself more than her and that once he gave in to his desire, she didn't have to worry about any repercussions as to how she had played out her plan. Apparently she had been wrong.

She lowered her eyes and stepped up to him. He didn't move. She put her fingers on his chest. "I'm sorry I didn't trust you. Uncle Ben made me think no one ever kept their word, but I should have known better about you. Please forgive me."

He took her hand and moved it off his chest. "I forgive you. But we're still not sleeping together until I know I can trust you."

Startled, her gaze flew to his face. "Trust me?" She saw desire in his eyes again, but another emotion shone in them, even stronger.

"Yes, I need to know I can trust you. You almost—" His voice choked, but he hardened his tone and pushed through. "You almost ran off with another man. What happens the next time you decide to do that?"

She stared at him, amazed that his refusal to be with her wasn't from anger but fear. She moved closer, and he let her touch her body to his. Conflicting emotions struggled in his gaze. She willed tenderness into her own. She traced his ribs longingly with her hands. "I won't leave you, Caleb. I promise. I've only wanted you. I won't hurt you."

"You already have." He stepped away. "I'm going to relieve Rye. Take a taxi and get your stuff from your parents. You can have the bedroom. I'll sleep on the couch. Don't wait up for me."

Astonished, she watched as he strode out the door, leaving her alone.

Rye sipped his 7-Up in a back corner of Al's Friendly Bar as he watched Sweeney chalk his pool stick. His cell phone vibrated. Noting Caleb's cell number, he pressed Answer. "Where are you?"

"Just leaving my place. Where are you?"

"Al's Friendly Bar. Sweeney's been here for the past hour. He seems to be a regular. The bartender greeted him by name."

"Kenneth?"

"Yeah. But he's not registered at the motel by that name."

"Do you know his room number?"

"206."

"I'll hack into the motel database later to find out his other alias. Are you planning to search his room?"

"As soon as you get here."

"I'm ten minutes away."

Caleb signed off, and Rye finished his drink. Ten minutes later, Caleb walked into the dimly lit bar. He strode to the counter and ordered a drink.

Rye strolled out the side door and slipped into the Pinto. He drove to the Porter Motel and climbed the staircase to the second floor.

An elderly lady passed him as he slipped his lock pick into Sweeney's door, but she didn't seem to notice that he wasn't using a key.

Rye waited for her to enter her room several doors down before fidgeting again with the lock pick. After several tries with various sizes of picks, the lock clicked. Rye slipped inside, locking the door behind him.

An unmade double bed took up most of the space of the interior. A small dresser and straight-back chair sat next to it. An unzipped suitcase lay at the foot of the bed.

Rye strode to the suitcase and lifted the lid. He carefully moved aside layers of clothing, but found no weapons or papers inside.

He poked into the dresser drawers and the closet. He lifted the mattress of the bed and felt the pillows. Sweeney was playing it safe. Nothing discriminating had been left behind, nor did Sweeney have a laptop to hack into.

Rye made sure nothing looked disturbed, then exited the room. He and Caleb would have to keep tailing Sweeney to discover the granddaughter's identity.

Arianna clicked through the channels on Caleb's television and stopped at one airing a romantic flick from a decade ago. It was a quarter past eight. After obeying his instructions to get her belongings from her parents', she had spent hours mulling over her options. She had encountered Caleb's stubbornness before and doubted she could convince him to give up his anger, at least for a few days.

However, with enough time and enticement on her part, she felt certain he would eventually cave in. After all, his rules said that now she was the only one he could have.

She smiled to herself as the romantic flick paired off two people at odds with each other until something snapped, rotating their strong dislike into mutually strong attraction. It reminded her of Caleb, intensely passionate whether he was angry with her or in love with her.

When a commercial came on, she muted the TV and wandered to the fridge. She hadn't bothered fixing supper just for herself so she helped herself to Caleb's ham and cheese for a sandwich. Perhaps tomorrow she could use the Ford to get some groceries.

Before falling for Caleb, she would never have considered being a housekeeper. At her previous social standing, couples hired maids. She was glad to know that Caleb wasn't the poor stable hand he had pretended to be, but she knew he would expect her to manage their home. Which was fine with her. She wanted Caleb all to herself.

A knock on the door interrupted her thoughts. Carrying the sandwich, she swung the door open. "Uncle Ben!"

He smiled with amusement at her surprised tone. "Can I come in?"

"Sure!" She gestured him inside, feeling pleased that her uncle was her first visitor in her new home. "So... did Mom tell you?"

He raised his eyebrows as he sat and crossed an ankle over his knee.

"She did. Congratulations. I think."

She laughed, amused by his sardonic attitude. "You think Caleb's not worth it, I know."

"I think marriage isn't worth it. But that's your call." He glanced around the small living room. "You've definitely downgraded in living style."

She brushed the comment away with her hand. "I don't care about that."

"No?" He looked her up and down, as though trying to see something different in her. "So is his lovemaking everything you hoped for? I can't imagine he's had any experience."

Arianna suddenly wished she hadn't invited him in. Sometimes he could be too crass even for her. She flicked her gaze away, not wanting to admit the part where her marriage lacked. "I don't mind inexperience."

"Obviously." He studied her. "But do you mind experiencing nothing at all?"

She dug her fingernails into her palms. "You don't know that."

He laughed softly. "I can read you like a book, Nan. I always have. But don't give up. I'm sure even a Jew will succumb to base need, especially since you're his only choice."

Only moments ago that exact sentiment had made her feel secure. Now it made her feel second-best. She frowned. "Maybe you should go."

"Okay, but don't be mad at me. I could have warned you he wouldn't be easy to manage." He stood to his feet and headed to the door. "By the way, I stopped at the Y and heard Cora had been in an accident. Do you know how she's doing?"

"She's in the hospital, but she's getting out tomorrow. I guess she has a concussion." She noted the intense interest in his eyes. "You like her, don't you? I don't see why. She's not your type. She breathes religion, and she's so sweet it's like walking in honey. Not to mention the fact that Caleb would kill you if you ever went near her. He's more protective of her purity than his own."

Uncle Ben's eyes darkened. Then he slid nonchalance over the emotion. "I'm just concerned, that's all. Of course Caleb should be protective of her. She's a sweetheart, and David Hauzen is a lucky man."

Arianna didn't believe the act. She had been around his womanizing for too long. Feeling the need to goad him just like he had been goading her, she said, "David wasn't at the hospital, and she didn't mention him at all today. But Rye sure made her blush, and Caleb got mad over that. He doesn't think Rye is good enough for her."

"Who's Rye?"

"Caleb's best friend." She remembered to stick to Caleb's cover, not wanting to give him another reason to get angry at her. "They came from LA together, looking for jobs here. But Rye quit his job at the resort so he has plenty of time to hang around Cora when Caleb's not around."

Anger registered on her uncle's face and Arianna felt a cynical satisfaction at twisting the knife of jealousy. *Serves you right, Uncle Ben. You shouldn't have provoked me with all those comments about my marriage.*

She waved at the door as she settled back on the couch and unmuted the TV. "Come back anytime."

He took her hint and headed out the door.

Chapter Twenty-three

Good afternoon, Miss Abrams. It looks like you've checked out with a clean bill of health."

Cora nodded at the female orderly's words where she sat on her hospital bed. The doctor had examined her a half hour before and told her she could get dressed to leave. She had lost her sunglasses in the accident, but had donned the tank top and shorts she had worn back from Sandy's house.

Her roommate had wanted to spend some time with her parents and had invited Cora to join her. Cora enjoyed her time with the hospitable family, wishing she didn't have to return so soon to the Y, but she needed to be back at camp in time for her children's music rehearsal. Only they hadn't made it.

Instead the brakes had failed, and Sandy had cried out in terror as the car flipped. Cora beseeched the Lord to receive her spirit if this was the end of her purpose on earth. But He had kept her from serious harm and sent Rye once again in rescue.

She smiled. Rye should have called himself her knight in shining armor instead of her prince charming that first day they met.

"Cora?" The orderly's voice brought her back to the present. "Do you have someone to pick you up?"

"My uncle's supposed to get me, but he can't come until four."

"It's barely after one now. Do you want the TV on while you wait?"

"No, thanks. I'll be fine. Maybe I can see if his wife can pick me up instead."

"There's a phone on the left side of your bed if you want to call her."

"Thank you." Cora stood as she trailed her fingers along the top of the desk and located the phone.

She didn't dial, however, because the orderly exclaimed "Oh, wait. I think your uncle's here." The orderly left her side to let the visitor in.

Cora waited, wondering why Caleb had changed his plans.

"Cora, so nice to see you're safe," Dean greeted her. Her heart jumped into her throat. Where was the orderly? *Jesus, help me.*

"Are you feeling okay?" He came close and put a hand under her arm. She shrank back. "I'm fine. What are you doing here?"

"I came to pick you up. Nan said you were getting out today, but she needed to go shopping for groceries. She's endeavoring to be quite the little housewife now that Caleb's married her." Amusement colored his words.

His touch seemed to burn her. Cora pulled her arm from his hold and stepped back, bumping the bed. "I think I'll just wait for Caleb."

"I'll take you straight to the Y. Wouldn't you rather be there than here?"

She swallowed. She tried to remember the Scripture about not having a spirit of fear, but she couldn't grasp hold of it. Had the Lord given it to her only the afternoon with Caleb so she could share the gospel? Her every instinct commanded that she not leave with Arianna's uncle, regardless of his reassurances. She forced steadiness into her voice. "I'm sorry you made the trip for nothing, but I'm just going to wait."

"I see no reason—" His words stopped when a new set of footsteps entered the room.

"Cora," Rye said cheerfully, "the orderly said you're released. Oh, hi, Dean. Didn't know you were here."

"Rye." Incredible relief swept her, and she stepped his way even though she didn't know the lay of the room. Her arm bumped a table, causing something metal to clatter. In the next moment, Rye's warm presence saturated her. She breathed in his clean pine scent, thankful when he slipped his arm around her waist.

Dean's cool voice intruded. "I'm sorry. I don't think we've met."

"No, I guess not," Rye responded. "I'm Rye Nelson, a friend of Cora's. Sorry to cut your visit short, but I think Cora's had enough of this hospital so I'm going to take her back home."

"Really?" Dean's tone was suave. "She was just telling me she needed to stay here until her uncle arrives."

Cora swallowed, but Rye remained unperturbed. "Well, perhaps she told *you* that, but I'm more than just an acquaintance. Take care of yourself, Dean." Rye guided her out of the room, keeping his arm around her until they entered an elevator. It hummed as it descended, and she breathed a sigh of relief.

When Rye broke contact, she wondered if he had held her so closely to send a message to Dean or to be moral support for her. Either way, she felt grateful for the security his touch had given her.

"So… what was Dean doing in your room?"

"He said he was there to take me to the Y. But there's no way I was going to go with him."

Rye's voice held a frown. "How did he find out you were here or that you were getting out today?"

"He said Arianna told him."

"Of course." Anger touched Rye's tone. "She dotes on him. If he asked her about you, she'd tell him everything he wanted to know."

Cora didn't like the way he had jumped to a negative assumption about Arianna's motives. "I doubt she did it to be malicious. I'm sure she just wanted to help me."

"Do you always do that?"

"Do what?"

The elevator chimed, and Rye guided her out. "Assume the best about people even though you don't have any idea what they're like or what they've done."

"What do you mean?" A breeze blew across her face as he escorted her out the hospital door.

"Yesterday you assumed that Caleb wanted to marry Arianna and that she is God's choice for him."

She stopped walking. Rye paused with her. She turned toward him, wishing she could see his face. "Why wouldn't Caleb want to marry her? He's been dating her—"

"Yes." Rye's tone held exasperation. "He thought he could take her under his wing like he did me and help her change her ways. But Arianna's only wanted one thing from him, and she's manipulated him until now he's completely caught. I told him to annul their marriage, but he has this crazy idea about commitment. He wants to keep her from throwing herself away on the first guy who comes along, even though she did that long before she met Caleb."

Cora's heart hammered at the vehement words. She could scarcely believe what she was hearing. Caleb had said Arianna's world was different from his, but Rye's words made it clear in what way.

Rye combed his fingers into her hair. "I'm sorry I vented my frustration on you. I shouldn't have said anything. I don't think Caleb wanted you to know."

She took his hand and cradled it. "How can I pray if I don't know the truth? And how can God work if we don't pray for the people He brings into our lives?"

"God didn't bring Arianna into Caleb's life. She's done everything in her power to control him and make him do what she wants."

"Caleb has a strong will. If he's given Arianna anything, it's because he's wanted to. If he's trying to change Arianna, I fear she's the one who will break."

"What do you mean?"

Cora shook her head, not sure herself what the Spirit was trying to tell her. But she sensed opposing forces waging war over the uncle she loved so much, and now they loomed over the girl who had been pulled into the dark waters of his heart. She had prayed all her life for his salvation, but so far he had looked upon a crucified Savior with contempt. Was it because he never had reason to doubt his own goodness? She beseeched the Lord to deal with him gently even as He broke his pride.

"Cora, are you okay?"

She smiled, knowing Rye couldn't understand. He was lost as well. But for some reason she found herself explaining anyway. "Sometimes I have to stop and listen to what God is saying."

"God speaks to you?"

"He speaks to all His children. He'll speak to you if you ask Him to."

"I don't think so." She could tell by the variance in his voice that he had turned away from her.

She squeezed the hand she still held before releasing it. "It's okay to doubt. Just don't let it keep you from pursuing the truth."

"The truth?"

She smiled. "Jesus."

"Cora…" His voice sounded hoarse. "Why are you willing to be alone with me and not Dean? Sometimes I don't think we're that much different."

"You don't think you're different? Why? I never feel scared around you like I do around him."

He groaned. "Baby, you make this so hard."

Her pulse leaped at the desire in his voice. Yearning swept her at the memory of his arms around her.

But her heart ached as she put her response in light of eternity. Hadn't he heard a word she said about God? Did he spend time with her only because he enjoyed her kisses?

She lowered her head. *Jesus, You told me You love him then You told me to forgive him. What now? Am I supposed to walk away from him because he wants me?*

The Lord's answer settled into the quiet pain of her heart. *Just love him, child. Love him like I love him and trust Me to keep his desire restrained.*

It wasn't what she had expected to hear, but she had no doubt of the command. She sighed, wanting to struggle through the issue in the solitude of her prayer closet. "Rye, can we go to the Y?"

"Sure."

She grazed his arm with her fingers. "God wants me to love you, but not the way you think. If you have a Bible, you can read in 1 Corinthians 13 the way God describes His love. Maybe that will help you understand."

He stayed silent a long moment. "I'm glad you aren't afraid of me."

"How could I be when you've rescued me so many times? Only let me pay you back the best way I know how—by having you look at Jesus and not at me."

Pain touched his voice. "I'll try. But I'm not sure He wants me anywhere near Him."

"Do you know that He hung between two thieves on the cross where He was crucified? One derided him, but the other begged for Him to remember him when Jesus came into His kingdom. Jesus told him, 'Today you will be with Me in paradise.' The Lord has no favorites. He loves everyone the same. Even you."

"You make it sound easy. But you're good, and I'm not." He drew in a deep breath. Before she could respond, he said, "Please, let's not talk about it anymore."

He took her arm and guided her across the parking lot.

She walked silently with him. Only the Spirit could blow conviction and hope into the depths of his soul. The depths he didn't want her to see.

Dean narrowed his eyes as he watched Rye help Cora into an older-model Pinto. He had hung back in the hospital lobby, unable to hear their conversation, but reading their actions loud and clear.

Covetousness had bit hard when Cora held Rye's hand, tenderness flooding her face.

From the moment he met the blind girl, Dean had wanted her. At first he hadn't understood why, since her manner was unassuming and her beauty soft. But after their meeting at Caleb's, he decided the compelling factor was her incredible innocence. He had never come across a girl as pure and unspoiled as Cora Abrams, and he hadn't been able to get the picture of having that innocence for himself out of his mind.

Arianna had been right when she said he didn't stand a chance at satisfying his desire for Cora when she was surrounded by protective friends and family. Hoping to find her alone, he had gone to see her at the hospital. Luck had played into his hands. Not only had she been unchaperoned, but the orderly had thought he was her uncle coming to take her home.

The fear on her face when she heard his voice had only fed his hunger. Most of his old loves lived lives of promiscuity just like he did, and the ones who didn't, he had seduced within days by soft promises and persuasive charm. Cora, however, was different. Regardless of what role he played, her faith would compel her to hold strongly to her chastity.

Now, watching her drive away with Nelson, Dean clenched his hand. Regardless of her fear, he *would* have gotten her alone with him if Rye hadn't shown up.

Rye had held his gaze when he slipped his arm around Cora's waist, his message clear: *She's not for the having.* Dean had a hunch that whereas Caleb had lived like a puritan all his life, Rye had a vast amount of worldly experience. The kid's desire for Cora had been no less raw and powerful than his own. It was amazing Cora trusted Rye when she obviously didn't trust him. Perhaps she knew the kid would restrain his desire while Dean had no such intention.

He strode to his Mustang and revved the motor. His mind raced as he headed back to Summerland. With both Caleb and Rye hanging around Cora when she wasn't at the Y, his chances of being alone with her again were slim. He needed an edge, something to give him the opportunity he needed.

Caleb and Rye had come up from LA together, but he knew little else about them. What if there was something in their past he could use to distract them from constantly playing chaperone?

There was a guy in LA who could obtain information on anyone if given enough time. He cost a bit of money to employ, but the memory of Cora reaching out to Rye with gentle sweetness heightened Dean's resolution. He had never denied himself anything before, and he saw no reason to start now.

Chapter Twenty-four

"Dean, it's Manney. Do you have time to talk?"

He pushed back from his seat at the poker table in Summerland's casino as he spoke into his cell phone. "Give me one minute."

He excused himself from the poker table. He hadn't been winning anyway, and he'd been waiting for Manney's phone call for three days.

He exited the casino and slipped into his Mustang, where he could speak in privacy. "What did you find out?"

"I found a Rye Nelson in the LA phone book, but he's a family man who's still in town. Caleb Lindon isn't listed."

Dean frowned. "So they're not from LA?"

"That's what I figure. I followed up on the girl's name. Cora Abrams has an uncle named Caleb, the right age. He's a private eye who's currently out of town. His partner is Rye Tyler, a kid out of the ghettos, who's also out of town."

Jackpot! "Do you have any information about what they're doing up here?"

"The last person they visited in LA was billionaire Patrick Sunnel. I understand he's a relative of yours."

"He is. I didn't know he'd hired private investigators, though."

"He's kept it quiet, but one of his security guards thinks they're searching for a missing granddaughter. Apparently Patrick was ready to head to Summerland Resort a week ago, thinking Abrams had found her."

Dean drew in a deep breath. He had his trump card, but he kept his tone casual. He didn't want Manney to realize his connection with the situation. "Anything else?"

"Nothing that's relevant to their presence at the resort. Do you want me to dig back further?"

"No, that's okay. Take care."

Manney ended the call, and Dean stared out the windshield of the Mustang. So Patrick knew about Douglas's daughter. Jackson needed to know about the presence of Patrick's spies, but only if it benefited Dean as well. Abrams and Tyler wouldn't have free time to spend around Cora if they were busy guarding the granddaughter. Or at least someone they thought was the granddaughter.

He thumbed Memory on the cell phone. A moment later, Jackson answered. Dean didn't waste time on pleasantries. "We have a complication."

"What?"

"Douglas's daughter."

"Sweeney's taking care of that."

"Patrick knows. He's hired a pair of private eyes. They're here at the resort."

"Who are they?"

Dean shook his head. "I'm not giving out more free information. I want Sweeney's help."

"With what?"

"Arrange a place to meet. Then I'll explain."

Rye rubbed at the grit in his eyes as he drove toward the YMCA campground. Caleb had relieved him at Sweeney's motel, and Rye would have headed to his hotel room after a long night of tailing Sweeney while he visited bars and prostitutes. But Caleb had let slip that he had taken Arianna to visit Cora just before he left. "Cora said she'd teach her to bake, but she'll probably preach at her too."

Rye had hid a grin at Caleb's mutter, then pulled away before Caleb remembered to warn him not to pay his own visit. He figured his two pure motives for going to the cabin outweighed his selfish one. First, Cora wanted to convert him, so he might as well keep giving her the opportunity. And second, he had a hunch that if Dean found out Arianna was visiting Cora he'd be making his own social call.

His hunch proved correct. When he arrived, he saw Dean's Mustang in front of cabin ten. Rye was glad he had once again given in to the temptation to seek Cora out. He had risked Caleb's anger by picking her up from the hospital, but he had been just in time to save her from Dean's intrusion. Her gratitude over his intervention had been easy to see.

He mounted the steps, hearing voices from inside. Only the screen door was shut. He rapped once before entering.

Arianna scowled as she glanced up from kneading a mound of dough. "What are you doing here?"

"Visiting Cora."

Cora smiled as she used a fork to mix apples covered in spices. "Hi, Rye."

Rye grabbed a chair on the opposite side of the table from where Dean sat. "Caleb mentioned you were granting one of his wishes."

Arianna frowned. "What wish?"

"That you would learn to cook."

Arianna narrowed her eyes. "I don't know why he cares. He's not home for meals anyway."

"One day he will be. Unless you're planning to sever the ball and chain before then."

"Rye!"

He winced at Cora's reprimand. "Sorry, Cora."

She tipped her head toward Arianna, and he realized she thought he hadn't apologized to the right person. He glanced at Arianna. "Sorry, Arianna."

"My, my."

Rye sent Dean a pointed look. "What?"

Dean absently pressed some wrinkles out of his khaki pants. "I think Arianna would love it if she could get Caleb to be that compliant. Wouldn't you, Nan?"

Arianna glowered at him, then pounded on the pie dough.

"Ready to roll out the bottom crust?" Cora asked Arianna, her voice a soothing sound in the room.

"Yeah." Arianna grabbed a rolling pin and pushed it over the dough until it thinned into a circle. "Okay, now what? How do I get it into the pan?"

"Use a spatula to fold it in half. Then do it again. It should be easy to pick up after that."

Arianna frowned in concentration, then unfolded the crust once it was in the pan. "Do I add the filling now?"

"Yes."

Arianna scraped the apple mixture into the pan. "Okay. Now what?"

"Take the other half of the pastry and roll it out. Cut some lines in it, then put it over the filling."

Rye watched, fascinated, as Cora helped press the pie crusts together in a simple design. Caleb would get a treat when he arrived home.

Arianna shoved the pie into the oven and set the timer.

Rye doubted Dean would leave before the pie was done, but he didn't feel like waiting in the strained atmosphere for a chance to talk to Cora. He walked over to her. "I wanted to talk to you some more. Do you mind if we go for a walk?"

Arianna startled, and he could sense Dean's instant displeasure. But Cora smiled with relief. "Sure."

She felt for the walking stick propped against the wall, and he wondered if his actions would get back to Caleb. Even if they did, he could defend himself by saying Cora had wanted to get away from Dean. Meanwhile, he could enjoy saturating himself with her peacefulness once again.

Dean flipped open his cell phone as he stopped behind a group of palm trees on the public beachfront across from the Y campground where Rye had taken Cora. He punched in Sweeney's number, having obtained it at the meeting Jackson had arranged between the three of them two days ago.

The time together had proved productive. Dean had refused to relate Abrams's and Tyler's names until Jackson agreed to let Sweeney help him. Then he and Sweeney had worked out a plan that would free both of them of the partners' restrictive presences.

Dean kept his voice low as he spoke into the cell phone. "Tyler's at the beach across from the YMCA. I see the lifeguard you said they think might be Sunnel's granddaughter. If you come now, we can switch cars so Abrams will follow me. Plan for fifteen minutes. I'll meet you inside the public restroom here."

Sweeney responded in the affirmative, and Dean snapped the cell phone shut. He sent one last glance toward the pair walking down the path to the beachfront. Tyler had his hand on Cora's elbow even though she had her walking stick to find her way. Dean felt immense satisfaction over the fact that he finally had the means to keep both Tyler and Abrams away from her.

Caleb pulled into the coastal parking area across from the YMCA campground two minutes after Sweeney, having followed the signal of the tracking monitor. The red Mercedes sat empty, so Caleb stepped out of the Ford. He strolled along the sidewalk that created a scenic lookout point.

The beach spread below, but Sweeney wasn't in sight or on the stairs that led to the beach.

Caleb glanced around the parking area, noting the large building with signs for men's and women's restrooms. Had Sweeney needed to use the bathroom?

He checked his watch, then double-checked the beach area. It was littered with occupants, some sunbathing and others lounging in deck chairs. More people swam in the sparkling blue water. Sweeney couldn't have blended in so quickly.

Caleb returned to the Ford to wait for Sweeney to emerge from the restroom.

After five minutes, worry gnawed. At ten minutes, he left the Ford. The tracking device would tell him if Sweeney drove off in the Mercedes. Meanwhile he needed to check the beach.

He descended the stairs swiftly, scanning faces of the men he passed.

The tracking monitor vibrated. He pulled it out of his pocket and exhaled in relief. The Mercedes was pulling out of the parking area.

Caleb ascended the stairs two at a time, then jumped in the Ford. He exited the parking lot and accelerated to regain a visual on Sweeney's car.

Rye caught the salty scent of the sea as he walked with Cora along the firm sand several yards from the shore. The ocean spread before them, shimmering with blue waves. Its white line met the brilliance of the sapphire sky. A warm wind blew against his skin, and he felt alive and free like the seagulls that circled above a ragged rock jutting out of the water.

He laughed at a sudden thought. "So, did that count as rescue number four?"

Cora's smile held amusement. "If you're including the times you've helped me escape Dean's attention, I'd say it's number five."

"That's right. The cruise." He slanted a look at her, feeling incredibly relaxed, like he had when she had just been Hershey. Was it because Caleb hadn't been breathing down his neck lately? Or was it because Cora made it so easy to be with her, even though she knew how he felt about her? Smiling in memory of the night on board ship, he teased, "You took a walk with me then, too, though if I remember right, you weren't sure if you should. Apparently I was the lesser of two evils."

"Is that why you think I went with you?"

"Isn't it?"

"No. I went with you because I knew I was supposed to share Jesus with you. Only I didn't get very far." She paused. "I'm glad I've had the chance now."

He studied her, realizing that she had the same depth of passion that Caleb had. Only it didn't look like Caleb's intense rigidness, because it was centered on the mercy of a loving Savior. Curious at the variance between the two, he asked, "How long have you believed in Christianity?"

Cora's face grew tender. "My grandmother became a Christian shortly before I was born, and she raised me to believe in Jesus. He's been real to me ever since I can remember. He's everything to me."

Rye drew in a shallow breath at the ethereal beauty shining from her eyes. It was the reason he had almost kissed her in the hospital parking lot. When she said the name of Jesus, he had seen clear to the depths of her soul, and there was no darkness there.

His heart rate increased in longing, and he struggled to refocus his attention. With a strong effort of will, he pushed his desire to the far corners of his mind and looked out at the blue expanse of the ocean. A number of resort members swam in the deeper waves while several children played merrily in the shallow waters.

He guided her closer to the ocean until the firm turf gave way to softer sand that sifted into his shoes with every step.

He removed his shoes, letting his feet sink into the warm sand. "Wanna take off your shoes? The sand feels wonderful between my toes."

Cora smiled. "And I thought I was the only adult to think so." She slid her sandals off her slender feet. She dangled them from her fingers and gave a happy sigh as she squished her toes into the sand.

Rye grinned. "Come on. Let's walk closer to the water."

The warm sand gave way to cooler sand, stained brown from the continual ebb and flow of the tide. Cora laughed as a wave splashed over her bare feet. "Close your eyes."

He obeyed, waiting for the tide to wash over their feet again. This time, since he couldn't see the water coming, the sensation was different, awakening his senses of touch and smell.

Absorbing the realization that he had just experienced a taste of Cora's world, he asked, "What do you miss most about not being able to see the world?"

Another wave rolled in, sloshing her feet and legs. She stepped a foot away from him as though to embrace the sea. At last she said softly, "I miss knowing what people look like. Caleb usually tells me, but he's been so busy lately he hasn't been around to ask."

Rye hesitated. "Who are you thinking of?" When she didn't answer right away, he teased, "Dean?"

She shook her head. "I don't care about him. But I'd like to know about Arianna."

"Arianna just turned eighteen. She's tall, probably six feet. She's voluptuous and has blue-green eyes. I think exotic is a good word to describe her because of the way she carries herself and exudes passion for life. Her hair's jet black and she used to wear too much makeup, but she knows Caleb doesn't like it. She used to dress provocatively, too, but Caleb refused to hang out with her until she started wearing modest clothes."

"Thank you."

Cora remained facing the sea, and Rye gazed at her profile, noticing the tendrils of long hair that whipped around her neck and shoulders. What would he do if he couldn't see her?

He stepped closer, removing the distance she had put between them, as he realized the answer.

The freedom she had given him to be himself in her presence pushed aside the weight of Caleb's boundaries. He took her hand as he stepped in front of her.

She drew in a startled breath when he touched her fingers to his face.

"You can see, Hershey, if people will let you close enough." He guided her sensitive touch over his features, willing her to see him.

"Rye." Her breathing intensified.

He pressed a kiss into her palm and yearned to do much more. Everything in him ached to pull her into his arms and drown himself in her kisses. He longed to immerse himself into her. Oh, why wasn't he allowed to have her? "I want so much to make love to you."

"Rye, no!" She pulled her hand from his face. His mouth went dry as he realized he had whispered the words out loud.

Her face distraught, she turned as though to move away from him, but he couldn't let her go. Catching her arm, he said hoarsely, "I didn't mean it the way it sounded. I just…"

She waited, completely still.

He searched for the words to explain what he was feeling, but instead realized he hadn't spoken honestly. The right to make love to her was exactly what he wanted. Only he was certain he could never have it.

"I'm sorry I said that or even thought it." He willed himself to mention the one name he had avoided above all others in his conversations with her. "I know you belong to David, and it's wrong to covet what belongs to someone else."

She didn't move, but her breathing seemed shallow. Watching the struggle on her face, he let go of her arm and walked several feet away. He wished he had the power to rid himself of all wrong thoughts and impure desires. His enjoyment of her peace and happiness only escalated his desire for her and not for the One she said gave her the peace. His heart was so easily led the wrong way. He ought to walk away from her and save her from being contaminated by his sins.

"If you didn't mean it the way it sounded, what made you say it?"

Amazed at her willingness to talk about something so intimate with him, he turned to face her. Searching his soul, he remembered all the times he had made love to other women out of base desire. But with Cora, a singular longing drove him, increasing every time he saw the all-pervasive peace in her eyes. Peace he ached to have.

Lifting his gaze to her face, he said, "I guess I feel it's the only way I could have some of the peace that's so deep inside you."

Tears flooded her eyes. "Oh, Rye, you can't get peace from me. You can only get lasting peace from Jesus. He's the One who needs to live inside you. That's why I said you need to look at Him."

Desperation filled him. "I try. I do. But all I see is you."

She shook her head. "You've got to try harder. Either that, or I'll have to stop spending time with you."

"Don't say that!" Anguish twisted his heart. "What do I need to do so I can look at Jesus instead?"

She stilled as though listening, closing her eyes as he had often seen her do to pray.

The laughter of children sounded in the distance, and for a moment it seemed that heaven began to reach down to the earth where he lived. But before the feeling could solidify within him, a scream rent the air. He whirled toward the ocean.

The woman screamed again from where she treaded deep water. "Help! She's drowning!"

Rye flung his shoes on the sand. He ran out into the glistening water until the waves engulfed his chest. He flung himself forward, stroking powerfully to reach the frantic woman he recognized as Lydia, close friend of Terri the lifeguard.

"Where is she?" he asked when he reached her.

"Under me. Please help her!"

Rye dove deep into the surging waves. His pulse jumped as he saw Terri struggling on the ocean floor, a heavy chain wrapped around her leg.

He pulled on the weighty piece of anchor chain, freeing it after a dozen seconds. Terri's head dropped as he kicked hard for the surface. Her head broke the water with him, and he breathed in deeply, but she remained a dead weight in his arms. He stroked for the shore with his free arm while Lydia swam beside him, crying.

His feet touched bottom, and he swung Terri's unconscious form into his arms. He ran through the rolling tide, then hit the shore. Dropping to his knees, he lowered Terri to the ground and began artificial respiration. After pumping on her breastbone several times, her chest heaved.

He turned her onto her side and she bubbled up water then gasped in oxygen.

"Oh, thank God!" Lydia wrapped her arms tightly around her friend. "I can't believe that just happened."

Rye waited until Terri had breath enough to answer, then asked, "Do you know who put the chain around your leg?"

Terri shook her head, tears streaming down her face. "A man grabbed me under the water and wrapped it around my ankle. I couldn't get away."

Rye looked around the beach as he stood, but Sweeney was nowhere in sight.

Cora made her way toward them with her walking stick, and Rye pressed his lips together. So much for leisure time. The case had finally cracked open, and it appeared Sunnel's granddaughter had been found.

The only part he didn't like was how Sweeney had given Caleb the slip. Why had Caleb lost track of the assassin long enough for Sweeney to almost succeed with another murder?

Chapter Twenty-five

After Sweeney left the beachside restroom, Caleb followed him for an hour along country roads. Not wanting him to realize he had a tail since there were few vehicles on the roads, Caleb increased his distance. Although he disliked losing a visual, the tracking monitor told him that the Mercedes didn't stop along the way.

It seemed odd, though, when the drive took him back to the town of Summerland. When he caught up to the Mercedes in the parking lot of Al's Friendly Bar, Sweeney had already vacated it.

Disappointed that Sweeney was beginning his night of drinking already, Caleb entered the bar, but Sweeney wasn't in sight.

Caleb glanced toward the restrooms. Was Sweeney's stomach giving him problems? Had he needed to use the bathroom again?

Wanting to blend into the atmosphere while he waited, Caleb walked to the bar and ordered a drink. To his left, Dean raised his beer in a mock salute. "Arianna driving you to drink?"

Refusing to acknowledge the cut, Caleb accepted his beer and carried it to a far table. He pretended to drink, but after fifteen minutes, Sweeney still hadn't emerged.

Caleb headed to the restroom. Inside, all the stalls were empty.

He strode out of the bathroom. Sweeney must have slipped out the employee door, but the Mercedes remained in the parking lot.

Caleb jumped in the Ford and scoured the blocks around the bar, but he didn't catch sight of his target. Sweeney must have hailed a taxi. Had he suspected that he was being tailed? Angry with himself for losing him, Caleb hit Memory on his cell phone to warn Rye, but the kid didn't answer.

Hitting the End button in frustration, Caleb analyzed his best move. If

Sweeney had gone to such efforts to separate himself from his normal mode of transportation, he must be planning to go after the granddaughter. Mayla had bodyguards, but Terri was an open target.

Caleb punched in the resort's phone number. The desk clerk informed him that Terri's shift had ended two hours before.

Caleb drove to her apartment just in time to see Rye's Pinto pull up. He startled as Terri and a blonde-haired friend stepped out of the backseat, shivering in wet clothes. Rye stepped out as well, then followed them to the apartment door.

Caleb jumped out of the Ford and jogged across the street. "Rye!"

He turned and waved. Then he murmured something to the women before striding down the sidewalk. Caleb met him halfway as the women disappeared inside. "What's going on? I've been trying to call you, but you didn't answer."

"I lost my phone. Sweeney went after Terri. She almost drowned, but her friend called for help. Sweeney had wrapped a chain around Terri's leg, but I managed to get it off. My phone ended up in the water somewhere. So what happened on your end? How did you lose him?"

Caleb shook his head in disgust. "He slipped out of Al's bar before I got inside. He must have gotten edgy and decided to take a taxi to the resort. Have you told Sunnel yet?"

"No. I've been at the police station with the women for the last hour. "

"The last hour? I lost Sweeney twenty minutes ago."

Caleb sucked in his breath as realization hit. "Someone else must have been driving the Mercedes. It's like he knew I was following him and needed to get me out of the picture."

"Who would he have switched with? Jackson?"

"Maybe, but I didn't see him at the bar. Dean was there, though."

"Dean! He falsified the will for Jackson. And he was at the Y—"

Caleb narrowed his eyes. "You were visiting Cora, weren't you?"

Rye shrugged. "Dean was there too. I took her to the beach to get her away from him."

"There was no reason for you to get Cora away from him, not with you and Arianna in the cabin. You had your own reasons for getting her alone. I've warned you: keep away from her."

"She has her own mind, Cal, and she doesn't have a problem being with me."

"And her generous nature makes you worthy of her?"

Pain crossed Rye's face, and he looked away. "No. I know it doesn't."

Silence hung for a moment.

Rye drew in a deep breath. "It bothers me that Sweeney wrapped the chain around her leg. Why didn't he use it to strangle her instead? It doesn't make sense that he would take the chance she would be rescued. He knew there were people around who could help."

"Maybe he's squeamish about using his hands."

"Nobody hires a squeamish assassin. It seems more likely he wanted to divert our attention."

"We can't take the chance that Terri isn't the granddaughter. We need to guard her."

"She and her friend, Lydia, asked me to stay with them. They're scared to death."

"Did you show them one of our pictures?"

"If I did, I'd have to explain why I have it. And I don't want Terri to think she's going to inherit Sunnel's billions if she's not really the granddaughter."

"I'm going to stake out Sweeney's apartment. He has to get his stuff at some point. Then I can begin tailing him again."

Rye looked dubious. "He didn't have much of value in the apartment."

"In that case, he's probably going to make a move soon. At least we know it's either Terri or Mayla. And they're both protected."

Rye nodded slowly.

"I'll talk to you later." Caleb strode to the Ford and drove to Sweeney's motel. His gut told him that Rye's assessment was correct. Sweeney suspected a tail and had taken great pains to escape surveillance. He wasn't going to return to his apartment where he might easily be seen and tailed again.

His cell phone rang, and he glanced at the number. Arianna. He hit Answer out of sheer obligation.

Her voice was warm. "Hi, Caleb. Have you talked with Rye?"

"I just saw him. I take it you know what's going on."

"Yes. Rye dropped Cora back at her cabin before taking those two women to the police station. How horrible that woman almost drowned! Do you think she's Uncle Douglas's daughter?"

"I don't know. Rye doesn't think so. We're going to wait a couple more days to see if Sweeney attacks again."

"Are you still trailing Sweeney?" Disappointment touched her tone.

"No. I lost him. We think he figured out that we were following him."

"So are you guarding that woman and her friend?"

"Rye's staying with them."

"Does that mean you can come home? Cora helped me make an apple pie."

Caleb's chest tightened. It was still early. She would expect him to spend the whole evening with her and compliment her on the pie she had made. He could imagine the warmth she would respond with. But he couldn't handle her affection. Not right now.

"I need to visit Cora first. I'll be home later."

"Why?" Jealousy touched her voice.

"I'm tired of how much time Rye is spending with her, and I'm going to put a stop to it. You don't need to wait up for me." He pressed End before she could respond.

He drove to the YMCA campground, his mood darkening as he thought about how Rye had deliberately broken his command to not spend time with Cora. Twice. This time, though, he had not only gone to see Cora but had taken her to the beach. The kid was lucky Sweeney had struck, forcing him out of reach of Cora instead of Caleb doing it.

However, it was obvious Rye wasn't the only one who needed to understand that the relationship couldn't continue. It was time he set some things straight for Cora, too, especially since he hadn't seen anything of David, which meant the other man really was letting the betrothal fall to the ground.

Anger wouldn't accomplish his purpose as far as Cora was concerned, which left only one way to convince her that Rye wasn't suitable company.

Not looking forward to the upcoming conversation, he pulled the Ford up to Cora's cabin, strode up the steps, and knocked.

One of Cora's roommates answered the door. "Are you looking for Cora?"

"Yes. Please tell her Caleb's here."

"Sure." The girl looked him up and down with approval before going back inside.

Caleb stared grimly at his wedding ring. The girl's look reminded him of Arianna when they had first met. Would he ever be certain that her gaze wouldn't stray to other men? The way she had almost gone with Sweeney felt like a raw wound inside him.

Cora appeared in the doorway, her walking stick in hand and a surprised smile on her face. "Caleb! I didn't know you were coming."

"There's something I need to talk to you about. Mind if we take a walk?"

"Of course not." She stepped onto the porch, and he guided her down the steps. He let go of her arm as they began walking on the gravel path.

He didn't see any way to start the conversation except with a blunt question. "Cora, why did you go to the beach with Rye?"

She startled. "I didn't know I needed a reason. He said he had questions for me, and I didn't want to be around Dean any longer."

Caleb frowned. Dean was almost as persistent as Rye, except the kid had the advantage of Cora's friendship while the other man did not. "When you broke off with David, was Rye part of the equation?"

Her breath caught, and her face gave away the answer.

He steeled his resolve. "David may not be the man for you, but Rye definitely isn't."

She blushed. "I know that."

"Do you? Your actions seem to say otherwise."

A dismayed look crossed her face, and she seemed to struggle with her emotions. "I care about him, but he knows I want him to have a relationship with Jesus, not me."

Caleb shook his head. "You're setting Rye up to be a false convert."

"What?" She stopped walking.

"Do you think that if Rye does make a profession of faith he'll be doing it because he wants your Jesus? I don't think so. He'll do it because he wants you. I don't know how much he's told you, but when I found him, he was living as a gigolo in the slums of LA. He made love to women for money."

Strain washed over her features. "He told me it was just pretense for the case."

Caleb tightened his jaw. "It was. Here. But that's what he was for four years before I found him. Long enough to experience every depravity known to man. And Rye's admitted that he didn't refrain from anything when it came to women."

"Oh, Jesus." Cora slid her eyes shut, and Caleb felt pity for her. He should have known Rye's light-hearted demeanor and charming boyishness would affect her soft heart. But he couldn't let pity precede his adamancy that she sever the relationship.

He waited silently for several moments, letting her take in the impact of his words. Then he said, "You've got to stop hanging out with him. Whatever your motivation, I can tell you there's only one motivation for him. You have to stop leading him on. He can't offer you purity, and a man of his experience will never be content with just one woman. There's no way he could be faithful to you, even if he went so far as to offer you marriage."

Her lips moved silently.

He frowned, irritated. "Praying isn't going to change anything. You have to accept the facts."

She opened her eyes and turned toward him, anguish on her face. "How can you say that praying makes no difference? I know you believe in an almighty God, so why do you limit Him?"

He had never heard her reprimand him so strongly, and it took a moment for him to get past his astonishment. "Are you defending God or Rye?"

"God changes hearts. He could change yours, too, if you'd let Him."

He grasped her arm, provoked enough to let anger surface. "Don't you dare preach at me, Cora! You should be ashamed of how self-righteous you sound. As though you're the only one God will let into heaven."

She began to weep, covering her face with her hands. "I'm not the only one. But you have to accept God's provision. Our sins are greater than we can pay for without a Savior."

Caleb released her arm, frustrated with both of them for fighting over a subject they had agreed to disagree on years ago. He pulled his thoughts back to the argument he had to win. "Fine. Have it your way. But regardless of how much you believe God can wipe the slate clean for Rye, I'm telling you that people's pasts remain. He will be influenced by the things he's done all his life, even if he seeks to make it otherwise. Now, will you promise me to stop spending time with him?"

She pressed her fingers to her mouth. Tears glistened on her cheeks. "I can't make that promise. Only God knows when I've completed all He wants me to do."

Caleb clenched his fist. She could be so stubborn beneath her aura of peace!

He willed himself to try one more time to make her understand. "How long do you think Rye's self-control will last if you continue to put yourself in situations alone with him? You may think he would never hurt you, but he's trained his body to follow base instinct. For the past three years, he's followed my command and stayed away from girls. But in this last month he's started bending the rules—because of you. How long do you think it will take before he weakens and totally ignores the moral code I've taught him? I do not want you to be with him when his self-control snaps."

Her face went pale.

Finally he had gotten through to her. Just to make sure, he added, "You don't want to end up like your mother, do you?"

"Caleb!" Emotion choked her voice as though she couldn't believe he had pushed so hard. "Rye's nothing like that man!"

"How would you know?"

"I just do!" She spoke with desperation. "With Dean I feel fear over what he might do if I am ever alone with him. But I've never felt that way with Rye. Even when he—" She broke off, as though realizing she had almost admitted to something she shouldn't have.

Caleb said it for her. "Even when he tried to seduce you on the beach?"

"He didn't try to seduce me. He just kissed me."

Caleb couldn't believe how she continued to defend the kid. "And how many times has he done that? How many times has he lacked the self-control to respect your betrothal to David? Or did you not tell him?"

She trembled under his attack. "I told him."

"And you think he'll stop with kisses?"

"He has stopped." Cora pulled in a ragged breath. "He hasn't kissed me since he found out my name."

Well, that was something. Caleb frowned. "Does he know you've broken your engagement to David?"

She shook her head.

"Good. Don't tell him. Maybe believing you belong to someone else and fear of retribution have held him at bay."

Cora gasped. "Retribution? What are you talking about?"

Caleb grimaced. In his fear for her, he had said too much. "Never mind. He hasn't touched you at all since finding out who you are?"

She hesitated.

"What has he done?"

"He's kissed my hand. That's all, I promise."

She bit her lip as she apparently thought of something else, and Caleb refused to let her protect the kid any longer. "What else? Tell me, Cora."

"He said he wanted to make love to me."

Caleb swore then caught her arm as she shrank away. "See? There's only one thing on his mind. You've got to stay away from him!"

She trembled, and silence hung between them for a long moment. Finally, Caleb pulled her into his arms. "I'm sorry. I just want to keep you safe."

She embraced him in return. "I know you do. Sometimes I think you feel that if you don't, God will let something terrible happen."

"Something terrible did happen. Or have you forgotten?" He brushed his hand over her sightless eyes. "God didn't stop that, did He? Why do you think He'll stop a worse thing?"

"He loves me. He won't let anything happen that He can't redeem."

Caleb grasped her arms. "I don't want you salvaged. I want you whole!"

"He won't fail me. God never fails."

He couldn't keep from scoffing as he let go of her arms. "He failed seven years ago. Come on, I'm taking you back to your cabin."

She walked silently with him. At her cabin, he acknowledged her quiet good-night then stepped into the Ford. Glancing at the time, he realized it was only nine o'clock. He had planned to stay longer with Cora, but her stubbornness had frustrated him too much. Sighing, he headed back to Summerland.

He didn't go to the bungalow, though. It was too early, and Arianna would still be up. Instead, he headed to a small café and nursed coffee for over an hour. Finally, he paid the bill and headed home.

The lights were off when he arrived, and he breathed a sigh of relief. However, it was short-lived, for as soon as he entered, the bedroom light switched on. It cast a block of light across the living area floor, with Arianna's shadow in it. His stomach tightened. She was wearing one of his T-shirts, and her hair was disheveled, making her look young and much too inviting.

She walked closer, her gaze holding too much emotion for his good. He looked away, and she stopped from coming closer.

"How long are you going to punish me for just wanting to be your wife?" Her voice held longing.

He could imagine holding her. Imagine how it would feel to have her melt against him as she had done in the past.

But she had manipulated him without a qualm and threatened to sleep with another man. He clenched his hand as anger flickered. "You were going to be my wife in one year. But you weren't willing to wait."

"I said I was sorry. What more can I do?"

"Prove you want my heart instead of my body." Prove she wouldn't tear his heart to pieces once he made her one with him.

She gazed at him with yearning and vulnerability. "I want all of you. Is that so wrong?"

An aching desire swept him. All he had to do was let go of his anger. All he had to do was believe that her desire for him would last.

But he couldn't do it. Not yet. She had to understand he wasn't like the other men she had known, where only the physical mattered. He valued the sanctity of marriage, and there were consequences to the choices she had made. He hardened his resolve. "Go to bed, Arianna. I'm tired of arguing, and I want to sleep."

Pain filled her eyes. His heart contracted with its intensity, and he looked away, not wanting to let her hurt dissuade him. She seemed to sense his struggle and stayed a moment longer. Finally, she walked toward the bedroom. The door shut harder than needed, and he sank to the couch, putting his head in his hands.

He felt incredibly weary, but it was deeper than a physical tiredness. Beneath his anger over Rye's behavior toward Cora lay hurt that the kid had failed to change after their years together. And if the kid's past still held that much sway over him, Arianna's would influence her as well. Why had he thought he could make such a difference in their lives?

Chapter Twenty-six

I t didn't work."

Dean frowned at Sweeney's assessment. They had met in the back of a roadside gas station, Sweeney driving a new rental car since he had ditched the Mercedes. He hadn't sounded happy on the phone when Dean had called, and he didn't keep his displeasure hidden now. "They didn't return to LA like you thought, and I need to go after the girl. Now. Before they figure out who she is. They obviously don't think Laven's the grand-daughter."

Dean thought fast. Words wouldn't convince Sweeney to wait, but money would if he offered enough. He took a deep breath. "I'll give you ten thousand if you'll wait a couple more days. I need your help getting to Cora. Then you can finish Jackson's job."

Sweeney frowned. "She hardly seems worth the bother. But that's your call. You'll need a way to get her away from the Y, where people are always watching out for her."

"She seems smitten with Tyler. I think I can convince her to go to his apartment. But I'll need you to create a distraction so the person who drives her there will leave."

"What if it's Abrams? He's been hanging out at her cabin in the evenings. I can't have him on my tail when you're done."

"Then I'll make sure he's busy elsewhere so she has to ask someone else to drive her. He's spent the last two nights at the Y, but I think he'll come running if he thinks Arianna's cheating on him. I'll get her to come to a club with me."

Sweeney's black eyes gleamed. "I'd love to see his face if she was with me again." He turned thoughtful. "A club isn't somewhere he usually hangs out. You'll need a reason for him to be there. If I let him tail me again, I could lead him there. Then you could leave Arianna with me. Abrams is sure to come out of the shadows if he sees me making out with her. I'm sure his jealousy will outweigh duty to his job. I should have plenty of time to slip away while he decides how to deal with his wayward wife. Then I can meet you at Tyler's motel. Do you know how you're going to convince Cora to meet you there?"

Dean grinned. "I've got an idea."

The next afternoon, Dean set his plan into motion. He drove into Summerland and rapped on the door to Caleb and Arianna's bungalow. Like usual, Caleb was gone, and Arianna opened the door.

She looked at him sourly. "What do you want?"

"My, my, aren't we in a mood this afternoon? Husband still hasn't laid you?"

She glared at him. "Why are you here? You haven't been nice to me once since I married Caleb."

"Marrying Caleb was a mistake," he said. "I just want you to see that and get on with your life. There's so much more out there that you could be enjoying. In fact, I know someone who's very interested in you. I'm meeting with him tonight and told him maybe you'd join us."

Arianna's gaze darkened. "Did you tell him I'm married?"

Dean shook his head. "Nan, Nan. When will you realize that a piece of paper is worthless unless a person actually does something about it? You need to get out. You've been cooped up in this room for a long time. Let Lindon get a little jealous. Maybe he'll notice you again."

She gazed at him with stormy eyes. He waited patiently, and at last she said in a curt tone, "Fine."

"Good. I'll pick you up at nine."

Caleb straightened in the Ford, where he had staked out Sweeney's old motel room, although he doubted the man would return. Time sat heavy on his hands. Mayla had refused to hire him back, and Rye was guarding Terri. With no other leads to follow, Caleb alternated his time between hanging out with Cora and watching Sweeney's room in the hope that he would risk coming back for his belongings.

He watched in hopeful surprise as a man in a long trench coat and hat inserted a key into Sweeney's door. He was too tall to be the landlord, and moments later, he emerged with Sweeney's suitcase. The man slipped into a rented Nissan, and Caleb turned the ignition. Remembering that Rye had lost his cell phone, he punched in Terri's home number as he followed the rental down a side street.

Rye answered the phone.

"I think I've got Sweeney. He grabbed his suitcase from his apartment. Probably thought we gave up keeping watch."

"Great! Call me if he comes close to this area."

"I will."

Caleb hit End and sped through a yellow light to stay on the Nissan's tail. Even if Sweeney became suspicious, he couldn't risk losing him before he had the chance to plant a tracking device and see where Sweeney was staying.

Arianna clenched her hands as the minute hand on the clock neared nine. Caleb would be angry with her if he found out she had gone out with Uncle Ben tonight. But her uncle's words had cut deep, especially after a week of Caleb's absence.

Caleb avoided being with her in the bungalow except to sleep and wouldn't respond to any of her pleas for a real marriage. She had pushed down the pain of his coldness by reminding herself that he needed time.

After all, his passion was the main character trait that drew her to him.

But since Uncle Ben's visit, the suppressed pain had begun to fester. She couldn't bear the thought of another night alone. Uncle Ben's company would at least keep the pain at bay a while longer.

She stood as car lights shone through the window. Grabbing her purse, she headed to the door.

Uncle Ben's eyes gleamed as she slipped into the Mustang's passenger seat. "Glad you're ready to go. A night out is going to be good for you."

He drove to a night club on the other side of town. Arianna frowned. "I'm still a minor, you know."

"You're with me. And every guy in this place is going to want to keep you here."

She scowled, not liking his casual assumption of what the night would bring. "I'm not stepping out on him."

"Of course not." He pulled the Mustang into a spot on the far side of the parking lot. There weren't any street lights, and the building nearby cast a long, deep shadow over the area.

Arianna stepped out of the car, but Uncle Ben paused when his cell phone vibrated. She frowned as he turned his back and walked a little ways from her, speaking in a muted tone. She crossed her arms, and several minutes slipped by. Uncle Ben walked farther into the darkness.

Movement caught her eye, and she straightened as the shape of a man headed toward her out of the darkness.

A flicker of fear grabbed at her throat.

Sweeney emerged from the shadows. His black eyes glinted with satisfaction. "Hello, Nan."

She sucked in a shallow breath and jerked her gaze to where Uncle Ben had been. But he had disappeared.

Sweeney stepped in front of her. "Looking for your uncle? He's already agreed to let me have the evening with you, so you don't need to expect him back."

Arianna stared. Uncle Ben had set her up?

Sweeney's gaze moved over her then returned to her face. Raw desire emanated from him, and heat poured into her. "I...I'm married."

He stepped closer. Too close. But she couldn't pull her gaze away from his.

He smiled sensuously. "From what I hear you still need someone to make love to you. Unlike your husband, I'm more than willing to do the job." He pulled her to him and absorbed her into his kiss.

The strength of his passion flooded her even as her mind cried out, *Oh, God, I don't want this!* But her body's hunger for pleasure betrayed her. She melted against him.

A harsh voice commanded, "Let her go."

She jerked her head around as Sweeney pushed away from her.

Horrified, she stared at Caleb's rock-hard face as he strode toward them across the parking lot. Sweeney stepped backward into the shadows while Caleb's wrathful gaze speared her. "Do you want to go with him and finish it?"

She pressed her hands to her mouth as tears poured down her face. "No, Caleb. I'm sorry. I'm so sorry!"

Caleb narrowed his eyes. Then his attention shifted. He dug his fingers into her elbow and propelled her in the direction Sweeney had gone.

The darkness seemed to have swallowed the other man, and Caleb broke into a run. Arianna sprinted beside him. Then abruptly Caleb halted. "He's gone."

She trembled. His voice was so hard. So cold. She looked up at him, but could barely stand to meet his gaze. Past the anger was deep, soul-throbbing pain.

Tears welled. "Uncle Ben set me up."

The hardness in his eyes didn't lessen. But why should it? How could she expect him to believe she hadn't wanted Sweeney? Caleb had feared she was too weak to remain faithful, and she had proven him right.

She began to weep. "I didn't want him, Caleb. But I couldn't pull away."

"I know. I almost let you go. But for some reason, I thought you might want me to stop him."

She choked on a sob. She reached for him, desperate for his strength. He let her cling to his chest for a long moment. Then he slipped his arms around her, closing her into a place of safety.

Dean slipped a lockpick into the doorknob of Tyler's hotel room then eased inside when the lock clicked open. He glanced at his watch. Barely five minutes since he had left Arianna. Anticipation hummed along his veins. He picked up the room's phone and dialed Cora's cabin. He hoped she wouldn't be the one to pick up, and luck played into his hands. One of her roommates answered. "Hello?"

Dean strained his voice as if in pain. "Is Cora there? I need her to come. Right away."

"Who is this?"

"Rye. Just tell her I need her to come before Caleb gets here."

"Are you okay?"

"Just tell her. Grandview Hotel, room 14."

Dean ended the connection and smiled. Cora refused to be anywhere near him, but for Tyler she'd do anything.

Not wanting Cora to realize immediately that he wasn't Rye, Dean pulled open a dresser drawer and found Tyler's shirts. Tossing aside his polo shirt, he slipped into a loose tee. How well it fit didn't matter because Cora relied on her other senses. Tyler's scent would keep her defenses lowered long enough to give him the upper hand.

"Rye said he needed you to get to his room before your uncle. And he sounded like he was hurt."

Cora's breath caught. Her roommate, Sybil, had hurried into the room they shared in Cabin 10 to tell her about Rye's strange phone call. Rye was hurt? What had Caleb done?

Fear of retribution has held him at bay.

Caleb's words from last night haunted her. Had something happened to incite him to attack Rye? "Do he say what hotel he's staying at?"

"Yes, the Grandview."

"Will you find the phone number for me?"

"Sure. Just a minute."

Cora waited nervously until Sybil said, "You want me to call?"

"No, just tell me the number."

Cora punched in the numbers as Sybil dictated.

A desk clerk answered within two rings. "Grandview Hotel."

"Could I have room 14?"

"Sure."

The connection rang, and Cora's heart thumped. Her anxiety grew as the call went unanswered. Had Caleb already arrived at Rye's room? What if he was keeping Rye from answering? What if his anger had led him to severely hurt Rye? Whatever fight the partners were involved in, she felt responsible since she was certain it concerned her. She hung up the phone. "Sybil, can you take me to Rye's hotel? He's not answering."

"Sure. I'll get my keys."

In the car, Sybil asked, "Do you think your uncle beat him up?"

Cora swallowed. "I can't imagine..." But her voice trailed off because, unfortunately, she could.

Caleb pulled out his cell phone to call Rye at Terri's house to tell him that Sweeney had escaped his surveillance again, but his phone didn't turn on. He hadn't realized his battery was getting so low. Grimacing, he slipped the phone back into its case.

Arianna sat silently a foot from him, her shoulders hunched.

She should be ashamed, Caleb thought as he pulled the Ford to the front of bungalow. Though he had let her step into his embrace, the pain of her wantonness burned through him.

When he saw her with Sweeney, rage had swept him. She was his wife, but she had willingly kissed another man. He wanted to lay all the blame of her adulterous actions at her feet and walk away from the folly of their marriage. But his conscience had goaded him. *Your stubbornness brought her to this point. You know sex is her weakness. So why did you withhold it where it is permissible and leave her vulnerable to the lure of someone else?*

He had fought the tentacles of guilt that wrapped around him. But they had singed him with responsibility for her actions. If he was part of the reason she had been tempted elsewhere, he couldn't stand by without giving her the chance to choose again.

When he appeared, she hadn't given Sweeney another glance. Instead she had reached out to him with anguished tears. Maybe he really was the only one she wanted. But that meant he had to somehow bring her flesh into subservience to her will.

He stepped out of the Ford, then slammed the door shut. He unlocked their room and looked over to where she sat in the truck. She seemed to be waiting to make sure he really wanted her back.

Finally she stepped out of the Ford. He watched with turbulent emotions as she walked to him. She kept her head down as she entered the bungalow.

He stepped inside and closed the door. She didn't look at him as she crossed to the bedroom. She closed the door, and he gazed at it angrily. She had not gone a night yet without offering herself to him. But it seemed her guilt wouldn't let her do so tonight.

Conflicting emotions struggled for mastery within him. Though he had vowed not to have her on her terms, it appeared that if he held to his intense standards, he wouldn't have her at all. She was too easily tempted, too weak to resist taking what every man offered her except him.

He should have let her go the first night she lit a cigarette on her father's porch in defiance of him. Instead, he had thought he could change her and had let her wind herself into every corner of his heart. Now it was too late to undo the past or the commitment he had made. A commitment that so far had only cost him and given him nothing in return.

His heart rate intensified as the reasons for withholding himself shriveled away. She was his wife, and he wanted her.

The telephone hung on the wall, reminding him that he hadn't warned Rye about losing Sweeney. But he ignored it. He was certain Terri was the granddaughter, and Rye was guarding her. He had used the case as an excuse to neglect his marriage. But not anymore. Not tonight.

He opened the bedroom door without knocking. She sat up in bed, startled.

He took in the tear streaks on her face and felt a raw sort of satisfaction. She hadn't wanted Sweeney, but he had given her nothing to empower her to resist another man. Well, now she would be without excuse.

He drew off his shirt, and her breathing accelerated. He smiled grimly. "I'm joining you tonight."

When she drew back the covers, he slipped in, finally willing to play the game her way.

Cora could tell Sybil was driving faster than usual through town to Rye's hotel. The car leaned sharply at every curve. Then Sybil braked abruptly. "Here it is. Come on, I'll help you find the room."

"Thanks." Cora waited on the sidewalk for Sybil to join her, then felt her way forward with the walking stick.

Sybil instructed, "There's a stairway to the second floor on your right."

Cora hesitated, remembering the first time she had met Rye. A nudge of caution urged her to double check her friend's information. "Could you go to the office first and make sure 14 is actually Rye's room?"

"You don't think he'd remember his own room number?"

"Just go ask, okay?"

"Okay."

Cora had to swallow her anxiety over Rye's welfare while she waited, but soon Sybil returned. "Yep. Rye Nelson is renting room 14."

Cora remembered the false last name that Rye had given Dean at the hospital. "Okay."

Sybil started with her up the stairs. "Do you think he'll be hurt bad? I saw my brother beat up a guy one time and it was—"

Sybil halted abruptly, letting go of her arm. "Someone's breaking into my car!"

She clattered down the stairs, yelling at the thief. Cora hesitated. She couldn't get the image out of her mind of Rye lying on the floor, badly beaten. He had begged her to come before Caleb did, but it had taken thirty minutes to drive to town. Caleb could have already come and gone, leaving Rye severely hurt.

Carefully, she headed up the staircase alone. It creaked with every step, and when she arrived at the top, she traced her hand along the wall until she came to a door. The room number was embossed on it, and she traced the number 10.

Two doors down, she found the right number and knocked lightly.

A moan sounded on the other side. Her heart thumped hard. "Rye? It's Cora."

Another painful moan reached her, and she pressed aside her inhibitions. The door wasn't locked, and she pushed it open. The musty smell of an old room reached her along with the faint scent of pine. She stepped inside. "Rye? Are you okay?"

She turned as his warm presence came between her and the door. A click sounded. He wrapped a strong arm around her waist and pulled her close against his cotton shirt.

Confused and relieved at the same time, she tipped her head back. "I thought you were hurt."

He took her walking stick out of her hand and whispered against her cheek, "I knew you'd come."

Terror and unbelief poured into her. *Dean!* She screamed, but his mouth bore down on hers, smothering the sound.

She jerked her face away, screaming again. He backhanded her. Pain split through her head, but the steel hold of his arm kept her from falling.

"I don't want to get rough with you," he murmured. "But if you're not going to let me do this the easy way, so be it."

He tore the neckline of her dress, and she kicked out hard. He twisted her arm behind her back. She cried out as her knees buckled. He shoved her down, and her head hit the floor with sickening pain.

His breathing became hard and laborious, his hands going where she didn't want them. He had her at his will. Jesus was letting it happen again, just like it had to her mother.

The raw pain of abandonment rushed through her. Terror swept her into merciful darkness.

Chapter Twenty-seven

Rye paced by the couch for the hundredth time that evening, his gut churning for no apparent reason. Terri and Lydia took turns glancing at him where they played a card game at the kitchen table. They had invited him to join them, but he couldn't force himself to sit still.

Something was wrong. Something was really, really wrong. But he had no idea what it was.

He kept replaying the recent events in his mind. He twisted them in different directions to try to make sense of why Sweeney hadn't killed Terri outright. He had had plenty of time to do so underwater. Instead of wrapping a chain around her leg, he could just as easily have used it around her throat. So why hadn't he?

The question nagged, as did the matter of why Sweeney had switched vehicles. He and Caleb were trained to stay in the shadows. Unless Sweeney had been tipped off, discovering them would have been unlikely.

No answer made sense, and as the evening slipped into night, his anxiety heightened. He glanced at the clock. 9:40.

He needed to do something to reassure himself he was in the right place with the right girl. Terri's near drowning had tied him to her, making him feel useless.

He glanced at the clock again. 9:41. Desperate to stop the anxiety eating at him, he strode to the phone. If he had to stay put, he could at least talk to the one person who always brought a measure of calm to his spirit. Caleb had told him to stay away from her, but surely a phone call wouldn't be bending the rules. He dialed the Y and asked for Cora Abrams.

"One moment. I'll put you through to Cabin 10."

He forced himself to stand still as he waited through several rings. Finally, a girl picked up. "Hello?"

He tried to affect an easy demeanor. "Is Cora there?"

"No, but I can leave a message. Who is this?"

"It's Rye. Do you know when she'll be back?"

"Rye?" The girl sounded puzzled. "Isn't Cora with you? Sybil took her thirty minutes ago to meet you, like you asked."

His breath halted. "What do you mean like *I* asked?"

"Aren't you the one who said you needed Cora to come help you?"

"No. Where is she supposed to be meeting me?"

"At Grandview, Room 14. Is that your room?"

Adrenaline surged. "Yes. Call Grandview and tell them there's an intruder in my room. And tell them to stop a blind girl from going in there."

"Okay, but why—?"

Rye slammed the phone down. He sent one quick look at Terri and Lydia. "Sorry. I've got to go."

He threw the apartment door open. Terrified he was already too late, he ran to the Pinto. He had to stop whoever had called Cora, though he needed only one guess.

Dean swore under his breath. She had fainted!

He pulled back from Cora's limp form and regarded her grimly where she lay on the floor. She wasn't getting out of this that easily. He had no wish to satisfy his lust while she was comatose. He carried her to the disarrayed sheets on Tyler's bed and shook her shoulders. She didn't stir, so he went to the bathroom to wet a washcloth with cold water.

Bringing the washcloth to the bed, he frowned when a knock sounded on the door.

"Management." A deep, male voice called through the door.

"I'm busy," Dean grumbled. "What's the problem?"

"You all right?"

"Fine. Why?"

"Someone called in a prank. Sorry to bother you."

Footsteps retreated, and Dean frowned. Had one of the other residents reported Cora's scream to the manager? If so, he couldn't let her scream again.

He found a handkerchief in Tyler's dresser and tied it around her mouth. He retrieved the wet washcloth and rung its cold water onto her face. She began to stir, and he pinned her arms to the bed.

Cold horror swept her face.

He smiled with satisfaction. "Yes, I'm still here, and you might as well accept the inevitable. No one's going to come save you."

Her face whitened, and she fought against him. But he was stronger, and the God she served had deserted her to his pleasure.

Rye took the stairs three at a time, praying desperately that the hotel clerk had believed Cora's friend about an intruder in his room. He reached the second floor landing and slipped his key into his room's doorknob.

Tussling sounds reached him, and he slammed the door open. His pulse jumped with raw fury when he saw Dean on top of Cora.

He threw Dean off her and sent a hard right to the man's jaw, knocking Dean to the floor. Hauling him up, Rye hit him again. Blood squirted from Dean's nose. Then he fell to the floor, unconscious.

Rye yanked off his belt. He pulled Dean's hands around his back and fastened them tightly in place.

Behind him, Cora choked on a sob.

He walked to the phone and dialed 911. "I've got a rapist at Grandview Hotel, room 14."

"Patrol car's ten minutes out."

Rye dropped the phone. Ten minutes. He dragged Dean to the bathroom and stuck a chair under the doorknob. Dean wouldn't be going anywhere even if he awakened.

Cora's weeping filled the room. Rye stood a moment with his back to her. She needed something to replace the dress Dean had torn away.

He pulled open his dresser drawer and grabbed a T-shirt. It seemed pitifully inadequate when what she needed was for God to have given him just five more minutes.

God, why? Even though he had driven faster than he ever had in his life, the blood on his bed said he had been too late to save her.

Emotional pain seared him, and he wished Caleb had found her instead of him. She wouldn't want him near her. Not when he had told her he wanted what Dean had taken. However, neither did he want her to face the police uncovered.

He drew in a steadying breath. "Hershey, do you have the blanket around you? I've got a shirt to give you."

Her weeping caught.

He waited until she whispered in a choked voice, "Okay."

He walked slowly to the edge of the bed. Her countenance was etched with agony, and her disheveled hair fell on bare shoulders. She had pulled his blanket to her chest, her knees drawn up underneath it. Her whole body shook uncontrollably.

Compassion rolled over him in waves. "Oh, Cora... I'm so sorry, baby. Here. I'm gonna put the shirt over your head."

He slipped the T-shirt on her and held it out so she could put in first one arm then the other. Tears steamed down her cheeks. "I thought you were hurt. I came to help you, but he was here instead."

"I know." Grief overwhelmed him along with unaccountable shame. He didn't deserve the trust that had led her to enter his apartment alone.

In the distance, a siren sounded.

Cora gasped. She reached out to him blindly.

Rye took her hand.

"Don't leave me."

He tightened his hold on her fingers. "I won't. I promise."

But as he said it, he remembered Terri and the way he had deserted her. Even though Caleb was following Sweeney, he cringed over his abandonment of duty. He had been too late for Cora. What if something happened to Terri while he lingered here?

He glanced at the phone. "I'm sorry. I need to make a quick call. I'm supposed to be guarding Terri, but I rushed over here when I found out Dean had tricked you."

Cora let go of his hand and wrapped her arms around her drawn-up legs.

He made the call. Terri answered immediately, her tone upset. "Where are you?"

"I'll be back as soon as I can. Call the police if you think someone's trying to get in the house." He glanced at where Cora sat with her eyes closed and tears streaming. His heart smote him. "I've got to go."

He set the receiver down just as the door opened. A serious-faced policeman strode into the room, one hand on the hilt of his revolver. His gaze swept Cora. "I'm Officer Jetson. What's going on?"

Rye grabbed Dean's slacks and walked to the bathroom door. "The man you want is in here."

He opened the door. His gaze hardened as it fell on Dean, who was awake and infuriated.

Fear touched Dean's gaze as Officer Jetson appeared.

Rye felt a grim satisfaction until he recognized his T-shirt on Dean. Fury poured back in at the lengths Dean had gone to in order to deceive Cora.

Officer Jetson pulled his handcuffs off his belt. "Do you know who he is?"

"Benjamin Dean. He's been staying at the Summerland Resort. He tricked Cora into coming here tonight—"

Dean's foul curse cut him off, and Jetson snapped the cuffs in place. "All right, buddy. You're under arrest. You have the right to remain silent."

Dean cursed more, but Jetson jerked him to his feet. "Get dressed." He kept his hand on his gun as Dean obeyed, then prompted him out of the bathroom.

In the hall, Jetson paused to look at Rye. "Don't go anywhere. I'll be returning to take down statements. Dr. Miller is on his way too." Pity touched his face. "He has to get proof of rape, so don't let her shower."

Rye's stomach twisted. *Oh, Cora. I'm so sorry.*

He closed the door and walked to Cora. She was rocking back and forth, lost in inner turmoil. He could imagine the nightmare that kept replaying in her mind. Of course, the police would need to know every detail.

Dying inside for her sake and longing to wash away whatever images were tormenting her, he sat down a foot from her on the bed. "The officer took Dean away, but now the doctor has to come."

She gave no indication that she had heard him.

He drew in a tight breath and touched her arm. "Cora, you're safe now." Safe but not whole.

She continued to rock without response.

"Hershey." He grasped her upper arms. "Baby, please answer me."

She gasped as though coming up from deep water. She cried out with agony, "Jesus, help me!"

Rye stared at her. She called out to Him even though He had failed her?

He let go of her arms and couldn't keep the bitterness from his voice. "He didn't stop Dean. What can He do for you now?"

Her breathing grew ragged, and her face spasmed.

His conscience cut deep. Had he hurt her all over again? "I'm sorry. Forgive me. I know God means the world to you." He clenched his hands into fists. "But why didn't He stop Dean? I don't understand why He would let someone hurt you if He loves you so much." Wasn't God's love supposed to be greater than his own? If he had had the power, he would never have let Dean touch her.

She whispered something, but he couldn't distinguish the words. Her eyes closed, and his heart twisted. Always she prayed. In every situation and for every need. Even when he knew she didn't understand the reason for her pain.

A knock sounded on the door, and fear shot across her face.

He stood. "That'll be Dr. Miller. He has to… examine you."

New agony jumped into her sightless eyes.

He turned away, then walked to the door to open it.

The doctor who had given her the antivenom for the snake bite met his gaze with deep concern. "May I come in?"

Rye stepped out of the way.

Recognition touched Miller's face as he entered the room. Fatherly pity reflected in his eyes behind his glasses. He laid a hand on Cora's arm. "My dear. I'm so sorry, but…"

She lifted her face. "You have to get evidence, don't you?"

"Yes."

She shook her head, new tears streaming.

Miller glanced at the blood on the bed, then at Rye. "It'd be easier for her if you stepped out of the room."

Though Cora had asked him not to leave, Rye knew there was no way he could stay. He told her raggedly, "I'm just outside the door."

He stepped into the hall, closing the door after him. Then he put his head against the wall and wept.

Chapter Twenty-eight

As soon as Officer Jetson left for the second time, having obtained the details of Cora's attack, Rye tried to track down Caleb. For some reason, Caleb's cell phone was turned off, so Rye called his bungalow room. He received no answer there either.

Dropping the phone back on the hook, Rye ran a hand through his hair. Caleb could be out all night trailing Sweeney. But he couldn't keep Cora at his place. He needed to find her somewhere else to stay.

He walked to where she sat with her head buried in her knees and his T-shirt drawn over her legs. Jetson's detailed questions had been a nightmare for her. But there had been nothing he could do except hold her hand.

He sat next to her and waited for her to acknowledge his presence. After a moment, she lifted her head.

He drew in a deep breath. "I don't know where Caleb is, but I need to get you some clothes and a place to stay. Can I take you back to the Y?"

Anguish broke out on her face. "Don't take me there. Please. The girls are sweet, but I don't want them to see me."

Rye's heart tightened. Of course she didn't want to be exposed to public speculation and gossip.

"Okay, not there. But then I need to call the Hauzens. They can take care of you until I get ahold of Caleb."

She closed her eyes, the tears trickling down. "I don't want them knowing, either."

Rye clenched his hand in frustration. "You can't keep something like this a secret. David's going to find out after you're married. Better he finds out now so he doesn't assume something against you then."

She put her hands over her head and cried brokenly. "We're not going to be married."

Pain twisted his heart. Surely David would accept her. After all, the rape was in no way her fault. For her sake, he pushed himself to ignore his own torment to reassure her. "Cora, it's not your fault. David isn't going to hold this against you."

She wept more. "No, it's—I broke the engagement weeks ago."

He stared at her. She had broken the engagement? Was she crying because she regretted her choice?

He didn't trust himself to question her, and after a moment, she lifted her head, wiping the tears from her face. "Please. I just want to wait for Caleb."

He drew in a deep breath, then stood. "Okay. Why don't you lie down and try to sleep? It's almost eleven, but I'll keep trying to reach him."

"I don't think I can sleep. But thank you, Rye. You're always here when I need help."

She looked so vulnerable he couldn't pull his gaze away. He trembled with an urgent need to pull her into his arms. More than anything, he wanted to wipe away her nightmare. But would she accept such comfort from him?

His shoulders slumped. He knew. She hadn't told him before about the broken engagement despite her attraction to him. Rather than give in to it, though, she had always told him she wanted him to pursue Jesus. Not her.

Despairing, he walked to the phone. Frustration mounted as it rang and rang. He replaced the receiver with a hard jingle.

Cora had once again covered her head with her hands. Cursing silently because Caleb wasn't available when she most needed him, Rye walked across the room, then slumped into a chair. He shielded his eyes with his hand. He couldn't bear to see her in so much pain and do nothing to comfort her. He tried to pray as he had seen her do so often. But he felt only a bitter ache inside.

Beautiful peace had always existed in Cora's eyes before. But now her peace had been cruelly shattered. He didn't think even God could put the pieces back together.

Caleb rolled over in bed, hearing the muted ring of the phone once again. He had ignored it earlier in the evening, before he and Arianna had fallen asleep, but he knew it was Rye since no one else would call so late. Annoyed that the case couldn't wait just one more night, he swung his feet to the floor.

Reaching for his boxers, he took a moment to glance at Arianna. Her hair was disheveled from his kisses, and her features were softened by sleep. His pulse heightened, but the phone pulled his attention away. Pulling on the boxers, he strode out to the wall telephone and answered tersely. "This had better be important."

Rye's tone mirrored his irritation. "Do you think I'd call for anything else? Dean raped Cora."

"What?" Caleb went rigid with shock. For a moment he couldn't think or react. Rye couldn't be serious. Cora was always with someone, and she would not allow herself to be alone with Dean. His gut twisted. "Where is she?"

"He lured her to my apartment. I found them too late, but Dean's in custody now. The police and doctor have already been here. They have everything they need to convict him."

Black spots danced in front of Caleb's eyes. Cora had gone to Rye's hotel alone? After all his warnings? "Are you still at your room?"

"Yes. Cora wouldn't let me take her anywhere until you came." Rye paused, then said with obvious pain, "I need to go to the Y and get her some clothes after you get here."

Caleb pressed his forehead into the wall as pain swept over him in waves. Rape... again. It seemed the women of his family were cursed. Swearing at the One who would allow it to continue happening, he hung up and strode to the bedroom to get dressed.

Arianna stirred as he headed out the door. She pushed the hair from her face, looking at him with new depths of need and desire in her eyes. But she didn't ask where he was going.

He couldn't bring himself to speak the awful words about Cora, so he said in a hard tone, "I'll be back in a couple hours." He let his gaze run over her. "Stay here. I want more."

She nodded.

Satisfied, Caleb strode out to the Ford and headed to Rye's hotel.

Rye was thankful Cora hadn't heard him explain what had happened to Caleb. Despite her words that she wouldn't be able to sleep, she had fallen into an exhausted slumber around one, curled into a ball under his blanket.

Sighing, Rye waited for the minutes to inch by on the bedside clock. Ten minutes passed, then a sharp rap sounded on the door.

Rye jumped up, hoping the sound hadn't wakened Cora, but she remained hidden under his blanket. Pressing his lips together, he prepared himself for the forthcoming conversation and opened the door.

Caleb entered the room. His gaze swept Rye, then halted on Cora's dark head, the only part of her that was visible. He strode over to her. Before Rye realized what he meant to do, he shook her shoulder. "Cora, wake up."

Rye swore softly. "What do you think you're doing? She just fell asleep an hour ago. I'll answer your questions."

Caleb's gaze scorched him. "I don't want your version, Tyler."

Rye threw his hands into the air, scarcely able to contain his anger. "Fine. Then call the police and get the sordid details from them. Cora's already had to relive the nightmare one time tonight. Don't make her do it again."

Caleb frowned and looked back at her. She hadn't moved. He pushed the blanket down a little and brushed the hair away from her face, exposing her worn-out features. Rye had to look away. Even in sleep, she looked like she was in pain.

Caleb swore bitterly and put the cover back. "Dean's gonna pay for this."

Rye met Caleb's fury with his own anger. "Yes, he will. In a court of law, where Cora will have to face him all over again."

"I'll kill him first."

Rye had no doubt Caleb would do exactly that if he could get at Dean. But Dean was behind prison bars, protected from personal vengeance.

Rye made no attempt to bring reason into the situation. Instead, he muttered, "I'd better get her clothes. Then I need to get back to Terri. Do you know where Sweeney is?"

"No. I lost him."

Rye sighed. "I told Terri to call the police if anything happens."

He headed to the door. But as he reached it, Cora cried out in her sleep. His heart ricocheted with anguish, and he turned instinctively.

Caleb bent over her. "Cora, wake up."

"Jesus, help!"

Caleb brushed damp tendrils away from her face. "Cora, it's Caleb. I'm going to take care of you."

She sucked in a desperate breath and reached out to him. "Oh, Caleb, I'm sorry. I'm so sorry."

Caleb drew her into his arms, and she buried her face in his chest as he held her like a child.

Rye turned toward the door again, his heart wrenching. Why should she be sorry? Because compassion had brought her to his apartment? He felt guilty because concern for him had been the bait Dean had used.

"Did you take the abortifacient, Cora?"

Rye whirled around at Caleb's quiet question and stared at Cora. All the possible consequences of the rape played out in his mind because of Dean's lifestyle: any number of STDs, HIV, pregnancy. But why would Caleb drag them up before her now?

His stomach tightened as Cora shook her head. The morning-after pill was used like birth control in the neighborhood where he had grown up. No girl he had been acquainted with would have wanted a baby by a man she loathed or kept a child she wasn't prepared to care for.

But Cora wasn't like any girl he had ever known.

Caleb grasped her shoulders and shook her slightly, his voice rough as he apparently battled the same emotions as Rye. "Cora, think. Do you want it to happen all over again?"

Rye frowned. Want *what* to happen again?

Then he remembered. Caleb had told him his teenage sister died giving birth to a baby when he was five years old. Cora's mother must have been a victim of rape as well. Which meant Cora…

Rye suddenly understood why she would refuse to abort any child.

Caleb walked to the phone. "I'm calling the doctor back."

"No, Caleb." Cora covered her head with her hands. "I won't take it!"

Angry at Caleb's insensitivity, Rye put his hands on his hips. When Caleb looked at him, Rye made sure his eyes said it all. *Back off. She's made her choice.*

Caleb's gaze burned, but he moved back to the bed. He sat by Cora and pulled in a hard breath. "Okay, not tonight. But you have to think about this. Even God won't judge you for taking it." He pulled her into his arms. "I don't want to lose you too."

Cora shook her head.

Caleb sighed. "Rye's going to get your clothes, and I'll take you to my place after you're dressed." He stood, helping her up. "Right now, I'll help you to the shower."

Rye took his cue and headed out the door, leaving his heart behind.

Arianna stared out the bungalow window. She wrapped her arms around her middle as she waited for Caleb to return. She felt his absence like a drug addict felt the absence of a powerful drug.

His dark silence on the ride home had convinced her that he abhorred her and would put an impassable barrier between them. But to her shock, he had pulled her to himself, his passion sending her to a high she had never known. Desperate to be loved, she hadn't cared that his love-making wasn't gentle but demanding.

After he left, fear and guilt shot out of the dark recesses of her heart. Unable to handle the weight of her trespasses, she centered her every thought on Caleb.

At last the Ford drove into the gravel lot. She took a step to go open the door, but froze when Caleb went to the passenger side.

He helped Cora step out and guided her to their door.

Arianna stepped back in shock. Why would he bring his niece here? Tonight?

Before she could decide what she should do, the door opened.

Caleb guided Cora inside. His dark gaze met hers, but he didn't greet her. Instead, he took Cora to the couch and said in a low voice, "I'll find you a blanket."

He headed into the bedroom and came out with a spare blanket. He helped Cora lie down, then draped the blanket over her. He kissed her damp hair. "Call me if you need anything. And try to get some sleep, okay?"

Cora murmured something. Then Caleb straightened. Dark desire burned in his eyes, and Arianna's breathing shallowed. He came to her and moved her into the bedroom. When he closed the door, she asked, "What's wrong with Cora?"

He reached for her. "Does it matter?" He sank her back into a place where no one mattered but him.

Where was He? Where had the Lord gone when she needed Him most?

Cora wept into the blanket Caleb had provided for her. He had told her to go to sleep, but he seemed not to understand the darkness that tormented her.

Seven years ago, another type of darkness had swept her away from the world of living color and brightness. But Jesus had met her. He had provided refuge and sanctuary, allowing her to step into a realm of the spirit she had only heard of before. His home had become the place she could go anytime the loneliness of living blind overcame her.

But now… She couldn't find her way to that place or hear His voice. Had He deserted her in her greatest agony?

She wept over all that she had lost. The precious gift she had sought to reserve only for her husband. The peace that had always come to her in distress before. The comfort of being held in her Savior's arms simply because He loved her beyond compare. But where was her sweet Lord now?

She battled the darkness that taunted her. It whispered that if God really loved her, He would never have let her enter Rye's room alone. Or at least He would have stopped her desecration.

Five minutes, Jesus. That's all You needed to give me. But You didn't. And now I'm not whole any longer. I'm just salvage. Leftovers for someone, if anyone can ever love me. Jesus, why weren't You there to stop him?

Her tears increased, but she pressed the blanket into her face, smothering the sobs so that Caleb and Arianna wouldn't know how terribly she was doubting the Lord. They needed Him more than life itself, but she had made no difference in their lives. Even Rye had spoken bitterly of God, and she had not been able to utter a single word of faith that He still held her in His hands.

Oh, Jesus, forgive me! Tears racked her body, and she felt as though her soul was being poured out. *Why did You require this road of me? What purpose can it have? Wasn't the loss of sight enough for You? Wasn't it enough that my mother was raped and died giving birth to me so that I never knew her? Or is there still so much of self in me that You had to use this way to rip it from me so I can be more like You?*

Guilt and shame covered her in waves.

What did I do that required this punishment? Was it because of Rye? Did I put him before You? Was I too self-righteous in thinking that I could make a difference in his life? Or is it because of the things I said to Caleb and the way I ignored his wishes? Did I bring this on myself because of my rebellion? I thought I was doing what You wanted, but You didn't save me. You didn't save me.

Somewhere a clock ticked, pulling back her awareness of her surroundings. Movement came from the other room, but she shrouded herself with the blanket. Everything disappeared except her desperate need to search the realm of heaven for the One who eluded her.

Jesus, where did You go when Dean was smothering me with his hands and desecrating my body? Did You watch him and not care? Did You avert Your gaze so the enemy could have his way? Why would You do such a thing? I've always believed that You love me and that You redeem every circumstance to bring Your beauty into the lives of Your children. But where is Your beauty now? Where is Your redemption? I'm so filled with despair, Lord. So filled with malice and disillusion and bitterness. There's no peace left inside me, Jesus. Nothing but darkness.

Time seemed to stand still as she lay, cloaked in physical darkness and wracked with despair. The air seemed to whisper with the laughter of sinister voices.

But then a hushed silence began to fill the room. The air around her grew heavy with the weight of Another's presence. Slowly she breathed in His aura.

Child, look at My hands. Look at My feet and My side. I wore a crown of thorns once as I climbed a hill with the scorn of men all around. My body, too, was exposed for all to see. The blood poured from My wounds even though I had done no wrong. Child, I was wounded for your sins. I was crushed for your iniquities. Because of My suffering you can have peace, and by My stripes you can be healed.

Cora wept. "Why didn't You stop him if You know what it's like to be shamed?"

Quiet.

Her heart burned inside her, and she wept again. "Lord, forgive me. I want perfect protection while You offer perfect peace. What must I do, Jesus, to have Your peace again?"

Forgive him.

"No!" She cried out before she could think, before she could judge either the cost or the healing it could bring. "Jesus, I can't do that. Don't ask it of me."

Silence engulfed her again. Then there was nothing. His presence had departed. She sobbed brokenly because she hadn't had the faith to take hold of His command.

She fell into a fitful slumber, plagued by nightmares, some old, some new. Flames of fire intermingled with hot breath and hands tearing. She gasped as though she were drowning, but she didn't awaken. Demonic forms ran rampant across her mind.

Then a cross materialized before her. Blood flowed from the wounds of the Man who hung upon it. His head hung limp with a crown of thorns pressed deep into His skull. Death enshrouded her. She cried out against the ones who had nailed Him there, screaming that He had done no wrong and that they had no right.

Then, to her horror, she looked down and saw the hammer in her blood-stained hands.

Chapter Twenty-nine

Cora woke, sobbing. The nightmare stood emblazoned before her, and agony burned through her. She was the one who had nailed Him to the cross. She had refused to forgive, and He had been crucified in her place.

"No, Jesus. I would never do that to You."

But she knew she had. Sometimes unknowingly, other times purposefully. Every disobedience, every wrong choice or selfish thought that put her will above His, meant His sacrifice was the only way to redeem what she had done.

Cora wept. Slipping to the floor beside the couch, she surrendered everything. Her grief, her shame, her hatred, and her disbelief. Her life was not her own, and her body was only a tent for dwelling in. What He allowed while she lived upon the earth was not for her to resist or refuse. If she did, she denied Him as Lord and crucified Him again.

"Jesus, I love You. I can't live without You. If I must forgive Dean to have Your presence, I will. I surrender all my rights. I deserve nothing, yet You gave everything to redeem my soul. I'm Yours. I withhold nothing. Take it all, Jesus, and do what You want with me. I forgive Dean, Father, just as You have forgiven me for all that I have done against You. Help me to live in a manner worthy of the calling I have received."

Fire touched her deep inside. It seared her with purifying heat. Then a voice said, *"Your sins are forgiven, and your shame removed."*

Peace rushed over her. It swept her into the presence of her almighty Savior. Wave upon wave of sweetness overtook her soul, and she breathed in the aroma of life itself. Purity flowed like a river into her, and she felt herself drawn into the arms of the only One able to bring beauty from ashes or give the oil of joy for mourning.

Tears of healing streamed down her cheeks, and she raised her hands to the heights of heaven. "Jesus!"

Terri was gone.

Rye blinked at the note she had left taped to her front door. "Rye, I'm not staying around for some crazy guy to come after me. Thanks for your help. Terri."

Great.

Terri had no idea that Sweeney's attack hadn't been circumstantial. He wasn't just a local serial killer, looking for a victim. If she was Patrick's grand-daughter, she wouldn't be safe no matter where she went.

Did Sweeney know where she was?

Although Rye seriously questioned whether she was Douglas's daughter, he couldn't ignore how she fit the clues. Sweeney could already be on her tail, ready to attack now that she was traveling alone. He and Caleb had to find her as fast as possible, if just to warn her.

He picked the lock to her apartment and entered, hoping to find a clue in her belongings as to where she may have gone. He combed through her papers and personal belongings. After four hours of looking, he hadn't found any reference to friends or family. Had she removed all mention of them in an attempt to keep Sweeney from following her?

Rye rubbed his stinging eyes as fatigue from the long night hit hard. Caleb wouldn't be up yet, but they needed to hack into the resort's database as soon as possible. It should list Terri's next of kin, giving them a place to start looking.

Not wanting to disturb Cora or Arianna with a phone call, Rye drove across town to Caleb's. He rapped on the bungalow door, certain only Caleb would hear the knock where he slept on the couch.

"Who is it?"

Shock flooded him at Cora's voice. "It's Rye. I need to talk to Caleb."

"He's not up yet." The door opened, and she smiled.

His heart lurched, and he hurried forward. Shutting the door, he pulled her into his arms. "Baby, you can't keep doing that! You didn't know for sure it was me."

She tipped her head back. "Yes, I did. I know your voice."

How could she still be so trusting after last night?

He cringed as he realized she wouldn't want him touching her. He set her back from him. But his breath caught at the peace that glowed on her face.

He ran his thumbs over the smooth planes of her cheeks where last night there had been lines of deep pain. A rush of astonishment choked him, and he asked hoarsely, "Baby, how is it possible for you to look like this?"

"Like what?"

He couldn't tear his gaze away from the glow of beauty on her skin. "It's like your face is shining. But last night... you were so filled with pain I could hardly bear it."

Understanding settled over her. "I met with Jesus last night. He asked me to forgive Dean. When I did, He poured His peace back in."

Rye dropped his hands on her shoulders in astonishment.

Caleb's bitter voice came back to him. *She forgives everyone.*

Looking at the serenity in her sightless eyes, he knew she really had forgiven the man who had defiled her and that in return God had given her the comfort he had wanted so much to give. A yearning burst inside him so strongly, he ached. But he couldn't discern its meaning. All he knew was that she was so beautiful it hurt.

He drew in a shallow breath, then gradually became aware of the room. He stared at the empty couch, where a folded blanket lay. He jerked his gaze to the closed bedroom door. "Is Arianna here?"

Cora tilted her head as though wondering why he asked. "Yes. I heard her and Caleb talking."

Rye stared at the bedroom. He could scarcely believe Caleb had given in.

"Do you want some coffee?"

Cora seemed perfectly at ease with his touch, but if Caleb came out and found him alone with her…

He stepped back from her, feeling an immediate loss. "No, thanks. I'll wait outside for you."

"You can wait in here."

"No. He's upset with me enough as it is."

"It's not your fault I went to your room."

"Maybe you don't think so, but he believes otherwise."

"It doesn't matter what Caleb thinks. You're innocent."

Innocent! Rye laughed out of sheer incredulity. "No, Cora. I'm not innocent."

The weight of his sins was so great that it robbed him of hope, no matter how much he longed for life to play out otherwise. He turned toward the door. "Please tell Caleb I need to talk to him."

"Rye, wait."

He paused at the door. Head down, he drew in a ragged breath as premonition hit about what she wanted.

"Tell me what you've done that you feel God won't forgive."

Fear of rejection burned through him. "I can't."

He grasped the doorknob, but she spoke again, softly, poignantly. "'If we confess our sins, He is faithful and just to forgive our sins and to cleanse us from all unrighteousness.' Rye, God already knows everything you've done, but you have to be willing to expose your heart to Him." She paused, then whispered, "You don't have to be afraid."

He turned to face her. His heart felt ripped open. But looking at the compassion on her face, he knew he had to take the risk. If he didn't, his past would always stand between him and any hope he had of loving her. Between him and any hope of redemption.

He moved back to her and took her hand. "Okay. But you'd better sit down."

He guided her to the couch. She sat calmly. Instead of sitting beside her, he went to his knees on the floor. He grasped her hand like it was a lifeline. "Hershey, for years I lived in the ghettos of Los Angeles. I really was the person I pretended to be when we first met."

He drew in a ragged breath. God might know all he had done, but he had a desperate need for her to understand his past as well.

"I've broken every one of God's Ten Commandments. I stole, I lied, I cheated. I drank myself into oblivion and used hard-core drugs. I committed adultery with other men's wives." His voice faltered, but he made himself go on. "I prostituted myself in any way that a woman wanted. And I almost killed…" He stopped, his agony so great he could hardly breathe.

Silence filtered into the room. Then, amazingly, her hand went to the top of his head and combed through his hair. With unexplainable strength, she said gently, "Jesus covered it all. If you accept His payment, He'll trade your sins for a clean heart and give you the power to walk in His righteousness."

"What are you doing here, Tyler?"

Rye jumped to his feet. He turned to confront Caleb's angry countenance. Almost he bit back that Caleb shouldn't be one to speak about breaking boundaries, but the gold band on Caleb's left hand stole the words away. He groaned and stepped away from Cora.

Standing, she defended, "He's not doing anything wrong. I asked him to stay."

Caleb glowered. "I would think that after last night, you wouldn't want to be alone with any man."

"I will not live in fear. Or bitterness or anger."

"Don't tell me you've forgiven Dean too."

"Yes. I have."

Caleb swore. "I never will. People like that don't deserve forgiveness."

Caleb turned to Rye. "If you have a reason for seeing me, I'll join you outside. Otherwise, leave."

Cora gasped, but Rye didn't argue. "I'll wait outside."

He slipped out of the placd and leaned against the side of the Pinto. He crossed his arms and lowered his head. The difference between Cora and her uncle had become starkly clear. Closing his eyes, he made his choice.

"Jesus, I need You. Please forgive me for all the times I've broken Your laws. I believe You paid for my sins with Your own death and that You're alive now. You're the only One who could give Cora peace after she was in so much pain. If You can do it for her, then I believe You can take away my pain too. Please help me to do what's right."

Something stirred deep inside him. He didn't understand it at first. But then a weight pulled away from him. So far away that he drew in a full breath, as if he were a captive walking out of the darkness and decay of prison into the brilliant sunshine and clean air of freedom.

The moment crystallized. Even when Caleb stepped out the door and walked toward him, the incredible joy within him remained.

"So, what do you need to talk about?"

Rye drew in another beautifully free breath, as though to combat the darkness in Caleb's eyes. Then he said, "Terri's gone. She left a note saying she wasn't going to stick around. I searched her apartment for contact information, but she cleared everything out. You'll need to get into the resort's database."

"Okay. I'll do an Internet search as well. Her family might be listed. Anything else?"

"Where was Sweeney when you lost him? Did he seem to be going after her or Mayla?"

Caleb clenched his fist. "He was with Arianna."

Arianna had been with Sweeney again? "And you still slept with her?"

Caleb's eyes flashed. "That's none of your business, Tyler. She's my wife."

Rye got back on track. "I'm going to locate Lydia's address. She might have gone with Terri, but if she didn't, maybe she'll know where Terri is and be willing to tell me."

"All right. As soon as we know more, I'm calling Patrick. He needs to know what's going on. I also have to call Dad to come get Cora." Bitterness shrouded Caleb's face. "Finding out she was raped is going to rip his heart to shreds."

Rye's chest constricted. Cora needed her grandfather and the sanctuary of her home. He simply had to stop thinking of how much he wanted to be near her.

He slipped into the Pinto and drove away.

Chapter Thirty

Arianna pressed her forehead into the wood paneling of her and Caleb's bedroom door. His angry words to Cora reverberated through her mind.

"I'll never forgive that man. People like that don't deserve forgiveness."

Caleb had told her early that morning why he had brought Cora to their place. But she hadn't had the time to fully take in the horror of the tragedy. Only upon hearing him talk with Cora and Rye in the front room did she realize Uncle Ben was the one who had forced himself on Cora. She felt his sin almost as if it were her own. She had modeled her life after his, and now both of them had exposed the blackness of their hearts to the world.

Her breath grew ragged as Caleb's declaration of unforgiveness ran through her mind again. *People like that . . .* Who did he include in that statement? Murderers, rapists . . . adulteresses?

Beginning to weep, she realized what was wrong with their love-making. He had not forgiven her, and she was consumed with guilt. Though raw passion hid the wall between their hearts momentarily, every time he finished with her, darkness returned, eating away at her soul. She didn't blame him for his anger. She had known what giving in to Sweeney would do to him. How it would hurt him. Why had she lacked the power to resist and stay faithful?

She had hoped Caleb's rescue would give her another chance to love him like he deserved. But now she knew his demands of her came out of pain and anger, not love. Deeper than desire, darkness lived in his eyes, his voice, and his actions.

Sobs shook her body. *What have I done? I can't be the wife he needs. No matter how many times he makes love to me, I've already thrown his love away.*

Caleb didn't return to the room, and Arianna pressed her anguish into a hidden part of herself. She couldn't leave him. Not right away. She'd have to wait until she had a valid reason, or he'd suspect her of desertion.

She dressed, then drew in a deep breath. She hoped she could play the committed wife. Fortifying herself to face him and Cora, she stepped out of the bedroom.

Cora lifted her head from where she sat with her Braille Bible on the couch. A smile softened her mouth. "Good morning, Arianna."

Arianna cleared her throat. "Hi."

Not knowing what else to say, she glanced at Caleb, who was pouring coffee from the electric pot. He was so gorgeous she wondered if she'd really have the will to follow through with her decision to set him free.

When he glanced at her, dark desire flickered through his eyes. She dropped her gaze. If only she could believe he didn't see her in the same way he saw Uncle Ben. But betrayal was betrayal no matter what form it came in.

"Do you want some coffee?" He walked over to her, and her pulse hummed.

She shook her head. "No, thank you."

He studied her, and she forced herself to lift her gaze. She didn't want him to think she was avoiding his perusal. She swallowed, unable to smile, but he seemed satisfied.

Leaving her, he sat by Cora on the couch. "Dad should be here within a couple hours. He's going to take you home."

Arianna poured cereal into a bowl as Cora responded softly. "I assume Rye told you I don't want to go back to the Y. But I think I should. I can't run away, and the children are having a performance soon that I'm directing. They would be hurt if I wasn't there."

Caleb scowled. "Stop thinking of others for once and think of yourself. You can't just go back to life like normal."

"Why not? I'm glad Grandpa is coming. I want to see him and talk to him about... everything. But I have peace again. I'll be okay."

"You have peace." Caleb said it derisively, and Arianna caught the scorn in his gaze as he glanced her way.

She sat at the table with her cereal, trying not to draw attention to her presence. Inside she shuddered. Her soul was eaten up with darkness and so was his. There was no getting away from the awful truth that she had pulled him into the hell where she lived. If only he had never given in to her. At least he would have saved himself.

She finished the cereal, then found paper to make a grocery list. Maybe he'd let her go get the food on her own. Maybe he'd insist on taking her. But she had to at least try. When she finished what she thought was a validly long list, she gathered her courage and walked over to him. "If we're going to have company, I should get some things to make lunch."

He frowned at the list. "Are you sure we need more food?"

She shrugged, pretending indifference. "I could make peanut-butter sandwiches."

He handed the list back to her and pulled out his keys. "Here." His gaze hardened. "Don't take too long."

Arianna forced herself to hold his gaze. "I'll be back." She accepted the keys and slipped outside.

She didn't go to the grocery store. Instead, she drove to her parents' beach house. It wasn't the best place to go, since she was certain Caleb would look there first. But she needed to find Rebecca's phone number. She would be titillated at Arianna's scandalizing tale, but at least she could hide her from Caleb.

Arianna hoped he wouldn't keep looking once he realized she didn't want to be found.

Rye slipped into Lydia's empty apartment using his lock pick. He had found her address in the phone book, then driven to the six-plex on the edge of town. Whether she had gone with Terri or was at work, he hoped to find a phone number or address so he could contact her.

He located her address book beside the phone and thumbed through it. Several people with her last name were listed. He picked up the phone, noticing several of the same names penciled into the memory bar. Griffin's Bakery also held a memory space.

He hit the button for the bakery, assuming it to be her workplace.

A man answered. "Griffin's Bakery."

"Hi. I'm looking for Lydia."

"I haven't seen her in three days. If you find her, tell her she's lost her job."

"Okay. Thanks."

Rye hit End, then punched the top memory button, listed for Brad and June Meyers.

After several rings, an older woman answered. "This is June."

"Mrs. Meyers, my name's Rye Nelson. I'm a friend of Lydia's, and I need to get ahold of her. She's missed several days of work, and I think she left the area with her friend Terri. Have you heard from either of them?"

"Lydia called this morning. She said she and Terri are taking a trip. But I didn't know she missed work. Is something going on?"

"I'm afraid so. Three days ago, I rescued Terri from drowning after a man attacked her under the water. She's been afraid the man will try to come after her again. She left a note this morning telling me she was leaving the area. It's possible the man may have followed her. I want to make sure she gets somewhere safe."

"Lydia didn't leave a contact number or tell me where they were going." Worry flooded June's voice.

"Can I leave you my number?"

"Yes, of course."

Rye listed his motel number and Caleb's cell.

"Should I call the police?"

"It's doubtful they'll do anything since Terri left of her own accord. You could call relatives and friends, though, to try to track the girls down."

"I'll do that."

"Thank you."

June hung up, and Rye exhaled slowly. At least the family would soon be informed. Hopefully Terri was headed to a friend or relative who could help protect her. If not...

He hoped she had been attacked as a decoy, If so, Sweeney would still be in the area, focusing on his true target. Was it Mayla? At least Sweeney would have a tough time getting to her. He would have to try for a long-range assassination, either with a rifle or explosives.

Rye headed to his Pinto. Although he couldn't tell Mayla she might be an heiress, he could warn her in an anonymous tip of a possible assassination attempt.

He drove to a pay phone and dialed the resort. The operator put him through to Mayla's personal assistant. Rye kept his warning brief. "Mayla may be the target of a hired killer. Please tell her to be on her guard for explosives and a long-distance shooting."

"Who is this?"

Rye hung up without answering the assistant's question.

Tiredness hit as he stood in the phone booth. He hadn't slept since Dean's attack on Cora. His heart ached. He needed to find out if Caleb had discovered any information on the Internet about Terri. Although a phone call would be quickest, he slipped into the Pinto. He wanted to see Cora one more time before her grandfather took her home, even if he risked incurring Caleb's anger.

The ache in his heart increased. He could hardly stand the thought of going months or even years without seeing her. She had focused on his need for the Lord in all their conversations, but now he had given his life to Jesus. Would it make a difference in her affection toward him? She had also broken her engagement. Was he part of the reason she had done so?

His pulse skittered. For years he had yearned to be a part of the Abrams family. Did he now dare hope for acceptance? Surely if Cora gave him a chance, Caleb and her grandfather would be willing to receive him too.

He couldn't let her leave without finding out the answers to his questions.

Caleb accessed Terri's emergency information on the resort database, but her parents weren't home, nor did an answering machine click on. Irritated, he glanced at the clock and frowned. Arianna had left over an hour ago. Her grocery shopping shouldn't have taken so long. Realization hit. She had lied.

He called her parents' beach house, but no one answered.

He curled his fist. He had stupidly believed her story about getting food for his dad's visit and had let her take his only mode of transportation. Was she going off to meet someone? He didn't know. It didn't matter. Wanton that she was, she belonged to him.

His dad would be arriving in another half hour, but he couldn't wait that long to begin his search. There was a rental car lot a five-minute walk away, but it would take another thirty to drive to the resort. Arianna didn't have any friends living in town.

He walked over to where Cora sat on the couch. When she looked up from her prayer posture, he said curtly, "I have to go out. Dad should be here soon."

Worry crossed her face. "Are you worried about Arianna?"

Her discernment was uncanny, but he didn't want her to know about Arianna's unfaithfulness. "Tell Dad I'll be back as soon as I can. And if Rye calls, tell him I found the number for Terri's parents but they weren't home."

"Okay."

He strode out of the bungalow and headed down the road to the rental agency.

***

Sweeney could hardly believe his good luck as he sat in his third rental car. Cora was alone!

He had planted a bug inside both Tyler's and Abrams's hotel rooms after Dean told him about their connection with Cora. Time after time she had been rescued from his attempts on her life, and his frustration had turned into self-directed anger when Tyler found Dean with her.

The extra ten thousand Dean had deposited in his account had bought her an extra couple days, but he shouldn't have given in to the temptation of mixing jobs. Dean had promised to give him full access to her as soon as he was finished. Instead Tyler had found them and called the police.

Now, though, anticipation hummed along Sweeney's nerves. He had parked behind the abandoned barn across from Abrams's bungalow, expecting it to be days before he had a chance at her. But Abrams had left her alone to go searching for his wayward wife. Sweeney chuckled and touched his high-powered Glock where it hung beneath his jacket. Jackson was getting testy, and he had grown tired of trying to make the girl's death look like an accident.

He stepped out of his vehicle and strolled across the gravel road. Arriving at the first bungalow, he monitored the area. None of the other bungalow residents were in sight. The advantage was his. He withdrew his lockpick and took a step forward, ready to leave the shadows.

Tyler's Pinto turned into the gravel lot.

No!

The car stopped in front of Abrams's room, and Sweeney narrowed his eyes. Cursed luck. The kid might stay any amount of time, especially with Abrams gone. And in another half-hour, Hezekiah Abrams would arrive. Sweeney doubted Cora would be left alone after that. Perhaps his best bet was to take her out while she traveled home. Trees covered the hills around the highway, providing perfect cover, and his high-powered rifle had always proven reliable.

He headed back to his car. The time for waiting was over.

Chapter Thirty-one

Rye's pulse beat faster than normal as he walked up to the door of Caleb's bungalow. Concern about the case faded to a back corner of his mind as he knocked on the door. He lifted a prayer heavenward for God's favor. "Jesus, please let us have a chance. I want to be with her so much."

What about My will, Son?.

Rye dragged in a ragged breath at the gentle voice. He couldn't doubt who had spoken. He had committed his life to the Lord and begged for His guidance. Did God not want him to pursue a relationship with Cora?

His heart tightened, sending an ache all the way through him. Cora loved Jesus with all her heart. She would never want a relationship outside His will.

"Rye, is that you?"

At her voice, he pulled in a deep breath. "Yeah, it's me."

The door swung open. She smiled in warm welcome. "Caleb said you'd call."

Hesitation assailed him. How much could he say? "I wanted to talk to both of you. Is he here?"

"No. He left."

Rye frowned. "Where did he go?" How could Caleb have left her after all she had gone through?

"I don't know." Concern flickered across her face. "I think something's wrong between him and Arianna. She went to the grocery store more than an hour ago, and she hasn't returned. He's worried about her."

Rye's stomach tightened. "She ran off with a man last night. He must think she's run off again."

Cora paled. "Oh, Jesus."

Rye pulled his focus onto his responsibility. "Did he say if he found Terri's family?"

"He has her parents' number, but they weren't home. What about you?"

"I called Lydia's mom. Lydia's with Terri, but Lydia didn't tell her mom where. Her mom's going to have them call Caleb's cell as soon as she hears from them again."

"I hope they're okay."

"Me too." Rye drew in a deep breath. "There's something else I wanted to tell you. I accepted Jesus this morning after talking with you. I didn't believe God could forgive me, but when you didn't turn away from me, I realized God wouldn't either."

Amazement flooded Cora's face.

He continued, "Your reaction to Dean's attack struck me hard. You chose forgiveness while Caleb didn't. I see the same darkness in him that's been tearing my heart to pieces. I realized as I waited for him to come outside that he was wrong. Jesus isn't dead. He's alive, or He couldn't have given you peace after you were in so much pain. For the first time in my life, I feel like I can breathe freely."

Tears glistened in her eyes. "Oh, Rye. I'm so glad. I've been praying so much for you."

He touched her cheek. *Lord, surely You want us together, don't You?* "Cora, why did you break your engagement?"

She startled. Then longing crossed her face, and she whispered, "Because I can't be the wife David needs. I realized we don't fit together."

Rye spread his hand against her cheek. He had so much he wanted to say. But the phone rang, interrupting him.

He swallowed. Divine intervention? "It's probably Caleb." He walked past Cora to the wall phone.

An older man asked for either Cora or Caleb.

"Who is this?"

"Cora's grandfather. Who's this?"

"Rye Tyler, Caleb's detective partner. I'll get her."

He carried the phone to her, stretching its cord. "It's your grandfather."

Her eyes widened as she took the receiver. "Grandpa?"

She listened for a moment, then put her hand over the receiver. "His truck broke down on the highway. He's at an Exxon truck stop off the Oxnard exit and needs someone to get him."

"I'll go."

She spoke again into the receiver. "We're on our way. See you soon, Grandpa. I love you."

Rye accepted the phone and hung it up. Could he trust himself to heed the Lord's warning if he spent any more time with her? "Maybe it's best if you stay here."

"Why?"

"Caleb—"

"He doesn't run my life." She smiled kindly. "Let me come with you."

"Okay. Do you have everything you need?"

"I just need my walking stick."

Rye found it for her. "I'm going to call Caleb to tell him we're heading out."

Caleb's cell phone went to voice mail, and Rye frowned. Had Caleb turned his cell off to avoid interruptions? What was he doing? Rye left a message and hung up. "He didn't answer. Hopefully he'll be back by the time we are. If not, I'll take you and Hezekiah to the Y."

He locked the door and guided her down the steps. In the car, he wrestled with his desire. Didn't Cora deserve to know the truth about his feelings? How could he be accepted into the Abrams family if she didn't plead on his behalf? Was he to ask only for friendship?

He took the ramp onto the highway, silently begging God for permission to follow his heart.

"Are you okay?"

"I'm not sure Caleb will let me see you again after you return home."

She fell silent a moment, her features serious. "Caleb doesn't think God can change a person. He doesn't believe we can overcome sin once we give into it. I suppose that's why he's so hard on Arianna. But he's wrong, and eventually he'll see that in you." She paused. "And I'm not going home yet anyway."

"You're not?"

"No. Running away was my natural reaction. I just wanted to hide my pain. But Jesus has given me peace. The children's program doesn't finish for another three weeks. I'll leave after that. And you're welcome to visit Grandpa and me anytime."

"Caleb might tell him about my past."

"The Bible says God has a good future for you. In Ephesians, it says He does more for us than we can ask or think. Grandpa will come around." Her voice softened. "Especially when I tell him I want you to visit."

Hope and uncertainty filled him. "What do you think about God's will?"

"In what regard?"

"In the choices we make. Like when we want something, but it's not His will for us to have it."

A troubled expression crossed her face. "We have to submit to His direction. He knows what's best in everything."

Rye remained silent. He didn't know God's will. He had to wait.

He focused on the highway, turning the steering wheel around a strong curve. Hills rose before them.

The front window exploded.

Cora screamed, clutching at her chest. "Rye!"

Adrenaline shot through his veins. A rifle had discharged in the distance. A hunter? Not likely. No one would aim across a road.

He ignored the glass shrapnel stinging his face and hands and hit the gas.

Had Sweeney decided to take him and Caleb out? Oh, why had he allowed Cora to come with him?

The shattered window must have cut her badly because her breathing grew ragged. As soon as he could, he glanced at her.

He sucked in a searing breath. The front of her dress was soaked in blood. Dear God!

He slammed on the brakes. The moment the car stabled, he yanked off his top shirt, leaving only the white tee he had worn against the chill of the morning. Ripping a long strip from the bottom of his outer shirt, he angled himself to help her.

The blood spread in an ever-widening circle under her hands, and he gritted his teeth. "Sorry, baby."

She choked on her tears as he ripped the neckline of her dress. A jagged wound over her heart gushed blood. He pressed his shirt tightly against the bullet hole. "Can you hold this so I can tie it in place?"

She pressed a trembling hand against the bandage, and he unlatched her seatbelt. He shifted her forward and tied the long strip from his shirt around her.

Her head slumped against him.

The cloth was tight. He prayed it would be enough to stop the bleeding until they reached the hospital.

He angled her against the far window, then froze.

The long tear in her dress had shifted, exposing the scar burned into the soft dusky skin over her heart. The deeply etched cross looked like an *x* with one long leg. It identically mirrored the scar on his chest from the fire long ago. Two realities collided, and his skin went cold.

"No!" Black spots danced before his eyes.

But he didn't have time to give way to emotion. Putting the Pinto in gear, he spit gravel and begged God that the last puzzle piece of the case hadn't been fitted in place too late.

While Cora was in surgery to suture her wound and treat her collapsed lung, Rye placed a call to the Exxon truck stop where Hezekiah Abrams waited. Rye closed his eyes as he waited for the clerk to page Cora's grandfather. The ache inside him was so intense he could scarcely bear it. All this time, he and Caleb hadn't had a clue.

"Tyler, what's going on? Where are you?"

"I'm at the hospital with Cora. She's been hurt. Can you take a taxi here? She's in surgery right now."

"What happened?"

"I'll explain when you get here."

"I'm on my way."

The line clicked, then Rye dialed Caleb's cell number. It jumped to voice mail, and he said that Cora had been hurt. He left the hospital's phone number then hung up.

His heart ached over all Caleb was facing. *God, why did You allow him to marry Arianna? You must have known what she would do to him. And now Cora's life is at risk again. Haven't the Abrams known enough suffering?*

He reached into his pants pocket and pulled out the paper where he had listed June Meyers's number. When she realized who he was, worry filled her voice. "I still haven't heard from Lydia."

"You don't need to worry about her anymore. The man who attacked her didn't leave the area. Terri's not in any danger from him. She and Lydia are safe. I promise."

"Thank God!"

Rye said good-bye then found a seat in the waiting room.

Grief and anxiety gleamed on the faces of a young couple sitting in the seats opposite him. He slumped in his seat, putting his hand over his face. *Jesus, why did it have to be Cora?*

A clock ticked somewhere above him as his mind slipped back in time. Seven years had passed, but the flames of that fire were once again seeking to devour him. Though he had carried her from her home as it collapsed, it had been his hands pouring the gasoline and lighting the fire that had taken her sight.

If only there was a way to keep the truth hidden. But his crime was literally stamped upon his heart. Should Cora agree to a life with him, he would not be able to hide his one act of brutality from her. She would recognize the scar as soon as she felt it.

Trembling, he faced the horror of what he had done. *God, help me. I told her I almost killed a person, but I didn't give her the details. I didn't think it mattered. But now... Oh, Jesus! How do I tell her? How do I face this guilt?*

He covered his eyes in anguish. He had thought that confessing his life as a gigolo would be the greatest challenge. But his involvement in a racist group was far more personal. It had gouged a wound deep into the hearts of all the Abramses. Caleb's hatred toward the neo-Nazi gang had been a living thing.

But Caleb had also said that Cora had forgiven the perpetrators.

Rye breathed in deeply, a tinge of hope shining through his darkness. She had forgiven Dean, a man for whom she held no affection and who had stolen something precious from her. Rye squeezed his eyes closed. Surely she would forgive him for how he had handicapped her.

But Caleb and Hezekiah would never forgive him. The past would have to remain buried as far as they were concerned.

"Son, I thought you said your life was Mine to do with as I will. Are you withholding yourself now?"

Rye sucked in a burning breath. *God, no. That's too much.*

"Is it? You promised your life belonged to Me."

Pain seared him. Rye bowed his head to his knees, covering his head with his hands as he moaned. *Jesus, help me. Help me.*

Long moments passed. The voice didn't speak again, but conviction remained, a burning heat in his chest. Cora wasn't the only one the Lord wanted to know about what he had done to their family.

A distant voice penetrated his thoughts. He straightened as he recognized it, then looked across the waiting area.

A large, gray-haired man stood at the nurse's counter, his ruggedly handsome face tight with pain. The nurse pointed Rye's way, and Rye forced himself to his feet.

The man's hard, dark gaze swept over him. He looked so much like Caleb, both physically and in expression. Rye swallowed. How could he ever bear their pent-up hatred, even with Cora's forgiveness?

Hezekiah strode toward him, and Rye pushed down his pain to deal with the present.

Hezekiah held out his hand the moment he was close. "Tyler. Good to finally meet you. The nurse said Cora was shot. Can you please explain what's going on?"

Rye gestured at the chair next to his. "Please sit down."

Hezekiah complied, and Rye let out a deep breath. "Caleb must have mentioned that we're here on a case. We've been at the Summerland Resort all summer, trying to locate the missing granddaughter of billionaire Patrick Sunnel. Have you heard of him?"

"Yes, but what does he have to do with Cora?"

"Patrick's nephew stands to inherit the Sunnel fortune, but word came out that he has an illegitimate granddaughter. So the nephew hired an assassin to kill her before Patrick could change his will. Patrick found out about the assassin and hired Caleb and me to learn the identity of the granddaughter and protect her. We've known her age range and that she's at Summerland Resort. We've also known she has an x-shaped mark and that the assassin is seeking to attack her."

Hezekiah stared, beginning to understand.

Rye blew out a hard breath. "Caleb and I made several false assumptions, never suspecting that Cora's accidents might have been orchestrated."

"She's had more than one? I only know that her friend's brakes failed, causing the car to roll with them in it."

"Yes." Rye clenched one hand into a hard fist. "Caleb and I neglected to investigate that incident. I'm guessing that Caleb forgot about Cora's scar. Also, Cora was staying at the YMCA campground instead of the resort." Throat tight, he asked, "You don't know who her father is, do you?"

Hezekiah's square face reflected the same bitterness that Caleb's did whenever he talked about Cora's mother. "No. Hannah couldn't identify the man who raped her, though she was sure he had known her."

"Did Cora tell you about being bitten by a rattlesnake?"

"Yes. You think that wasn't an accident either?"

"No. I believe the assassin put the rattler in her bed. Pest control never found an entrance for the thing. But once again, I assumed the snake had gotten in by freak chance." Caleb had assumed it more than him which meant he was even more to blame for not following his instincts.

Rye could scarcely believe how badly he and Caleb had failed the person who meant the most to them. He beseeched the Lord to preserve Cora's life.

Chapter Thirty-two

Arianna twisted her wedding band as she waited for Rebecca to arrive at the Sunnel beachhouse. At last her friend rapped on the front door. Arianna opened it, and Rebecca's eyes gleamed as she entered. "I can't believe you've finally given up on this guy."

Arianna swallowed. "Well, I have."

"Then you need to get rid of that." Rebecca pointed at her gold band.

Arianna mutely obeyed her friend's command and took off the wedding ring. Rebecca held out her hand, and Arianna gave her the band.

"You think he'll come here?"

"Yes." Caleb was a private detective. He wouldn't have a problem breaking and entering to search the beach house.

"Okay. We'll leave your ring with a note so he'll know for sure you're done with him." Rebecca grabbed pen and paper off the counter. "What do you want it to say?"

Arianna's eyes stung. "Just write, 'You're free.'"

Rebecca scowled, apparently not liking the implication that Arianna had been the one ensnaring Caleb. But she dashed out the note and dropped the ring on top of it. When she straightened, she eyed Arianna. "So, do you really want to get rid of this guy? Or are you just going to hide for a couple days then go back?"

The sarcastic question would have stung if Arianna hadn't already been in so much pain. But she couldn't go back. It had taken only one night to bring him down to her level. If he let her go, she was sure he would find his way to wholeness again.

Her heart twisted. Maybe she loved him after all. Why else would she want him untainted by the darkness driving her, even when she desperately wished it could be otherwise?

"I don't think you're gonna give this guy up." Rebecca turned toward the door.

"Becky, wait!"

Rebecca's gaze cut into her. "If you won't let me help you my way, I won't help."

"What's your way?"

Rebecca walked back, studying her. "Come with me tonight to the party Vance is throwing. That stable hand has worked some magic spell over you. The first thing you've got to do is break free from his ridiculous idea about abstaining from any sort of fun."

Arianna had heard about the kind of parties Vance threw. They included drugs, alcohol, and sex. Caleb would kill her. But then, that was why she was walking away from him. So he wouldn't feel compelled to rescue her from herself ever again. Rebecca was right. If she didn't give Caleb every reason to hate her, she might eventually go back to him. She ached over how much she still longed for him, but she couldn't stand to see him destroyed by her demons.

She pulled in a shallow breath. "Okay. I'll come."

Rebecca smiled. "Then let's get you changed out of those prudish clothes. We also need to make sure there's nothing in your room with my address on it. I don't want your husband tracking us down and crashing our party."

Caleb found the Ford parked outside the Sunnel beach house with the keys in the ignition. He slid his lock pick into the beach house door.

He discovered Arianna's ring on the kitchen table. He narrowed his eyes as he read her note. *"You're free."*

He knew what she meant. But she didn't understand that God had designed sex to mesh two souls into one. For him, it had done exactly that.

He couldn't let her go even if he wanted to.

He jabbed the ring into his pocket and crumpled the note, then searched her bedroom. The place looked like it had been swept through by someone looking for something. He gritted his teeth. Arianna had known he would come, and she had tried to remove everything that might give him a lead for tracking her down.

But he was a professional and she wasn't, so he went through the tossed-about items carefully. The clothes he had picked out for her were abandoned on the floor, and her vanity had been cleared of all makeup.

After a half hour, he found the photo of her and the red-haired girl with whom she had smoked a cigarette weeks ago. He turned it over. *To Nan, From Rebecca*

Rebecca. If Arianna had turned to her last time, it was likely she had gone to her again.

A car pulled up outside. He hurried downstairs and slipped out the back door. He angled around the beach house, catching sight of Aurora Sunnel as she stepped out of her blue Crown Victoria. She looked like a waif the wind could blow over.

Caleb regarded her thoughtfully. Maybe she would give him the answers he needed. He stepped into sight. "Mrs. Sunnel?"

Her eyes widened, and he walked closer. "We haven't met. I'm Caleb. I married your daughter."

She startled. "Arianna told us she got married. Are you still together?"

"Yes. She's visiting a friend right now. Rebecca. But I lost her address, and I'm supposed to pick Arianna up. Do you know where Rebecca's staying?"

"Her family's staying at Beach House 31, but I doubt Rebecca's there. She has a new boyfriend who has his own beach house. I've seen her hanging out with him there. It's at the south end of the beach. You can't miss it. There's always a loud party there."

Caleb nodded. "Thank you."

He stepped off the porch.

"Wait." Aurora gazed at him in puzzlement. "Aren't you going to ask for money? Jackson said that was the only reason you'd marry her."

Caleb grimaced. "That's not the reason. Thank you for your help."

He slipped into the Mazda he had rented. Later, he would return for the Ford. He followed the road to the southern beach front and stopped in front of a house where two young children played in the yard. They stared at him as he walked up the sidewalk. He knocked on the door.

A pale blonde answered. "Yes?"

"Could you tell me which of these houses is 31?"

She startled. "Are you the police?"

"No."

"Second on the end."

"Thanks." Caleb headed down the sidewalk and along the gravel road to Vance's beach house. A compact car sat in the driveway.

He felt tempted to force his way in. But the last thing he needed was to be arrested for trespassing. Although he doubted Arianna would come willingly, he walked up the porch steps and knocked on the door.

Movement sounded inside, but no one responded to his knock. He tried again, harder. Just as he reached for the doorknob, the door swung open. Rebecca's eyes narrowed. "What do you want?"

"Where's Arianna?"

She smirked. "Not here."

She was lying. He was certain of it. She had obviously talked with Arianna or she would have been surprised at his presence. "I'm not leaving without her."

Her eyes narrowed. "Didn't you find her note? She's done with you, Lindon. And unlike the age in which you pretend to live, nowadays husbands can't drag their wives back."

Anger burned, but she was right. Caleb gritted his teeth, then made himself walk away. Striding back to the Mazda, he ran through his options. He didn't have many if he didn't want to risk arrest, but he had to find a way to get Arianna away from the influence of her worldly friends. Although she had left of her own accord, he was certain her willpower wouldn't hold once she was in his presence. He had always been able to pull her back to him before.

However, he could think of only one way to get to her. He would need to watch Vance's beach house and wait for the next party. With a dozen or more people entertaining in the house, he should be able to slip inside, find Arianna, and get her out before her friends discerned his presence.

He headed to his bungalow. He had left his cell phone there to recharge since he had forgotten about it the night before. He needed to call Terri's parents again, then get ahold of Rye. He would return that evening to Rebecca's beach house. If luck was with him, there'd be a party tonight. If not, he'd stake out the house every night until he retrieved Arianna.

Rye stared at Cora, watching the rise and fall of her chest as she lay on the hospital bed, sleeping off the anesthesia from her surgery.

On the other side of her bed, Hezekiah frowned. "Why isn't Caleb here? Is he following leads on the case?"

Rye hesitated, seeking a safe answer. Caleb wouldn't want Hezekiah knowing about Arianna's waywardness, but he didn't want to lie. "He's trying to find a girl who ran away."

"He took on another case?"

Rye shrugged and looked back at Cora. In a sense, the assumption was true. Caleb would need all his detective skills to track down Arianna if she didn't want to be found.

Cora's eyes moved under her eyelids, and he leaned forward. "I think she's waking up."

Hezekiah took her hand. "Cora, it's Grandpa. Can you hear me?"

Her lips moved slightly, and Rye held his breath.

"Grandpa?"

"Yes, Cora. I'm here."

Her eyelids flickered as she fought the effects of the sedative. "Rye?" she whispered.

His heart tightened, preventing him from speaking.

"He's here," Hezekiah answered.

She moved her head. "Can I sit up?"

"Sure. I'll move the bed up." As the button whirred, Hezekiah looked at Rye. "Will you call a nurse?"

"Sure." Rye walked to the door and caught the gaze of a middle-aged nurse at the nearby work station.

She hurried over. "Is she awake?"

"Yes." He followed the nurse in.

She checked Cora's vitals, then touched Cora's hand. "Looks like you're doing well. It will take a week or so for your wound to heal completely. You'll be staying here tonight so we can monitor you."

"Thank you."

The nurse smiled in a motherly fashion. "You're welcome, sweetheart."

The endearment reminded Rye that Patrick Sunnel would be getting his wish for a sweet-hearted granddaughter after all. Cora's kindness would win him over the moment he met her.

"Rye?"

"I'm here."

"What happened?"

He walked to her bedside. "Someone shot you."

She sucked in her breath. "Was the assassin you and Caleb were after trying to kill you?"

"No. You're the girl we were hired to protect. You're Patrick Sunnel's missing granddaughter."

Her face registered shock. "Me?"

Rye repeated the explanation he had given to Hezekiah. Astonishment crossed her features. Quietly, he said, "I'm going to go call Sunnel and let him know. He promised to come get you."

"Oh." She seemed unable to say more.

Rye gave a tight smile. "I need to try to get ahold of Caleb too."

She gripped the blanket. "I'll be praying."

"Thanks."

He found a pay phone in an out-of-the-way corner. After punching in the private number he had for Sunnel, he waited through several rings. At last the old man answered.

"It's Rye Tyler, sir. We've identified your granddaughter."

"You'd better not tell me it's Arianna."

"No, sir. You'll fall in love with this girl. She's in ICU right now. She took a bullet to the chest, but she'll live. Her name is Cora." He paused. "Actually, she's Caleb's niece. Her mother died giving birth to her after being raped."

"Douglas." Sunnel spat out his son's name. "You and Abrams stay with her around the clock. I don't want Jackson's assassin to finish the job. I'll be driving up in an hour."

"Yes, sir."

He hung up the phone. Leaning his head against the pay phone wall, he prayed, "Jesus, keep Cora safe and help Caleb to find Arianna soon. And please... help me to do what You want."

Drawing in a deep breath, he pushed down his emotional turmoil over the past and called Caleb's cell phone. A recording played, telling him it was turned off. But when he called Caleb's bungalow, Caleb picked up.

"Tyler, where are you? Where's Cora?"

Rye frowned. "Didn't you get my messages?"

"No. My phone's been recharging, and I just got home."

"I'm with Cora and your dad at the hospital. She's in ICU. Sweeney shot her."

"What?"

"She's the granddaughter, Cal."

"I don't believe it."

"She matches every clue, and there's no doubt he was aiming to kill her. The bullet missed her heart by two inches."

"Does Sunnel know?"

"Yeah. He'll be here in a couple hours. I also called Lydia's mom and told her that Lydia and Terri are out of danger."

"Good."

"Have you found Arianna?"

Caleb's tone darkened. "I'm pretty sure I have. But I can't get to her yet. She's staying with some friends who know she's hiding from me. I'm going back tonight, and I won't leave until I get her."

"Why are you so determined to get her back if she doesn't want to be married to you anymore?"

"Arianna doesn't know what she wants. You haven't told Dad about her running away, have you?"

"No. Does he know you're married?"

"I told him when I asked him to come get Cora. He was shocked that I had eloped, but he was more anxious about Cora than me. Did you tell Cora what I'm doing?"

"Yes. She had already guessed Arianna was the reason you left."

Caleb's tone hardened. "Just make sure she doesn't tell Dad."

"I'll warn her if I get the chance."

"Talk to you later."

Caleb hung up, and Rye replaced the receiver slowly, his heart aching. Why had the Lord allowed so much hurt to come out of Caleb's relationship with Arianna? Why hadn't He protected Caleb from her wantonness?

Son, you think only to spare others pain. But I want their hearts. For some, light is sought only in the deepest darkness.

Rye caught his breath. Caleb's marriage had seemed like sheer folly to him, but the Lord's ways were above his. His despair had driven him to the Cross. Would Caleb's pain do the same? Would he surrender his self-righteous pride in order to be forgiven and forgive? Would Arianna seek the Lord to free her from the sin wound around her soul?

Rye bowed his head in prayer for both Caleb's and Arianna's salvation.

Chapter Thirty-three

I can't do it." Arianna stared at her reflection in Rebecca's bedroom mirror as her friend straightened Arianna's hair with a flat iron. She hadn't worn heavy eye shadow and lipstick since blackmailing Caleb into marrying her. But the revealing clothes were what created panic inside her.

Rebecca set down the iron abruptly and left the room.

Arianna slumped and shielded her eyes with her hands. When Caleb had knocked at the door, only Rebecca had saved her from throwing herself back in his arms. Rebecca said she had warned Caleb not to come back, but Arianna was certain he would. His nature was like hers: relentless and passionate.

She longed to return to the days before their marriage. Back then she had been intoxicated with him, and he had been falling for her. But she had been impatient and had not recognized how sweet his affection was. She had pushed for passion, not knowing it would draw him into the darkness of her soul.

She willed herself to look in the mirror again. Depths of horror and anguish stared back at her. If only she had the will to free him instead of merely waiting for him to find a way to take her back.

In the mirror, she saw Rebecca appear in the doorway. Vance followed, his gaze cool. Arianna turned around, and Rebecca tipped her head toward her boyfriend. "Vance says he can help you."

"How?"

He held up a syringe. "Becky said you needed courage."

Arianna knew a hard-core drug when she saw it. She shuddered and closed her eyes. If she took it, every inhibition she had would be gone as would any fear of Caleb's vengeance. But it was the only way she could follow through with her plan to sever herself from him completely.

She opened her eyes and gave a single nod. Vance slid the needle into a vein in her arm.

He smiled. "Welcome back, Nan."

Cars began pulling up to Vance's beach house at nine o'clock, but Caleb didn't leave his observation point on a beach dune until more than a dozen people had gone inside. Since drugs were no doubt available, Vance wouldn't let strangers inside for fear of an undercover cop breaking up the party. Although it would be easier to wait until everyone was inebriated or stoned, after an hour Caleb decided he couldn't wait any longer.

Slipping down the dune, he stayed in shadows until he reached the back of the beach house. Blinds had been drawn in every room except one.

He noted a washing machine and dryer inside the room. Hefting his crowbar, he pried open the window. Thankfully, the vibrating rock music covered the sound of wood tearing. He hauled himself up to the sill, then landed lightly on his feet. Forcing a casual attitude, he walked across the room and opened the door. No one would recognize him except Rebecca. Hopefully he'd have time to find Arianna.

Half a dozen people glanced at him from the living area. All of them held wine glasses and marijuana joints. Arianna wasn't among them, so he headed for the stairs. A tall blonde slid her fingers across his chest as he tried to pass her on the steps. "Who invited you, gorgeous?"

"Rebecca. Do you know where she is?"

"Back bedroom, but Vance isn't giving her up. Why don't you stick with me?"

"Thanks, but she said she has a friend waiting for me."

The blonde pouted. "If you mean Nan, you're a little late. Becky already has the guys lined up for her."

Caleb's blood ran cold. "Where?"

Something in his eyes must have startled the blonde, for instead of answering she mumbled a good-bye and hurried the rest of the way down the stairs.

Caleb took the final four steps in one leap, then marched down the hall. Whatever Rebecca had scheduled for Arianna, there was no way he was waiting in line.

He yanked open a bedroom door and startled a couple intimately involved. He slammed the door shut, then grabbed for the next one.

At that moment Rebecca stepped out of the far bedroom.

Their gazes collided. Her slow, self-satisfied smile made his skin crawl. "So… you did come back. Nan thought you would. I'd call resort security, but she can tell you what she wants." She smiled cruelly. "Or I can show you."

Caleb clenched his fists. "Then show me."

He knew he was already too late to preserve Arianna's fidelity. Rebecca's self-satisfaction had to come from believing he wouldn't want Arianna back after he had seen her. But he was more determined than ever to get her out of the hell she was in. Whatever had driven her here, he would find a way to drive it out of her.

As soon as he was close, Rebecca murmured maliciously, "Enjoy the show."

Caleb steeled himself for whatever was inside the room as she swung open the door.

Obscene comments rushed over him.

Half a dozen people ringed a king-sized bed, leering at the couple on it. He stepped closer. The girl being made love to was Arianna.

Fury shot through him. He pushed a couple out of his way, grabbed the man off the bed, and threw him to the floor.

Several people shouted angrily.

The guy bounded up and threw a left at his face. Caleb launched his fist into the man's stomach. Then he cracked a hard right into his jaw.

The man dropped like lead, and shock vibrated across the room.

Caleb glared at the others, but no one else had the guts to try to stop him. He turned to the bed and twisted the top sheet around Arianna's nakedness.

She smiled hazily as he lifted her into his arms. "Hi, Caleb. Wanna have some fun?"

Infuriated, he carried her out the door and down the stairs. He forged through the crowd of people gathered in the living area.

No one tried to hinder him as he stepped out the front door. Arianna rested her head limply on his shoulder as he carried her away from the house of destruction.

"Where are we going?" she murmured.

"I'm taking you home."

"Don't you hate me now?"

He gazed at her darkly. "Why did you take the drug?"

She frowned as though it was hard to think. "Vance said it'd give me courage."

Caleb gritted his teeth. "Why did you think you needed to free me?"

She stared at him. Then the drug dropped a haze back over her expression.

Caleb shifted her in arms that were beginning to ache from her weight. He would have to wait until the drug wore off to ask more questions. The trouble was, he doubted she would remember any of this night, whereas for him it would be burned forever into his soul.

He reached the Mazda and slid her inside.

Her head stayed against the window the whole drive home, as though she didn't have the strength to lift it. When they arrived at the bungalow, he unlocked the door before returning for her. Hoisting her in his arms, he carried her inside, then kicked the door shut.

He carried her to their bed. Laying her down, he breathed in her scent. Jealous desire converged over him. It would be so easy to take what was his. She wouldn't resist. She was still too stoned.

With a heavy inhale, he drew away. He didn't want his wife limp in his arms. He wanted her passion in response to his.

Returning to the front room, he sank down on the couch and let torturous thoughts roll over him. How could he love a harlot so much he was willing to bring her home even though he feared she would rip his heart out yet again?

Arianna opened her eyes slowly. She felt as though she had come out of a long, deep slumber. She stared at the ceiling, then moved her head and looked around the room. She gasped as realization dawned. She was back in her and Caleb's room.

"No!" She sat up, and a sheet pulled away from her bare skin. She glanced down at her arm. The bruise from the needle gleamed at her.

She couldn't remember anything after receiving the drug, but she doubted Caleb was the one who had undressed her. Yet here she was back in the bungalow's bedroom.

She jumped when the door opened. Caleb stepped in. Scared and ashamed, she pulled the blanket over her chest.

He walked to the side of the bed, regarding her darkly. "Why are you hiding from me? I've seen everything you have. And so has everyone else."

She couldn't speak above a whisper. "Everyone?"

His gaze pierced her soul. "Yes. Your so-called friend made sure of that. Do you even know how many times you betrayed me in full view of everyone? How many men got to you before I came?"

Coldness washed over her. *How many?* What had she done? Caleb's knowledge of her betrayal brought more shame than she could bear. She cringed away from him. "If you saw, then why'd you bring me back?"

He tilted her chin up, forcing her to look at him. "Because your body isn't yours anymore."

Her breath caught so hard it hurt. She stared at him, hardly believing he would touch her. Desire emerged in his gaze, and he said with intensity, "Despite what you may wish, I can't be free. God says marriage means one flesh."

She trembled. His resolve was overwhelming. When he lowered his head to kiss her, his dark passion flooded her veins.

Rye called Caleb from a hotel near the hospital where he had rented a room at Patrick's urging the night before.

"Hey, Cal, glad I caught you."

"Yeah?" Caleb growled. "Well, you've got lousy timing."

"Does that mean you've got Arianna back?"

"Yes."

"That's great. I've been praying you'd find her."

"Praying?" Caleb's tone hardened. "Why didn't you pray for her to be faithful while you were at it?"

Rye's heart twisted at the pain behind Caleb's words. "I'm sorry."

"How's Cora?"

"The doctor says she'll be released tomorrow afternoon. Patrick wants her to live with him. He still fears for her life."

"What did Dad say about that?"

"Patrick invited him to stay in LA with them for as long as he wants. Patrick's footing the hospital bill, and dotes on Cora like crazy. He's promised to get her a seeing-eye dog."

"Sounds like a fairy godmother."

Rye understood Caleb's sarcasm. Cora's world was brightening while Caleb's had gone as black as midnight. Rye bowed his head. His world had been void of light as well, until the truth of the Cross had penetrated the fear inside him. "Cal, there's something else you should know."

"What's that?"

"I accepted Jesus as Savior yesterday."

A hard silence came across the line.

"My pain and guilt are gone, and He speaks to me."

"Christianity is a perversion of the true God."

"Is it? Cora has peace even though she just went through hell."

"I don't want peace. I want retribution."

"For whom? Cora? Or yourself? Retribution only brings darkness and death."

The phone on the other end slammed down.

Rye bowed his head, beseeching heaven to break through where he could not.

In the quiet, the Lord's gentle voice infiltrated his thoughts. *Son, do you love them?*

His heart burned as he thought of Cora, Caleb, Hezekiah, and Arianna. Love from an outer Source poured into him, becoming an uncontainable longing for them to experience the power of an almighty God. He clenched his hands. "More than my life."

Then accept My way above your own and do not hesitate to obey My will.

Rye drew in a deep breath. He had sought the Lord's leading, and now the Lord had made His way plain. It was the way of sacrifice.

Chapter Thirty-four

"C ora, you must tell me if there's anything else you want."

Cora smiled at the question. Ever since his arrival, Patrick had asked her numerous times what he could buy her with his immense wealth. "You've already given me so much, Grandpa Pat. I have a new grandfather, a new family, and you are going to give me a seeing-eye dog. There really isn't anything else I need. I'm very happy."

"Well, if you're sure."

Grandpa Kai spoke with pride from where he sat on the other side of the bed. "Cora's always been content with her life. She's adopted her late grandmother's standard of never complaining. Even with the difficulties she has faced."

"I greatly admire you for that, my dear. You've been very kind to an old man. I'm only sorry I did not know about you sooner. I'm also deeply grieved for all you've gone through because you're my heir. I want to make it up to you."

Cora shook her head. "It's not your fault. Please don't let it bother you anymore. God protected me. He sent Rye every time to rescue me."

She smiled warmly in Rye's direction. He rarely participated in her conversations with her grandfathers. She assumed he was letting the older men have priority.

Grandpa Kai acknowledged, "We owe you a lot, young man. It's definitely providential that you were able to step in to help Cora when Caleb was unavailable."

Grandpa Pat complimented, "I'm very pleased with your and Caleb's endeavors on this case. I want you to continue the investigation so we can find evidence against Jackson and Sweeney. They must both be put behind bars." He squeezed Cora's hand. "I don't want to fear for your life anymore, my dear. But I'm afraid Jackson won't give up just because I know who you are."

Cora nodded. Her chest hurt if she moved wrong, reminding her of how close she had come to the end of her life. Thankfully, Grandpa Pat had a secure estate with armed guards. She would be safe there while Caleb and Rye sought for evidence against Sweeney and Jackson.

The conversation drifted along the topic of crime and random violence. Grandpa Kai talked bitterly about the brutalities committed because of racism, and Grandpa Pat agreed that LA had more than its share of gangs.

Grandpa Kai explained, "After losing our home in a fire started by a neo-Nazi gang, I rented a small apartment and began saving to move to a smaller community. I knew a good job would be harder to get there, so Caleb helped me invest in my own business. I've never regretted the decision. It's saved us much heartache." Bitterness touched his voice. "Until recently."

"I will make sure Cora is always protected. I'm glad my wealth can at least give her that."

Cora faced Patrick's direction. "I'm thankful for your protection, Grandpa Pat. But it's the Lord who's in charge of my life. He's the only One who can protect us from everything that happens. And sometimes He chooses to allow tragedy for His own purposes."

Grandpa Pat asked aghast, "How can the tragedies you've faced be considered good?"

Cora felt reluctant to share Rye's story without asking him first. "Very recently a friend I've been praying for accepted Christ. He said it happened because he saw the peace Jesus gave me after one of the darkest nights of my life. If God had not allowed that tragedy, I don't know if my friend would have accepted the Lord."

Across the room, Rye inserted quietly, "You're right. I would have continued believing my pain couldn't be taken away, even by God. But He's done exactly what Cora said. Circumstances no longer rule my life because now He does. I don't have to fear pain anymore, even though it's not my desire to embrace it."

Cora smiled. Rye's answer poured renewed confidence into her heart. He wasn't the troubled man he had been before, and she sensed a strange maturity in him. New believers seldom understood the concept of trusting God through tragedy.

The conversation picked back up on a new topic, and Rye said little more the rest of the evening. When nine o'clock came, Grandpa Pat said, "Rye, you're looking tired. Hezekiah and I will keep watch over Cora. Go ahead and get some rest."

"Thank you. I'll see you in the morning."

"Night, Rye." Cora smiled.

After Rye left, Grandpa Kai asked an orderly to wheel in two beds for himself and Grandpa Pat.

After they'd settled in, Cora pulled the covers over her shoulders. She looked forward to getting out of the hospital, but regretted that she wouldn't be returning to the Y. Neither Grandpa Pat nor Grandpa Kai would allow it. Not with a hired killer after her.

Silence descended over the room. Cora let the quiet seep into her. The day had been full of conversation and laughter, and she was grateful for so many unexpected blessings.

Rye's testimony continued to fill her with amazement. Would Caleb keep holding the past against him when Rye's deep contrition was so obvious?

She prayed silently. "Jesus, please let Caleb see the change in Rye. Let him believe it really is possible to become a new creation. And please help him to deal gently with Arianna. I don't understand why she would run away after pursuing him so hard. They must both be in so much pain right now."

She shifted to her side, but interwoven thoughts kept her awake. Caleb, Grandpa Pat, Arianna, Sweeney, Dean. No matter what situation she prayed for, her thoughts always brought her back to Rye.

A fear flickered in the back of her mind. Rye had seemed distant ever since she awoke from her coma. Was it because of the presence of her grandfathers? Or did something else hold him back from showing her the affection he had lavished on her before?

Oh, Jesus. She squeezed her eyes shut. *Did You bring us together only so he would come to know You, and now that he's saved Your purpose is finished? Please... I don't want him out of my life.*

She had never longed to belong to David like she now ached to belong to Rye. She could hardly bear to think of life without him. She was blind, but he had made her blindness irrelevant. She wasn't a beauty, but Rye had made her feel beautiful. His voice held deep desire and tenderness whenever he called her "baby."

Baby. A new fear flashed across her mind, and she sucked in her breath. Had he been there when she told Caleb she wouldn't take an abortifacient?

Her heart burned as she remembered. He had been!

Though he hadn't said a word during her talk with Caleb, she remembered the room door opening and closing when Caleb took her to the shower. So many things had happened since then that Rye had probably forgotten about her choice. But what if it had come to mind while she lay unconscious? What if his emotions had begun spiraling away from her because he'd started thinking about what it meant if she were carrying another man's child? A rapist's child?

Cora wept into her hands as fear consumed her. In his past, Rye had likely fathered one or more children who had been aborted. Had he been glad he wouldn't be responsible for providing for a child? Though Rye was a new creation now, Caleb had warned her many times that old thought processes would always influence a person. How could she hope that Rye agreed with her decision?

Oh, Jesus, help me! I know every life is from You, no matter how You allowed it to come into being. You're the only One who can breathe spirit into a body and make a soul come alive. I won't destroy any life You have created, even if I have to give my life for the baby like my mother did, or even if it means losing Rye. But please help me. I love him, Jesus.

She wept into her pillow, smothering the sound so her grandfathers would not awaken.

In the quiet of the buzzing hospital monitors, she heard Jesus' gentle voice. *Why don't you ask him, child, and lay your fears to rest?*

She wiped the wetness from her face. Asking him would mean exposing her heart. Rye would know how much she wanted him in her life; otherwise, her question would be irrelevant. Could she risk rejection? What if he had already given her up?

"I'm going to get another cup of coffee from the lounge. Does anyone else want some?"

Rye smiled at Hezekiah's offer where he sat near the door of Cora's hospital room. "I'll take a cup. Thank you."

Hezekiah glanced toward the white-haired billionaire. "What about you?"

"No, thanks."

"Cora, would you like some tea?"

"I'm okay, Grandpa.

"Okay. I'll be back in a few minutes." Hezekiah left the room.

Sunnel paced to the window. "When do you think Caleb will get here?"

Rye shook his head. "I don't know. I can give him another call."

He headed for the door, but Cora interrupted. "Rye, wait."

He turned toward her. She sat in a chair wearing the lavender dress Sunnel had bought her in preparation for their departure. The neckline rounded sweetly across her collarbones, and her hair hung in a soft wave down her back. Rye's chest constricted at the thought of being apart from her.

She bit her lip. "Grandpa Pat, will you go call Caleb? I'd like to talk to Rye for a minute alone."

Sunnel raised his eyebrows. "Sure. I'll keep Hezekiah company in the lounge." He headed out of the room, closing the door.

Rye's mouth went dry. He had been waiting for Caleb's arrival to reveal his part in the fire that had stolen Cora's sight, but his confession sat like a lead weight in his chest.

"Rye?" Cora said his name hesitantly, as if she wondered if he was still in the room.

He cleared his throat and came forward, but paused a few feet from her. "I'm here."

Pain flickered over her features, and his heart smote him. She had acted more subdued that morning, but he had had no idea why. Now her reaction to his distance told him she wanted him close. Forcing down his pain, he knelt on one knee then slipped his hand into hers. "I'm here."

She clasped his hand like it was a life preserver. "Do you think I should have taken the abortifacient?"

He pulled in his breath in surprise. She had seemed so certain of her choice before. Was she now worried she had chosen wrong? Compassion flooded him. "No. I think you did the right thing."

She drew in a trembling breath. "Caleb was upset with me for not preventing the possibility. I thought maybe you were too."

He had battled fear of rejection too often not to recognize it in her voice. Had his reticence caused her to doubt the affection he had always shown her? Though the Lord had not told him if they were meant to be together, he did not want her to doubt his friendship and caring.

Standing, he drew her into his arms. "Any child would be blessed to have you for a mother. I know you trust God's perfect plan, and so do I." He pressed her head to his chest, holding her there.

She tightened her arms around him and seemed to soak in his presence.

His heart constricted. He needed to tell her about his past soon. Perhaps he shouldn't wait for the others to come. Cora was the one who had been hurt the worst by his sin. She was also the most likely to forgive. Perhaps he could bear the others' anger more easily if she spoke to them on his behalf.

He set her slightly away from him. "I need you to do something for me."

"Okay."

"I need you to feel the scar."

"The scar?" Confused, she touched the place where her own scar lay.

He slipped off his shirt. "Not your scar, baby. Mine."

He took her hand and touched her fingers to his bare chest.

She sucked in her breath as raw current leapt between them. He moved her fingers slowly over the deeply burned cross close to his heart. After a moment, her face registered recognition.

Her lips parted in astonishment. "You're the one!" Trembling violently, she moved her hands across his chest, then up his arms to his neck and finally to his face. "You're the boy from the fire. The one who rescued me."

He clasped her hand against his cheek. "The one who stole your sight."

She shook her head, slipping her hands around his neck. She held on to him as though she were afraid he would run away, like he had seven years ago. "You weren't the only one there that night. And I forgave all of you when it happened. I couldn't live in bitterness. But I always wanted to thank you. I kept praying for you."

Rye stared in astonishment. "You did?"

Her smile poured love all over him. "Yes."

In that instant he knew the Lord had fashioned them for each other. He ran his fingers into the soft hair at the back of her head.

Longing filled the depths of her unseeing eyes, and he knew she had given him the right to love her as he had yearned to for so long. Drawing in a shallow breath, he lowered his head and tasted the sweetness of her mouth. She melted against him, and he thought he had entered heaven.

"Cora Abrams! What do you think you're doing?" Hezekiah's harsh voice jerked them apart.

Rye let go of her and turned toward Hezekiah. The older man glowered at him.

Beside him, Sunnel lifted his hands in apology. Behind them, Arianna stood with Caleb, who glared at Rye. "I knew you converted just to have her."

Rye shook his head. "No. I needed His peace."

Caleb's eyes narrowed.

Hezekiah grasped Cora's arm and pulled her away from Rye, his eyes burning. "Cora, I'm ashamed of you. Sunnel said you needed to talk to Tyler. But I come back to find him with his shirt off, kissing you!"

Cora's face flushed with anger.

Rye stepped forward. "I did not take my shirt off to make love to Cora." He touched his chest. "Do you see this scar?"

"No!" Cora gasped with horror as though she knew he had just thrown himself in the lions' den.

Everyone in the room looked at Rye's bare chest. But the deeply etched cross held meaning to only two of them.

Caleb stared as if struck. "You—you said it was a brand."

Rye shook his head. "No. I just didn't correct your assumption. I'm surprised you didn't recognize it before."

"You took her sight?"

Arianna and Sunnel gasped.

Fury blazed in Hezekiah's eyes. "Every part of her life has been changed because of you and that gang who burned our home."

The accusation gouged deep.

Caleb jumped in as well. "It's your fault she was raped too. If not for her blindness, Dean could never have tricked her."

"Don't listen to them," Cora cried out. "God's in control of my life, and He uses everything for His purpose."

Rye gazed at her, loving her more than he ever had before. "I know, baby. But they don't."

Tears poured down her cheeks. "Oh, Jesus!"

Hezekiah raised a finger at him, trembling with anger. "You will never be welcome in our home or anywhere near her again. Now, leave!"

"No, Grandpa! You can't do this!" Cora reached out her hand. "Rye, I'll go with you."

Hezekiah glared at Rye, daring him to try to take her.

Within him, the quiet voice of Jesus spoke clearly. *Follow in My footsteps and bear the cross I've given.*

"I'm sorry, baby. It's not about us. Please… just pray."

He walked quietly past his judge and jury, past the two silent spectators, and out into silence.

Separated from the ones he loved with all his heart, he drove to his hotel room, where he knelt by his bed and prayed. He couldn't walk back into the Abrams' lives until the hatred had been released and forgiveness embraced in its place. Giving up Cora was the cost of serving the One who had saved him. He prayed that when the Lord's purpose was accomplished, his future would be restored.

Chapter Thirty-five

M y boy, you gave me a scare."
Surprised to find Sunnel waiting in the parking lot outside his hotel, Rye raised his eyebrows. He had gone out to purchase an easy-to-read study Bible in order to fill his soul with God's truths and promises. With his new purchase tucked under his arm, he waited for Patrick.

"I was afraid I wouldn't be able to find you after you ran off."

Rye leaned against the side of the Pinto. "Do you need something?"

"I still want you to find evidence against Jackson."

"I'm sure Caleb isn't employing me anymore."

"He doesn't have to. I've asked him to follow leads in LA for cementing the case against Jackson. But my nephew is scheduled to be at the resort for another week. I'd like you to search his premises for information against him."

Rye considered the option. He needed a job, and everyone else was going back to LA with Cora. "All right."

"Thank you." Patrick hesitated. "You know, I don't make it a habit to interfere in other people's affairs, but I'm guessing you knew what would happen when you told the Abramses about your scar."

"Yes."

"Then why did you?"

"Because until Caleb and Hezekiah forgive me, they'll never be free of the bitterness that's eating them alive. As long as the issue is suppressed, they'll never have to face the consequences of their choice not to forgive."

"Cora told them the same thing after you left. She said Caleb and Hezekiah have to forgive you or they'll only bring more pain into the situation."

Rye remained silent.

Patrick studied him. "You're different from any man I've ever known."

"Jesus changed my heart. Every day of my life I lived with guilt and fear of my own lack of self-control. But when I told Jesus I believed in His death on my behalf as well as His resurrection, He purified my heart and gave me the power to live a life that pleases Him." He held Patrick's gaze. "We're all sinners, sir. No one deserves forgiveness, but God extends it to each of us through Jesus Christ."

Patrick seemed to mull the idea around. "That's why you and Cora want Caleb and Hezekiah to believe in Jesus. You believe He can help them forgive."

"Yes. Do you know what first drew me to Cora?" Rye asked. "It was her peace. I craved the serenity she had. She kept trying to tell me that it came from Jesus, but I couldn't get it through my head that He would give such a gift to me. Every time I rescued her from some physical danger, she always turned my attention back to Jesus. But what finally got through to me was how she chose to forgive Benjamin Dean."

"The man who raped her."

Rye nodded. "I saw her the night it happened. There was so much pain on her face, I could hardly bear it. But the next morning, when I visited, she radiated peace. She told me she had chosen to forgive. That's when I knew Jesus is real and gives us power to make choices we could never make on our own."

"Like you did at the hospital."

"Yes. I've always tried to preserve my life, but Jesus asks us to lay our lives down for others."

Patrick shook his head. "I'll have to think about the things you've told me."

Rye pushed himself away from the Pinto. "God will answer if you ask Him for the truth of who He is. Sometimes it's not a truth we're ready to receive, but He always answers."

Patrick held out his hand. "Cora and I are going to miss you. Take care of yourself."

Rye returned the handshake. "I think Someone is already doing that job."

Patrick smiled. "Maybe." He released the handshake, then walked to his black Cadillac.

Rye looked down at the new Bible in his hands. He traced his fingers over the leather cover as he reminded himself of a verse he had read that morning in the Gideon Bible at his hotel. *"God's word does not return void, but it accomplishes the thing for which He sent it."*

He closed his eyes in silent entreaty. *Please, Lord, let Patrick turn to You, as well as the others. Oh, God, there's so much pain right now for them. But I know You can heal and restore. Please let Caleb and Hezekiah choose You. Speak to Arianna and give her the power You've given me to live righteously. Work in their hearts, Jesus, and don't let them live any longer without You.*

Arianna stared out the side window of the Ford as Caleb took the highway back to LA. Patrick had given him his address before leaving the hospital with Cora and Hezekiah. For a brief moment, the old billionaire had held Caleb's gaze with hard eyes. "You're wrong about Tyler. Dead wrong."

She had disliked Rye when they first met. However, his quiet admittance to his past guilt, and his refusal to defend himself against Hezekiah and Caleb's angry accusations, had told her he didn't deserve their continued hatred. There was no way he could walk away, giving up his personal happiness with Cora, unless he was different from the person he had been before.

If only such a change had occurred in her before she gave in to her old weakness. But it was too late for her now. She had thought she could sever the connection between her and Caleb and had allowed her soul to be stolen from her. However, Caleb had told her he couldn't be parted from her, and for the last two days he had relentlessly made love to her as if to prove it. Desperate to make amends, she had given him everything he wanted, but she was more convinced than ever that nothing could heal the place she had impaled with her adultery.

She feared he was beginning to realize the truth as well, for he rarely spoke to her and his eyes held unrelenting anger. Rye was the focus of his hatred now, but that left her even more afraid. Caleb had once referred to Rye as a friend as close as a brother. If Caleb could hate Rye so intensely after having so much affection for him, where did that leave her?

"Here's your room, my dear."

Cora thanked Grandpa Pat. He had shown Hezekiah to the guest room on the second floor, but said he figured it would be easier for her to have one on the first floor. Caleb had driven Arianna to his place in the city, to the house he had shared with Rye for three years.

Anguish simmered in her heart over her family's anger. Now that she was alone with Grandpa Pat, she asked, "What did Rye say when you talked with him at his hotel before we left?"

The door clicked as though Grandpa Pat wanted to make sure they had privacy. Compassion filled his tone. "He said Hezekiah and Caleb have to face the consequences of their choices not to forgive."

Cora closed her eyes in grief. She had wept until she had no tears left after Rye departed, but it hadn't seemed to make a bit of difference in her grandfather's wrath. Caleb had viewed her only with derision too. "He's not worthy of your forgiveness, Cora. Your infatuation is misplaced, and you need to get over it."

She had turned on him, swept by an uncontrollable surge of anger. "I love him, and he'll have my heart until my dying breath! Your hate is hurting me more than he ever has!"

Caleb stared at her, but her words seemed to bounce off the iron wall of bitterness around his heart.

She had known the effect of unforgiveness upon her own soul after Dean raped her. But now she saw what bitterness did to the souls of the ones who allowed it to remain unchecked. Couldn't Caleb and Grandpa see that the anger which was supposedly for her sake was destroying her happiness and forbidding the future she longed for?

She brought herself back to the present. "Did Rye say anything else?"

"He said he wants them to seek Jesus. And that he knows you'll wait."

Tears welled in her eyes and spilled over. When Hezekiah had ordered Rye from her presence and Rye had gone without resistance, asking her only to pray, she had known he wouldn't return to her until her entire family could accept him. But knowing didn't make his absence any easier to bear. Her shoulders shook as weeping overcame her.

Grandpa Pat pulled her into his arms and patted her back in a soothing fashion. "I'm sure everything will work out. Just give your family time."

It had been seven years, and they were still so bound up with bitterness they couldn't see how their hatred was tearing her heart to shreds.

Resentment touched her.

"Be careful lest any seed of bitterness spring up in your heart and defile the truth."

She startled. How could she be a witness to help others forgive if she herself slid into bitterness and anger? The enemy had laid his trap so cunningly that only the warning of Scripture had saved her.

She straightened out of Grandpa Pat's embrace. With a trembling hand, she wiped the tears from her face. "I have to forgive them too."

"Caleb and Hezekiah?"

"Yes." She drew in a deep breath and felt the Spirit pour His strength into her soul. "It does no good to be angry at them for the way they act. They don't have the power to go against their pain. But I do. Jesus prayed for those who beat Him and forgave those who nailed Him to the cross. He has given me His Spirit so that I can make the same choice."

"But won't Hezekiah and Caleb think you've simply accepted your fate if you don't argue with their decision to exclude Rye?"

"I won't stay quiet, Grandpa Pat. But I need to talk to them about Jesus instead of about me or Rye. Jesus is the One they need."

"Rye said the same thing."

For the first time since Rye's departure, she felt peace and the beginning of hope. All her life she had prayed for her family's salvation, and now God was relentlessly on their trail.

"I haven't been able to reach Caleb and Grandpa with the truth of salvation all these years. But perhaps that's why God put Rye so strongly on my heart when I first met him. He knew Rye was the boy from the fire, and He knew what it would take to make Caleb and Grandpa face the pain in their hearts."

Grandpa Pat took her hands in his wrinkled ones. "I have pain too. Douglas ripped my heart out long ago. But now I'm beginning to think I chose the wrong path by casting him away from me in hatred."

"All you have to do to have peace is ask Jesus to forgive you, then choose to forgive Douglas. It's the only way to be free from pain."

Grandpa Pat was silent a long moment. Finally he asked, "What do I need to say?"

Rye slipped into the Sunnels' beach house, the moon covered by dark clouds. He had dressed in black clothes for his midnight endeavor, then used the security code Caleb had given him weeks ago to turn off the alarm system.

Although Dean now resided in the county prison, Jackson and Aurora slept soundly upstairs. Rye had decided to risk entering the house with them present in order to access Jackson's laptop and cell phone. Jackson always took both accessories with him wherever he went, but tapping the cell phone seemed the best way to find out Sweeney's whereabouts. And the files on Jackson's laptop could provide valuable evidence.

Darkness shrouded the downstairs, but Rye didn't flip on his small flashlight. He waited for his eyes to adjust to the shadows, then explored the living area. However, Jackson hadn't left either of the items Rye was searching for within immediate sight.

Rye glanced toward the stairs. Most likely, the cell phone and laptop were in Jackson's bedroom. However, with Cora's identity now known, he didn't need to fear alerting Jackson to his investigation.

Rye tiptoed up the stairs. Thankfully, Summerland Resort kept its higher-priced accommodations in good condition, and none of the steps creaked.

Jackson's door was closed but not locked. Rye eased it open, then held his breath, waiting. No movement.

He poked his head into the room. A tiny crack between the heavy curtains gave enough light to discern Jackson slumbering in bed.

Rye scanned the room, locating the laptop on the desk near the head of the bed. The cell phone was plugged in beside it.

Rye would have to take both devices downstairs before powering them on. Silently, he crept across the room, pausing every few steps.

Jackson didn't awaken, however, and ten minutes later, Rye had the laptop turned on at the kitchen table.

While the interface loaded, he pulled out several tools from the pouch belted onto his waist. He unscrewed the back of the cell phone and slipped a small bug into it. He attached the wires to the bug and replaced the back of the cell phone. Now Rye could monitor any call that Jackson received or sent through a cell phone coded to duplicate Jackson's.

A creak sounded upstairs. He slipped into deeper shadows and waited. Five minutes later, a toilet flushed, then silence reigned again.

He let out a shallow breath and moved back to the laptop.

The initial screen required a password, but the hack program on his jump drive inserted the correct code within seconds. Not taking the time to review the files, he copied the documents folder to his jump drive. He searched the other folders, but they contained only programs. He shut down the computer and carried the laptop and cell phone back upstairs. He held his breath as he replaced the items on Jackson's desk. Then he vacated the house, reactivating the alarm system.

Cora pulled her violin bow across the instrument's strings, filling her soul with the melody of an old hymn. Grandpa Pat had bought her an exquisitely made violin two days ago, and she spent long hours on the instrument, finding release for her emotions in its lilting tones.

When she paused at the end of the hymn, Grandpa Pat said, "That was beautiful."

Surprised she hadn't heard him enter, she turned in his direction and smiled. "Thank you."

His footsteps neared. "Rye called. He had information for me to give Caleb about Jackson. I tried to get him to talk to you, but he said he wasn't going to go behind Hezekiah's back. I'm sorry."

Cora nodded without speaking. Only prayer could change the situation.

"Also, a letter came for you. It's in Braille."

Cora accepted the missive, then slid her finger under the seal. She traced her fingertips across the heading. It was from the State Department of Justice. "Benjamin Dean's trial date is in three weeks. I have to appear as a witness."

"I'll go with you. I'm sure Hezekiah will too."

Even though she had forgiven Benjamin, Cora wished she could avoid the procedure that was needed to condemn and sentence him. The jury would have to know all the terrible details and hear from her lips what had happened. They would also hear Mr. Dean's case for himself. The thought made her stomach revolt.

But then she remembered someone else would be there, testifying because he had found the rapist on her.

She inhaled deeply and closed her eyes. Longing and hope intermingled. Rye would testify on her behalf, but would she get to go near him? Reality stole some of her hope. Grandpa Kai would be there with her, and Rye wouldn't come to her if he sensed he hadn't been forgiven.

Tightening her hold on her bow and violin, she battled again the temptation to anger. If only she could *make* Grandpa Kai let Rye back in her life. If Grandpa loved her, wouldn't he give in if she said she was going to elope with Rye no matter what?

She trembled at the thought. She longed so much to be Rye's wife, to be held in his arms and to bear his children. But Rye wouldn't elope with her. He had told her their dilemma wasn't about them.

She lowered her head. If Rye, who had been saved only a few days, could have the patience and self-control to wait for God's intervention, she had to hold to the same resolution.

She sighed. If Rye wouldn't come near her at the trial, she would have to be content with hearing his voice when he testified. She would pray night and day for Grandpa Kai and Caleb to forgive him.

Swallowing her yearning, she raised the violin back to her shoulder and sought the realm of hope through the poignancy of her music.

Chapter Thirty-six

C aleb, call me when you get this."

"Caleb, I have news for you. Call me soon. Patrick."

Caleb scowled where he sat in his home office as he played the messages on his cell phone. Patrick had called twice in the last half hour. He'd asked Caleb to search for evidence against Jackson, but in the three days since his and Arianna's arrival in LA, Caleb hadn't left the house.

Since Cora was staying within Patrick's secured estate, fear for her safety had been superseded by a fear much more personal. If he left the house, would Arianna leave as well?

In Summerland, she had acted frightened and ashamed. But since coming to LA, she had seemed to shut down. She did what little housework needed done, but spent most of her days sitting on the couch. Not speaking, not moving.

Caleb ignored her most of the time, letting her punishment take its toll. She couldn't expect him to try to console her. She had committed the worst offense a wife could, and he hoped his silence would embed in her a fear of righteousness. Wasn't the fear of the Lord how the Israelites had learned obedience? When they turned from the Lord by worshipping idols, the Lord allowed ruin and devastation from their enemies. Eventually, the Israelites cried out for rescue, recommitting themselves to Yahweh as the Lord. Arianna would have to learn the same lesson.

The Internet sufficed as a distraction as he waited for enough time to pass. He kept in contact with friends, did his banking, searched Web sites for further information on the Sunnels, and played Internet games.

When something triggered his need for her, he sought Arianna out. She was his wife, after all. Her marital duties remained.

She never resisted, but the vacancy in her eyes stirred his anger. It seemed she was simply waiting to be free of him. It compounded his fear that she would leave the moment he gave her the chance. But if she left, she'd make their suffering to have been in vain.

His cell phone rang. He hit answer.

"Caleb, it's Patrick. Did you get my messages?"

"Yes. What do you need?"

"I need you to bug Jackson's office. He's coming home in two days. You should bug his study as well, and open his safe. I couldn't get into it when I searched his house."

"Anything else?"

"Yes. Rye found Jackson's account numbers listed in his computer. I want you to hack into his bank accounts to find all the large payments he's made in the last month. We need to find a connecting point between him and Sweeney that will stand up in court."

Anger stirred at the mention of Rye's name, but Caleb held it in. "Fine."

Patrick listed the account numbers. "Call me tomorrow. I want to know what you find."

Caleb scowled as he hit End. Patrick apparently suspected he hadn't been following leads for the case.

He opened his hack program and created a search for the accounts Patrick had listed. Jackson had an account for personal use, one for business, and another for savings. Five transactions stood out. The first was a transfer of $50,000 to an account in Switzerland. Caleb shook his head. Swiss banks were well known for their unbreakable security codes. He wouldn't be able to hack into the foreign account.

The four other transactions were cash withdrawals of $10,000 each, ten days apart.

It seemed odd to have so many payments. Usually an upfront fee was paid for a job, then the remainder given when the job had been completed. Was Sweeney blackmailing Jackson?

He hit Memory and called Patrick.

"Caleb. Did you find something?"

"Yes. Jackson wired fifty thousand dollars to a Swiss bank account the day after Brinnon's death. I can't trace the owner of the account, but I'm sure it's Sweeney. Jackson also withdrew ten thousand in cash four different times. There's no way to trace it, but my guess is that he's been paying Sweeney off. It seems like a blackmail setup. Perhaps Sweeney kept the letter to Cora that he found in Alan Brinnon's safe to make sure Jackson didn't rip him off."

Patrick's voice held excitement. "If Sweeney has the letter, perhaps Rye can find it. I'll let him know. Thank you."

"No problem."

Caleb disconnected, then stared at the clock on his computer. 8:20. He couldn't bug Jackson's office during the day. He would have to leave. Tonight.

He walked into the living room. Arianna sat in her usual spot on the couch, her unfocused gaze on the front window. He tied his shoes and grabbed his keys. She didn't move until he stopped in front of her. At last her eyes lifted, void of life.

Fear clenched his heart. He couldn't assume she'd stay. He spoke in a hard tone. "Wherever you go, I'll find you."

Nothing registered on her face. He firmed his lips and strode toward the door. Slamming it shut, he wished with all his heart he could speed time up to the day when faithfulness was burned into her soul.

Arianna sat in the silence of the little house for hours.

"Wherever you go, I'll find you."

She squeezed her eyes shut in utter desolation. Even knowing how much Caleb wanted her, she felt more alone than she ever had in her life.

The only time he touched her was to make love to her, but there was no intimacy in the action any more. Only base need. Then it was over. She had played the harlot, and now he used her like one.

Day after day, Arianna felt her strength drain away. Whether it was because of Caleb or her own shame and guilt, she didn't know. But when he walked out the door, she had no willpower to make herself leave. So she stayed.

The sun set, cloaking the house in darkness. She didn't have the motivation even to get up to turn on the lights. The darkness seemed fitting, anyway. It matched the looming emptiness within her. Whatever life that had once drawn Caleb to her had now been sucked away, leaving her despising her own existence.

I wish I had never been born.

The thought struck her, pulsating anguish yet at the same time offering a tantalizing taste of freedom. If she had never been born, Caleb would never have met her or married her. He would have been able to marry some other girl.

The thought circled over and over in her mind, like a bird waiting to land. Her parents had never loved her. The boys she had given herself to before Caleb had been driven by lust not affection. And now Caleb despised her too. Her existence was a matter of vanity and shame. But her non-existence would free both her and Caleb. He could find someone sweet and pure to love, and she would no longer live every moment in soul-consuming pain.

Arianna glanced out the window at the street lights. She drew in a shallow breath. Freedom. What would she give to taste it? Or at least to end her anguish?

She had a friend once who had taken his own life, and she had looked upon the action with disgust. Back then she thought life had much to offer, and she had been full of passion, wanting to embrace it fully.

But she had already gone down that road, and just like Caleb had told her, the end was darkness and emptiness. Nor was Caleb able to give her back everything that she had thrown away. Everything that was precious and made life worth living. Her manifold sins had pulled her worth out of his reach, and she could almost hear the hordes of hell laughing.

She began to tremble. She didn't believe in an afterlife, because her demons were present now, taunting and shaming her.

She covered her ears with her hands and rocked as if she could somehow drown out the sound, but it only intensified. She had to find a way to stop the laughter and the swirling accusations. But she could think of only one way.

She went to the kitchen and searched for the right drawer. She stared at the razor-sharp blades of Caleb's kitchen knives. Her trembling increased. But she willed herself to grasp the handle of the largest one.

An outside streetlight glinted off the blade. She thought she saw the reflection of a hideous face in the metal. A seductive voice whispered in her mind.

You'll be free if you do it. You'll be free from pain, and Caleb will be free from the darkness you've wound around his soul. You want that, don't you? You want to free him just like you want to have the peace that's always eluded you. But it's here now. You're holding it in your hands. Just use the knife like a tool... cutting away the bonds of captivity and releasing you to freedom. It will only take a moment.

Arianna drew in a trembling breath, feeling the ice-cold pulse of her blood inside her. Could she do it?

She had to. Death was the only place from which Caleb couldn't bring her back.

The blade gleamed. Tears pouring from her eyes, she steeled her resolve. Then she plunged the blade deep into her heart.

Caleb considered not returning home from his night accomplishing Patrick's errands. He was certain Arianna wouldn't be there, and despite what he had told her, he didn't know if he had the strength to hunt her down again. Maybe it was best if he let her slip from his hands. No matter how many times he had united himself with her, her eyes told him he still hadn't found a way to drive out the demons inside her. The demons that would always pull her back to destruction.

Sitting in the truck outside their home, he pressed the heels of his hands against his forehead. "God, why did You let this happen? Haven't I loved You and served You all my life? Didn't I hold stringently to Your standards of righteousness? Give You my love? I thought You wanted me to make a difference in others, but You've only mocked me. Not only is Arianna beyond my reach, but Rye lost his soul years ago. He fooled me, but there's no way his actions against innocent people can be overlooked on judgment day."

There is a Way.

The barest whisper brushed words across his mind.

Caleb cringed. It couldn't be the voice of God. Cora had spewed out her belief so much in the last weeks that it must have wormed its way into his thinking. He refused to believe God had become a poor Nazarene or that a crucified prophet could rise from the dead. It simply defied his understanding.

Pulling back his anger to cover the voice, he stepped out of the truck and walked grimly up the steps to his house.

It had taken him longer than he liked to plant the listening devices in Jackson's office and home study. Cracking the safe had added another hour without bringing satisfactory results. The papers inside had been irrelevant to the case. He could only hope Rye had better luck with the safe deposit box.

He slipped his house key in the lock, entered the dark living room, and flipped on the light.

"Arianna?"

No answer.

He went to the bedroom. Her belongings were still in place. He frowned. Perhaps she had been so anxious to escape him she hadn't taken the time to haul down the suitcases he had thrown in the attic.

He rubbed his hand over the back of his neck, tired and feeling more alone than he ever had. *We're one flesh*, he had told her. *And I'll always want you back.*

The words were still true. Somehow he would find her once again.

He started for the door, figuring he would check the bus stations. Most likely she'd try to get as far away from him as possible. If he had to, he'd persuade Aurora Sunnel to give him a list of Arianna's out-of-town friends. Arianna didn't have the strength to survive on her own. She'd have to run again to someone who would help her.

His stomach growled as he reached for the doorknob. The sudden hunger pains reminded him he hadn't eaten since he left. He was running on adrenaline and anger, but he'd wear out soon without food or sleep.

Although he had no time to rest, he could take a few minutes to make a sandwich.

He moved to the kitchen and flipped on the light.

His gaze froze as the acidic scent of blood struck his nostrils.

Arianna lay crumpled on her side, a dark pool of blood beneath her. Her face held the whiteness of death.

"No!"

Caleb dropped to his knees beside her. He rolled her into his lap and stared in horror at the knife she had plunged into her heart. He pulled it out, but no blood flowed with it. He was too late.

"Oh, God, no! *No!*"

He put his fingers to her throat. There was no pulse. Nor was there any breath from her lips.

"No! No!" Violent weeping took hold of him. He pulled her tightly against him. It seemed as if vultures circled overhead, gloating over their prize, ready to feast upon her death.

He lifted his gaze to heaven. "God, not her! It should be me. I drove her to this. If I had forgiven her, she would never have wanted to end her life."

He sobbed, broken by the depths of his sin. He had thought he was righteous and that his anger was justified. But he was guilty just like the others, perhaps even more so because he had been the one to condemn them.

Rye. Arianna. Both had sought to please him, but he had turned on them, casting stones when the truth was that he had no right to act in God's place. His own soul was steeped in the sins of self-righteousness, anger, and pride.

"Oh, God, help me!" He bowed his head over Arianna's limp body, weeping. "I was so wrong. And now Arianna's gone because of me. All she ever wanted was to be valued and treasured. But I stopped cherishing her because of how much she hurt me."

He tightened his hold on Arianna's lifeless form. "God, is what Cora's said all along right? Did You really take on flesh and die on a tree? I won't fight it anymore if it's true. I've already dishonored You by assuming I knew Your truth. I don't want to dishonor You again."

A breeze swept through the room.

His hair stood on end. He lifted his head and looked around the kitchen. There was no window open. The breeze touched him again, and he heard the hordes of hell shriek in terror.

His blood ran cold. Cora had told him about the spirit realm, but he had paid little attention. Of course a blind girl would need another way to make sense of her world. But now he was experiencing the clash of two dominions himself.

The air of the kitchen intensified, charged with electricity, as if a great unseen battle was taking place. In a moment it was over, and utter stillness surrounded him.

He held his breath. Then he heard a deep inhalation. Only it wasn't his.

Arianna stirred.

Shock swept him. He loosened his hold and stared as she pulled in another breath. Her face twisted in pain, and he glanced to the hideous wound below her ribs. Blood trickled from it.

He laid her on the floor and pulled out a dishcloth from a nearby drawer. He pressed it into the gaping hole.

She moaned, rolling her head.

He pulled his cell phone off his belt. A man answered his call on the first ring. "911."

"I need an ambulance. My wife tried to commit suicide. She has a severe knife injury to her chest."

"What's your address, sir?"

Caleb told him.

"The ambulance will be there in seven minutes. How bad is the bleeding?"

"There's a trickle. But she's in a lot of pain."

"All right. Just keep her still so you don't increase the bleeding."

Caleb laid the cell phone on the linoleum. He closed his eyes and prayed fervently, unashamedly, to the only One in history who had come back from the dead by His own will and power.

"Jesus, I believe in You. Heal her, I beg You. Don't let her leave me again. You brought her back to me so I would know You are God in heaven. Please have mercy on me and let her remain. I don't deserve her, I know, just like I don't deserve Your forgiveness. But that's why You came, isn't it? To provide a better way. A new and living way, just like Cora's tried to tell me for years. Forgive me, Jesus, for refusing to believe that You would humble Yourself and become a man, making Your own provision for our sins. 'We're not righteous, no not one. We have all gone our own way, and You took upon Yourself the sins of us all.'"

The words of Isaiah flooded his mind. Words he had never understood before but which now revealed the truth. God had prophesied long before the birth of His Son that a sacrifice had to be made. Only then could the King come.

Arianna moaned, and he glanced at her face. It seemed the pain had lessened. He lifted the dishcloth just enough to look under it. The blood flow had stopped.

His shoulders slumped with gratitude. "Thank You, Jesus. You are the Way, the Truth, and the Life."

Love beyond compare flooded him from a Source outside himself. He shifted Arianna into his arms. Even though the clerk had said not to move her, he figured if God had brought her back from the dead, he could get away with moving her enough to hold her close. He hadn't cherished her since the day they were married, but that was going to change, starting now.

Her eyes flickered, and hope poured over him.

"I'm sorry, honey. I'm sorry for all the ways I've hurt you. And I forgive you, for everything. Please forgive me."

She didn't respond, but it didn't matter. He would tell her over and over how much he loved her. And one day she would be ready to receive the healing that flowed from Calvary's cross.

"Will she be okay? Is she awake yet?"

Cora's voice drifted toward Arianna as though from far away.

"Not yet," she heard Caleb reply. "The doctor said she's very weak. Once she wakes up, it could take a while before she can get out of bed."

A thick fog hung over her, but gradually it cleared away. Afraid to open her eyes, Arianna lay completely still and listened to Caleb speak again. His voice held a humility she had never heard in it before.

"I was so wrong. It shames me that I didn't see the consequences of my unforgiveness and anger before. Not only did I hurt Arianna, but I hurt you and Rye as well. Please forgive me."

"I forgive you. I'm just amazed God brought her back to life."

"He's given me more mercy than I ever imagined possible." Awe filled Caleb's voice. "I just pray Nan will be able to forgive me too."

Arianna's heart tightened. Nan. He had never called her by her nickname before. It sounded beautiful the way he said it, but she didn't understand. Caleb had left the house angry, certain she would leave him again. And in a way she had. Or at least she had tried. She didn't understand why the knife hadn't ended her life.

She couldn't remember anything else until awakening just now, but it sounded as though Caleb had brought her to the hospital and that she would live.

A moan touched her lips. She didn't want to live. She didn't want to be burdened by the pain in her soul any longer. She had wanted to be free. But even death had been snatched from her.

The back of a warm hand touched her face. "Nan? Are you awake, honey?"

Her breath shuddered. Never had he called her an endearment. She slowly opened her eyes.

"Oh, thank God!" He slipped his hand under the back of her neck.

She blinked at the compassion and gentleness in the depths of his eyes.

"Nan, honey, will you forgive me? I hurt you so much. I know that now, but I was wrong."

She lay still, scarcely able to think. Caleb was asking *her* forgiveness?

He must have seen the disbelief in her eyes, for he said it again, his passion the only thing she recognized. "I was very wrong to stop cherishing you. I know that's all you ever wanted. To be safe and feel valued. I'm sorry I didn't make you feel that way after we were married. I'm sorry I used you."

She could hardly process the change in him and didn't know how to respond. She licked dry lips and realized how terribly thirsty she was. She tried to use her voice. "Water. Please."

"Sure, honey. Just a minute." He slipped his hand out from under her and left her side.

She closed her eyes, relieved that for a moment she didn't have to deal with the unexplainable change in him. She supposed she should be grateful, but he felt like a stranger. Even before she had betrayed him, he had never looked at her with such tenderness. He had always been trying to change her. But now...

An emotional tremor swept over her as he came back.

The tenderness was still in his eyes, along with deep concern. "Are you cold? I can get another blanket."

She shook her head.

He sat on the edge of the bed and raised her head slightly. He put the cup to her lips.

She sipped the water, then tried to sit up but gasped in pain.

"Lie still, Nan. You don't want to move until your chest has healed." He laid her head down and smoothed the hair from her face. His eyes held the shadow of pain. "I lost you, you know. You were dead when I came home."

Dead?

He held her gaze sadly. "I drove you to take your life, didn't I?"

She licked her dry lips again, but at least the water had eased some of the roughness of her throat. "I just wanted us both to be free."

Tears moistened his eyes, stunning her. "I'm sorry, Nan. You shouldn't have had to suffer so much."

She had thought it only right, considering how much she had made him suffer. But she hadn't been able to bear the weight of her sentence. If only death had freed her. "I'm sorry I made you marry me."

Grief shone in his eyes. "Don't say that," he said with tender intensity. "I married you of my own free will. I'm glad you're my wife."

She couldn't stand the depths of emotion in his eyes any longer. She turned her head away. "You don't mean that. I scared you, that's all. But I'm still the same person I was. I'll hurt you again."

He turned her head back toward him with gentle strength. He waited until her gaze met his. Then he said softly, "Maybe you will, but it doesn't matter. You see, I'm not the same person I was. I asked Jesus to live inside me, and He's given me the same love for you that He has. And it's without condition."

He had promised unconditional commitment before, but this time he was promising unconditional love. Tears streamed down her face.

He thumbed them away, murmuring, "I love you, Nan. More than I ever could before."

Chapter Thirty-seven

Cora stood in the hallway of the hospital with her new seeing-eye dog, Sadie. She hadn't meant to eavesdrop on the conversation inside Arianna's room in the ICU, but she was held in place by wonder. Caleb's voice conveyed such gentleness and kindness as he spoke to Arianna.

Sadie thumped her tail against Cora's leg, telling her of someone's approach. Cora waited, expecting Grandpa Pat, who had come with her to the hospital after Caleb's phone call. Sure enough, he came close enough for her to smell his aftershave.

"How's Arianna? Any change?"

Cora smiled. "She woke up. Caleb's talking to her. It's beautiful how tender he is with her. He keeps asking her for forgiveness even though she's the one who ran away."

"Ran away? I thought she committed suicide."

"She committed suicide because he wouldn't forgive her for running off with another man. But now he's promised to love her unconditionally, and I know he'll point her to Jesus so she can receive the power to turn away from sin as well."

"You must be so happy, my dear. You've been praying for your uncle a long time."

"Yes. I want so much for Arianna and Grandpa Kai to come to know Jesus too."

"Cora?"

She turned at Caleb's voice. "Yes?"

"Would you like to come in and sit? Arianna's awake and I don't want to leave her, but I have some things I'd like to talk with you about."

"Of course. Can Grandpa Pat come too?"

Patrick patted her hand. "I don't need to, my dear. I'll leave Ralph standing guard out here, and he'll take you home when you're ready."

Cora nodded, aware of the silent presence of the security guard who had driven them to the hospital. "Thank you."

"It's my pleasure. Caleb, I don't know if Cora had the chance to tell you, but I accepted Christ as well, just a couple days ago."

"I'm glad. You've given Cora the best thing she could want from you."

Patrick laughed. "Right you are. I'll be sending an invitation for dinner at my house as soon as Arianna is better."

"Thank you."

Grandpa Pat headed away, and Cora prompted Sadie forward, grasping the special harness that enabled ease of guidance. Sadie led her into the room and took her to the hospital bed, wagging her tail at the presence of another person. Cora located Arianna's limp hand and squeezed it gently. "Hello, Arianna."

The young woman didn't respond right away. Finally, she said in a weak voice, "Hi."

"I'm glad you're safe." Cora laid Arianna's hand back on the bed. She signaled Sadie to take her to a seat.

"I'm not sure I like your new independence, Cora," Caleb said. "It means you don't need my help anymore."

"I thought that was a good thing."

"Maybe. But I bet Rye doesn't let Sadie usurp him."

Cora's pulse quickened. Caleb had already told her how sorry he was for the wrong things he had said to his erstwhile partner, but they had both focused their attention on Arianna's condition. Now, though, she followed the yearning of her heart and asked softly, "Are you going to tell him?"

"I've already tried to reach him, but he hasn't been in his hotel room."

"Are you sure he's still at the same one?"

"Actually, I'm sure he's not. He wanted Jackson to think he had left town, but Patrick gave me his new number."

"Oh." She sat silently, not sure what else to say. Caleb's forgiveness would mean the world to Rye, but it was still only half of the equation.

Caleb seemed to read her thoughts. "I need to find time to sit down and talk with Dad."

"Do you think it will make a difference?"

"That I've forgiven Rye? I hope so. But what I really pray will impact Dad is the change in me." He paused. "Do you remember why Mom became a Christian?"

"Yes. It was because my mother had been raped."

"That's right. Hannah reacted much like you did, and Mom felt her pain with every beat of her heart. I was too little to understand anything except the terrible weight of oppression over the house. One Sunday, Mom attended a Christian church meeting and accepted Jesus. Dad thought she was weak, and unfortunately, I followed his example, but Hannah followed Mom's. They both chose to forgive and gave up their anger. You'd think I wouldn't have made the same mistake, but I did. I'm sorry."

Cora stroked Sadie's head. "The Bible says Satan blinds the minds of the lost so they can't perceive God's truth. He also holds us captive to committing the same sins, over and over. But that's why Jesus came to earth. His death on the cross paid for our sins, and His resurrection from the dead defeated the powers of hell. When you accepted Him into your heart, He gave you the power to step away from sin and walk in newness of life."

"I think Dad will recognize that the change in me is the same change that occurred in Mom and Hannah when they accepted Jesus." Caleb sounded thoughtful. "Mom raised you to love Jesus, so Dad's told himself the same thing that I have: that you are just naturally sweet and kind and forgiving. When Dad saw the change in Mom and Hannah after they received healing and comfort from the Lord, he accused them of being too weak to hold on to their righteous anger. But he won't be able to lay that charge against me. I've held on to mine much too long. But today I finally let go."

Arianna reluctantly met Caleb's gaze where he sat beside her hospital bed. She understood only parts of his and Cora's conversation about Christianity, but one thing stood out. Caleb was different, and he attributed it to his new belief in Jesus.

And now he was looking at her as though he desired her input about his conversion.

"Do you mean you aren't angry at Rye anymore?"

"No, I'm not. I should never have gotten angry at him in the first place, but I let my bitterness over Cora's blindness fester for years. When I found out he was one of the gang who caused the fire in our house, all my hatred spilled over onto him." He glanced toward Cora. "Rye deserved none of my accusations, especially about his part in Benjamin Dean's attack. Dean used Cora's blindness to set her up, but if she hadn't been blind, he would have looked for another way. God could have stopped it from happening, but for some reason He didn't."

"I know why," Cora said softly. "Rye told me it was only after seeing the difference in me that he finally believed Jesus was real and could remove his pain too."

Arianna's chest tightened in longing. The deeply embedded pain in her own soul had driven her to plunge a knife into her heart.

Caleb apparently caught the look of yearning on her face, for he moved onto the bed, facing her. "Nan, you can be free from pain too. Jesus is the way to the peace and freedom you crave. All you have to do is ask Him and He'll make you new."

Arianna trembled. Tears welled up from the intensity of her desire, but she felt helpless. She could barely move and seemed hardly able to think. The change in Caleb was amazing, but she didn't think she had the strength to believe like he did. Jesus seemed like a fairy godmother who came and made good people better. She couldn't believe that a heart as defiled and black as hers could be made whole.

Caleb waited, his gaze filled with compassion as she struggled. At last she shook her head. She couldn't do it. She didn't have the will to believe.

A voice in her head accused her of hurting Caleb all over again, but Caleb pressed a kiss to her forehead. "It's okay, honey. It's new. But you're going to get well, and we're going to have our whole lives to spend together. Someday you'll see Jesus loves you too."

Tears slipped down. *Our whole lives.* Gone was the assumption that she'd run away. Gone was the driving force to change her. Instead, his words told her he accepted her just as she was.

That knowledge was more amazing than the compassion in his eyes.

"Rye! Glad I finally got ahold of you."

Rye sank onto his hotel bed, having entered the room in time to answer Patrick's call. "Sorry. I bought a new cell phone this afternoon."

Rye gave him the number. "I wish I had news, but Jackson and Sweeney haven't been in contact."

"That's all right. Caleb looked up the accounts you gave me. He discovered several large transactions to a Swiss bank account. He thinks Sweeney is blackmailing Jackson. Caleb's guess is that Sweeney kept Douglas's letter to Cora."

" I didn't find it when I searched Sweeney's room. Perhaps he put it in a deposit box or is keeping it in his car. If I get the chance, I'll look."

"Good. Caleb also wanted me to tell you that he wants you to call him."

"He does?" Rye sat up straighter. "Has something happened?"

"Yes, but I'll let him tell you. Take care, my boy. I hope to see you soon."

"Thank you." Rye hung up, his chest tight with uncertainty. Why did Caleb want to talk to him? Was it just about the case?

He dialed Caleb's cell and held his breath as it rang. When Caleb answered, Rye spoke hesitantly. "It's Rye. Patrick said you wanted me to call."

"That's right. I've been wanting to tell you that I was wrong to be so angry at you. Please forgive me for the horrible accusations I made against you at the hospital. I should never have said any of them."

A great burden lifted off of Rye's shoulders. "I forgive you. I know why you said them. If not for me—"

"Don't even go there. Cora's said many times God's in charge of her life. She saw much sooner than I did how amazing it is that God brought you into our lives again. This time for good. You rescued her many times, and you accepted Jesus. That's more important than anything else."

"What's changed your mind?"

Caleb shared Arianna's attempt at suicide, and the Lord's supernatural intervention."

Stunned, Rye asked, "God brought her back to life?"

Caleb laughed. "He sure did. She's at the hospital right now. It could take her some time to recover fully, but she's going to be okay. I hope you can visit soon."

"I will."

"I don't believe it."

Caleb tried not to wince at his father's angry words where they sat in Patrick's parlor. He had left Arianna in order to share every detail of his marriage so his father could understand the incredible way God had redeemed him.

Now he watched with pain as his father discarded the truth of her resurrection with an angry gesture. "People don't rise from the dead, Caleb. You must have assumed wrong."

"No, Dad. I've seen death. I know what it looks like. I know when there's no pulse or breath left. Arianna should be in a casket right now, with me standing over her grave. But God breathed life back into her so that I would know Jesus is real. That He is God in human form."

"That's blasphemy!" Hezekiah clenched his fist so hard it turned white. "You're saying the same things now that you were so angry at your mother for teaching Cora. And now some parlor trick has convinced you that Christianity isn't a cult? You've been deluded!"

"Dad, remember the peace that Mom and Hannah received when they accepted Jesus? Cora's had that same peace her whole life because she grew up loving Him, and now I know it too. Won't you at least consider the idea that Jesus might be the One God sent to satisfy our debt of sin? Isaiah declares that our righteous deeds are as filthy rags in comparison to God's holiness. But then he declares that the Lord's Servant has taken our sin upon

Himself. How can that not mean a sacrifice? The Messiah had to die in our place before He could come back to reign as King."

Hezekiah stared at him, a flicker of hesitation showing in his dark eyes.

Caleb leaned forward in his seat. "Jesus is the King we've been waiting for. He will judge the world with righteousness. But David declares in the Psalms, 'There is none righteous. No, not one.' He included himself in that statement. 'My sin is always before me.' If David, our nation's strongest king, admitted his need for forgiveness, why do we think we are exempt? There's no favoritism with God. The Torah teaches so plainly. If even the righteous deserve God's anger, then none of us will stand on judgment day. Not without a Mediator. Not without Someone to take our punishment in our place."

Hezekiah's shoulders slumped. "All these years I thought for certain that Deborah was wrong. I derided her when she tried to say to me the very words you just said. I refused to listen to Hannah before she died bearing Cora. I blamed God for not executing justice, and I determined to hold up the iniquities of others to His face until He repaid the evil of sinners upon their heads."

"God will judge evil, but when He does, there won't be anyone who's ever lived who won't be found guilty. That's why, before He judged, He had to provide a way for mercy. That way is through His Son, Jesus Christ, who is God in human flesh."

Hezekiah stared. Then he began to weep in broken, soul-deep sobs. "Oh, God! I have shamed You. I have judged You. I thought You weren't strong enough to demand payment of the man who hurt Hannah and of the boys who stole Cora's sight. But now I see it. You wanted mercy more than justice. Jesus, forgive me."

Tears stung Caleb's eyes. He had begged God to change his father's heart, but he hadn't really believed it could happen the first time he shared. He bowed his head, overcome with gratitude. *Lord, forgive me for ever doubting You.*

Rye grabbed the duplicate cell phone as it vibrated on the passenger seat. He hit Answer as he took the same turn Jackson had onto a coastal road.

He held his breath as the transmitter connected with the bug in Jackson's cell phone. Sweeney's voice came across clearly, frustration evident in his tone.

"She's only left the estate once to go to the hospital, but there were security cameras everywhere. I'm not going to risk getting caught to take her out. We have to wait until they get lazy."

"We're not going to wait. Patrick has the money to keep her guarded night and day for the rest of her life. You find a way to get into that estate. Poison a guard. Pretend to be a delivery person. I don't care. Just earn the money I've been paying you. It's your fault she's still alive."

"You said you wanted her death to look like an accident." Anger radiated from Sweeney's voice. "You didn't want any investigation. But Patrick's already changed his will. What good is her death going to do you now?"

"Once she's dead, I'm the only heir. And if Patrick tries to give his money away to some charity, I'll fight it tooth and nail."

"If you don't care what her death looks like, a bomb is the best way. Security guards can't save her from that."

"Do whatever if takes."

The connection broke, and Rye stared out the window of his car. Cora's life wasn't the only one that would be in jeopardy if Sweeney succeeded in his plan. Even if the guards searched everything that came into the compound, a bomb could easily be hidden and detonated from miles away.

He exhaled, running through his options. He didn't know where Sweeney was, but most likely he was watching Patrick's estate. Rye or Caleb could look for him, but Sweeney had the advantage. He would keep himself out of sight, and possibly shoot if one of them came near.

Caleb had friends in the police department who might help set up an ambush. They could provide transmitters for Rye and Caleb to communicate. Rye could sneak up on Sweeney's lookout point while Caleb walked with Cora close to the compound fence. Once Sweeney was arrested, he would most likely turn state's evidence against Jackson to receive a lighter sentence. Only then would Cora be safe from another hired killer.

Rye breathed in deeply. It would take a lot to convince the others to risk

Cora's safety, but he had to try. He punched in Caleb's cell number. A moment later, Caleb answered.

"Rye! Great timing. Dad just asked me for your number."

Rye startled. "Hezekiah?"

"Yes. Here. I'll let him talk to you. God answers prayers fast."

Rye's throat went dry. Could Hezekiah have forgiven him as well?

The old man cleared his throat when he came on the phone. "Caleb's spent the last hour sharing with me all that happened between him and Arianna. He also reminded me of everything Cora's told me about the Messiah in Scripture. I didn't understand until now that mercy had to be offered to everyone, not just the righteous. Although I'm sure you understand my anger against you for what happened to Cora at the fire, I've been wrong not to forgive you when you repented. But I forgive you now."

Rye blinked against the sudden sheen of tears. "Sir, I wish so much I had never believed the lies that group told me. And I wish with all my heart that I could give Cora back her sight. That I could go back and undo everything I did. I especially wish that it wasn't because of me that Dean—"

Hezekiah cut him off. "No. I was wrong to blame you for what Benjamin Dean did. You had nothing to do with that. He would have found a way even if she had her sight. You're innocent of that, and Cora says you've never disrespected her in any way. In fact, my granddaughter has told me many things about you. She's insisting that I invite you to come to Patrick's house as soon as possible."

Joy and amazement closed Rye's throat. *Thank You, Jesus. I don't deserve Your kindness. But then that's why You came.* He breathed in deeply. "Sir, I definitely want to come. But Sweeney is planning another attack. Could I talk with Caleb again? I've thought of a way to stop Sweeney and prevent Jackson from hiring another assassin."

"Of course. One moment."

A few seconds later, Caleb asked, "What's going on? I thought you'd want to talk to Cora as soon as Dad finished. She's waiting right here."

Rye's pulse jumped, but he forced himself to stay on track. "Sweeney called Jackson today. He's watching the estate for another chance to take Cora out, but Jackson's insisting that he doesn't delay. Sweeney's planning to poison a guard or plant a bomb. That means it's not just Cora's life at risk. I'm going to head to LA as soon as I can pack, and we can look for Sweeney together. The trouble is, I think he'll risk shooting us if he sees us around the estate. Even if we managed to arrest him, our evidence isn't concrete. A jury might say it's all circumstantial."

"Dana's testimony should be enough to convict him."

"Yes. If a jury believes her. They might not think her brief glance valid enough to sentence him for life. Meanwhile, Jackson could hire another killer. We'd have to keep Cora behind closed doors at all times, but that's impossible because we need her testimony. And there's no way we can be certain a bomb won't be sneaked into the estate. I think we need to give Sweeney another chance at her, one he can't pass up, and catch him in the act."

"Let him attempt to kill her? Are you out of your mind?"

"It's the only setup that nails both Sweeney and Jackson. Sweeney's sure to turn state's evidence if he knows we have a hard case against him."

Caleb pulled in a hard breath. "I assume you're planning to get the police department to help."

"Yes, but we'll need to act soon."

"I'll check out the estate tonight to see if there's a good spot for Cora to go walking. Sweeney will probably suspect a setup if I go walking with her in plain view. Cora's been careful to remain close to the house until now. But I don't think Sweeney would suspect her motives if she sneaked off the estate to meet with you. He's seen you together often. And he might guess that you've been ostracized."

Rye frowned. "Who would take her to meet me? Sunnel?"

"No. He's too protective of her safety. And it can't be me or Dad since we're the ones who supposedly don't want you near her. I think we can plan a safe route for her to take by herself. She's become quite independent with Sadie's help."

"She needs to be kept safe from a long-range shot. I don't want Sweeney getting a clear view of her until I'm close enough to protect her."

Caleb's smile touched his voice. "Don't worry. I want you protecting her too. Now, are you ready to tell her the plan?"

Rye tightened his hand on the phone. "Are you sure your dad understands?"

Caleb laughed. "He realizes she's as crazy about you as you are about her. He thinks you're already engaged. Are you?"

"No."

"Well, don't worry about us standing in your way anymore. Here she is."

Rye wiped the sweat from his hand as he waited.

"Rye?" Longing and joy spilled from Cora's voice. "How are you?"

Warmth flooded him. "I'm good. Your grandfather's forgiven me, and so has Caleb. I know you've been praying for them a long time. I'm so glad they've both accepted Jesus."

"So am I. When will you be here?"

"Tonight. But Sweeney needs to be stopped. Will you meet me tomorrow morning just outside the estate? Caleb's going to find a safe spot. It will give Sweeney a chance he can't pass up, and Caleb's going to have a police friend help nab him when he tries to shoot."

Cora's voice seemed breathless. "Of course I'll meet you."

"Good. There's something I've wanted to ask you for a long time."

Chapter Thirty-eight

Arianna's heart jumped at the sight of Caleb beside her bed. He had been gone all evening, and she had wrestled with tormenting thoughts before falling into a fitful slumber.

Seeing him sitting beside her bed, arms crossed and eyes closed, she felt an incredible moment of relief that he hadn't given up on her or left her to her tormenters. She averted her gaze, however, as soon as he stirred and looked her way. The change in him seemed too good to be true, especially when the voices in her head reminded her constantly that she deserved none of his affection. In time, he would remember to hold her sins against her. Right now, he was just scared because of how close she had come to death.

You were dead. Jesus brought you back to me.

An involuntary tremor swept her at the memory of his awed words, but she pushed the potency of the idea away. Even if God had that kind of power, He wouldn't have wished her existence back upon Caleb, regardless of what Caleb claimed.

"How are you feeling, honey?"

Arianna closed her eyes. Why did he persist in calling her by an endearment? It was as though he thought she was someone different from who she was. She swallowed against the roughness of her throat. Despite her IV, she always felt dehydrated.

"Do you need a drink?"

She looked at him, affected by his solicitous attention despite herself. Tenderness gleamed from his eyes.

A rueful smile touched his lips. "If you don't want to talk to me, that's all right."

She licked her lips. "My throat hurts."

His eyes twinkled. "I'm sorry, but I'm glad that's the reason."

"Did your dad forgive Rye?"

"Yes, he did." Caleb filled a water glass at the nearby sink. "He also accepted Jesus as Savior."

Arianna dropped her gaze. Another person accepting Christianity. It seemed she was the last one left. Poor Caleb. Always she was a disappointment. If only she could say she believed as well. But he would see that there was no change in her like she saw in him.

Caleb returned to her bedside, glass in hand. "The doctor said I can tilt your bed up a little today if you want."

"Okay."

Caleb pressed the button, and the bed motor whirred. "Tell me when to stop."

Arianna gave an involuntary gasp at the sudden tightness in her chest. Caleb immediately lowered the bed back down a little.

Arianna accepted the water cup, but her arms felt almost too weak to hold it.

"Let me help." Caleb held the glass so she wouldn't drop it. She accepted the help, drinking thirstily.

He set the cup on the table. "Does your chest hurt often?"

"Only when I move too much."

"Did you do okay while I was gone?"

Arianna slid her gaze away. "I was fine."

"Nan." He breathed her name like a caress. "You can tell me the truth. I want to help you get better inside as well as outside."

A tremor swept through her, but she suppressed the emotion his gentleness stirred. "I know."

He stayed quiet for several minutes, then asked, "Mind if I read some verses out of Psalms?"

"If you want to."

He opened his crisp-leafed Bible and turned its pages, but then sat, staring at the words.

"Is something wrong?"

He turned his attention to her. "I was going to tell you in the morning before I headed out, but I keep thinking about it, so I guess I'll tell you now."

Apprehension touched her. Was this how he prepared her to hear that he wanted out of their marriage after all?

"Rye located Sweeney. He's still trying to kill Cora. In the morning we're going to set up an ambush. We need to catch him red-handed so we can stop him for good."

"You're going to go after him? Why can't you let the police do that?"

"I have a friend from the police department who's going to help. But it would take too long to present all the evidence and get a full team together." He smiled. "Thanks for being worried about us."

She dropped her gaze. She wished he hadn't seen her fear, but if something happened to him, she would have no one to take care of her. Her parents didn't know where she was, and she doubted they were losing sleep worrying about her. She had been closest to Uncle Ben and Rebecca, but both had proven to be frauds. People who had taunted her with her weakness, taking advantage of it.

Tears stung her eyes. Caleb had taken advantage of her, too, in the last days in his home. But he had asked her forgiveness and promised to only love her from then on.

A tremor swept through her as her old longing struggled to resurface. What would it be like to be embraced with the gentleness that now underlay all his actions and words? She could hardly bear the thought of being made love to in that way. But she couldn't start thinking in that direction. She didn't deserve that kind of love—even if the impossible happened and he wanted to give it.

Rye met with Caleb and his police friend in his hotel room ten miles from Patrick's estate. "Rye," Caleb said, "this is Will Glendon. Will, my partner, Rye Tyler."

Rye shook Will's hand, noting the other's lean frame, close-cut gray hair, and serious gaze. "Good to meet you."

Will smiled, his navy blue eyes set in a kind, craggy face. He handed Caleb and Rye each a small microphone and earpiece. "These will enable us to be in continual communication. Since Sweeney is most likely armed, it's best if I'm in charge of taking him down. However, Caleb will stay close to me to warn you if Sweeney takes aim at Cora."

Caleb attached the miniature microphone to the collar of his polo shirt. "Patrick told me the safest route for Cora to take is along the south wall. It's protected by trees, and she can stay out of clear view until she reaches the corner. After that, there's an open field. If you linger near the corner, Sweeney will need to climb the hill across from the field. Will and I will be waiting in the trees there for him to set up for a shot. Will can take him down as soon as his intent is clear."

"Have you told Cora what to do?"

"Yes. She's going to leave the house at 9:45. The guard is supposed to act engrossed in a magazine and let her slip through. You need to give her about five minutes to reach you at the field."

"And you're sure Sweeney can't get a clear visual of her before then?"

"Not unless he exposes himself. In that case, Will has a rifle and can take him out from the hill."

Rye nodded. "Sounds solid."

"We'll head out first. Test the earpiece in five minutes. Be at the field in twenty."

Caleb and Will exited the hotel room, and Rye took a deep breath. He bowed his head. "Jesus, please go before us. Protect Cora, and Will also. Please enable us to capture Sweeney and end these attempts on Cora's life. Thank You for Your blood that covers us."

His earpiece crackled. Caleb's voice came through. "Rye, are you there?"

"I'm here."

"Good. Will?"

"I can hear you both. Remember, don't panic if something unexpected happens. The main thing is Cora's safety."

"Right. Talk to you again in fifteen."

Rye headed out of the room and jogged down the flight of stairs to the Pinto. He located Patrick's estate, then the open field, but he drove a quarter mile past it. He parked the Pinto on the side of the road and jogged back to the field.

Tall grass waved in the wind, ruffling his hair. His heart rate accelerated as the corner of Patrick's walled estate came into view. He spoke into the small microphone attached to his shirt. "I'm almost at the wall. Are you in position?"

"We can see you," Caleb whispered. "Will's several yards away from me. Sweeney hasn't appeared yet, but he might be coming up the other side of the hill. Remember not to look up here."

"Right."

Rye slowed his pace as he reached the southeast corner of Patrick's estate. Cora wasn't in sight yet, but he wasn't supposed to go any farther. He waited several seconds.

His pulse jumped when she came into view. Her hair was braided and she wore shorts. She gripped Sadie's harness as she walked with apparent ease along the tree line.

"Sweeney's at the top of the hill," Caleb murmured. "He's carrying a rifle."

"I'm ready," Will hissed.

Sadie wagged her tail against Cora's leg as they neared him. Longing swept her face. "Rye?"

He covered the last yard and touched her shoulder. "I'm here, baby."

She swayed toward him, but he didn't pull her into his embrace. He wanted to stay alert to the situation and be able to run with her if needed.

He took her hand. "Thanks for trusting me."

"I could hardly stand waiting another day to be with you, though I was sure I'd have to wait a lot longer before Jesus touched Caleb's and Grandpa's hearts."

"Me too."

He glanced down and noticed she still had hold of Sadie's harness. Not wanting to trip over the dog, he said, "Let go of Sadie. I need to be able to get you away from here fast."

She obeyed.

"Get ready," Caleb whispered. "Sweeney's moving into position."

Rye solidified his grip on Cora's upper arm. "So, did your grandfather decide I must not love you after all to risk your life catching the bad guy?"

She laughed. "Grandpa Kai thinks we're both crazy."

Rye ran his other hand down her cheek. "I love you, Cora Abrams."

Love spilled from her chocolate eyes. "I love you too."

"I hope you'll marry me at the soonest possible moment."

"Of course, I will. When—"

"Now!" The earpiece crackled with Will's command.

Rye twisted her away from the hill even as a streak of lightning seared his left shoulder. The retort of two gunshots immediately followed.

Caleb tensed in his hiding spot as Will crept closer to the spot where Sweeney had fallen. Will had fired a moment after Sweeney. He held his Beretta ready as he nudged Sweeney with his foot.

Was Sweeney badly injured or seeking to catch them off guard?

Sweeney moaned.

"You're under arrest." Will knelt as he recited Sweeney's rights. He grabbed his arms, drawing a more painful moan as he handcuffed them behind Sweeney's back.

Caleb emerged from his hiding spot. Blood seeped from Sweeney's side, his face ashen. Relief filled Caleb. Thank God for Will's excellent aim.

Will grabbed the radio at his belt. "I need a patrol car and ambulance at the Sunnel estate on Meridan. I have a wounded felon in the hills just behind it."

"We're ten minutes out."

Will dropped his radio and spoke into his small microphone. "Rye, are you or Cora hurt?"

"The bullet grazed my shoulder, but we're fine. Is Sweeney down?"

"He is. Your plan worked."

"Thank God."

Caleb agreed whole-heartedly. "We'll see you at the house."

"Okay."

Caleb closed his cell phone. Will had snapped on a pair of plastic gloves and was exploring Sweeney's pockets. He found a wallet in one pocket and pulled out a folded piece of paper from another. He carefully unfolded it. The paper was filled with writing, which he glanced over. He raised his eyebrows. "It's a letter, addressed to your niece. It's evidence, but perhaps you'd like to take a look at it first."

Startled, Caleb accepted one of the disposable gloves then took the paper. Amazement touched him. It was the letter Douglas had written to Cora. Not only had Sweeney implicated himself by keeping it, but the letter revealed Douglas' deep sorrow over his crimes. Caleb looked at Will. "Can I read this to Cora before we submit it? It will mean a lot to her."

"All right. But don't get fingerprints on it. Put it in a zip-lock bag when you get to the house."

"Do you need me to wait for the ambulance?"

"No."

Caleb nodded and strode down the hill. Gratitude welled up inside him. *Thank You, Lord, for all You've done in our lives.*

"You're hurt!" Cora ran her hands up Rye's arms at his declaration of a slight wound. Sticky wetness seeped from the back of his left shoulder, and anxiety filled her.

"It's nothing. Don't worry about it. I'm just glad he didn't get you." His voice held a trace of pain.

"Let's get back to the house. Sadie, come!"

She grasped the harness when Sadie neared, thankful to have her faithful canine so she could take charge. Rye let her hold on to his elbow as they walked, and after a moment he chuckled.

"Why are you laughing?"

"You're the one who's blind, yet you're guiding me."

"It's not really me. It's Sadie."

"Still, you're more independent now. Sure you're going to need me around?"

"You and Caleb! You're so used to me depending on you. But I want to be with you just for who you are, not what you can do for me."

"Thank God for that."

She squeezed his arm. "I wanted so much to tell Grandpa I was going to run off with you, but I knew you wouldn't let me."

He pressed a kiss to the side of her head. "You showed me that a person's salvation is more important than romance. Though I hope I'll soon get to kiss you without interruption."

She stopped walking to face him, and he curved his hand around the back of her head. She put her hand against his chest and slanted her face up. "I'm so glad you want me for your wife."

"Baby, I've wanted you since the first time Caleb spoke your name. But I was certain I could never have you."

Longing flooded her, and she stepped into his embrace. The warmth of his mouth drowned her with intimacy. His hold tightened, and the kiss heightened. His passion filled her with love and safety.

Finally, he slid his mouth off hers and murmured, "I hope you're gonna marry me at the soonest possible moment. I don't know how many more times I can pull myself away from your kisses."

She traced his features lovingly. "I'm sure we can get a marriage license in a couple days. If we get married at the hospital Arianna can be at our wedding too."

"That's fine with me. But if you want more time to have a church wedding, I'll make myself stop kissing you somehow."

"I don't need an elaborate ceremony. I'm sure Grandpa Pat can find us a minister by the time we get a marriage license approved. And I still have the white dress from the night of the cruise."

He sighed with contentment. "You're too good to me, Cora Abrams, but I'm gonna do the best I can by you."

She touched his lips. "I think that's saying an awful lot."

He firmed his hand around the back of her neck and kissed her again, but he broke away after a short moment. "I think I'd better quit, or I'm gonna need help leaving you tonight."

She laughed. "Do I need to lock my room when I retire so you're not unduly tempted?"

"Tempted I may be, but you don't have to worry. I won't go in your room until I'm wearing your wedding ring on my finger. However, if Patrick offers me a room here, I think I'll decline and stay at a hotel. Just to be safe. But I'll be back in the morning so we can go to the courthouse and any other place we need to go in order to get ready for the wedding."

"Have I mentioned that I love you?"

He hugged her. "I'm never going to get tired of hearing it. So keep saying it even after we're old and gray."

"You think you'll love me even then?"

"I know so, my chocolate-eyed beauty." He kissed her hand then took her arm so they could continue walking.

At the house, Hezekiah and Patrick greeted them. "Did the plan work?" Patrick asked. "Is Sweeney in custody?"

"He is. You don't need to fear for Cora's safety anymore."

"Thank God!"

Hezekiah apparently noticed Rye's arm. "Yes, thank God. But it looks like you need a bandage, son."

Cora's heart tightened. Her grandfather had never called anyone 'son' except Caleb. "Grandpa, Rye and I want to get married this week."

Patrick laughed. "You're sure not letting the grass grow under your feet!"

"After all the crying you did," Hezekiah said, "I didn't think you'd procrastinate."

Cora smiled while Rye hugged her shoulders and answered, "No, sir."

"Let's get that wound cleaned," Hezekiah declared.

Cora walked with them into the kitchen, where Hezekiah ran water.

Rye winced as Hezekiah applied antiseptic. After a moment, Hezekiah declared, "That bandage should hold. But I'd better get you a new shirt. I think one of mine will fit you well enough."

"Thank you."

Hezekiah's footsteps left the room, and another set entered.

"Hi, Cal," Rye greeted.

"Forget hello. I want a hug. You're in the family now."

Cora smiled as both men pounded backs. Then Caleb told her, "I have a letter to read you, Cora. It's the one that Sweeney stole from Alan Brinnon's safe."

"You mean the one that Douglas wrote?" Grandpa Pat asked.

"Yes."

Cora drew in a startled breath.

"Read it," Patrick urged.

Caleb cleared his throat.

"My dear daughter Cora, Not a day goes by that I do not regret my life and the evil I have used it for. Though I will be dead when you read this, I am in prison now, sentenced to thirty years for robbery, possession of an illegal weapon, attempted murder, and rape.

"It can only hurt you to hear from me, and that is why I will never try to contact you in life. But perhaps after I am gone, you will be able to find it in your heart to forgive me.

"You may wonder how I know that I am your father. A year ago I hired a private detective to find you. I knew your mother's name, and I saw in the paper the listing of your birth and her death. How I wish I might never have been born instead of inflicting pain on so many people, most of all your family. But your birth is the one thing I cannot regret and which I am sure God has used to bless others.

"I cannot blame you if you hate me, but one thing causes me to hope that you might forgive the man who hurt your mother so much. When my detective found your birth records and traced you to your new home, he found out that you have been the victim of other crimes. He told me about your blindness and the cross burned into your skin. It's my greatest hope that you were wearing the cross necklace out of love for the One it symbolizes. Could it be that you, too, have Christ inside you?

"You see, my darling girl, I found mercy at the cross of Calvary. Until I met Jesus, I was filled with cruelty and lust. Then one day I attended the prison chapel service and found my heart burning with need and desire. Life in prison holds only fear and darkness, and I feared death most of all. Until Jesus. Do you know Him? Do you know the Savior of our souls? The Healer of our scars and wounds? He gives such comfort

and is a Friend even to one such as me. If you do not know Him, please search out the truth of what I have just said. If you do... oh, my precious little girl, may He give you the grace to forgive me. I love you. I pray for you every day.

"Your Dad, Douglas Sunnel."

Tears poured down Cora's face, and she made no attempt to wipe them away, her heart overflowing with gratitude. "My dad was saved too! That's why he searched for me. Oh, how wonderful God is!"

Rye squeezed her hand.

"I can hardly believe it," Grandpa Pat said in a choked voice. "After all those years of cruelty and rebellion, Douglas accepted the Lord. I'll see him in the courts of heaven!"

Caleb breathed in deeply. "So much of the pain and hurt in our lives, God has turned into good. I believe He is going to heal Arianna, too."

"Yes." Confidence surged in Cora's heart. The Lord had already granted them so many miracles. More than anything He wanted Arianna to know Him.

Chapter Thirty-nine

Arianna watched the minute hand circle the clock numerous times after Caleb's departure.

Two nurses came and checked on her in their rounds. One of them removed her IV and suggested the bed be lowered, but Arianna asked to remain sitting up.

Caleb's Bible remained close to her bed where he had left it, apparently in case she wanted to read it for herself. But she didn't feel any desire to open its pages. He had read to her about Jesus' miracles, betrayal, death and resurrection, but the only part that had stood out was the betrayal. The thought taunted her that she was just like the man called Judas.

As the afternoon lengthened, fear welled inside her. Had Caleb been hurt in his encounter with Sweeney? He had promised to return as soon as he had testified at the police station, but surely it wouldn't take so long. What if he didn't want to come back?

She clenched the light sheet drawn over her lap with white knuckles.

"Are you all right, dear?" A nurse in her mid-thirties with curly blonde hair poked her head in. "You look exhausted. Perhaps you should take a nap."

Arianna shook her head. "Caleb said he'd be back."

"Oh. Poor dear." The nurse moved into the room, sympathy on her face. "He really seems to love you. But you've refused to see the psychiatrist and explain why you wanted to end your life. Are you sure it's safe for you to go home once you're fully recovered? You don't have to, you know, if your husband's been abusive in any way."

Pain rolled over Arianna at the nurse's words. Caleb thought he had driven her to suicide, too. How could she explain that his actions had been justified? That she simply hadn't been able to handle the consequences of her own sins? She looked away, tormented. "I'll be fine."

The nurse touched her shoulder. "You don't look fine. I don't want to see you hurt again."

She couldn't even defend Caleb's character adequately. She licked her lips and tried again. "I slept with another man. I couldn't stand the fact I hurt Caleb so much. So I tried to free him so he could marry someone better."

"But no one gets angry at affairs nowadays. Many husbands and wives have them. It's a mutual understanding."

"Not for Caleb. And I'd rather die than hurt him again."

The nurse looked disturbed. "I'm going to set up an appointment for you with our psychiatrist. He can help you understand you don't need to condemn yourself for following your feelings. And if you need to get away from your husband's judgmental behavior, there are safe houses where you can go to think about your choices and start over."

Arianna trembled. She had still failed to make the nurse understand. Just like she failed with everything else. She covered her face and let the tears come.

"Hi, Joyce. Nan, what's going on?"

Her tears stopped with her surge of relief.

Caleb sent a quizzical look at the nurse as he entered the room. The nurse shrugged and slipped out the door.

Caleb walked into the room then sat on the bed. "I'm sorry I was gone so long. I didn't mean to worry you."

"It's okay." Arianna wiped the wetness from her face. "I'm just glad you're safe."

He touched her cheek. "Is that why you were crying? Did you think something had happened to me?"

"Sweeney has a gun."

"He did. He's under arrest now. Rye and I gave our testimonies, along with my friend from the police station."

"Will Sweeney be convicted?"

"I'm sure. He shot Rye, just a graze across the shoulder, but it adds to the evidence of his intent to assassinate Cora."

"Is Rye with Cora now?"

"Yes. He went back to Patrick's when he finished testifying. He told me that he and Cora want to get married here in two days so you can attend the wedding, too."

"They must be very happy."

"Yes." His gaze traveled her features. Then he ran his knuckles down her cheek. "I love you."

Tears pricked her eyes. She averted her gaze, not letting herself believe she had seen the flicker of an old desire in his eyes.

He brushed his fingers through her hair, but she wouldn't meet his gaze. He said softly, "I want us to be happy, too. I hope I didn't ruin your desire for me forever."

She trembled. She longed for intimacy, but it was the last thing she dared hope for.

"I hope you don't mind, but I'm going to kiss you."

Her gaze flew to his. He smiled as he shifted closer.

His lips were soft and warm, and he kissed her the way he had before they were married. Her heart began to pound much too fast. She couldn't help but respond, filled with yearning. He framed her face as he took her deeper. She reached for him, touching his chest.

She didn't want the moment to end, and Caleb didn't seem to want it to either. Finally, he drew in a deep breath and eased back. Love shone from his gaze, and he brought her hand to his lips. "As soon as you're strong enough, I'm going to take you home so we can start over."

Start over. The nurse had said the same thing, but Arianna didn't want to start over without Caleb. Barely able to let herself hope, she asked in desperation, "What if I can't be good? What if I just hurt you again? What if something happens and I can't…"

She trailed off, unable to ask what would happen if temptation lured her away again. Caleb watched her face somberly. "Do you want to be good?"

Tears tracked down her cheeks. "Yes. But I wanted to be a good wife before, too, and all I did was hurt you."

"I wanted to do the right thing before, too, but I didn't even know what was right. That's why I ended up hurting you. I needed Jesus to change my heart so that I could understand His ways. You also need a new heart. It's the only way to have the ability to recognize lies and have the strength to do what you know is right even when someone tempts you to do something else."

Arianna sat quietly. What Caleb said was true. She needed power to recognize lies and not give into them or her own weakness. She hesitated. She didn't think she could believe in Jesus like he did. But she needed help not to hurt him again. She bit her lip. "What do I say?"

"Tell Jesus you believe He is God and that you believe He died to pay for your sins then rose again. Ask Him to give you a new heart and the power to do what He says is right. He'll answer you. He's been waiting for you to submit your will to His."

She dropped her gaze to her hands. She had submitted her will to Vance's needle. Why was it so hard to submit her will to Someone who was supposed to love her more than Caleb did?

She closed her eyes, trying to will herself to believe. But all she heard were voices raining down accusations once again. *You're no good. You're a failure. Caleb's giving you another chance, but even if you say you believe in his Jesus, you're going to blow it again. Pretend all you want you can be changed. It's never going to happen.*

She pried her eyes open, desperate to get away from the voices. She grabbed Caleb's hand, filled with agony. "I want to believe in Jesus. I know I need help. But… I can't."

He sat silent for a moment, and his gaze lost focus as though he was listening. Then he said, "You have free will to believe in Jesus or not believe. What are you thinking that's stopping you?"

She swallowed. What would he think if she told him about the voices that tormented her? Would he think she was schizophrenic? That's how the hospital psychiatrist would diagnose her, just like her mother's psychiatrist had told her.

At last she whispered, "I'm no good, Caleb. Even if I say I believe in Jesus like you, I know I won't change. I'll still end up hurting you, and I don't want to do that." Tears slipped down her cheeks. She turned her face away from him as the tears came harder. "You shouldn't let yourself be hurt again. You should just leave me."

"No." He said it emphatically. "I won't leave you, and I already told you: it doesn't matter if you hurt me again, though I want you to have the power to do what's right. I want you to stop hurting yourself. Nan, look at me."

He put his hand under her chin and made her face him. "The enemy wants to keep you from Jesus by telling you you're no good and Jesus can't change you. But those voices are lies. Jesus will change your heart, and you will receive power to make hard choices. But you have to choose. Arianna, believe in the Lord Jesus, and you will be saved."

The voices shouted, but Arianna ignored them, trying desperately to look past them in her mind. If they were lies like Caleb said, then where was the truth? Could it be what Caleb had told her? That God had created her for a purpose, unique and incredibly loved?

The voices seemed to become like a mist. If she could just exert the will to make it past them.

You are the one I want.

She drew in a soft breath. Whose voice had she just heard? It had sounded so different, so much more tender and compassionate than the others. She closed her eyes as yearning welled up inside her. *Jesus?*

I'm here, child. I've been waiting. Do you believe in Me? Will you give me Your heart so I can make it new?

Tears streamed down her cheeks. "Yes. Yes, Jesus."

A love more beautiful than she had ever imagined permeated her being. She saw herself immersed in dazzling light. A Man robed in white drew near. He stretched out nail-pierced hands. *I did it for you, Daughter. I did it all for you. Take My hand and walk with Me in the path I have chosen for you since the beginning of time.*

She pulled in a breath of wonder. The voices of fear and grief and accusation blew away like chaff in the wind. Then she felt the hand of God reach into the deepest cavity of her soul. He grabbed hold of the blackened heart she loathed so much and drew it out. Then He placed within her a heart glorious with purity.

Joy exploded inside her. Laughter bubbled up, soft and pure. She opened her eyes, overcome with amazement. "Oh, Caleb. I didn't know. I didn't know He was real."

Tears shone in his eyes. He brushed his thumbs across her cheeks. "I know, sweetheart. But you found Him, didn't you?"

"I started looking, but He found me."

"Then that makes two of us. Hold tight to Him, Nan. Temptation still comes, but He's promised to tell you the truth and give you the power to do His will when you're willing to obey."

Arianna nodded, feeling able to trust and obey for the first time. "Okay. I know I don't know anything about being a Christian, but I want to learn. Please help me."

Caleb smoothed his hand over her cheek again. "Jesus will have to help both of us. I'm learning, too."

"I love you. I'm so glad you didn't stop holding onto me."

"Jesus wouldn't let me. I know that now. He has a future for us, sweetheart. A wonderful future of hope and joy so that we can serve Him all our lives."

At ten the next morning, Arianna woke from the first peaceful slumber she had had in a long time. Immediately she felt so light she thought she could fly. She drew in a deep, cleansing breath. Jesus had met her. He had changed her from the inside out.

Caleb smiled at her from the chair, his Bible resting open in one hand. "Morning."

"Hi. So I didn't dream it."

Joy shone from his brown eyes. "I guess not. How do you feel?"

"Like new."

"I reckon that's why the Bible calls it being born again."

She shivered happily, then elevated the bed, feeling stronger. She shifted her feet to the side of the bed. Pain tugged at her ribcage, but she braced herself with her arms so she could remain sitting.

"You okay?"

"I feel stronger. My chest hurts a little, but I hope I can start walking today."

He looked alarmed. "Don't push it, honey. Just because your soul's recreated doesn't mean your body's brand new, too."

She laughed, ignoring the twinge of pain in her ribs out of sheer joy. "Laughter's supposed to be good medicine."

"Actually it's in the Bible. I guess God knew what He was talking about."

She touched her bare feet to the floor. "I suppose He would. Can you help me?"

He set the Bible aside. "I almost forgot about that competitive nature of yours. You're not going to give up, are you?"

"Should I?" She waited for him to slip his hand under her arm then pushed off the bed. Her legs buckled, and Caleb caught her with a groan. But Arianna pushed on her legs, forcing the weak muscles to hold her up. She grinned at him, causing a wry smile to touch his lips. "See. I'm doing it."

"Um… hmm." He eyed her then swung her into his arms as soon as her legs started to buckle again. She slipped her arms around his neck, and he murmured, "What am I going to do with you?"

"I thought you were going to take me home as soon as I got better."

"My Nan. Is that your motivation?"

The shame was gone, and there had been moments together that hadn't been dark. She ran her hand through his hair and kissed him lingeringly.

A knock sounded on the door, surprising both of them. Caleb laughed. "I hope the nurses don't bar me from your room if they find out I'm the reason you're overdoing it."

Arianna smiled, and he placed her back on the bed.

"Hello?" Rye poked his head in the door. "Sorry. Bad timing as ever I see."

Caleb chuckled. "Come in, Rye. Cora." He raised his eyebrows. "No Sadie I see. What did I tell you, Cora?"

She laughed, and Arianna said, "Caleb told me you're getting married soon. Congratulations."

"Thanks." Rye grinned as he led Cora to a chair.

"We'd like to have the wedding here if we can," Cora said, keeping her hand in Rye's.

Caleb said with amusement, "Well, Arianna's determined to be walking by tomorrow so you might get a church wedding after all."

"Oh, don't push yourself for our sakes," Cora implored.

Arianna smiled up at Caleb, loving the joy in his eyes. "I'm not."

Rye laughed. "It's all right, baby. From the look on these two lovebirds' faces, I think we should slip back out of the room."

"Oh!"

Cora began to stand, but Caleb inserted, "No, it's okay, Cora. Rye's teasing us. But it's true that we've agreed to start over in our marriage. I figure it's only right since I'm not the same person I was, and neither is Arianna."

Cora caught her breath, and hope shone in Rye's eyes.

Arianna confirmed, "I met Jesus last night. I really didn't think He could take away all the voices inside me telling me I could never be good and that He wasn't real. But He did."

Cora said softly, "Praise Jesus. We prayed for you last night. Now you're part of our family in every way."

They chatted for awhile about wedding plans, then a knock sounded on the door. Arianna's red-haired doctor stepped into the room. At the sight of visitors, she hesitated.

Arianna said, "It's okay, Dr. Ruth. Rye and Cora can wait outside for a few minutes if you need to check me."

"Actually, I need to talk with you one-on-one."

Cora stood. "We'll wait outside. I know doctors are busy."

"Thanks."

Cora and Rye slipped out of the room, but Dr. Ruth remained where she was. She regarded Caleb coolly. "I'll need you to leave as well, Mr. Abrams."

"What?" Arianna sat up straighter, wincing at the abrupt move. She tightened her hold on Caleb's hand. "He can hear whatever you have to say."

Dr. Ruth pressed her lips together. "This is a personal matter that concerns only you."

"We're married. Nothing concerns only me."

"Very well." Dr. Ruth shut the door then walked into the room. She sat on the edge of Arianna's bed, and studied her. "Do you remember the ultrasound I did yesterday to see how your heart and internal organs are healing?"

Arianna nodded. "Yes, of course." She glanced to Caleb and explained, "It was when you were helping Rye."

He nodded.

Arianna looked back at Dr. Ruth. Her gaze felt too intent. Arianna bit her lip, feeling nervous. "Is something wrong? Am I not healing right?"

Dr. Ruth explained, "I also took a look at your abdomen, just to make sure there were no unknown injuries, and you can rest at ease. You're healing well and should be able to leave on schedule."

"So what's the matter?"

"There's another problem. I'm sorry I can't handle it immediately for you, but I can't risk another procedure for a month or longer. You need to be fully recovered if you decide to have it done. And in your state of mind, it's recommended."

Her state of mind? The doctor must be referring to her attempt at suicide. But what did her mental health have to do with another procedure?

Then abruptly fear bit. Arianna caught her breath. Suddenly she wished she hadn't asked Caleb to stay. In agony, she whispered, "Caleb, please go."

"What?" He sounded struck, but she refused to look at him, already hurting inside for him... for herself.

"Just go. The doctor's right. This is just for me."

"No, Nan. You aren't listening to the right voice—"

Dr. Ruth cut him off sternly. "Every patient has the right to privacy. I won't tell her with you present so you might as well leave."

For a moment, he didn't move. Then he let go of her hand and strode from the room, shutting the door behind him.

Arianna closed her eyes. *Oh, Caleb, I'm sorry! Even with Jesus inside, the past is still there to hurt you. But I'll do everything I can so that it won't. I promise you that much.*

She opened her eyes, and Dr. Ruth said, "You're pregnant. But it will be easy to rectify in another month after I'm no longer afraid of you losing too much blood."

Chapter Forty

Rye sat with Cora on the bench outside Arianna's room while Caleb paced. After several minutes, Rye asked, "Why didn't Arianna want you in there?"

"I don't know." Caleb rubbed his neck in agitation. He stared at the closed room door. "The doctor said there's another procedure Arianna needs to do, but that she can't do it yet. The doctor said it's best for Nan to choose to get it done because of her state of mind." He frowned. "What does that mean, anyway?"

Rye sucked in a hard breath. "I know."

Caleb turned toward him. "What?"

"There's only one procedure Arianna could choose to do in order to supposedly benefit her mental health. The doctor thinks Nan should have an abortion."

Caleb looked at the door, shocked. "Nan's pregnant? No, that can't be it. If Nan thought that was what the doctor would say, why would she want me to leave? She must know I'd be happy. . ."

His words trailed off as the grim reality of their situation hit. Caleb paled. He whispered, "No. The baby's mine. I know it is. The other was just one hour."

Cora said intently, "The baby *is* yours, Caleb. God gave Arianna back to you and kept the baby safe, too. He preserved both their lives, and only God can make life. They're both yours."

Caleb clenched his fists. "She didn't want me in there. She must think the baby isn't mine, or she wouldn't have asked me to leave."

The old anger was fighting for a foothold once again. Rye couldn't bear to see his friend go back under its dark weight. "Cal, Arianna doesn't know who the father is. She's acting out of fear. Remember how she ran away because she didn't want to hurt you? She's doing the same thing now."

Caleb stared at him.

Rye sought for the right words. "From what you've just said, the chance is small that the baby isn't yours. But regardless, you chose to forgive her once. True forgiveness also accepts whatever consequences might come from the original sin."

Caleb looked at him in raw agony. "But a child, Rye… a child will be a reminder against us forever."

"And abortion won't?" Rye shook his head. "The baby shouldn't be punished for Arianna's choices. If you take a life, you give sin a foothold. You'll be holding onto bitterness and anger, hardening your heart to the precious gift God is giving you. Don't go back to hatred. Not to avoid pain, not out of fear. Jesus will take you through both if you let Him. He'll make your family beautiful."

Caleb's shoulders began to shake. He dropped to the bench next to the door, then covered his head with his hands as the sobs took him.

Tears slipped down Cora's face. Rye pulled her against him, inwardly beseeching heaven. Only Jesus could give Caleb the strength he needed to love and cherish Arianna and the baby, even if the child was not his own.

Arianna sat cloaked with internal darkness as pain dug its claws into her soul.

Dr. Ruth had told her that she was eight to nine days along. The time-frame had severed all hope that the embryo couldn't be a stranger's, and now cold permeated her entire being.

She had committed adultery, and though Jesus had held out to her His forgiveness, He had left her to deal with the consequences. But she couldn't bear Caleb's anger when he found out.

Dr. Ruth pressed, "You aren't strong enough to live with Caleb's condemnation a second time. He's the type to blame you for the pregnancy and try to punish you for it. But it's not your fault. You need to go somewhere safe so you can develop the strength to believe in yourself. It's too hard for you to know what's best for yourself when your husband is so domineering. You need to go to a safe house."

Arianna's heart twisted. She didn't want to leave Caleb. She loved him. But she feared his anger. Around him, her guilt would haunt her during every waking hour just as it had before. She buried her face in her hands. "I'll go to a safe house. I can't bear to face him like this."

"That's a wise decision, dear. I don't want you back in a situation that will drive you to try to commit suicide again." Dr. Ruth stood. "Don't worry. I won't let him back in here."

She walked to the door then exited the room.

Arianna stared out the window of her fourth floor room. The blue sky and fluttering leaves in the trees reminded her of the happiness she had felt only a short while before. Could she really have been so naive as to think that accepting Jesus would make everything all right?

As soon as Dr. Ruth emerged from the room, Caleb strode for the door. Dr. Ruth blocked the handle. "Arianna doesn't want to see you. You're not allowed in her room anymore."

Anger swept him. "You can't keep me out."

"I'll call hospital security and have a warrant issued placing you under restraint if you so much as touch that handle."

He clenched his hands, ready to remove the doctor by force. Arianna had been so eager to come home with him until the doctor had come. Then first she had told him to leave her room, and now her life? Never!

Rye came up with Cora and asked casually, "Is it only Caleb she's not allowed to see?"

"Yes." Dr. Ruth frowned. "But I don't recommend that you go in. She's in an extremely fragile state of mind."

Cora asked, "May I go see her?"

Dr. Ruth softened. "I'll take you in."

"No, it's okay. I've been in there before. I'd like to speak to her alone."

The doctor allowed Cora to slip in.

Caleb rubbed his hand over his neck then sat down on the bench, thankful that Cora was allowed to go in. Minutes ticked by. The doctor gestured for a nurse to come over. They whispered together then the nurse flicked a wary glance at Caleb before hurrying over to the work station and placing a phone call.

Caleb grimaced. A call to security no doubt. The law at work, keeping him away from his wife.

Rye paced for several minutes then joined him on the bench. He rested his head against the wall and closed his eyes. He seemed to be praying.

Caleb clenched his fist then bowed his head and began praying as well.

Jesus, help me. I need You as much now as when Arianna was laying in her own blood. She's scared. But I trust You. You work all things together for good to those who are called by Your name and love You. I know You've placed Your hand upon Arianna's life as well as mine. I choose to believe You've placed Your hand and calling upon this child's life, too.

Forgive me for doubting You. Forgive me for wanting what seemed to be the easy way out. But abortion wouldn't stop the pain. It would only fill our hearts with darkness. You formed this child in Arianna's womb. You knit him together and already have a purpose for giving him breath. Help me to be the father You want me to be. Help me to love this child as much as You do.

Cora found her way to the edge of Arianna's bed and sat down.

Arianna gasped, apparently not having seen her enter. "What are you doing here? Didn't the doctor tell you I don't want to be with Caleb?"

Cora answered gently. "Yes, but I don't think that's really what you want. You were so happy when Rye and I came here. So full of joy because Jesus had given you a new heart and you were going to start over in your marriage. Does having a baby change things so much?"

"How do you know?" Shock echoed in Arianna's voice.

"Rye figured it out. He grew up in a neighborhood where girls often had abortions. It grieves him that he believed the lie a baby's life doesn't begin until birth. If he had realized the truth, his own children might still be alive. But as it is the girls he got pregnant didn't want to have a baby out of wedlock."

"Is that why Caleb didn't think Rye was good enough for you? Because he slept around?"

"That's part of it. Caleb also didn't think Rye could change. He thought the things Rye had done would always have power over him. But Caleb knows differently now. He sees how Rye has changed because of Jesus, and he knows you're different, too."

"No." Arianna spoke tonelessly. "I thought I was different, but now I know I went too far. Whatever Rye's done, he's not as bad as me. He's never committed adultery or prostituted himself in full view for others to see."

Cora sat quietly for a small moment. Then she said, "Yes, Arianna, he has. Caleb found Rye when Rye was living as a gigolo. Rye has done things far worse than you. He slept with other men's wives, seducing them for pay, and he's admitted he refrained from no form of perversion when it came to women. But the moment he cried out for mercy, Jesus wiped his sins away."

"But why are you marrying him if he's done all those things? How can you be sure he won't end up hurting you?"

"You're thinking of how much you've hurt Caleb, aren't you?" Cora clasped her hands together. "As God's children, we are given the ability we didn't have before to do what's right. Caleb taught you and Rye about the righteousness of God and about the standards the Lord has placed upon us. Your soul has been eaten up with guilt and shame, much like Rye's has been the last three years, because both of you began to realize that you couldn't be good on your own."

She touched Arianna's leg kindly. "What Caleb didn't know is that we don't have the ability to please God or do what's best for others in ourselves. Caleb believed he was right with God, but he wasn't. His pride brought condemnation down on you, and you took your own life because none of us can bear judgment without mercy. Only when Caleb recognized the depth of his own sin and the way he was hurting you did he cry out for a Savior. That's when he began to offer you the hope each of us needs so desperately."

She paused, praying the quiet meant that Arianna was thinking about her words. Then she explained, "Rye cried out for mercy, too, with a heart completely broken before God. He received not only forgiveness but the power of Jesus to make choices that go against his natural desires. Jesus has given me to him because he's obeyed God's will even when it hurt and he's proven that he can be trusted.

"Yesterday you made the same choice he did and Jesus has given you the same power to do what is right instead of giving into fear or weakness. Sin no longer has power over you because you're God's child. Caleb, too, has committed himself to live by the grace and love of Jesus. You don't need to fear his judgment anymore—"

"Don't I?" Arianna cut her off, her voice filled with agony. "Rye must have told Caleb I'm pregnant. What did Caleb say to that? What did he say to the fact that the baby might not be his?" Her voice broke as she wept. "I can't assure him that it's not."

Cora stood. "Why don't you ask for him to tell you himself? It's the only way you'll be certain he has chosen to live by mercy instead of judgment."

Arianna drew in several deep breaths. Finally, she choked, "Okay. I can't bear to live without him. But I've been so afraid I'll only be living with his anger. Tell Dr. Ruth I want to see him, just for a few minutes. And if Dr. Ruth comes in here to make sure it's what I want, come back in with her." Her voice broke again. "I'm afraid she'll try to convince me not to let him in."

"Okay." Cora moved toward the door, her heart bursting with hope and prayer.

"She what?"

Caleb's heart pounded heavily as Dr. Ruth stared at Cora.

Dr. Ruth strode into the room, not believing Cora's words that Arianna wanted to talk to Caleb.

Cora whispered, "It's what Rye said, Caleb." Then she went back in the room as well while Caleb's heart tightened. A baby. For sure.

Rye sat on the bench, elbows on his knees as he continued to pray. Then Cora and the doctor came back out. The doctor's eyes were angry. "Five minutes. That's it."

Caleb exhaled. Five minutes was all he needed. He entered Arianna's room, shutting the door behind him.

Arianna gazed at him numbly. He realized she knew he was aware of her condition and feared his response. His heart ached. Except for the grace of God, he would have reacted in the old way.

He sank onto one knee beside her then took her limp hand. He held her gaze with all the love he had inside. "Honey, it doesn't matter who the father might be. I want to be your husband, and I want to be this child's father. God's the One in control of every circumstance, and He gave this baby to us."

Her face paled. Then a torrent of tears flooded her eyes, and she began to weep.

He shifted onto the bed then drew Arianna onto his lap.

She clung to him as she drew in great gulps of air. "I never… I never thought you'd want it. I was going to get rid of it. But then I knew you'd know why, and I couldn't bear to hurt you all over again. The doctor said I needed time to think for myself." She broke down. "I'm sorry, Caleb! I did it again. Just like you said. I listened to the wrong voice."

He cradled her in his arms. "It's okay, honey. We're learning. We're learning how to do things God's way. I almost gave into fear and pain, too. But Rye and Cora reminded me of the way God thinks. We need them, Nan, and we need each other."

He tipped her head up so she could look at him. A sheen of tears stood in her eyes. "Let's promise each other to always seek Godly counsel before we let the world tear us apart."

She nodded, trembling as she clung to him.

Caleb leaned his forehead against hers and closed his eyes. "Jesus, we desperately need Your help in every part of our marriage and in raising this child You've given us. Please fill us every day with your unconditional love and the power to do what's right. We want our home to glorify You. Thank You for sending Rye and Cora this morning because You knew we needed

Your wisdom to overcome our fears. In Jesus' name."

Arianna whispered, "Amen", and Caleb gazed down at her. The joy of the Lord began to fill him once again, and the pain cleared from her face as well.

"I love you, Nan. Thank you for giving me a chance."

She wrapped her arms around his neck. "I hope the baby looks like you."

He squeezed her. "I know. But what I want most is for the baby to grow up to look like Jesus."

Arianna framed his face with her hands and kissed him with all her heart. Nor did she pull back when the door opened.

"All right, five minutes are—"

The doctor cut off and abruptly left the room, slamming the door behind her.

Caleb laughed while Arianna smiled. "I guess that means she's angry I succumbed once more to your influence."

"Ah, honey, let's get you well and out of here. Rye's not the only one who's tired of waiting."

She laughed softly. "Why don't you tell them they can come in? I'm sure they want to know that we've decided to be a family."

"All right, though I think they already know." He shifted her off his lap then walked to the door. He smiled when he saw Cora and Rye sitting on the bench close together.

As soon as Rye saw him, his eyes lit up. "Cal! Praise the Lord! He hears and answers prayers."

Caleb hugged him as soon as Rye was close. Then he hugged Cora too. "We couldn't have made the right choice without you two. I hope you know that. Thank you."

Rye squeezed his shoulder. "I didn't want you to make the same mistake I did." He grinned. "And besides it's gonna be fun watching you be a dad."

"Hmm. That reminds me." Caleb gestured them into the room. "Come inside. There's something I forgot to mention to Arianna, but it includes you as well."

"All right." Rye guided Cora into the room.

Cora stepped close to the bed and found Arianna's shoulders with her fingers. She leaned down and gave the girl a strong hug. "We love you. You and Caleb are going to be good parents."

Arianna blinked at tears and returned the embrace. "With God's help we will."

Rye guided Cora to a chair. Then he turned to Caleb. "So what other news do you have for us?"

Caleb took Arianna's hand. "You can tell me if you don't like the idea, Nan, but I've decided to sell the house and buy a horse breeding ranch. I was thinking about it before, but now that we're going to have a family, I'm certain it will be better for all of us. Both you and the baby are going to need me around a lot more than PI work allows."

Arianna's face lit up. She reached out her arms to embrace him. Caleb hugged her then sat on the chair and looked at Rye. "Sorry about throwing you out of a job, but I figure you can't get too angry at me since you're marrying an heiress tomorrow."

Rye grinned.

Cora clarified, "You're not going to be partners any more?"

"No, but Rye was only doing that job by default anyway. Now that he's given his life to Jesus, I'm sure God has something specific He wants him to do. You wouldn't want to have to keep worrying about his safety, anyway."

"No. What do you think you'll do, Rye?"

"I don't know. I guess I'll take our honeymoon to pray about it."

Caleb laughed, and Rye grinned. "Okay, maybe I'll end up doing most my praying afterward."

Caleb squeezed Arianna's hand. "I keep thinking that God's love is a lot like Cora's blindness."

Rye glanced at Cora's dark brown eyes. "How's that?"

"God wants us to love each other so greatly that we don't see each other's sins or the ways we can be hurt. God asks us to be blind to those things and reach out with complete trust for Him to take us in the way that He has chosen for us to go."

Rye hugged Cora's shoulder. "Amen, brother. Amen."